UNDER HIS GUARD

UNDER HIS GUARD

RIE WARREN

A Don't Tell Novel

FOREVER
YOURS

New York Boston

Forever Yours

Hachette Book Group

1290 Avenue of the Americas

New York, NY 10104

Hachettebookgroup.com

Twitter.com/foreverromance

First ebook and print on demand edition: February 2015

Forever Yours is an imprint of Grand Central Publishing.

The Forever Yours name and logo are trademarks of Hachette Book Group, Inc.

The publisher is not responsible for websites (or their content) that are not owned by the publisher.

The Hachette Speakers Bureau provides a wide range of authors for speaking events. To find out more, go to www.hachettespeakersbureau.com or call (866) 376-6591.

ISBN 978-1-4555-7416-2 (ebook edition)

ISBN 978-1-4555-7519-0 (print on demand edition)

Acknowledgments

It's time for the Don't Tell journey to end. It's been an awesome ride for me, and I have many folks to thank for being with me every step of the way. Gillian Littlehale was my beta reader, my middle-of-the-night cheerleader, and the fact-checker who helped me keep my sanity. Jenna Barton, Kari Haines, Lisa Pinney, and Tracey Porcher provided constant feedback and support. These amazing women helped me bring the entire series together from the first days of the Revolution to the final endgame.

Thanks to my new editor, Scott Rosenfeld. He took up this last book and helped me shape it into something awesome. I have much appreciation for my agent, Saritza Hernandez, and her team at Corvisiero Literary. They've been great supporters of this series. Ron McAulay was on call through all three books with his weapons and military expertise. Joanne Sato, a dear friend, came through with the Japanese translations. I'm indebted to both of them.

I'm most grateful to my readers, my street team, and the many bloggers who championed the series through all of its twists and turns. Even when I'm sure they wanted to throttle some of my characters.

Last but not least, of course, is my family. They back me up, support my dream, and *almost* never bat an eyelash at the crazy hours and unpredictable schedule I keep.

UNDER HIS GUARD

CHAPTER ONE

July, 2071, Chitamauga Commune

The meadow was a landscape of bonfires and boisterous revelers. Music swelled from Eden's and Nate's guitars as they took over from Smitty's painfully out-of-tune banjo playing. The Freelanders were in the full throes of merrymaking as they gathered in celebration of Liz and Linc's betrothal announcement. For one evening we forgot about the cruel facts of the war in favor of reveling in a moment of all-too-rare joy. The scene was a one eighty from the months spent in the urban Beta Territory, where bombs dropped, guns fired, and the Revolution had almost been lost.

Victory had been ours in the end. As always, it was paid with a high price. A similar rebel win in Alpha Territory had cost the lives of my two lovers. This time the cost was Leon's memory of me and our time together. And the son of a bitch responsible—CEO Cutler—had managed to escape unscathed once again.

But this wasn't the time for such dark thoughts. Perhaps that was why my mother had named me Darke. I'd always assumed it was because of my incredibly black skin and inky eyes, but maybe I'd just been a broody little bastard from birth. I nearly laughed at the thought, but I couldn't do that either. Not when the one person who knew how to lighten my mood danced in the middle of the meadow, as carefree and unbelievably sexy as always. Leon gave the type of wicked smile he'd previously reserved for me to some young buck named Jake or Jack or Jackal. My jealousy flared as I watched Leon twine his arms around the other man's neck and gyrate against his hips.

What very few knew about me was I felt too much, from all sides. Emotions came at me in clouds and bursts and spikes. While it was a boon on the field of battle, since I could get an immediate read on my warriors—who was a cool hand versus who was too freaked to fire their weaponry—this *ability* was a bane to my barren love life. I'd cut Leon loose when his memories went on a leave of absence, thinking it was the higher road. Now I trudged my path alone.

After giving my congratulations to Linc and Liz, I'd ambled away from the group I'd been with through the battles of Beta. It was mostly to get away from Leon, yet I still couldn't take my eyes off him. I finally turned my back on the intoxicating movements of his body and decided to mingle with the other villagers. I danced a fast-paced jig with one of the women but declined a second dance when the music became slower and more sensual. I ended up drinking a couple tankards of ale with my buddy Micah as we laughed over his twin girls. They made their *uncles* Caspar and Nathaniel squire them about the field, which meant Smitty was back on the banjo, much to the agony of everyone's ears.

"Your girls are gonna be heartbreakers, man," I said, knocking my mug against Micah's.

"Shit, Darke. You don't need to tell me that. Jesus. They take after their momma." He pushed a faded green cap off his brow and winked at me. "Kamber had my nuts twisted tighter than a blue-balled bull the first time I met her."

I grinned and took a swill of the alcohol in my cup.

"Mind now, that'un over there's a heartbreaker, too—ain't he?"

I looked in the direction he pointed and let loose a groan. Leon had switched partners. As Smitty warbled a raunchy song, Leon grinded his ass against a guy called Dixon. Or Dickhead, as I called him.

"Yeah, he is," I answered, trying to pass off my gritted teeth as a smile.

I'd made avoiding Leon my latest detail, going out of my way to eat at opposite ends of the mess hall, ensuring Caspar was the one to head up any military training with him instead of me. Despite my efforts, I still knew where he was and what he was doing almost every second of every day.

Three more teasing dances from Leon later, I couldn't hold back any longer. When I saw him leaning against the fence, his own mug of ale in hand, I stalked toward him. The moon had long since risen and was making its way across the other side of the sky. The glow from the white orb above outlined his striking features and his shoulder-length hair in silver. He was stunning. The sight of him stole my breath and cooled some of the jealousy he'd stoked. He always wreaked havoc on my too-vulnerable emotions.

As I approached, his golden gaze found mine. He leaned his head back and dragged the hair away from his face, affording me a mouthwatering view of his clenched biceps and the cords of his neck. I ran a finger down his throat, which elicited a small gasp. He lifted his head as I sucked my fingertip, licking off the salty taste lingering there.

"You about done making a spectacle of yourself out there with Jackal and Dickhead?"

"Who?" Leon's chest was shiny with perspiration, his shirt long gone.

Copper-colored nipples sat on his tight pectorals. I wanted to kiss them, lap them until he cried out my name. His chest was smooth until a thin line of soft-looking dark brown hair ran from his navel to the top of his pants, nearly dripping off his Adonis belt.

My gaze rose from wandering all over his body. "Jack. Dixon. And that other one who was all over you."

He finished taking a long, lazy sip of his drink and cleaned his lips off with a slow roll of his tongue. "What do you care? I know you won't help my momma and Miss Eden tap into my memories. I know you're hidin' somethin'." He rubbed his stomach like a lion preening itself, muscles rippling beneath his hand. "But guess what? The world don' revolve around you."

The words were eerily similar to something he'd said the night I'd tracked him to Farrow's apartment in Beta. He'd been downright pissed off at me for following him when he'd wanted only to get away from me. He didn't remember any of that now.

Leon was right. I used his amnesia to keep him at arm's length, for all the goddamn good it did me. Fresh emotion boiled through me.

I grabbed the rail behind him with both my hands, caging him against the fence. "I care," I bit out. I'd cared then, and I for damn sure cared now.

"You jealous?" Leon didn't shrink from my presence. Instead he arched into my body. A breath hissed from me as his chest came into contact with mine and the contours of his lean legs brushed my thighs.

I swallowed hard. "Yeah."

Winding his fingers through his sun-streaked hair, he licked his lips. They were red, and juicy, always plump, begging to be kissed. I couldn't look away. He slid one long thigh between mine and drew it back slowly. The ache in my groin exploded into a full-blown erection from that teasing stroke alone.

"Then why don' you fuck me already?"

It was as if lightning struck my body, sizzling right down to my balls. My hands clenched the fence rail, but I wanted nothing more than to drive them inside the back of his pants, pull him against me. Find some relief from this longing, this raw seduction that had been building for six months whether he remembered or not.

I jerked away when his lips sought mine. A kiss, one kiss from this man, and I'd be a goner. I couldn't. I just *couldn't* get involved with Leon. My chest billowed in and out with the effort to put a stop to this one more time.

Words, harsh and low, fell from my mouth before I even considered them. "Because I don't fuck. I make love."

Leon's face crashed in an instant. "And you don' love me." He moved as far back from me as he could.

I scowled at him. There was no answer to that. None I was ready to give. I turned away and vaulted over the fence, almost tripping over my feet to beat a hasty retreat. But I couldn't move fast enough to outrun the guilt and desire that battered me. Leon always flew too close to my emotions. I couldn't let him in enough to hurt me.

From behind, I heard Liz shout, "Hey!"

My shoulders drooped. I slowed my sprint to a stop. She'd been looking out for Leon since he'd arrived in Beta. She hadn't stopped just because we were back in Chitamauga. Liz was as much a woman as a soldier, and I had a sinking feeling she was about to kick my ass and then give me love advice.

"What the hell are you playing at?" She grabbed my arm, tugging me around.

So it *was* to be the ass-kicking first. At least she was predictable. She stood a good few inches shorter than me but was formidable nonetheless, even without her usual weapons holstered at her hips.

"I'm not playing anything. This isn't a game you can tactically decide from the sidelines, so back the fuck off."

"Not gonna happen. Why don't you tell me why you're running away from Leon again? What was all that shit you spouted when Taft brought him back to you?"

I folded my arms across my chest. "Ignorance, arrogance, and blind stupidity."

"You know what? All that fucked-up emotion? That was the

first honest feeling you've shown toward Leon." Her finger pointed at me, and if she'd had one of her guns, it probably would've gone off right then, too.

"I don't know what you're talking about." When faced with a woman going all mama bear, it was best to play dumb.

"I got eyes in my head. I know what I see. It just so happens I saw you last night, Darke, at the lake, watching Leon."

Ah fuck. "You saw me?"

I hadn't intentionally followed Leon, but I'd heard him whistling. Then playing in the water. I'd kept to the tree line, shaking with need. Leon swam, and his sleek body teased me from the lake—a flash of his perfect ass rising above the waves, the splash of water running down his chest. It'd taken all my restraint to keep from joining him, to walk away.

I glared at Liz. "Wait. You saw him naked?"

"Easy there, big guy. I got a man of my own, and you could, too, if you pulled your head out of your ass. So why don't you tell me what the hell is going on?"

I clamped my fingers into my hair and pulled hard. A rumbling groan grew from my chest in sheer despair. "I don't know."

"Are you shitting me? Do you remember sobbing over him when he was gone? I do. Because I was right there with you."

"Maybe the amnesia thing is better for him, a clean break…"

"I'm gonna clean break your neck." She got right in my space, shoving her finger in my face. "Look. Did you see what he was doing out there? He was making you jealous, and it worked because you're about one step away from devouring him on the spot every time you see him. He wants you. So it doesn't matter what the hell he does or doesn't remember, Darke. He's into you. He is yours. Still."

"Not my problem anymore." I dodged Liz's eyes, squared my shoulders, firmly setting myself on the path of probable personal destruction.

"Wrong. He is always gonna be your problem and your man. You need to grow a pair already."

She looked thoroughly disgusted with me when she pivoted on her heel and took off for the meadow. It didn't matter. No one could be more ashamed of me than I was.

* * *

I walked back to my caravan. I had to stop before going up the steps. As always, I shut my eyes for a moment to prepare myself for the scene inside. After closing the door gently behind me, I bent to unlace my boots and place them aside. I tried not to look around too much. Tam's and Wilde's belongings—their books, clothes, weapons, and trinkets—were how they'd left them. I hadn't moved or removed a single thing. I couldn't bear to touch them. I couldn't bear to part with them. Though Wilde and I had spent one summer cobbling two caravans together and the place was bigger than most others, I felt suffocated.

Their ghosts still lingered.

There was no room for Leon here. I'd made the right decision, but even so, he'd filled the hole in my chest for a little while, back in the winter. Now it simply gaped open.

Broody bastard? I'm downright maudlin. I snuffed out a smile.

Lighting a few candles, I undressed and washed quickly. The big, empty bed was another torment, but instead of memories of old, it filled me with fresh, increasingly hot fantasies. No, it wasn't Tam or Wilde I thought about. It wasn't either of them who kept me up night after lonely night, awake and so aroused I had to relieve the physical ache with fingers I pretended were long and slim and tanned, a hand I wet with my tongue so when I wrapped it around my jutting cock, I could imagine I was being sucked and teased and blown by the poutiest, reddest pair of lips beneath two heavy-lidded, honey-flecked eyes. Even when I came so hard I had to bite back a holler and mop away strands of milky liquid all the way up my chest, I was left unsatisfied. The emotional turmoil I felt never disappeared.

Tonight was no different. I thrashed around the bed, sleep chased away by images of Leon—laughing, dancing, flirting—the scent of him that was earthy, his guttural accent spoken in a soft, low voice. My hunger for Leon never waned. It became harder with each passing day to maintain distance. I hoped like hell he'd gone to bed alone and not with Jackass or Dickhead or any number of randy males he could pick from.

It felt like my eyes had only just shut when my Data-Pak went off over and over, showing no signs of stopping its piercing alert. I snatched the handheld comms device from the floor beside the bed and checked the incoming. *Linc Cutler.*

I barked into the thing, "Thought I said congrats earlier, man. It's too fucking late for you to be on the horn on your betrothal night."

"I've just gotten word from Denver." I went on high alert

at the mention of CEO Cutler's personal bodyguard. "This is strictly on a need-to-know basis, so I'm not gonna spread it over the D-P. Be in the town hall in ten minutes." The tension in Linc's voice sounded clearly through the airwaves.

Instantly, all weariness fled. After yanking on the clothes I'd taken off only hours before, I slammed outside. I didn't even bother with my bootlaces.

The town hall became a tunnel through which I saw only Liz and Linc at the opposite end. Linc stood behind the table, Liz at his side. Hatch—the brains of the commune—Nathaniel, and Cannon hurried in after me. Both Linc and Liz nodded at them, but they skipped over me.

"What the hell's going on that this couldn't wait until the morning?" My boots resounded on the wood floors as I marched up to Linc. When he didn't answer and still wouldn't meet my gaze, dread funneled through me. "Give it to me straight, right now."

"Denver came through with some intel."

"You already said that."

Liz placed a hand on my arm, her touch not soothing me at all when she said, "It's bad, Darke."

I swung my gaze to her and then back at Linc. His eyes looked bleaker than I'd ever seen them, and seeing as we'd been through hell ten times over in Beta, I wasn't sure I wanted to hear Denver's info.

Linc passed a hand over his face. "Leon's a human time bomb."

"What?" Sweat trickled down my back, as cold as the fear slicing through me.

"This is what our *father* meant when he told Liz he had a second wave planned. It's why he didn't really give a shit when Taft blew up the DCICs. The asshole masterminded a human delivery system. Leon's infected with the new Plague." Linc exchanged bitter looks with his twin brother, Nathaniel. Once again the evil wrongdoings of their father, CEO Lysander Cutler, came home to roost. "I should've killed that fucking bastard when I had the chance."

"What?" I asked again, grasping the edge of the table as my legs threatened to collapse from under me. My body, my brain, my heart, all shut down.

"To kill the Plague, we'd have to kill Leon—his body is a Trojan horse we won't be able to destroy, because…because…" Words failed Liz.

Bile rose in my throat. I swallowed it back. "Because he's ours." *He's mine.* "That's why no one else showed at the water tower. There was to be no handoff, no delivery except to us."

"The virus is implanted in Leon, but it's dormant." Hatch scanned through the message that had been sent to Linc via Denver. Denver was feeding info to Linc because he played a dangerous game, straddling both sides of the war, or so he claimed. I wasn't quite a believer yet.

"Leon's body is a weapon for the Company." Numbed through, I could barely raise my eyes to the others.

Nathaniel's hand was heavy on my shoulder. "Father let Leon go because he knew we'd take him in. Our exposure to the virus will be guaranteed. He wants us all dead."

An incendiary blaze of hate for CEO Cutler fired inside me. "I'd still take Leon in, no matter what."

Cannon rose so slowly, bearing such pain, it appeared the big, broad-shouldered man was made of no more than vapor. His voice was just as thin. "Imagine how many others Cutler's infected."

"When?" All the life was leached from me in an instant.

"When what?" Linc asked.

"WHEN DOES IT GO LIVE?" I bellowed.

"Middle of August." Linc grabbed Liz's hand.

"But that gives us only a couple weeks. There has to be an antidote, a cure, something!" I spun around, only to halt when I saw Leon just inside the door. Shock, fear, and concern all clashed within me. And want, foremost.

I could never get enough of him. I never would. No matter how hard I tried to push him away, I always pulled him back. His bright eyes looked almost kohl black and suddenly too big for his face. His hair was wild, tangled, down around his shoulders. I tensed, reaching for him. I didn't want him to know. *I* didn't want to fucking know.

Leon walked toward me with his loose-legged swagger.

My heart pounded. My mouth went dry.

He ambled closer, and everyone moved away from us. They fell silent, became nonexistent.

"Thought I heard a commotion." He stopped in front of me.

"Leon." *Angel.* "How much did you hear?" My hands clenched beside me. I was desperate to touch him.

His slight smile was tremulous around the edges. "Jus' a little of this, a little of dat. Somethin' 'bout me bein' an incubator for the new Plague and set to infect." He clicked his tongue against the roof of his mouth. "*Mais,* I always wanted to be famous."

CHAPTER TWO

Leon." I struggled to breathe.

"Guess we know what that Dr. Val did to me now, yeah?"

I let out a hoarse cry.

"Darke." His hand ran along my jaw. "I wanna know who you are, what you mean to me before I die, 'cause I can *feel* this thing between us," he whispered.

Leon closed his eyes when I groaned at his touch. There was no one else. Never. Not like this. Guilt wormed its way into my gut, thoughts of Tam and Wilde warring within me. But I wouldn't deny this passion. I couldn't. Not anymore. Not if Leon was going to die as a pawn in the InterNations war.

"*Cher,*" he whispered against my neck.

A great gasping sob broke through my lips. I crushed him to me. He hadn't called me *cher* since his abduction. He'd forgotten what we'd started, what I wouldn't let myself have.

Now it was too late.

He pulled back. Courage fought with sadness in his eyes as if he were looking at something that would never be his. I felt the same, and it made me clasp the back of his neck, bringing him against me once more.

"There might not be a cure." His words, warm on my skin, instilled coldness in my heart.

"You do not say that. You do not *think* that." I lifted him against me, strengthened by a new resolve. "You are not going to die, Leon."

Nuzzling his hair, running my hands over his body, I barely noticed when the others departed. Filled with arousal and torment, I slid him down and stepped back. I was barely holding on by a thread. To love him and make him mine once and for all. To lash out and kill something, someone. "Go wait for me at my place. I won't be long."

Leon brought his hands to my face. He kissed me sweetly, just a brush of lush lips. "You know there's only life or death between us now."

I groaned against his lips, tasting mint and scotch. "I need you in my bed."

"*Mais*, you din't want me earlier." Leon stepped away.

Despite his recent, intimate words, he stood defiantly in front of me. How could I have forgotten about his fire? The bright flame that had first surprised me and then enthralled me.

I grabbed his arm as he spun away. "Yeah, I did."

He wrenched free. When I advanced, he slammed a palm to my chest. "Pull me one way, push me another." He flicked his hair back, his eyes going from soft and sultry to hard and flinty. "Changed my mind. I'll be fine without you."

I wouldn't be. I'd never be fine again if something happened to him. But words failed me as I watched him sweep out into the night. I barely contained myself from running after him, dragging him home with me. If I went after him right now, I'd have him bent over and screaming for my cock. Just to be inside him where nobody and nothing—not the Revolution, not fucking Cutler, not my ghosts—could touch us.

After he left, I waited as long as I could until rage overwhelmed me. I overturned the table, roaring to the rafters, "NOT HIM!" Tears ran down my cheeks unchecked. "Not Leon, not now. Please. If there's any god at all. Don't. Don't take him, too."

I hunched over as pain gripped me from the inside out. "I've already lost everything once."

Eventually I reined in the dry, racking sobs coursing through my body. It felt like a lifetime had come and gone during the past hour. I looked around the room. The town hall had seen some of the best moments of my life. My handfasting with Tammerick and Wilde. My nomination as the head of the Chitamauga militia. The night Cannon and Nathaniel had promised themselves to each other and Leon had caught my eye. He'd coaxed that first smile from me, and I'd thought he might be someone worth living for again.

Now the town hall was the scene of one of the most dreadful moments I could ever have imagined. I had to leave.

Outside, the village was quiet at this late hour. Only the loud, blaring crickets sounded as agitated as I felt. The humid July heat hit me and clung to me as I headed down to the forge.

As I entered the barn where Smitty did his ironwork, the smell

of hot coal and metal stung my eyes. I made my way to a pallet
covered with a ratty blanket, a mirage of all the different sides
of Leon swimming around me. Bold, confused, hurt, protective,
playful…sexy as hell.

The pallet creaked when I shifted, and the red haze of the
never-ending fire in Smitty's cavern reminded me of the last time
I'd been in here with Leon. Before he'd run away from me in the
dead of winter to Beta and straight into harm's way. I'd asked him
to tattoo me with Tammerick's and Wilde's names.

*I tore off my shirt and tossed it aside. As I stretched on the pallet
on my stomach, the heat of the fire beside us baked across my skin.
Leon sat back on his heels, sweat forming in the hollow of his throat.
He shrugged off his shirt. In the orange and yellow and red light,
his skin glowed. A dusting of caramel-colored hair thinned from his
belly button to his pants. His smell was mouthwatering, and I swallowed through the need to touch him.*

"Do it. Mark me." I lay my head on my arms.

*He found his pouch and perched beside me, cleaning the sharp
bone awl that would pierce me. A vial of black dye was set beside my
head. I arched and hissed when he touched me, not with the tool but
with his hand. I had to lift my head and watch him. He swept under
the waist of my pants. My muscles tensed, and I threw my head back,
on the brink of coming from one little touch from this gorgeous man
who had marked my heart as indelibly as he was about to mark my
skin.*

*"Mais, I don' wanna hurt you, Darke." The white shard of his tool
quivered above my skin.*

"Been hurt through a lifetime. A little tattoo won't kill me." I

rolled over and caught his wrists, bringing him across my body. "Do me, my angel, my devil. Make it so I'll never forget my lovers."

Leon cursed quietly, prodding me onto my belly. I moaned when the bone cut into me. Leon groaned through every needle tap that pushed ink into my skin.

For Tammerick and Wilde. Not for him.

I burrowed my face deeper into my arms as the guilt washed over me.

He took his time, but the pain didn't affect me. It was his touch that had me on tenterhooks for hours. His breath washed across my shoulders when he leaned close to fill in the lines. I bit into my arm to muffle a moan when his moist lips roamed up my spine with soft kisses, the tools set aside.

No one had touched me like this since Tam and Wilde had died, and now their names were etched onto my skin by Leon's hand.

Leon's forehead rested against my neck. His hot tears splashed against the warm blood. "I want my name on you, too, cher.*"*

As soon as he cleaned me up, he pressed a small kiss to my shoulder and left. The agony I felt wasn't just of the flesh. It was of the heart. But it didn't stop me from sliding my pants to my thighs and gripping my cock. My hand came away slick with precome, as sticky as the blood that had dripped from my back, the same blood that was on my soul. My shaft throbbed thickly with veins, and my head craned back. Three strong strokes and the sting of the tattoo was all it took. Come splashed my sweaty chest and slid to my groin. It was the first time I'd let myself orgasm since Tam and Wilde had died.

They weren't the ones I thought about when I came.

I growled into the dark room. Every place held memories of

the two of us when what I really needed was to be with him. I'd almost made it to the door when Old Tommy and his mutt shuffled in.

Tommy, he was the town crier. Knew just about everything about everyone. It came as no surprise he and his dog—the shaggy gray mongrel he simply called Gal—were up and about at this otherwise deserted hour, or that he already seemed to know what had gone down earlier.

Instead of laying on the pity, he looked me over with his fierce bushy brows pulled low over his eyes. "Is hidin' in the dark any way for a warrior to behave?"

"I was just heading home."

"Shoot. You ain't goin' nowhere 't'all." Taking my spot on the pallet, he motioned Gal to one side of him and me to the other.

I grumbled but took a seat anyway, and he started right in.

"Lemme see if I got this straight. Now, remember, Old Tommy here ain't the sharpest tool in dis here shed." He flashed me a mostly toothless grin. Summer teeth, he called them.

I fought the urge to tell him to mind his own business, but the nosy old son of a bitch wouldn't pay me any attention at any rate.

"So your boy—"

"He's a man."

"I'm mighty happy to hear dat, the way you coddle him like he's still in a romper one minute, then run from him like he's gonna jump dem big bones of yours the next." He plugged a wad of raw tobacco inside his lower gum so his speech slurred even more. "Your young man got taken from you up in Beta and you went off your rocker. And when he came back, he din't remember you."

I was hit by all the memories I didn't want to relive.

"But y'all decided after a fashion there was a good way to play dat mind-scrub thing of Leon's, yessir. Keep dat son of gun at arm's distance 'cause you're too damn scaredy-cat to get close to anyone again." At the mention of *cat*, the dog's ears perked up, and her long, wet tongue rolled out. "Ain't no cat here, Gal. Jest me and Darke settin' things straight."

"Where's this going, Tommy?"

He spat a line of brown juice onto the rough wooden floor and scrubbed it in with his boot. "See now, I don't rightly know. You were fixin' on lettin' Leon go all this time. In fact, ya never did claim him as yer own. But you ain't cut him loose yet. I know dis 'cause I see the way you watch him, and so does ever'one else with eyes in their head."

I exhaled a frustrated curse. Tommy the goddamn gossipmonger was good for nothing but telling me my fucked-up love life was the talk of the town. "I should probably be on my way. Make sure he's all right."

Tommy locked a wiry hand onto my thigh. "I reckon you ain't ready to face dat demon yet, son. Leon's got dat sickness now, and you fell apart as soon as nobody was watchin'. Ain't no good for him if he sees you like dat."

"Dammit! Have you got the whole fucking commune wired or something? Yeah, I lost it." I shoved his hand away and jumped to my feet. "He's gonna die. Do you get that?"

He didn't blink in the face of my outburst. Gal growled at me but put her head back down on her paws when he petted her. "Cool dem heels and sit down. Won't do if Gal takes a bite out of you. We don't need to add rabies to the list of ailments."

Dropping beside him, I rested my head in my hands.

"Do you want dat boy to remember you? Because it sure do look like he loved you before and he's fixing to get dat way again."

"That doesn't really matter now." My hands curled around my head, but there was no use blocking him out, not when he hit me with the bare-knuckled truth.

"Never thought I'd see the great warrior Darke defeated."

I lifted my head and glared at him. "Fuck you, old man. I'm not defeated."

Leaning over to spit again, he wiped his mouth on his sleeve. "And I never thought I'd see you get attached again. Not after Tam and Wilde. That was some love right there between the three of you. Don't imagine I've ever seen the likes of it before; nor will I again. Dat don't mean there's not enough room in dat big ol' chest of yours for someone like your boy to be given some space. I seem to think he might deserve it, and you're just a stubborn jackass."

"I am not attached," I spat.

Tommy went right on ignoring me. "Don't know what's happenin', all dis love in the air."

"I'm not in love." My demeanor quickly changed from defiant to defeated. "Leon scares the shit out of me."

"*Mm-hmm.* There's some truth right there." His gnarled hand moved to my shoulder. He squeezed and then patted me, like I was his dog. "What're ya gonna do about dis here Plague business?"

"Keep him alive. Fight for him." Steely determination pulled me upright.

"Don't dis seem like a damn fool place to spend the night? Me and the old girl are gonna hit the hay." Tommy made a big show of cracking his back and wincing, trying to make me feel sorry for him.

The old coot wasn't getting any sympathy from me. "You're the damn fool."

"Hey, now. My place is right next ta Nathaniel and Caspar. Dem boys are screamers. I gotta wait until they pass out from fucking before I get any shut-eye. Oughtta be old enough to be deaf already." He slapped his scrawny thigh and whistled. "C'mon, Gal."

"You know, Liz thinks Gal's a guy," I called after him.

"That's 'cause she don't want no competition when it comes to her menfolk." His eyes twinkled with glee.

Left alone once more, I walked to the door and looked out. Up and down the lane, lights were off in the mess hall, the schoolhouse, the trade hall. In the distance, beyond a sentinel of trees, the lanterns glowed from the neighborhood of caravans.

I squared my shoulders and walked down the road, alone but resolved.

No one was gonna take Leon from me. Not Cutler, not the Revolution, and certainly no fucking Plague.

CHAPTER THREE

After a mere two hours of lying on top of my bed, I stomped into the town hall the next morning. My demand that Leon go to my place last night had apparently failed to convince him, since he'd never showed up. Maybe being a domineering prick wasn't the way to play things with him, but damned if I could remember how to woo someone.

Cannon and Nate sat side by side at the long table that had been returned to its proper place, along with the chairs I'd kicked out of my way last night.

I overheard the tail end of Hills—our commune elder—saying, "Wrecked the place a little bit."

I settled in an empty seat next to Liz and grabbed a cup of coffee to hide behind. "Sorry 'bout that."

The air around me was cloying with pity, thick as the mud I needed to knock off my boots after my walkabout last night. I kept my head in my cup and held up a hand to ward off everyone's sympathetic glances. "Aw, shit. Don't start pussyfooting around me now. Whatever the CEO dishes out, I can take, so long as Leon doesn't have to."

There were coughs and mumbles and more looks I chose to ignore. Linc, Eden—who was Nate and Linc's mom as well as the Chitamauga healer—and Hatch, the tech guru, took their seats.

Liz turned to me. "How was Leon last night?"

I blew across the steam rising from my coffee.

"You pissed him off, didn't you?" Her tone turned icy.

"He's got a hairpin trigger; you know that." I took a scalding sip from my cup, not even wincing as it burned my tongue.

"And?" she pressed.

"I was a dick."

"Well, there's a surprise."

The door opened and I shot to my feet, expecting Leon.

In swanned Farrow, who looked ready to reign over a tea party in her swishy dress, only the dark circles under her eyes giving away her fatigue. She'd been our go-to girl in Beta, the real mole as far as I was concerned. "Ah'm sorry to be late, y'all. It was a rough night after Ah told Sebastian about Leon."

Her brother, Sebastian, and Leon had become friends in Beta while Leon worked to infiltrate the *Posse Omnis Juvenis*, the hardcore crew of militants Cutler had under his thumb.

Farrow swept behind me, running a hand along my back. "Ah'm purely distraught for you, Darke."

I grumbled a response and returned to watching the door. Two minutes of chatter later, Leon still hadn't showed. "Where the hell is Leon, anyway?" I asked.

Guess I wasn't so good at playing it cool after all.

Hills hooked a white strand of hair behind his long pink ear-lobe. More of the crushing weight of sympathy rolled from him. "We thought it best he didn't sit in on this meetin'. If you find you can't contain yourself, perhaps you'd be better off trackin' him down."

Like hell. "I can control myself."

"Good man." Hills nodded at me. Easing back, he asked, "What do we know?"

Hatch launched into a detailed description of the Pneumonic Plague, the disease that had been spun as the Gay Plague back in fifty-nine to sixty in order to wipe more homosexuals off the map. When she was being tortured by CEO Cutler, Liz had found out the virus wasn't originated to kill gays—it'd been created to infect rebel masses. Created by Liz's father, Robie Grant, and his InterNations counterpart, Dr. Val. It was this Dr. Val who'd not only wiped Leon's frontal lobe but had also made him a human incubator. She was on Liz's hit list, too, for perfecting her mind-scrub techniques years before on Robie Grant.

"It'll be total genocide of the rebel faction if Cutler has his way," Hatch said. "He wants complete control of the government, total adherence to the Company, and death to all who stand in his way. A handful of those infected with the sleeper virus are our fellow rebel leaders. Cutler's savagery is very well planned." Hatch's keen eyes landed on me.

Cannon joined in. "From the records Liz gave us from her father's lab, we know this new manifestation will spread faster than ever once it goes live." He kicked his chair back, his hands scrubbing down his face. "Jesus fucking Christ. I remember what happened to my folks, my sister when they got sick. This thing's gonna rip through all of us until our guts are bleeding out on the floor."

The thought of Leon becoming sick from this disease, dying from it, was not a reality I was willing to face. "It's exactly what the Colonial Americans did when they sought to lay claim to Native American land. He's using Old History against us. They delivered diseased blankets to the indigenous, killing them quietly."

"We won't go quietly." Liz gripped my hand.

"Lysander's just waitin' to wipe us all out." Miss Eden twined her fingers together, looking down.

She'd know better than anyone what the CEO was capable of. She'd been married to the monster, forced to abandon her two sons when they were young because her husband, the rising CO star, had beaten her mercilessly. She'd been reunited with both Nathaniel and Linc only recently.

Lysander Cutler might've been defeated in the Territories of the former North Americas, but he was blazing a new trail across the Pan-Atlantic pond. Worldwide, he'd either assassinated leaders or simply slick-talked his way into the director's seat in places like Zeta—home of the Siberian citizens—Delta and Kappa in the Europa continents, and Omega Territory. We might be free, but our brethren overseas were not.

I barged to my feet, unable to contain my rage any longer. "You were right last night," I said, glaring at Linc. "You should've killed your motherfucking dad when you had the chance."

Liz tried to placate me while Cannon was ready to restrain me, rising from his seat.

Linc merely nodded. "I know."

Nate spoke in a calm drawl. "It wouldn't have mattered. Leon was already infected by that point."

I wrenched free of Liz's hands.

"If we can track down Father, we can find the cure. When we finally take him out, it will be with the antidote in hand and total InterNations victory on our side." Linc drew Liz close to his side.

"Sorry. Sorry, man. I'm just really screwed up about this," I apologized.

"No shit." Liz huffed a little laugh.

"You have every right to be upset, Darke, which is why I asked if you needed to step away from our meeting." Hills frowned at me.

"I'm not going anywhere." Taking my seat, I laid my palms flat on the table. I thought for a moment. "What about this Denver? You trust him? Because he seems like a sketchy dude." Both Linc and Farrow considered him a double agent, but I wasn't convinced he was working for the good of the people. His only saving grace so far was he hadn't killed Liz when he'd had the chance back in Beta.

"Got no choice," was Linc's not-so-comforting reply.

Liz leaned onto her forearms. "I say we send out our feelers for Dr. Val. She created this thing. She infected Leon. She'll have the cure. And as soon as we get it, I've got first dibs on slitting her throat. A little bit of justice for my dad."

I listened to them go around for another hour before I snapped. "All this yammering is getting us nowhere. What's the strategy?" I was used to formulating a plan, not sitting on my ass while people flapped their gums.

"We can't just go off half-cocked—" Cannon started.

"The hell we can't. Maybe you want to twiddle your damn D-Ps until Cutler destroys every last rebel and Freelander Outpost, but I don't. I'll go it alone if I have to."

Linc shook his head. "We don't even know Dr. Val's true whereabouts. We don't have any solid leads yet."

"Or contacts." Cannon rapped his knuckles on the arms of his chair.

"Ah reckon Ah might know one or two people here and there…" Farrow interjected.

"Is there any Territory you haven't plundered, Farrow?" Liz snaked a grin at the other woman.

Farrow pinned a loose curl back into her hairdo. "What's that old sayin'? Every port in a storm."

Linc chuckled. "I think it's *any* port in a storm."

I growled in frustration.

Suddenly Hatch jumped up from his seat. He'd had his ears on the conversation and his eyes locked on his D-P, constantly scanning the channels. "Holy hell. I think y'all are gonna wanna see this."

Our D-Ps bleeped as he sent the link. I dug mine out of my pocket, tuning in to a black screen that showed only the word REVOLUTION in bold red letters.

"Where's this coming from?" I asked.

"There's no origination signal. It's being broadcast from one hundred and fifty different locations, and my guess is they're all false leads." Hatch pushed his glasses farther up his nose.

A voice came across the wire. Distorted and deep, it echoed around the town hall:

"The Revolution is one step away from being defeated by the Company. Activism, equality, freedom will be dictated by a newly unilateral militarized government controlled by one man only: CEO Cutler."

"Who the hell is this?" Cannon curled over the D-P he shared with Nathaniel.

Shivers raced up my spine. "Who's this going out to?"

Hatch threw his smudged glasses onto the table. "Everyone. Everywhere."

"Holy shit," Nate whispered.

The blank screen changed to an image of what had to be Omega Territory—a red desert dust bowl to begin with—followed by more images that flashed quickly on the screen. Omega on the Aafricans continent had always been the most forward-thinking Territory. There the Company *allowed* the population of Freelanders to do the daily drudgery for them in this sunbaked land my ancestors hailed from. In exchange for their workforce, the CO let the Omega Freelanders live within the Territory walls instead of outright persecuting them.

Now the D-Ps streamed pictures of the Freelander people being hounded and harassed by the military from every corner of the vibrant city of bazaars.

"We rebels now know a certain number of the subpopulation in each Freelander stronghold has been infected with a new strain of the Plague. The CEO wants to rid the InterNations of what he calls our pestilence. This strain goes live on August sixteenth, 2071."

"Aw, shit. That's not good."

All eyes swung to me.

"Are you thinking riots?" Linc asked.

"More like killing sprees since word of the infected is being broadcast live."

"There is a cure, my friends! It's in the early phases. We think it can be synthesized with the right medical instruction. Our shamans are working on it. It all begins in Omega. Remember: Love Free or Die."

The transmission ended with that rallying cry. Omega was where Cutler was reported to be. If the cure was there, too, it was a kill-two-birds-with-one-stone scenario.

"Who the fuck was that?" Cannon cussed.

Hatch shook his head. "Unknown voice, untraceable broadcast."

"Some bastard's out there making bold statements. He better hope to hell he can back them up once we nail his ass." I rewound the transmission and watched it again.

Everyone pulled closer to the table and started speaking at once, their voices rising above one another.

"Omega's the point of origin."

"Especially if Cutler's there, too."

"I'm going. Make the arrangements pronto." I just needed a starting place, my weapons, and transport.

"We're going," Cannon announced. A round of fists pounding the table sent a jolt of energy through me.

We were decided then. There were two races: to find the cure or steal Doc Val's antidote, and to take Cutler down once and for all.

Time was our biggest enemy.

More talk spun around me. I listened with half an ear, more attuned to finding out where Leon was than on who was going, who was staying, and why.

"Sebastian's with us." Farrow spit green fire from her eyes.

Hills sighed. "He hasn't been through the coming-of-age rites yet."

"Ah don't need a communal ceremony to tell me my baby brother is a grown man. He did his time in Beta."

"Ooh boy. Territory girl's got a temper. Maybe you need to get that itch scratched, Farrow." Liz's lips lifted.

Linc groaned.

Liz swiveled to him with a *tut.* "I wasn't offering, baby."

As head of the Chitamauga militia, this was my call. "Sebastian can come."

"Speaking of ceremonies, we want to get married first," Linc said. He looked at Hills, making his appeal to the commune elder.

I tried to ignore the knock to my chest. He and Liz deserved to be happy for one damn day, and I deserved exactly what I got, too—the solitude I'd all but demanded. I tuned out, lifting my head only when I saw a flash of gold skin and long hair pass beyond the windows. Leaning back in my chair, I followed Leon with my gaze. He strolled down the road, his shirt hanging from his back pocket. The muscles in his back shifted and shined in the sunlight.

I shoved away from the table. On my way out the door, I heard the usual guffaws, this time tinged with an air of sadness.

"Cock on a leash, like I always said," Liz halfheartedly joked.

Farrow drawled, "Ah'd be more inclined to say it's his heart on the leash."

* * *

Outside, I jogged to catch up with Leon. The sun worshipped his body, deepening the tan on his honey-colored skin. He wore cut-off denims that hung low enough on his hips to reveal twin pelvic cuts when he turned at the sound of my approach.

I swept my hands up his sides to gently clasp his shoulders. "Where've you been?"

"Out in the fields. Micah needed some help."

My already-stressed emotions hit the red line. "What the hell are you thinking? That can't be a good idea in your condition."

"I'm not six feet under yet."

I felt my stomach bottom out. "I know you're not. And you won't be. We just had some news. There's a cure in the making. We're headed to Omega."

He aimed a somber smile at our feet. "Are we?"

I lifted his face to mine. "Yes, we are."

"Bien." He remained distant.

It was so not fucking *bien* I tripped over my tongue. "Good, uh…I'll see you at the handfasting later?" *Come to the handfasting with me,* I should've said.

"Handfasting?"

"Linc and Liz. They wanna do it before we head out. Because…"

"We probably ain't gon' come back." He leaned in, fingers splayed on my chest before shifting away. "I guess I gotta go pack."

"Wait. Where'd you spend last night?"

"In my momma's wagon—not dat it's any of your business."

Leon walked away, back straight, head high. *So much for treading softly with the man. Shit.* It seemed like everything I tried with Leon ended with me planting my size-sixteen boots in it again.

But there was one thing I *could* do.

I set off for my place. It was time to say good-bye to my ghosts, even if Leon never knew it. Turning the corner, I slowed to a stop and wiped my eyes. *Forgive me, Tam. Let me go, Wilde. Be at peace.*

Let Leon live.

I let the door bang when I entered the two-roomer. I yanked the heavy curtains wide open over the windows and then ripped them entirely off. Sun streamed in. There was no hiding anymore. Throughout the rest of the afternoon, I filled boxes with their belongings. I lovingly laid Tam's favorite boots on top of her clothes. I packed Wilde's books carefully—the heavy tomes about husbandry and veterinary medicine. I added Tammerick's pistols after I cleaned them to a bright shine.

I kept only two things—the ivory-handled dagger Wilde had etched with my name and a lock of hair from Tam tied in a deep red satin ribbon. I placed them in a small wooden box I locked inside the bottom drawer of my dresser, and then I knelt on the floor and laid my hand over my heart.

"Good-bye, my loves."

It wasn't as if I felt freed when I walked over to Eden's caravan with boxes piled in my arms. There was no jaunt to my step. My burden was too heavy for that. I did take in the birdsong, the chatter of squirrels, and the heat of the sun. I thought about the room I'd made for Leon and I felt lighter.

Eden answered my knock, her haphazard bun of strawberry-blond hair collapsing on top of her head. She peeked inside the crates, and her hand flew to her mouth. "Oh, Darke."

Swallowing several times, I passed the boxes into her arms. I made my way back down her steps and onto the grass. "I figured you could disperse their belongings as needed to our villagers."

Eyes as vividly blue as the wings of a swallowtail butterfly found mine. "I'll do just that so long as you remember you deserve happiness, too."

"Yes, ma'am. I'll try." I retreated, blinking back the final pain.

She called after me, "You're a good man, Darke."

* * *

I hadn't dragged in a deep breath since last night. Fuck that. I hadn't inhaled a goddamn normal breath since I'd heard Leon had been snatched right in front of Cannon and Liz in Beta. And, fuck me, my heart had stopped when Tammerick and Wilde were killed. Today I'd said good-bye to them, because of Leon.

It was Leon who'd kick-started my heart again, Leon who ignited the fire in my blood and loins, Leon I didn't want to love but had to save.

My path to the meadow later was no less lonely for having laid my loved ones to rest. I padded softly among the tall stalks of wildflowers, careful not to crush them underfoot. I dawdled in the open fields that led to the small knoll beyond which the handfasting would take place. Everything now would be rushed: love, life, death, coming so swiftly upon us.

I was caught up in my meandering when a small hand snuck into the crook of my elbow. Jonquil kept her gaze ahead as she joined me. She was everyone's favorite former flirt, well, except for Cannon's. She'd taken great pleasure in terrorizing him with her feminine wiles his first few days in the commune. Now she was married, more mature, and well on her way to motherhood.

"Surely you'll walk a mother-to-be to the gathering, Darke."

"And where is your husband?" I fell into an easier gait beside her.

"I do believe he took to the merrymaking early."

"As he did with you."

She patted the proud swell of her belly with a secret smile. "Yes. And I have no complaints on that, either."

The meadow had been transformed during the afternoon. An altar was swiftly raised beneath an arbor dripping with blooms of brightly colored lilies. The table before Eden and Hills held the priapic wand and a length of red ribbon.

The villagers assembled, dressed in their finest, whatever shape that took on this muggy July evening, but always with the Freelander hint of red. Votives lit the path down which Liz would walk, and more candles on the altar added a beautiful glow to the night as dusk descended in dark blues and vivid violets.

Leon made his way to the ceremony after me. He didn't stand beside me or anywhere near me. He wouldn't look at me, although I stared at him continuously. I couldn't help it. His hair was tied back and tamed for once. His shirt was bright white against his skin, and his lips moved rapidly as he made little Calliope—one of Micah's young daughters—laugh.

A hush fell over the crowd. Cannon appeared on the crest of the grassy hill, Liz on his arm. She wore some sort of ivory dress that could have come only from Farrow's collection, baring her shoulders and part of her midriff. I chuckled when my gaze fell to her hips, where her Desert Eagles were holstered. They were her only accessories, except for a circlet of white flowers in her softly spiked black hair.

I glanced at Linc to see his mouth drop open before he snapped it shut. When Liz passed me, I noticed the way she kept blinking, trying to keep her tears at bay. Next to her—tall as a tree and as large as me—Cannon did the same. He deposited her in front of Linc at the altar, where they exchanged a few terse words before Liz drew their gazes to her gun belt with a wide smile.

The opening kiss Liz and Linc shared was slow and passionate. I stared at the side of Leon's face, willing him to look at me, to share this moment with me, but he trained his sights steadfastly ahead. I felt a sharp poke in the ribs from Tommy, which returned my attention to the couple in front of us.

Their vows were spoken in low voices—a rumble from Linc as

he clasped her face, a throaty whisper from Liz when she kissed the tips of his fingers, placing his hand against her heart. Tears slid down their cheeks, their eyes fastened on each other as their lives soon would be. I didn't need to hear their words to feel the power of their love.

Rings were exchanged once the ribbon was wound around their arms and hands, binding them together, no matter what might come. Linc closed his eyes and smiled at something Liz said as she slid his wedding band home. When his ring came to rest on her finger, the villagers went wild. Shouting, whistling, clapping, and hugging one another.

I was embraced by one person after another as I slowly made my way to the center circle trying to locate Leon. Goose bumps erupted on my skin when I found him a meter away, his eyes locked on me.

Neither of us moved until a flurry of red ribbons from each Freelander's hand waved and weaved into the air amid shouts of "Live in Freedom! Love at Will!"

The barrage of hollers and the press of people carried us away from each other and across the meadow. I fumbled in my pocket for my own ribbon and set it loose in the wind. It curled and coiled, then whipped from my hand, flying bright as a poppy across the dark sky.

* * *

Hills got his wish that Sebastian be sent off properly for our mission. In the town hall directly after Liz and Linc's handfasting, I conducted a quick ceremony to initiate him into manhood.

At the age of eighteen, Sebastian had been through his own ordeals in Beta. I deemed the tall, rangy youth with the white-blond hair and charming southern manner ready to face the hardships to come. He stood still and straight when the flat blade of my ceremonial dagger pressed onto one of his shoulders and then the other. His near-violet–colored eyes were somber as he kissed the cool metal laid against his lips.

After accepting my formal congratulations and my less-formal handshake, he gave me a small bow. Then he laughed. "Shoot. That was a breeze compared to the test of manhood in the bedroom Territorians have to go through. I didn't even have to get my equipment out."

"Tell me about it, baby brother," Farrow said. "At my ceremony, Nathaniel here ran out on me like his pants were on fire. Not in the way one would want, Ah'm afraid."

"I'm afraid that's because *you* had the wrong equipment." Sebastian mock punched his sister.

"Oh, just go and fetch me a drink," Farrow commanded.

Before he turned to leave, Sebastian shook my hand. "Thanks, Darke. I know we got off to a rocky start."

I tried to forget how I'd wanted to shoot him on sight because I thought he had the hots for Leon. "Water under the bridge." Unless he ever decided to look at Leon with anything even remotely resembling carnal interest again.

All the while I kept a lookout for Leon, who managed to always stay beyond my vision. I wondered if he watched me, if he was thinking about me. I wanted to initiate Leon, too, in a much more sexual manner, except I knew he'd had other lovers and I was probably the least of his concerns.

Jesus Christ. After that I found myself a frothy mug of ale. Nathaniel started his guitar playing, and Liz and Linc took to the cleared floor beneath rafters decorated with brightly colored banners.

An air of urgency tempered the jubilant celebration, or perhaps that was just my goddamn pining. I laid eyes on Leon just as Old Tommy and farmer Micah took up their usual bookend stances beside me at the plank-board bar. I quaffed quietly, ignoring their bickering about who originally wrote the song Nathaniel sang, his voice ringing clear and dropping to a gritty growl at turns.

Cannon hauled up beside us, licking his lips while he watched his mate strum. "Van Morrison," he pronounced, ending the debate. "Fuck."

I handed him a drink. "You got it bad, man."

Cannon turned his attention to me and arched an eyebrow. "And I'll be getting it in bed later, unlike you. What are you waiting for?"

"Dance with Leon?" I asked.

"Why not? Everyone else is."

Don't I know it. I'd found him, all right. He'd sucked back one drink and then another before taking to the floor. The way he moved his body invited unwanted fantasies I was trying to drown in alcohol. Leon danced with everyone but me. He acted like nothing was happening. Not to him, not between us.

"Don't think so." I crossed my arms, intent on staying where I was. Staring, stalking, waiting to strike.

Knocking against me, Tommy bared his summer teeth in a ghoulish grin. "G'on. Get 'im, son."

Micah pinched my ass, and I jumped forward. Cannon pushed a hand between my shoulder blades. "Now or never."

I'll take never, thanks. My palms grew damp, and Micah took my beer from me. *Assholes, the lot of them.*

I watched Leon, preparing to close in. He was dancing alone finally. His hips swiveled, his hair had come loose, and his eyes were shut.

Aligning myself behind him, I bent to let my breath brush his ear. "I want to dance with you."

My hands found his waist and he leaned in to me. "Darke."

I was no longer nervous. My voice deepened as hunger struck me. "Turn around, babe. Let me feel you."

Leon slid into my embrace. Tall and lithe, his body was enfolded by mine. My hands settled just above his ass, stoking the heat between us. Our groins met, both cocks hard. Music played somewhere, but the rhythm we moved to was the primal beat of rutting male bodies. Reaching beneath the tails of his shirt, I thumbed the dimples above his ass. His hips lurched. His lips and teeth found my neck, mumbling those crazed, lusty Cajuns words I only half understood. Explosives went off inside my body, shivering up my spine, shuddering down to my rigid cock.

"Good God, I want you." I leaned him back, finding his studded nipples beneath his shirt with fingertips that twisted, tapped, teased.

"*Dieu,* yes."

I loved watching my dark skin play against his tawny flesh. Too bad the damn shirt was in the way, as well as our pants—and hundreds of onlookers. Beyond our first month, I'd never given a second thought to taking both Tammerick and Wilde in public during the annual orgiastic festival, but there was no way in hell I'd share Leon with anyone here.

I growled, bending my knees, catching his cock against mine, grinding until my eyes rolled back. I smoothed a hand down his chest to the front of his pants, jerking him against me. Hooded eyes, tousled hair...I wanted him just like this for me, only me, every day of my life.

His lips parted when my mouth sought his, but at the last moment he turned his face. I was granted only a kiss on his cheek. My muttered oath was drowned out as people started clapping, whether for our show or Nathaniel's vocals, I didn't know.

Leon pushed off of me. He shook his head and stumbled away, glancing back only once. The hunt was on. My blood sang, and my body was on high alert. I barely said good night to Liz and Linc before I started after him.

Outside I heard him whistling as he ambled down the road. Perhaps he'd had more to drink than I'd thought. When he hiccupped, I smiled. Catching up to him, I ran an arm around his waist and pulled him back against me. His long sigh ended with a low moan.

"Darke, this ain't a good idea."

At that point I didn't really care. He smelled fresh and clean, spicy and a little sweaty. The pulse at the side of his throat ticked like a fast-running clock, and I nipped him there.

"Where are you going?"

Turning in my arms, he slid his hands along my waist. A current of heat raced between us, trapping my breath in my lungs. "To bed."

His mouth was so juicy and red. So ripe to kiss. I ran my thumb across his bottom lip, shuddering when he touched me with his tongue. "My bed."

He backed away. "I don' need a keeper. I'm not a boy. And I ain't your boy. You made dat clear."

I grasped his hair in a fist, softening my hold to cup his neck. "You're right. You're a man. My man. So stop fucking fighting me for a change and get your sexy ass in my bed. Now."

Fuck. Wrong words. Leon took another step back. Before he could let fly with another earful, I strode forward. "Please, Leon." I raised my hands to his face. "I need you. I want you in my bed, just once." My voice stuck in my throat. "We don't have to do anything, I just…"

"Oh, we're probably gonna do somethin'." He turned his head until his moist lips brushed my wrist. His playful grin was back, but then again he could just be three sheets to the wind.

"Will you wait for me in my caravan?"

He nodded.

"I'll go to the kitchens, find some food." He headed off toward my place while I did an about-face to the mess hall, grumbling, "Something to soak up all that alcohol, at least."

CHAPTER FOUR

Carrying a tray of food, I stepped quietly inside. I noticed the glow of the lanterns scattered around. When my gaze found Leon, my caravan grew impossibly small, reducing the world to him and me. The sight of him in my room, sitting on my bed, was something I wanted to remember forever. I closed the door, running a hand down my face before the image of him burned holes through my eyes. He was too goddamn gorgeous, too young. Too young to be mine. Too young to die.

I set the tray in the middle of the bed. I felt his regard as I removed my boots and unbuttoned my shirt. His eyes widened with every bit of skin revealed down the center of my chest. Leaving the shirt on, I crouched on the balls of my feet in front of him. His hand rose to my face, over my jaw, down my neck, where it rested while I took off his boots. I skimmed my palms up his legs, feeling the heat of his skin beneath the cloth. When I reached his thighs, his breath fanned across my face. I kissed his neck, took his earlobe between my lips and nibbled.

Leon's hand darted to my waist, but I gripped his wrist. "You can touch." He moaned, trying to twist free. I smelled the sweet scent of whiskey on his breath. "After you eat." I needed him to dry out a little bit.

"Blackmailin' me?"

"You got it." I grinned.

With a groan, Leon flopped back onto the bed. I climbed behind him and pulled him into my arms, my legs on either side of his. Resting with him against my chest, I arranged the tray beside us. He made a grab for a chunk of crusty bread, but I had him drink a glass of water first. He narrowed his eyes at me as he drained the glass.

"Let me feed you."

His tongue wet his lips. His voice turned husky. "Okay."

I dipped a piece of bread in a saucer of rich honey. "Open your mouth for me." His lips opened and I couldn't help but imagine the head of my cock pushing through them to be welcomed by his tongue.

Honey dripped down my fingers. It drizzled onto his tongue. He sucked it inside, and I groaned. I swiped more honey from the bread over his lips until his mouth was shiny.

"Take a bite," I forced out.

He tore off a chunk with a grin. The gorgeous bastard was playing with me.

The seductive dance continued with cubes of cheese and slices of fruit. Watching him eat was one of those simple pleasures I hadn't let myself enjoy. I soaked it all in, not knowing how long any of this would last. With that thought always in the back of my mind and Leon stretched against me, I dipped my fingers into the honey and fed them to him one by one. Watching his smoky eyes, listening to him hum as he suckled my flesh took simple pleasure to heightened intensity. When a drop of honey clung to the corner of his lips, I gave up resisting. I licked his mouth, pausing to dip just inside.

Eyes hooded and heavy lifted to mine. "Now I can touch you?"

"Yes." I barely got the word out.

He got off the bed, put the tray on the small table by the window, and returned to crawl between my outstretched legs. Grasping both sides of my shirt, he slid it down my shoulders and off my arms.

"I could eat you up, *beb*." His fingers sliding along my torso, trailing as if counting the muscles clenching at his touch, he sank his teeth into the sinew between my neck and shoulder.

My head cranked back. My hips surged up.

He soothed the bite with his tongue. "So many muscles. I like my men big, but you're like a fuckin' tank."

He squeezed my pecs, rubbing his palms in circles. His mouth joined his hands. His wet, pink lips and flushed skin stood out against my black body. When his tongue flicked one nipple, I growled at the harsh pleasure. My cock reared up, looking for an escape from my pants. I felt it press against Leon's hip. He sucked my other nipple and grinded down on my length.

My need was a bright hot coil low in my groin. "My turn," I said.

Taking him by his hips, I swiveled him around until he flipped to the bed beneath me.

He gripped my biceps. "*Mmm.* I like it when you use dem muscles on me."

Fucking hell. I could barely see straight, thinking about what it would be like to rip his pants off and attack his body, grab his tight ass and pull the cheeks open. I sucked hard on his neck, laughing when his back arched and his words became garbled. I gave him another love bite at the muscular hollow of his collarbone, bruising his skin until it turned red, then purple.

I tugged his shirt off, throwing it behind me. I undid his belt and quickly whipped it away. I stared at his swollen lips, remembering how he'd turned away earlier when I'd tried to kiss him.

I inhaled sharply and retreated from the bed. "I think you better do the rest."

"You wan' me to take it all off?"

I shook my head *no,* meaning *yes,* of course.

"Too bad. 'Cause I'm commando under these."

Jesus fucking Christ. That was a visual I didn't think my cock could withstand. I turned away, keeping my back to him through sheer force of will as I heard the rustle of clothes. When I heard his pants *thunk* to the floor, every single muscle from my calves to my shoulders tensed.

"It's safe to look now."

I doubted that very much.

He lay on his back. He regarded me with a smile on his lips, arms crossed behind his head. Tufts of soft-looking hair under his arms mirrored the thin line that trailed from his navel and beneath the sheet around his waist. His biceps were two tight hills of muscle. He wasn't a massive brute like me but a tasty, perfect package of slim strength and sexuality.

"So all's I gotta do to get into your bed is find out I'm destined to die in a few weeks?" Biting his lush bottom lip, Leon sent me a wink.

Fire traced hot fingers down my stomach to my groin. "Jesus, Leon." His bravado was insanely erotic, as if he needed more of that shit going for him. There was no explanation for the gut-deep reaction I had every time I saw him.

Turning to the basin, I glanced at him and then away. "Please tell me you're really wearing something under there."

"Yeah, *beb,* I'm wearin' my birthday suit like I told you. Did you know dat's what they used to call it? Bein' naked?"

I heard the bed shift. When I glanced over my shoulder, his smile was sinful. A long stretch pulled the sheet all the way down to his lean hips and the muscles carved into his pelvis. A dark shadow of hair peeked out, hinting at a cropping of pubes below. But that wasn't all. A lyrical-looking linear design was tattooed right there, on the left side of his groin, where the skin was smooth and golden.

I started to speak, but I couldn't. My mouth went dry and then totally wet. My eyes traced the tat like I wanted my tongue to do. It was suddenly hot as a furnace inside the caravan. I quickly splashed myself with cold water from the jug, hoping to cool down. In the cramped quarters, Leon's scent washed over me as I quickly dried. It became stronger the closer I got to him—musky, spicy, man.

I sat on the edge of the bed. "Maybe we should talk."

One hand ran from the nape of my neck down the center of my back. "Maybe you should get in bed."

My fingers contracted against my thighs. I shuddered at the sound of his invitation. Closing my eyes, I tried to steady my labored breath and quickening heartbeat, which matched the pulsing of my heavy shaft. When I rolled onto the bed, sinking in beside him, he moved against me. Intense, almost rabid lust for him made me jerk and shiver.

Rising onto an elbow, Leon watched his hand wander over my skin. My deep muscles flexed while he lazily explored my chest and abdomen. I pulled him against me. His flesh was hot, skin so silky soft when I dragged both hands up his back to grab hold of his head. The sun-streaked locks felt downright decadent between my fingers.

His eyes were nearly black when I pulled my face from the crook of his neck. "I want to kiss you."

"*Non*. Not until I'm sure you won't change your mind at the last second." Pushing me onto my back, Leon crawled over me. All that sleek skin slipped against me. He was small enough to curl on top of me, but strong enough to grasp my wrists and slam them to the bed beside my head. "Where you gonna go now?"

I lifted my head. "Nowhere."

He dipped his mouth to mine, and I nearly exploded at his sweet taste. It was a first kiss in almost every sense. Leon didn't remember any of the others we'd shared, and this one blew my mind. At first it was just a whisper of his mouth. A wetting of our lips together. I licked his upper lip, the lower one, too. He pursed his mouth with a low mewl, and I sucked on him, plucking on his lips again and again. He rose. I tried to follow, but he shook his head. So slowly, he lowered again, brushing his mouth against mine. He stopped and moved away. A hairbreadth separated us.

"Leon," I gasped.

He relented, sliding our mouths firmly together. Every lunge of his tongue against mine had him whimpering and moaning. Licking down my neck and up over my chin, Leon pumped his hips, and the pungent addictive aroma of precome drifted up to me.

I clenched my fingers around his, letting him take me any way he wanted. "*Ahh*, fucking hell, Leon." Months of self-enforced celibacy had me clinging to the edge by my fingertips.

His stubble streaked across my skin in a hot burn. He dug his teeth into my shoulder, provoking a low shout that tripped out of my throat with every ragged breath. Tugging my close-cropped hair, he slanted his mouth to mine. The rough kisses mashed our mouths together, drugging me. I almost jumped out of my skin when he began moving down my chest. His moist lips pulled and teased the dark beads of my nipples. My hips moved, my dick chafing down the leg of my pants.

Leon hooked a finger into the front of my pants, teasing through the curls and almost touching the base of my cock. A spurt of precome pushed from my slit at that mere brush. With a low moan, I grabbed his wrist and pulled his hand up to the less-dangerous territory of my chest.

"Not taking these off because I won't be able to control myself if I do."

His eyes were feverish. "I don' care. I'm ready."

"I'm not. I don't want our first time to become another lost memory."

He sat back on his heels, the sheet covering him from the hips down and foiling my sight. "And I don' want our first time to be our last time!"

The truth was chillingly cold as it swept through me.

"Leon."

He refused to look at me.

"We will make love and not just once." Pressing the butt of my palm to the hard length yearning to break free of my pants, I gave a low laugh. "I promise you that."

After a moment of huffing, he nodded.

I pulled him to me and rolled him onto his back. Studying the high color of his cheeks, his kiss-bright lips, his half-lidded eyes, I traced the fan of his eyelashes. "You're so sexy, babe."

Leon arched into my little touches. His hand drifted to my thigh, pulling it across his hip. "You jus' want me for my body," he said. "Diseased as it is."

"That's not funny."

"You'll have to get used to my sick sense of humor."

"You'll have to get used to this." I teased his lips open and drove inside deep and fast. I waited for his hot gasps before slipping away to lick and kiss his neck and his ear. He purred for me.

I tipped his face to me for one last lingering kiss. "We need to sleep sometime tonight."

He murmured softly, wrapping his arms around me. When sleep took Leon, I remained awake. I held him in my arms, cherishing every one of his breaths and every moment with him next to me. Because I knew better than to take anything for granted.

* * *

I woke up when Leon's lean body was replaced by a cool breeze. Propping up on my elbows, I watched him wash from the stand in the corner. His hands—those long fingers—rinsed the cloth after each sweep down torso to groin. From the back, his arms and shoulders flexed, and I could just see the deep dimples at the top of his buttocks peeking above the waistband of his pants.

He wrung out the cloth and slipped into a shirt.

"Where are you going?" I asked as he combed his hair back.

He swung around, color splashing his high cheekbones. There was an obvious tent under the sheet that fell about my waist, but I didn't bother to hide my reaction to him. In the dead of the night, I'd disrobed completely, wanting the closeness of his nude body against mine.

His eyes darted up and down my body. "Doc wants to finish up my blood work dis mornin."

"But he's sure it's a sleeper virus until the sixteenth, right?"

"Yeah." He fiddled with the buttons on his shirt.

I stretched my legs. The sheet dropped just below my hips. Leon's gaze slid right along with it. "How about a kiss first?"

I liked it when he flushed even deeper at my unexpected request. His wide brown eyes flicked to mine and away.

He edged to the door of my caravan. "Not sure how sick I am yet. Better not."

"Considering what you did with me last night, it doesn't really matter, does it? Besides, Doc already assured us it's spread through contact with contaminated blood. You're not... It's not live yet. Kissing isn't going to kill us."

He said nothing. He avoided looking at me.

"Hang on. You weren't gonna let me kiss you at all, were you?" I frowned at him.

"*Non.* Because something *is* gonna kill me. You know nothin' can come of this," he said sadly.

I jumped from the bed and strode toward him, the sheet draped negligently around me. "That's bullshit."

"I don' wanna lead you on. I know how much that hurts."

His words stopped me in my tracks. "You said you didn't remember."

The warmth from our nighttime embraces was extinguished by Leon's icy demeanor.

"I don't, not really. Just feelings. Wanting you and you turning me away. I feel it here." He thumped his chest. "I don' know why you wouldn't have me, Darke." His eyes met mine, brimming with tears.

"Whatever I said, whatever I did before, it doesn't matter. Everything's changed, Leon."

"*Non.* The only thing dat's changed is me. If you just want me now 'cause I'm gonna die, none of dis is true." He clenched his fists at his sides. "It does matter, Darke."

The door slammed behind him.

CHAPTER FIVE

I didn't blame Liz and Linc for their rush to get hitched. I didn't blame any of my comrades for getting involved in the fight for Leon's life. I admired their guts. Each one of them was stubborn, difficult, and too goddamn brave. Made up of warrior material, all of them.

That was all well and good in theory. The reality was much more gut-wrenching. I really started wishing they'd decided to fall back when it came time to depart Chitamauga. Early on the morning of July 27, we left the commune for what might be our last time. The good-byes were excruciating to witness.

Heavily pregnant, waddling, and wiping her eyes, Jonquil was the first in line to give her blessings for a safe journey. "Oh, these damn hormones. The baby's makin' a mess of me, and I haven't even had it yet." She sighed, cradling the globe of her belly. She kissed Nathaniel and Cannon full on the lips before they could protest, the rest of us on both cheeks. "There'll be a new little runt waitin' for you to return, so y'all make sure to get back here quick as you can—you hear me?" Breaking out in a fresh bout of weeping, she waved us away.

Hills stood in front of the circle of villagers. His strong stance belied his advanced years, his proud bearing reminiscent of the day he busted up the dirty fistfight between Cannon and our homegrown traitor, Kale.

"I remember telling you, Caspar Cannon, you had to earn your worth with these folks. You've done that, son, many times over."

Cannon went to bump fists with him, but our leader pulled him into a hug. Afterward, Hills turned to me. He looked me in the eye, measuring my mettle. I returned his stare, lifting my chin and straightening my shoulders.

"You give 'em hell, Darke."

Shouts went up around us and fists punched the air. Hills grinned at me, the old rabble-rouser, before he clasped my hand. "You bring 'em all home to us."

"You have my vow."

Eden pushed her way to us, giving everyone hugs, asking if we had our first-aid kits with her special poultices. She kept nattering nervously until Nathaniel brought her into his embrace. She broke down in his arms. Her family had grown so much in less than a year, her two sons finding their way home, her son-in-law, Cannon, and now Liz as the newest members of the Rice clan.

She patted Nathaniel's cheeks. "Oh, let me go already. I'm fine. I'll be right as rain." She stepped back only to be embraced by Linc. "Oh, you boys. Why aren't you always this sweet? Just wanna see your ma spring the waterworks? Lemme go, I tell ya." Her laugh was colored by sadness, but Linc released her. "You take care of each other. You're all family in one way or the other."

"Yes'm," the eight of us replied in unison.

Seeing Evangeline give her send-off to Leon was the most difficult. She kept a flowery handkerchief continuously pressed to her cheeks even while she laid into him.

"You got da gumbo, boy, but don' be thinkin' 'bout givin' dat *Monsieur* Darke a hard time."

Leon glanced at me, unable to mask his pain. "Try not to."

She grabbed him in a tight hug as her long, loose hair flew around them both. *"Je t'aime, mon fils."* She clasped his face. "Come back. Be safe."

In front of me, Evangeline shook her finger. "And you, you no cause *la misère* anymore, yes?"

"I'll try not to."

Leon chuckled. His momma glared at me. She relented long enough to draw me against her, letting me go with a hearty slap to my ass. My face reddened.

"You play up over there in Omega and there's more of dat when you get back."

Old Tommy was last. Too bad he wasn't too late. "Got you a bunch of hens peckin' at ya when what you need is a rooster, eh?" I rolled my eyes while my compadres laughed. He squinted around the group. "Well, I ain't gonna miss ya. 'Cept there won't be hardly nothin' to gossip 'bout now with all you randy youngsters headin' out."

Cannon and Nathaniel started down the densely wooded lane. Linc and Liz trailed them. Bas, Farrow, and Leon walked three abreast after them. I started to follow, but Tommy grabbed my arm.

"You remember what I said to you. No more hidin' in the dark."

Catching up to the group, I sent one last look behind me. The sentry pine forest surrounding our commune, the one road to and from, the meadow and the fields flush with flowers and summer crops...The deep lake reflected the sun. A crowd of people stood behind us, calling out good-byes and well-wishes, waving. Chitamauga had been my home my entire life. Now it was off to the unknown.

Dragging my eyes away, I walked beside Leon. We didn't touch. No one spoke.

Leaves, pinecones, twigs snapped beneath eight pairs of feet, making our silence even louder. Tension crackled between us.

Liz pushed a low-hanging tree branch out of her way and almost let it slap back to hit Linc. He rushed her with a growl, lifting her in his arms. Just like that, the mood snapped.

"You know, Darke, you can stop guilt-tripping about taking us away from our home and duties now," Liz called back.

"Oh, I can, can I?"

Linc placed her on the ground, prodding her forward.

"Yep." She grabbed a leaf and flicked it at Farrow. "*Ah reckon* Vance, Moxie, and Ginger Johnson can't do much more damage to Beta than has already been done."

We all laughed, falling in step together.

* * *

A day and a half later we arrived at our meeting point. Our flight captain, arranged by none other than Farrow, was to

convene with us at the edge of the forest overlooking Alpha-
Beta Route One, which was to be our airstrip. During the
intervening thirty-six hours, while we'd hiked and camped,
what had gone down between me and Leon? Absolutely fucking nothing. We were at a stalemate just like this goddamn
never-ending war.

As we waited for our escort to show, we rechecked our supplies. Cammos and ammo, that was how Cannon, Linc, and
Liz—former elite Corps soldiers—prepped for battle, and since
we were headed into a hotbed of insurgency amid a swarm of
Corps, the rest of us followed suit.

Our ears suddenly perked up at the sound of a branch cracking. When the curtain of greenery parted, the woman who appeared found eight guns aimed at her.

"Well, that's a fine how-de-do," she said. "Mind standing
down?" As soon as we safetied our weapons, she approached us.

"Flight Captain Darwin," the woman said. I realized she was
in a jumpsuit, her helmet stowed under her arm. She was Corps
through and through. Reformed Corps.

When the introductions were done, Darwin led us in the direction of our transport. We broke through the trees to get our
first visual of the Alpha-Beta airfield, and I missed a step on the
grassy slope. I almost skidded down on my ass. Directly below,
sitting fair and square in the middle of the tarmac, was a massive
unmarked air vessel. It looked just like the Corps planes that had
almost razed Beta Territory to the ground.

"That's a Predator…" I felt queasy. I'd never been in an air vessel, and these particular motherfuckers took off from a standstill,

rising vertically before the wings expanded and—*zoom*—they were gone.

Darwin raced down the hill to her machine. "How'd you think we were gonna get to Omega, swim the Pan Atlantic?"

We approached the Predator. It eclipsed the road and made me feel like an ant beside its big black hull.

"Hey, Leon. You might need to take your man's mind off the flight," Cannon quipped.

"Not my man." Leon walked me up the back ramp like I was a doddering old fool.

Christ, I'm not even a man at all at this point.

I continued to grumble as we made our way into the giant belly of the aeroplane. Leon's lips twitched, and his eyes sparkled. I'd make goddamn good and sure he saw me as virile warrior…later, after I upchucked my guts onto the iron-gridded floor. As I harnessed myself into a seat in the cavernous cargo area at the rear of the Predator, I felt dizzy from the nausea.

"Feelin' green around the gills?" Leon belted himself in beside me.

"Huh?" I felt like puking up the contents of my stomach. A cold sweat broke out on my forehead as I imagined us hurtling through the air with nothing above us and nothing below us.

Cannon snorted. "Fish out of water…"

"Seasick!" Sebastian joined the fray at my expense.

"Airsick." Nathaniel punched my thigh, a move that would've meant a broken wrist if I hadn't been ready to hurl.

Assholes.

Each of their ha-ha comments made me more ornery. "See how much y'all are laughing when I vomit all over the place."

My strained grip threatened to break my seat right off the floor. Leon placed a hand over mine. He slid it up my arm to my neck. "Relax, *beb*. It's an adventure."

Okay, yeah. Death sentence, adventure, same thing.

Darwin had watched the whole debacle with no amusement on her face. "Forgot to mention," she said. "I'm down one copilot."

Death trap it is.

Then she proceeded to walk down the aisle, stopping in front of each of us. She sized up Linc. "Too stern."

"Way too many weapons to be allowed near my control panels," Darwin said as she passed by Liz.

In front of Cannon, she wrinkled her nose. "Too bulky."

"Smiley," was her comment about Nathaniel.

Darwin leaned over to peer at me. "Oh dear. Do you need a sick bag?"

Before I could answer in the affirmative, she moved on to Farrow with one shake of her head.

Sebastian raised his hand.

She gave him a cursory glance. "Too young. And cute. I bet you're gay, too. The good ones always are."

He blushed.

"And bashful. I don't do bashful."

He stood from his seat, now towering over her. "I assure you, I can handle this machine and probably two more at the same time if you give me ten minutes alone with the manual."

Darwin blinked in surprise; then she grinned. "So you're brash as well. I do brash. Come with me."

They strode to the front of the Predator, leaving me sweating bullets and the others watching with their mouths agape. All but Farrow.

"What just happened here?" Linc asked.

"We got told," Cannon grumbled.

"Sebastian can fly?" I asked Farrow.

She rolled her eyes. "The brat can commandeer anything mechanical."

"Let me rephrase: Does Sebastian know how to fly a Predator airplane?"

"Ah guess we'll find out."

Thanks for the reassurance.

Darwin's voice came over the headsets:

"Buckle up, y'all! We'll be traveling at, oh, supersonic speed. Wouldn't want you to get thrown around back there."

I groaned. The others laughed. Good fucking thing Tommy the town crier wasn't here to record my humiliating moment. *The great warrior Darke turned into a pussy. Afraid of falling in love, not to mention a fear of flying.*

The rockets roared. My knees locked, and my feet braced on the floor. The thrusters engaged. Suddenly we were airborne, but before I could quail, Leon slid his lips across mine, easing his tongue inside. Every ounce of my focus aimed on him, I grabbed his head, massaging his lips with mine.

His cheeks pink and eyes soft, Leon drew back.

"Feel better?" he asked.

Hell yeah.

CHAPTER SIX

Twelve hours later, the Predator took a downward dive that had my gullet defying gravity. I gripped the armrests in terror.

Leon stared at me. "Is dis another ploy to get me to kiss you, big guy?"

The harness was too tight around my chest. I forced shallow breaths in and out. "Just tell me we're landing soon."

"See for yourself." He pointed to the small window across from us.

Through the square of glass, I watched a speck of land approach at Mach speed. Darwin leveled out before we nose-dived into the ground, circling several times around an airfield. Flight towers and hangars lined the runway, all bearing the CO symbol.

Fucking hell. Darwin's landing us in a Corps-sanctioned airbase.

Our boosters powered down as we went vertical and then softly plopped horizontal on the ground.

Over the comms, Sebastian drawled, "This is your flight crew speakin'. Please wait until the passenger in front of you has disembarked. We hope you had a—"

Static fuzz filled the intercom and then Sebastian squawked, "Ow! I always wanted to say that."

Darwin appeared from the hatch between the cockpit and the cargo area. "Keep your flight suits zipped over that ragamuffin commune attire you call clothing and keep those helmets on." She walked up and down our rank and file like a sergeant at a drill line, ignoring at least two higher-ups in her presence. "This is the sorriest motley crew I've ever had to manage. Most of you couldn't pass for bred-to-the-bone Territorians even if you were in uniform. Piercings"—she flicked Nathaniel's ear—"tats, and unruly hair." She paused in front of Leon, who skimmed the soft wavy locks off his face. "You look almost as freaky as the First People Freelanders we're supposed to meet, which ain't gonna happen unless we get off base undetected."

I'd never seen Cannon's eyebrows shoot so high. "Is there some reason you decided to put down in the middle of a Corps base?"

"Are you questioning my tactics, *former* Elite Tactical Commander Cannon?"

Cannon marched up to Darwin. "You bet I am."

"You've got balls, sir. I approve." Her fierce glare relaxed into her first grin. "I have transport lined up, and this was the quickest way in. It's not like we can just touch down in a CO Predator in Omega undetected. Eyes and ears everywhere. So be sure to keep those balls on straight." She looked him up and down, adding, "So to speak."

Sebastian ducked out after Drill Sergeant Darwin, and she

spun on him. "And Bassy boy, zip that flight suit back up. We can see your nipple piercings straight through your T-shirt." With a stiff salute, she pivoted back. "Welcome to the hot zone, *y'all*."

"Ah reckon she's got the biggest balls of all. Ah like her." Farrow settled her helmet back on her head.

"I think I found my long-lost twin." Liz grinned, buckling her chin strap.

Linc rumbled, "Why am I not surprised?"

I hadn't hurled yet, and I wasn't about to start. Not walking down the gangplank and straight into enemy territory. We held formation, striding across the landing strip toward the base. Three officers approached as we got near the depot on the far side of the airfield.

"Shit," I muttered.

"Stay frosty, people," Darwin said. "Standard debriefing."

She met the officers while we hung back. The sun was broiling, sending a trickle of sweat down my spine. I watched Darwin as she kept cool answering their questions.

"Care to explain the extra self-loading cargo?" A rough-looking soldier wearing an eye patch pointed at us.

My fingers flexed on impulse to reach for my weapons.

"Sir, you told me to recruit where I could. Found these troops in Alpha Territory and convinced them they were better off fighting over here than shoveling shit trying to rebuild over there." She dropped her voice and leaned in. "Turns out I can be pretty convincing when I wanna be."

The man clapped her on the shoulder with a laugh. "Damn good job, Darwin. Damn good. Put them through a full workup:

health, background, ranks, and specialties. See that they report to me at seventeen hundred hours, and we'll decide if these drifters make the cut—or get their throats cut."

"Affirmative, sir." She waited until the three departed before returning to us. "We gotta hustle. The hangar on the left. Move out, now."

Keeping a purposeful pace, we made it to the building without any further interference. Inside was a commissioned vehicle built specifically for Omega's desert terrain. It was sand colored with high, fat tires and small, heavily tinted windows.

"This thing bulletproof?" I asked, climbing inside after Leon.

"Depends on the artillery. It sure as hell isn't RPG proof." Darwin hit a button and the engine revved.

* * *

We made it through the two checkpoints, our cover holding solid. Past the danger zone of the gun towers, we let out whoops and hollers, speeding to Omega city proper. Across the flat horizon shimmering in the sun-soaked heat, the city of bazaars rose up like a glittering gold oasis.

"We've gotta be at the meet point in Sector Five in forty minutes. Think we can make it, Darwin?" Linc pulled up the coordinates on his D-P and held it in front of her face.

The last comms we'd had from Denver instructed us to locate one of his insiders in Omega, a man who could set us on the path for the cure.

"Does a bull have two balls, Commander?"

Farrow laughed and turned to Sebastian. "Well, ain't our new sister a sweet talker?"

A glimmer appeared in Darwin's eyes through the rearview mirror. The read I got from her was steady, unwavering, and mission-oriented. She earned my immediate respect.

"Lose the threads, folks." She unzipped her suit with one hand, wriggling out of the dark blue jumpsuit while keeping a foot on the gas.

We dressed down to our normal garb as Omega filled our sights. At the first and second gates into the city, Darwin simply had to flash her badge to get us through. The Territory opened her walls for us. Up close the buildings jumbled together in an ad hoc fashion so unlike the gridded streets of Beta and Alpha. The old-looking structures were gold instead of our bland silver and steel. The color reflected, making Leon's skin gleam more than ever.

Language was standardized in all the Territories, just like scrip. We could hear people haggling by the roadsides as we drove past. The discord in the area was evident from the graffiti on the sides of buildings and in the soldiers roaming the streets. The strong Corps presence stood out amid the flamboyant surrounds, injecting fear onto the faces of people hounded here and there at rifle point.

Poverty, affluence, and anarchy made the air electric.

I couldn't tell the Freelanders from the regulation Territorian stock—both factions inhabited this city side by side with the CO's consent. Yellow, black, tan-skinned, the citizens were a mishmash of heritage from different continents. I felt an aching kinship with these people, something unknown and unrecognized that pulled from deep inside me…until a bullet hit our tire, jarring me from my thoughts.

"We've got heat," Darwin muttered.

There was another screaming whistle, and the second tire on our right side blew out. People who'd been hawking their wares alongside the road fell to the ground as if this was a drill common to their daily life.

Cannon drew his gun. "How the hell have we been made already?"

Darwin took a hard swerve to the left, clipping the corner of a building. "Oh, I don't know. Maybe because I've got a vehicle filled with the Company's most wanted?"

"The cameras can't possibly see inside," I said, pulling out my guns. In every Territory, indestructible cameras were mounted right next to the huge public D-Ps on each street.

"Ever heard of spyware and a little something called zoom?" Darwin sped down the alley.

Sparks flew off the sides of the Rover, which was too big for the narrow breach between two tall buildings. The brakes squealed.

"We're ditching the vehicle!"

No shit, Darwin.

We raced on foot. I stayed beside Leon as we hurried away from the center of the city, worried he might be feeling the effects of the Plague injection. He kept pace with me, hurdling over the spreading squalor from a Territory under siege.

Omega was a maze, allowing us to lose our pursuers. Sectors

One and Two fell away, and with them the harsh rebound of boots at our heels. We broke into S-5 at a full-out run. The area was blindingly bare, almost completely destroyed. Vacant bomb-riddled buildings had blank eyes instead of windows. The earth was charred to cinder.

"What happened here?" I asked.

"The CEO decided Omega citizens were getting too big for their britches. He blitzed the sector last week." Darwin wiped her hand across her brow.

"What now?"

She grinned. "Now we find this guy Raine you've been told about."

CHAPTER SEVEN

After carefully exploring the wreckage of the Sector's neighborhoods, we finally picked up a signal on Linc's D-P. I took the lead, sneaking a look around the corner and into an area that might've once been a small courtyard for the four remaining structures surrounding it. A man with a full beard and long, rust-colored hair leaned against a building smoking a hand-rolled cig. The sweet scent of tobacco wafted to me.

"I'll make contact. The rest of you stay here." I exited the alley, keeping one pistol lowered at my side.

The tall man stubbed out his cigarette when I approached, his eyes glinting curiously. He didn't give me a greeting, but he didn't pull a weapon either.

"I'm looking for Raine," I said, less than a meter away.

Peering up at the cloudless sky and down at hard-packed earth, he smiled wryly. "Aren't we all?"

Bingo. That was the code Denver had given us.

"I see black skies ahead." I held out my hand and he grasped it firmly. "I'm Darke."

"You sure are." Raine made a quick scan up and down my body. "Denver sent you."

"And who's Denver to you?" I still didn't have enough reasons to trust Denver, especially not with Leon's life on the line.

"Someone to trust when most others can't be." Raine gave an easygoing wink. "You can tell your friends to come out now. We gotta hustle to get to Karesh Commune before nightfall. Don't wanna be stuck in the middle of the desert at night."

At my whistle, the others appeared. Once we'd taken care of the how-dos, Raine jerked his head to the building behind him, indicating we should enter.

Inside, he smirked in the low, cool light. "Get rid of the rags. You look like something straight out of a Company promo. You're liable to get yourselves shot within three klicks of Karesh." He kicked several bundles of clothes toward us.

What the hell? This was the second time we'd been asked to change in less than an hour, for exactly the same reason: fitting in. Farrow was probably in her element. Sure enough, she'd reinvented herself into a colorfully skirted Freelander in record time. When Leon began to disrobe, I fought between turning my back and watching every article of clothing leave his body. In the end, I faced away from him, and stood in front of everyone else in an effort to provide a shield from all other eyes.

By the time I dressed in long pants and a loose tunic, Leon was ready. He wore flowing gypsy pants that gathered so low on his hips the teasing tip of his tattoo showed. There was no shirt on his torso, just an expanse of bare skin I wanted to run my hands all over.

Raine beckoned us out the back of the building. I was blinded by the harsh sunlight, and it took a moment for my sight to adjust to the open expanse of terrain where Omega Territory left off.

"Welcome to your transport." Raine waved toward a group of tall, gangly animals roped up to a ramshackle shelter.

I stared at the two-humped beasts. And I'd thought the Predator was bad.

"Camels." Raine led us over.

The giant animal closest to Cannon hissed at him. The former Alpha commander looked like he might piss himself—or pull his Glock.

"Careful. They bite," Raine warned with a chuckle.

I cautiously sidled up to a camel, gathering the reins.

"Two of you will have to double up," Raine said. He mounted his ride as it took the opportunity to spit and bare big square teeth.

Sebastian seemed to be getting into his element after proving his worth in the Predator. He slapped me on the back. "Just like riding a horse, big guy."

I wished to hell Leon would start calling me *cher* again. No one else would dare call me that for fear of reprisal. Ambling over, Leon let me hoist him onto the blanket-saddle.

Holding his hand down to me, he grinned. "C'mon, *beb*."

I seated myself behind Leon and ran one arm around his waist. I touched my heels gingerly to the camel's flanks and we took off at an awkward gait.

"Giddyap!" Leon whooped.

There was no cover in sight as we galloped away across dusty plain. Or maybe not galloped, but more like bucked. The animal's coarse hair scratched through the thin fabric of my pants, and I leaned forward to touch my lips to the back of Leon's neck.

Half an hour later, he grumbled, "My ass is gettin' chafed."

"Don't worry. I'll massage it for you later." I lifted him onto my thighs, cushioning the ride.

* * *

We rode hard for nearly an hour before an outcropping of squat structures dotted the horizon. The sun had begun to set, sending streaks of orange across the sky and over the sand that shifted like waves on water. Leon had relaxed into my embrace, his hand curled across mine over his stomach. I thought he'd had fallen asleep, but leaning over, I saw his eyes blink heavily.

"We're here, baby."

"Aye yi yi yi yi!" Yips went up from inside the village, and Raine returned the call.

Streams of men, women, and children raced from between the round rustic buildings. Clusters formed around us, people in bright colors, their hair covered from the ever-present sand. Beaded necklaces dripped from their necks, bangles adorning the lengths of their arms. They gestured wildly and welcomed us with grins, taking the reins from our hands. I dismounted first and then helped Leon off, keeping an arm around his waist.

"Come, come. They've prepared a feast for our prestigious visitors." Raine unwrapped the cloth from his hair, shaking his red waves loose.

Karesh Commune wasn't protected by boundary walls, fences, or even trees or mountains. Nothing stood between the village and its surrounds. The situation was unsettling. I was more determined than ever to keep a close watch over Leon.

Domed huts crowded close together in the settlement that stretched as far as the eye could see. There were no roads but winding paths, one of which we followed to a central gathering point. A large tent-like structure opened over a huge fire pit in the middle, roasting meat sizzling from a spit. Rough blankets covered the seared, stubby grass. Cushions were thrown about for comfort, and camels, horses, cattle, and goats roamed in the distance on the plain.

Raine drew us under the tent. He began introducing us to the villagers awaiting their first look at their cousins from across the Pan-Atlantic Ocean. The Freelander way of life had begun long before the Purge had drastically reduced the world's population, a two-decade environmental annihilation that ended in the year 2020.

The back-to-earth movement started with our ancestors seeking a simpler existence not subordinate to the government, which had increased its focus on making war in far lands and money hand over fist. They adhered to the principles of careful balance between tending the earth and everyone's right to their own ideals.

The first Freelanders harvested not just the land but also the sprightly minds of their generations, espousing ingenuity in the arts and technology. Each of our communes was linked as one family by a shared hope for a life that wasn't meted out by strict rules. Our ultimate commonality was hope for a future not suppressed by CO dictates.

Linc and Liz fell in with a group of warriors, no doubt gathering what intel they could. Cannon and Nathaniel lingered by the fire, Cannon nearly salivating at the succulent scent of roasted meat. I watched Sebastian entertain a group of children as he juggled four large pebbles while his sister Farrow indulgently looked on. Each time he dropped a rock, he handed out a piece of hard candy he'd brought from his time in Beta. Bas was fast becoming an instant favorite, smart man.

Leon grasped my hand in his, settling us on a blanket.

"Are you tired?"

"Not a bit." He stifled a yawn.

"Here, lean on me." I smiled as he worked closer to me. After days of getting the cold shoulder from him, I was soothed by his reciprocating touches.

I was almost ready to drop off myself when he bolted upright. "I think there's someone we're supposed to meet."

Directly in front of us stood an impressive man. The long darts of his kilt were fashioned from animal pelts. His chest was bare, and he bore the marking of a black mamba moko across his left pectoral. Head shaved except for a round patch on his pate, from which a long black braid fell to his waist where several weapons rested, including what looked like a gleaming silver cleaver. His earlobes stretched with large-bore metal plugs. His lips were set in a grim line.

I shot to my feet, bringing Leon with me.

The man nodded to Raine at his side.

"This is Chief Shehu," Raine said.

"Thank you, Chief, for welcoming us to your commune." I clasped his hand. "This is Leon, my…"

"Partner?" He dipped his chin down, inspecting Leon.

"Friend," Leon quipped. His face flushed, and he took a step away from me.

I pinned him with my gaze.

"I'm gonna go check on the others." Leon swaggered away.

I kept him in my sights until Shehu cleared his throat. When I turned back to him, Raine had also disappeared.

"Not your lover?"

"Not yet." My jaw pulsed.

"But you want him to be."

"Yes."

"He is of fine making, firm and young. And a high spirit, one that can't be broken and shouldn't be tamed." Shehu was not doing me any favors, pointing out Leon's best qualities.

"I am fully aware of his attributes, Chief."

He laughed then, relaxing his stance. "Call me Shehu." He pulled me toward the fire and compared our coloring. "But you are not from Aafricans?"

"No. The former colonies of North America are where I was born and raised."

"Your ancestors, though, they hail from this continent." Shehu nodded to a slight boy who wore an eager-to-please grin. With the echoing sound of a large gong, Shehu ordered the feast to start.

As drums began to beat, dancers streaked in and out of the tent and a crowd surged toward the food.

I answered Shehu, "Many centuries ago."

"This Leon, he who is not your lover, he's the one infected? The reason for your journey?"

"Yes, but I don't want it known. It's too dangerous." I studied the fierce-faced chief. "How did you figure it out?"

"You hunger for him as that one hungers after meat." He gestured to Cannon, who was loading his plate, and I chuckled. "You look at him as one parched for love like our land thirsts for rain. Pain covers you, pain from the past and fear of what the future brings. It all centers on Leon."

I was taken aback. "You can read me so easily?"

"Only because I know the hardships of the heart."

Leon joined Sebastian. They attracted an ever-growing circle of youngsters with their two-man juggling act. I listened to his laughter, so low and deep, as he fumbled for one of the airborne rocks. Sebastian tossed out another piece of candy when Leon landed on the ground, having missed his catch.

"And the boy, Leon, he is under your skin, like a disease?"

"Not a disease." I rubbed my chest. "He's the sun, warming my cold soul."

"Ah, I understand." Shehu passed me a bowl and we sat together. "You are like me. You sense the emotions of others."

"I try not to. It was a treasure my mother honed and used well." I took a bite, savoring the taste. "When she died, I learned to close off that part of myself. I'm more suited to war."

He chewed thoughtfully. "If your prowess in battle is as

strong as your powerful emotions, I would believe it. Do you feel something from all of them?" He motioned toward my companions.

"When there's a convergence of the same feeling, yes. Most often it's with only one or two people. I lost the ability completely before Leon came along."

"His bond is the strongest."

"If we have one at all." I watched as the others joined the gravy train, filling up on the hearty smoked meat and the warm flat bread accompanying it. Mint tea was passed around, the hot drink somehow refreshing in this sun-drenched climate.

Gesturing to our contact, red-haired Raine, Shehu said, "He is one of our shamans. He's searching for the cure."

I wouldn't have pictured Raine as a medicine man, more of a hustler. "Is he close to finding it?"

"We think so."

"Are there any people infected here?" I asked.

Placing his empty bowl on the ground, Shehu wiped his mouth. His vision became distant, his posture regal. "We had one. A female. She was found yesterday, her throat slit."

My body went rigid. "She was murdered because of the Plague?"

"I believe so, yes."

"Now you understand why Leon's status needs to remain under wraps." I cast a worried look at Leon, who talked animatedly between taking huge mouthfuls of food across the tent.

"We will keep it so."

A woman worked her way over to us. Her skin was the color of cocoa, and she wore a large, glittering jewel around her neck. Her unlikely silver eyes shined like the ruby set against her throat.

Rising to his feet, Shehu took her hand. "And this is my woman, Pyra."

She slapped the formidable man's arm. "His wife. Although considering he all but dragged me to this godforsaken Outpost from the Amphitheater, where we met fifteen years ago, I might just as well be his concubine." Pyra was almost as tall as her husband and just as imperial, even while she handed out a light-hearted tongue-lashing.

I bowed over her proffered hand. "Darke of Chitamauga militia, ma'am."

She tapped my head. "No *ma'am* here—just me and the chief."

Pyra was obviously from a different life, yet she seemed well suited to the role of chieftess.

"And here is our offspring." She grabbed a girl by the arm and wrangled her back. "Lilith."

"It's a pleasure, Lilith."

"You as well, sir." The young girl was a mirror image of her mother in stature and posture, although her sigh was thoroughly that of a teenager. "May I go now?"

"They are in a world of their own." Shehu watched his daughter roam away.

"Blissfully so, I'd say." Pyra bade us both sit back down.

Cannon, Linc, Liz, and the others joined our powwow as the night darkened.

"Any sightings of Cutler?" Liz asked.

"None so far. We've got our eyes on the sky," Shehu said. Darwin smiled at the mention. "And our ears to the ground." The chief patted the soil by his hip.

I turned to Raine. "What's the next step to finding this supposed cure?"

"Man must heed Mother Nature's warnings. Life and death are her business, as evidenced by the Purge. This Plague though, this is a mutation of humankind's making." Raine leaned on his elbows. "The Earth Mother can be vengeful, but there is veracity in her fruits."

Oh Christ. Riddles. As if my day hadn't been long enough. Hills would've thought this guy was a genius. I was beginning to think he was another one of Denver's decoys—and a crackpot, shaman or not.

I wasn't alone. Cannon scowled at the guy. "Do you ever speak in plain old English, man?"

"She is giving us guidance on what herbs and roots and shoots to use. Rare plants are cropping up, vegetation that has not been recorded for centuries. How's that?" Raine didn't really explain anything.

"Pathetic," Cannon said.

"Ah, well, there are those who reach the higher realm of being and those who just be." Raine shrugged. "You'll have tomorrow to recuperate from your travels before a meeting at the Amphitheater."

"Is it safe to return to the Territory?" Linc asked.

"About as safe as it is out here in the desert—sitting ducks if the CEO decides to make a quality show of killing more Freelanders." Raine tossed his cigarette butt into the fire and loped away.

"Ah'm not feelin' the warmth from that man." Farrow had one of her KA-BARs in hand, whetting it on a flat stone.

"Maybe he'll grow on you." Sebastian lit a rolled smoke from the hot embers of our fire.

Cannon grumbled, "Like that mangy fucking beard of his."

We all laughed for a moment before I interrupted the chatter. "One of Shehu's people was murdered yesterday," I said, keeping my voice hushed. "The one infected with the Plague."

Everyone glanced at Leon, who continued to chew nonchalantly on a piece of grass. I felt his anxiety spike, though, like hot needles thrust under my nail beds.

"Christ." Cannon reached over and squeezed Leon's leg.

"So I think we can all agree keeping Leon's situation classified is of the utmost importance."

Liz popped her knuckles. "And have someone with him at all times."

"*Alors*. I don' need a bodyguard."

"*I'll* be with him," I said.

Although I could tell Leon wanted to protest, he held his tongue. His fear calmed slightly, but he was quick to change the subject. As he eagerly recounted the games he and Sebastian had played earlier with the children, we all began to relax once more.

Sometime later, the encroaching cold swept over the desert. But it was no match for Leon's increasingly heated stare. I whipped off my tunic, balling it behind my head.

Clearly turned on, Leon licked his lips and a breathy "*Mon Dieu*" rolled out of him.

I cast a glance at the abode Leon and I would be sharing. Leon looked at me with deep, starving eyes. A look I couldn't ignore.

"Come to bed, baby," I said.

Reclining on his elbows, Leon flirted. "Baby? Gonna touch me tonight, Darke? Or you gon' leave me hot and hangin' like you always do?"

I leaned over until our lips hovered a scant distance apart; then I pushed one hand through Leon's shoulder-length locks and gripped a fistful of his hair. His lithe body curled toward me.

"Lemme guess. My casbah awaits?"

One day had bled into the next, and I wanted nothing more than to find some sort of solace with him. "Yes. As do I."

After a lazy stretch, Leon leaped nimbly to his feet. "Lead on."

CHAPTER EIGHT

The circular abode was just tall enough that I didn't have to duck my head. The walls were fashioned of heavy woven fabrics tacked to wooden beams. The floor was tamped-down earth covered in a variety of blankets.

"This is—"

"Cozy." Leon lounged against the door as I placed our packs to the side.

"I was gonna say small." With the temperature dropping outside, it was cooling off in here. I hunkered in front of the little wood burner and started the kindling.

His hand brushed my neck, sending a spear of desire through me. "Not all of us are big as buildings."

"Pure, solid muscle." I rose to my feet.

Leon's lusty stare hit me hard and fast. "Don' I know it."

I moved away. He advanced with his prowling gait, stopping in front of me when the backs of my calves hit the side of the low bed. Leon came up only to my chin, but his presence had a more powerful impact on me than any other man. He grazed one hand up my chest, his fingers stopping to press against the hammering pulse in my throat.

"Lemme ask you somethin'. Do I make you nervous?"

I laughed harshly, my fists in balls beside me. "Yeah."

He ran his thumb across my nipple, chuckling when my flesh hardened. "Just me?"

"Yes." I closed my eyes, reeling from the speed with which my cock filled.

He sucked my nipple between his lips, his fingers running up and down my ribs.

"Wait." I grabbed his hands. "I want to make sure you feel okay."

Flouncing onto the bed, Leon licked his lips. "Wanna take my blood pressure, too? Maybe a full-body workup?"

"Are you having any symptoms?" I sat next to him.

"Oh yeah. A big one. In my pants. You can inspect dat, too." Leon winked.

I started to get up, but he grabbed my hand. "I'm fine. I feel fine. Ain't nothin' wrong with me except I'm real fucking horny for you."

"There's something else, Leon."

"Yeah, yeah. Get on with it so's we can get to somethin' more fun."

"Do you think anything...?" My voice drifted off. Maybe I didn't want to know. "Would you remember if anything untoward happened to you when you were kidnapped by Cutler?"

"Untoward? You mean did someone rape me?"

I winced. The nausea I felt during the flight was nothing compared to this.

Seeing my reaction, Leon rushed on. "I don' think so. Remember, I tol' you I've been getting flashes, feelings. I think I'd know if I'd been used like dat. *Mon Dieu.* It's happened enough to me before. I just took the scrip for it…"

"You sold your body." My jaw locked, and my fingers tightened on his.

"Yeah. I din't have a whole lot of other options when we needed money. I've got a pretty face. I'm good at keepin' dat stuff where it belongs. They could have my body but not my heart." He shrugged. It was all cut-and-dried to him. "They paid good, treated me all right. I made sure *Maman* had enough to live by. She don' know. She don' need to know."

I'd suspected as much from a few things he'd mentioned and from Cutler's slurs. Hearing the truth from Leon's lips crushed a part of me where I hadn't even realized hope had sprung, but I'd never let him know. In spite of everything, he remained pure and bright as always.

"I'd never treat you like that." I caressed his face.

Rubbing against my touch, Leon asked, "How would you treat me?"

"Like a man who is very much desired for who you are. I'd treat you with honor." My hand moved into his hair. "There's no one here now but you and me, baby."

"And everyone within hearing range." He angled his neck to my searching mouth.

I tugged his hair in a fist until his lips were almost at mine. "I can be quieter than you."

"Is dat a dare?"

I needed him. I couldn't hold back any longer. "Yeah." I crushed my mouth to his, seeking quick entry. All control snapped. "I want you to suck my cock," I breathed. Then I remembered my avowal. My hands disentangled from his hair and I sat on my heels.

"Ain't it a good thing I want dat, too?" Leon rolled me over, shyly pleased when he pinioned me to the bed. Sure fingers trailed to my pants. He pulled the fabric down, revealing me bit by bit.

Arching up, I kept my gaze trained on him. He wet his mouth when the tight black curls appeared and then the base of my cock, hard and ready.

"Oh yeah." Breath whistled from him.

"Like the look of that?'

"I think I'm gon' like the taste of it more."

Impatient, he snapped the pants down my thighs and off my feet, exposing thick-corded legs and a large, turgid erection.

"Big as the rest of you, huh?" He peered at me with an impish grin playing around his lips. "More than a mouthful there, eh, *beb*?"

"Maybe you should stop talking and find out." I flexed my cock.

"Fuck, dat's hot." He sighed, leaning down toward it.

His warm breath blew across me first. It was enough to make me clench my ass. He spiraled his tongue, teasing feathery brushes of his lips across the broad crown.

Leon's sweeping touches brought forth an instant flow of pre-ejaculate, which he loudly slurped up. Fingers tickled through the tight curls of pubic hair down to the pouch of my balls. He traced the seam there with a fingertip, lashing me with more teasing tongue action, never taking me into his mouth.

My shaft turned even darker, even harder.

I finally begged. "Please, baby. Suck it, please."

He quickly engulfed as much as he could, raising a shout from my throat with his hot, wet slurps.

Looking up hungrily with swollen lips, he fisted my wet shaft. "*Mmm*. Taste fuckin' good. Can't wait to swallow all your come, *beb*, but I gotta figure out how to get more of this cock down my throat."

My thighs trembled. My voice grew hoarse at the sights and sounds of him going up and down on me.

"Need more," Leon growled.

I watched him through a sexual haze as he lay down on the bed, his head pillowed at a perfect angle. "Straddle my face. Feed me that cock."

My face hardened. I had to squeeze the base of my shaft in order not to come right then and there. I moved over him until my knees rested beside his shoulders and brushed his lips with a knuckle. "You sure?" I asked.

"Yeah. I'm starvin' for you." His cheeks were flushed, his lips swollen.

I pointed my cock down toward his lips. He pulled me in, his fingers gripping my ass. With more than half my length seated inside his throat, I yelled at the wet heat constricting my cock. Thighs shaking, toes curling, I grabbed his head, his hair. I groaned and fingered his stretched lips.

His encouraging noises, his gorgeous cocksucking lips, tore a burning path of desire down my spine to my balls. He twisted his head with each thrust. So incredibly wet was his mouth, he sucked my cock like it was a sloppy last meal. The sounds alone were enough to send me over.

Falling onto my hands above his head, I looked down at him. "*Ahh,* fuck, Leon!"

A hot rush of come spurted from my cock, filling his cheeks with my seed. I held the nape of his neck, coming so forcefully it felt like he was sucking the very essence from me.

Muscles finally releasing, I spread my shaking thighs wider. I jerked when he skimmed his fingertips down the root of my shaft to my aching balls. I lifted off of him. He swallowed noisily, a sound that pushed another round of arousal right into my still-hard cock. When I collapsed beside him, he licked and nuzzled me all over.

I took his lips in a long, slippery kiss, my taste lingering in his mouth. "Get enough?"

"*Mm-hmm.*" He smiled against me.

I flipped him onto his back. "Good, because it's my turn."

"Oh yeah?"

My breath left me in a groan as soon as his pants slid away beneath my hands. Staring at him, I felt like a wild animal unleashed. The firm muscles of his thighs and the arrow of his pelvis all pointed to his groin. His cock rose toward his belly, long and lean, just like him. It was gorgeous, with a slight hook toward the bell-shaped head.

"Oh fuck."

Rolling his hips, Leon smiled. He reached a hand down and jerked himself languidly.

"You trim yourself." Saliva pooled in my mouth.

"Yeah." His fist moved up and down until I grabbed his wrist, resting his hand at his side.

"I want to do that."

His moan reverberated in my ears, but I was focused on the tattoo I'd never fully seen before, curving thin black lines that interlocked. It called to me. I traced it with my fingertips.

"Holy fuck, Leon. Who put this on you?"

"I did."

His skin reacted in goose bumps wherever I touched. Even better, he writhed and gasped when my pointed tongue trailed the intricate design. "What is it?" My voice had never sounded deeper, almost sticking in my throat as arousal—gut deep and so hot—made my cock fill completely again.

"An infinity circle. The end is the beginning."

"Alpha and Omega. You and me." I licked him again and he cried out. From hooded eyes, I peered up at him. "You are my end and my beginning."

"Darke," he moaned.

I desperately wanted to hear him call me *cher* again. He hadn't since the night in the town hall. But that could wait. I turned my face and drifted my hand to his cock. Liquid welled at the tip. Throbbing with a thick vein up the center, his shaft was deeply red, the head a perfect size for my mouth. He was incredibly rigid.

"Mon Dieu!"

I grazed the head across my cheek and swiped the bubbling liquid across my closed lips.

Leon watched. "Why does it feel like I've waited so long for dis?" His voice was strained.

I licked my lips. "Because you have." But no longer. Surrounding his cock, I sucked him deep, greedy for every damn thing Leon had to give me. Pain and pleasure, fury and fear, future and hope. *Everything.* Including this moment right now when I feasted on his body, worshipping him with my mouth as I meant to do with my soul.

I pulled his hands to my cheeks and brought mine to his hips. Moving him back and forth, I heard him choke and curse when his shaft bumped against my stretched cheek. It was the hottest thing I'd ever known, his grip tightening, his fingers stroking himself where he butted inside my mouth.

Murmuring, sucking, lapping at him, I snaked my hands to his ass. I slapped my palms against the rounded curves, filling my hands with the taut contours and my mouth with his cock. Rubbing, kneading. Licking, lunging. I gripped his ass cheeks hard and separated them, sliding the side of my hand into his cleft, feeling the smoothness. My pinkie circled his hole, which puckered out like lips needing to be kissed. I dragged my hands around and up his chest, plucking his silky nipples until he began to moan a litany of Cajun words slurred together.

His skin was feverish from arousal. And his arousal multiplied mine.

I took all of him in. He bucked his hips, enflaming me with high-pitched gasps. I pulled off just as his motions became jerky, lightly running my fingertips over the smooth weight of his balls.

His chest heaved with each breath. His eyes bored into mine. "What—"

"I want you to watch me when you come in my mouth."

His cock swelled; fluid dripped over my fingertips. He nodded frantically, biting his lip.

I gave him a savage grin. "Ready for me to blow your mind?"

His arousal leaped to another level, singing through my soul, singeing my nerves. "Oh, yes."

I kissed his belly, which trembled. I sucked on his tat until he whimpered. I pulled one testicle into my mouth and then moved on to the other, all the while pumping him loosely. I kept my eyes on his lust-dazed gaze the whole time.

Flicking the tip of his cock over and over, I moved with his circling hips. Then I dove over him, taking him deep down my throat. Leon's head thrashed until I stopped, looking up at him expectantly. His eyes flew to mine, wide and begging.

I sucked back up, then twisted my mouth one way over the head of his cock, my hand gripping him in the opposite direction. This way, that way, I sucked and licked until his moans echoed, his back arched, and I swallowed him down for one frozen second. His seed jetted out. Rising back up, I focused on the spurting tip, my eyelids drifting shut in the pleasure of tasting him for the first time.

Afterward, I cocooned him with my body, the blanket long forgotten. "You are so gorgeous. So precious."

Shivers raced down his torso, and I trailed them with my lips.

"*Oooh.* Dat was...dat was...*mon Dieu.*" He shifted against me.

"*Mmm.*" I kissed along Leon's neck to his ear, satisfied I'd made him come like no other. "I think you were louder."

His hand skimmed down to my cock, which lay hard and heavy against his thigh. "I think I get another round to prove you wrong."

I drew in a deep breath. The next place I wanted my cock wasn't in his mouth or in his fist. "Tomorrow."

He relaxed his hold and his breaths slowed. When I thought he was asleep, I pushed off the bed. I'd noted a jug of water earlier. I wanted to clean Leon up, to show him I cared for him more than this urgent desire to brand him as mine.

"Your back!" He gasped behind me.

I turned to see him sitting up. *Fuck.* I'd forgotten about my moko and the fact I'd kept them hidden from him since his return. Deep scars marred the design he'd so painstakingly marked me with. Not only had he forgotten tattooing me, but he didn't remember the night we'd almost died during the factory explosion in Beta last April. That night I'd protected him, Liz, and Sebastian, forming a human barrier between them and the fiery debris falling down around us. We'd survived intact. My moko had not.

"It's nothing. Just wounds of war." I found a cloth, dipping it into the water. Returning to the bed, I swiped his stomach, his legs, his groin, placing a gentle kiss upon his lips.

"Does it hurt?"

"Not anymore." Nothing hurt as much as knowing he might never remember the times we'd shared together.

"Let me take care of you."

My brow furrowed. "How?"

He gave me a cunning smile, looking down at my lap where my cock lay.

"Leon."

His fingertip hovered over my mouth. *"Shh."* At his pack, he pulled out Miss Eden's famous first-aid kit. "On your stomach."

I rolled over as he opened a tin of salve.

The feeling of Leon's long fingers warming my skin, massaging the scars that marred the moko across my upper back created a level of intimacy that astounded me. I hummed with each touch, relaxing into it.

Suddenly, he went cold, and his fingers stilled. Swirling depths of confusion doused the tender mood. I was stupid to let him do this. He had to recognize his work, memory or not.

"Whose names are these on your back?"

I didn't want him to know the depth of my deception. I swallowed. "People I lost."

Leon said nothing more.

CHAPTER NINE

When I woke, warmth spread through me. Leon stretched beside me, huffing in his sleep. His knee crooked across my thighs, and his head was on my shoulder. His hair fell over his face and onto my chest.

He murmured something and his nose wrinkled. His hand slipped from my stomach to between my legs, causing my muscles to contract. Holding the steely brand of my shaft, he blinked his eyes open. Sleep shifted into sultry awareness. Then that drowsy sensual look disappeared. He sat up abruptly, pulling his hand off of me.

"Good morning?" My voice was hoarse with the first words of the day.

He plucked at the lightweight blanket tepeed over his knees. "Mornin.'"

The same sense of coldness from late last night drifted off of him. I brushed a length of his hair behind his ear, studying his somber profile. Attempting to smile, I took his chin in my hand and turned him to me.

"You seemed to sleep well."

His gaze stole to the blanket barely concealing my obviously rigid cock. His cheeks turned pink, and those dreamy brown eyes swung to my lips.

"Are you shy all of a sudden?" I murmured, drawing my fingertips along his jaw, lingering on the soft feel of morning stubble.

He shook his head and took a deep breath.

"Do I make you nervous?" I replayed his words to him.

An almost smile worked across his lips but evaporated. He pulled away from my hand.

I was unwilling to let him close me out like I'd done to him so many goddamn times. "Tell me what's going on then."

"Fragments again." Leon knocked on his head. "Dreams dat felt so real they were palpable."

"Dreams of what?"

"You an' me. It's always dat…dat anger and sadness. Can't get rid of it." He rubbed his sternum as if he could rub the gnawing ache from his soul. "I don' know what the truth is anymore. What happened to us?"

I reached for him, but he stopped me. His eyes met mine, his agitation growing. "There *was* an 'us,' wasn't there?"

They weren't just dreams. It wasn't fragments. It was all the fractures between him and me beginning to show. When I didn't answer, Leon swung his feet to the floor.

I grabbed his arm. "Baby, I—"

"Knock, knock. Stop sucking cock." Liz's voice outside interrupted us.

Leon sat on the edge of the bed. I took the opportunity to trail a hand down his back. When he didn't move, my head fell to his shoulder. I kissed the silk of his skin, breathing in the warmth of his flesh while I could. As I brushed my lips against his ear, he let out a moan that was part whimper.

"Just give me a few more days," I rasped.

He turned and rested his forehead against mine for an all-too-brief moment. "Time don' seem to be on our side."

Liz stuck her head in with no further announcement. I leaned over, grabbed a discarded boot, and chucked it at her. She ducked with a laugh, stepping inside. Hands on her holsters, her gaze swept over my arms around Leon's middle. I lifted one unmistakable finger at her. Leon's belly clenched in silent laughter.

Undaunted, she crossed over. "Chow time. Rise and shine…" Her gaze cut to Leon's lap. "*Oh*, my bad. I see someone's already risen."

I growled then, jumping up to stand in front of Leon, stark naked.

Liz's hands flew to her eyes. "Ooookay. Did not need the whole show, Darke. Jesus. You got a permit to carry that thing?"

Clicking his tongue, Leon swatted my ass to move me out of his way. He pulled on pants while Liz's eyes remained covered.

I grabbed my own pair of pants. As I dragged a shirt over my head, I heard Liz swear. "Holy shit, Darke."

I peered over my shoulder to see both her and Leon staring

at my scarred-over moko. "Goddammit." Yanking the shirt on, I pivoted. "It's fine, all right? It doesn't hurt. That was four months ago."

"During the time I don' remember," Leon said in a flat tone.

"But all that work. All those hours spent—" Liz jerked with a sudden awareness and glanced at Leon.

I gave a nearly imperceptible shake of my head. Not imperceptible enough. Another icy storm of emotion swirled around Leon.

"I'll see y'all later." He opened the flap and was gone.

"I'm sorry, Darke. I haven't seen your back since that night. I didn't mean to—"

I cut her off. "Just tell me what the detail is for today."

The day's detail turned out to be anything but the resting up Raine had suggested. That was fine by me. I wouldn't be able to sit still until I got my hands on Leon or at least talked to him again. After a morning meal with what seemed like half the villagers—during which Leon ignored me to a far better degree than I'd ever done him—I decided to help out the Freelanders wherever I could.

Karesh might've been in the middle of nowhere, in the harshest of climates, but with a unique irrigation system from rain-captured water, their many small plots of native crops flourished. The livestock were free to roam, but they knew where their water supply came from and always returned home. Foragers scoured far and wide for wild fruits and liquid-filled gourds. Resourcefulness in abundance proved once again humanity could survive and thrive, without the CO's intervention.

I busted my ass all day long in an effort to keep my mind occupied. Lay a whole new plot for planting? *You got it.* Clean out lean-tos for horses more wild than tamed? *No problem.* Do a weapons demonstration for young warriors in the making? *Right up my alley.* Catch Leon's eyes during the intervening eight hours? *Not gonna happen.*

Exhausted from the day, I sat beneath the big awning in the center of Karesh, taking a break in the shade. I made sure to get an unimpeded view of Leon, who helped the women prepare the early-evening meal. They fawned over him. Their men grumbled from the sidelines.

I smiled, watching him beguile them all.

"You've got some drool." Cannon hunkered down beside me.

"Need I remind you how you blubbered all over yourself at your and *Blondie's* handfasting?"

"I have allergies."

"And it was cold. That explains how pink your face got. Yeah, I heard it all."

The smile on his face was all encompassing until he said, "The tables have turned, huh?"

My fingers dug into the ground.

"Listen, Darke, I know you loved Wilde and Tammerick. I saw you with them—"

"This is not about them."

He rocked back. "You're done mourning?"

"Yes." I was too busy yearning for Leon.

"But what about…?" His face flushed so bright I had to laugh. "Being bi?"

"I'm not bisexual technically. I love who I love. Man, woman, why does it matter?"

He rubbed the back of his neck. "Just don't get two loves."

"All love, one love. It's the same as you being gay. When it happens, it hits you in the chest. There." I knuckled his sternum with force. "The Company decrees one life, one order, *straight* love. That's not the natural way."

"Are you always so philosophical?"

"Only when I'm horned up." Leon and his god-fucking-damned pants riding low on his hips. Of course he'd taken his shirt off in the heat of the day, wrapping it around his head like a native.

"Probably more info than I needed to know." Cannon leaned back on his elbows and watched me scoping out Leon. "He's damn lucky to have a warrior like you watching out for him."

"I don't think he agrees."

"What'd you do to him now?"

"Nothing." Nothing apart from deliberately withholding the truth. "He's being cautious because of his circumstances."

"How unlike Leon."

I snorted.

"You mean you didn't throw him down last night?"

My face burned. This was not a conversation I'd ever imagined having with a former Elite Corps Commander.

"Hell, yeah, you did!" he shouted, calling the attention of half the people around us.

I neglected to meet his fist bump.

"You weren't up to snuff?" Cannon asked.

"Fuck. Off," I bit out.

"So you just didn't do it for him, huh?"

My jaw clamped tight. "I didn't say that."

He crowed so loudly Leon finally looked over.

"Do you and Liz compare journals or something?" My dig at his unlikely pastime shut Cannon up at last. "He's starting to remember little things."

"Hey, that's great, man." He squinted at me as I frowned. "Or maybe not."

"I really don't know anymore."

Clasping my shoulder, Cannon stood. "You gotta set shit right before it's too late, Darke."

He ambled off, no doubt in search of his man to rock their yurt.

* * *

Later that evening, while we readied to saddle up our transport—aka the spitting, hissing camels—Farrow launched into a conniption fit. "Y'all are tellin' me Ah gotta sit around and babysit mah little brother?"

To say she was unhappy about being left behind with Sebastian was putting it mildly.

I leaned over her. "You wanted him on this mission. Now suck it up, spy girl."

She scowled at me, her eyes brittle green and murderous. "And here Ah thought Linc was the only bullheaded bastard of the group."

"Bull something," Liz murmured, staring at Linc's lower half. Then she smirked at me. "Although, from what I saw of Darke this morning, and I saw a lot—"

Linc clamped one hand over her mouth and the other over her eyes. "At least he's covered up now."

Covered up? I was sweltering in meters of finely woven cloth from my neck to my feet, with a cowl-like hood over my head. Only my arms were bare, circled in tight silver bands on my biceps. The midday sun had felt like a warm spring breeze compared to the harsh heat crawling up my spine, but I bore up my deep disguise, squaring off with Linc.

He hit me with an acidic glare. "Next time don't even think about parading around naked in front of Liz."

"She was the one ogling, my man…"

"All I did was ask if he had a special license for his weapon." Liz was dressed in a fringed skirt and a short top that barely skimmed her midriff. She kept tugging at it distractedly.

Linc grabbed her hands, stilling them. He covered her taut stomach with his palm. "No one else needs to know how much you like handling weapons, sweetheart."

"Just yours…" she purred.

"Well, I guess we know why Leon calls Darke *big guy*," Sebastian drawled.

Leon shot me his first grin all day. One of these days I was gonna get him naked and slap his perfect ass until all that came out of his mouth was *more* and *please*.

I abandoned that train of thought when Cannon groused, "Hate this shit."

He scratched the two-days' growth of beard on his face that completed his transformation from commander to Free-lander.

"And I'll take pleasure in shaving you tomorrow." Nathaniel kissed his jaw.

I mounted my animal and turned to Raine. "You're sure tonight is necessary?"

"My guy Colt thinks he's found a rare plant we can use for the cure. So yeah, if you wanna save"—he quickly scanned our crew, "*someone's* life, it is."

Riding toward Omega was a lesson in trying to keep my cock under wraps, literally. With Leon in front of me once more, and bouncing up and down against my crotch, I had a hard time breathing, let alone thinking, strategizing, or planning an escape route if shit went haywire tonight. He wore an open animal-skin vest and no shirt, his hair dyed shocking black from a rinse of in-digo over henna. A kilt similar to Chief Shehu's hung from his waist, and I was willing to bet he didn't have anything on un-derneath. New henna tattoos on his chest entranced me, but not nearly as much as the real one low on his groin I'd licked and sucked and bit.

"My ass is startin' to hurt again." He jostled against me.

"Consider this practice. You probably won't be able to walk by the time I get through with you." Though my response was gruff, I drew in a breath of relief he was talking to me again.

He leaned back against my shoulder and turned his head, lick-ing the rivulet of perspiration that ran down my throat until my fingers convulsed on the reins. "I'm still mad at you."

"Sure feels like it." I bit his pouty bottom lip, smiling when he moaned.

The ride ended abruptly outside of Omega. The dusky twilight was shot through with vivid neon spots radiating from the area we approached. A stone-block fortress pulsed from the noise inside. It was so close to Omega walls, it was practically part of the sprawling, bustling city jam-packed with buildings one on top of the other. This appeared to be another case of the CO *generously* turning a blind eye to the lifestyles in this Territory.

Cannon tied his beast beside Raine's. "Fuck's sake. Just put up a sign already: *Round up Freelanders here.*"

"The Corps usually leave us alone," Raine said, shrugging. "They tap our livestock and crops, use us for workers.

"Welcome to our Amphitheater." He spread his arms out toward the network of buildings made of pale yellow stone. "This was once El Badi Palace. We call it now by its nickname: *The Incomparable Palace.*"

The palace was extensive, taking up what would be at least two city blocks. The structures may have been ancient and aged, but it was easy to imagine an era when they'd been sparkling with marble, gold, and murals. I was certain the CO had confiscated every piece of priceless art and architecture they could from the ruins, leaving only this surviving shell.

Crowds of Freelanders roamed outside the entrance to the Amphitheater, passing bottles back and forth and toking from the slim metallic pipes of hookahs. From the open door, grinding bass music jolted through my body, sending reverberations through my brain.

Raine reached an arm across me when I would've walked over the threshold. "We have to wait for Madam."

A tall woman came forth from a purple velvet curtain that obstructed our sight of the club's interior. She wore a corset that constricted her flat chest even more and lacy black stockings under her short skirt. Her obsidian skin and shaved head added to her sharp looks.

"Madam." Raine's red hair flowed over her hand as be brought it to his lips.

"Raine. And who is this?" Her long, bloodred painted fingernail scratched down the center of my chest.

"Darke."

Her slivered eyes never strayed from me. "Oh, but he is." She dragged in a deep breath. "I can feel him."

Jesus Christ. Is everyone an empath now?

Leon stood rigid next to me. His jealousy pierced my skin like hot knives. Something about the way the woman looked at me sparked a territorial urge in him.

I captured Madam's trailing hand and gently guided it back to her side. "A pleasure," I said with a dip of my head.

"The pleasure is mine. Perhaps we'll catch up later."

"Perhaps she'll catch a case of pubic lice later from some other stud," Leon muttered beneath his breath.

The tall black woman had already turned to sweep the curtain aside. She ushered us into the Amphitheater. "Condoms are free. Drinks are not. Weapons are allowed"—her hand snaked to the front of my pants—"only when kept on safety."

Leon knocked her hand aside. "I'll make sure he keeps it on safety, unless he's usin' it on me."

I grabbed the back of his neck and pulled him to me. His eyes popped wide before my mouth crashed down on his. My tongue twisted against his, thrusting quickly inside. Biting his lip, I broke away. Leon gasped, his lips wet from mine.

Madam watched with greedy pleasure. Silently acknowledging our connection, she swept away. The others cleared their throats, trying to look busy while surveying the scene before us.

Liz grinned. "I guess I don't have to break you two up tonight, huh?"

The last time I'd been to a Theater was outside of Beta, with Leon, Liz, and Linc. The moments before it was blitzed by CEO Cutler's unmanned drone planes still haunted me. Leon had said he was tired of my games. He'd never looked back as he marched away from me.

I released Leon's neck and grabbed hold of his hand. I quickly shut down the unbidden memory to gain a read on our whereabouts. The room was cavernous and dark, lit only by bars of bright strobe lights that flashed across the chamber in dizzying speeds. Smoke pumped from the corners of the octagonal room, adding to the impenetrability of bodies twisting to the beat of primal music. The walls were dotted with passageways and tunnels that snaked away from the main chamber. There were too many people, too many rooms, and too much chance of getting lost.

"Split up in pairs—that's why I chose y'all tonight," I instructed. "Work this room only. Keep your D-Ps on. Let's track down this Colt and get the fuck out of here pronto."

"Affirmative." They slid off, blending in with the dancers.

I kept Leon's hand tight in mine when he started moving away. "You're with me."

"What about *Madame la pute*?"

"I don't want her, and I think I made that pretty damn clear." I held his wrists gently behind his back and nuzzled his neck. "I want you."

"Possessive," he gasped.

I let go of his wrists to grab his ass. I thrust against him. "Obsessed."

Pushing away from me, Leon danced right into a throng of people throwing their fists into the air. I sent him a glower. He grinned. Wrapping his hands behind his head, he moved to a sinuous rhythm, his body slowly corrupting any thoughts of recon. Barely controlled chaos jumped around us, but the crowd moved like a wave, bringing us closer together.

Music invaded my body. The woman on stage threw herself about, her long pink hair covering her face as she riffed speedy raps. The vibrant energy was hypnotic. I locked sights on Leon. He rolled his hips, one hand cupping his crotch. There was no denying his sensuality as he pushed his kilt lower, licking his lips. A crisp line of hair curled around his fingertips.

I wanted to suck his cock right down my throat.

People tossed their heads back, bouncing against one another. Mashing bodies, sweaty skin, and the scent of sex propelled me to him. The energy was a flagrant *fuck you* to the CO, the CEO, and the anemic Corps. The air seethed with desire in every permutation. Man on man. Woman on woman. Threes, twos, a hundred titillating scenes made the air muggy with rebellious lust.

Nothing and no one was as riveting as Leon, who pressed his hips to mine when I reached him. I ran my hands down his bare chest inside the vest, tucked my fingers into the top of his kilt, and hauled him to me.

"You're a damn tease, boy." My lips brushed his ear; then I outlined it with my tongue until he shivered.

"Thought I wasn't a boy to you no more." He tossed his hair back. The black locks were disconcerting.

"Good boys get what they ask for." I nipped his earlobe and he sighed. My palm slid between his thighs, grazing the hot hard bar of his cock inside kilt. "What they beg for. Are you my boy?"

He lifted one eyebrow. "Are you man enough to take me?"

Just as I moved in to claim his lips, the music stopped. The flare of lights halted. I reached for my gun, shoving Leon behind my back. As I searched the vast, crowded room, I didn't discern any immediate threat, but I didn't relax my stance until an enormous D-P screen materialized over the stage as if from thin air.

Cannon and Nathaniel appeared beside us, sweat streaming off their bodies.

"Damn. I want one of those." Nathaniel's mouth dropped open.

Cannon gently pressed it closed. "Hatch would jizz his pants over that."

I turned to the screen when the multitude burst into loud jeers. CEO Cutler appeared, doing one of his thrice-daily promos. Having never met the man myself, I knew Nathaniel and Linc's father only through their horror stories, from Liz, and from Miss Eden, his estranged wife. Now I couldn't wait to slit his throat and watch him bleed out. Preferably over a crisp, clean white shirt like the one he wore for tonight's broadcast of bullshit.

"Hello, friends. Freelanders…freeloaders."

Asshole was not doing himself any favors, insulting my fellow revelers, who *boo*ed and threw bottles at the screen until alcohol dripped down it.

"Why are they showing this here?" I asked Raine as he sidled up to us.

"Revving up the Revolution. Nothin' gets the masses hotter than a nice nighttime parable from the paramount douche bag himself."

"By now you've heard about the Plague II." Cutler folded his hands in his lap. "It doesn't have to be like this. There are many of you out there, my little time bombs, ready to spread the disease…All of you were chosen for willful disobedience against the Company. Of course, *of course*, there is a vaccination. Company officers and Corps have been inoculated, as have all trusted citizens of the InterNations." He leaned in. His eyes were filled with hate he could not hide. "Do you want to face mass extermination again?"

His voice continued to boom over the razzing shouts of the Amphitheater crowd. "All you have to do, rebels, Nomads, is stand down. Accept One Rule. If you continue with this insurgency, I will begin to release the names of the infected. You may do what you must to curb the virus headed your way."

A shudder went through Leon, and I felt the same cold chill envelop my body.

I hugged him tight. "No one will find out, baby."

"You can't be sure of dat."

No sooner had Cutler shut the fuck up than the screen scrambled. People quieted once more as a voice came over the speakers and everyone cheered: "THE VOICE! THE VOICE!"

"Someone should tell him to get a better nickname." Liz sighed beside me, appearing from the vaporous stretch of the room with Linc at her back.

"Accept One Rule? Accept nothing but total victory!" *The Voice* sounded off from the fuzzed-out D-P that provided no visual, just a background. It was the same speaker we'd first listened to in Chitamauga.

"We will not accept the yoke of slavery around our necks for another half century. The CEO is scared. He's using fear to tie our hands and turn us against each other. We can defeat his virus. We can heal the carriers."

The swarming mass surrounding us roared with deafening shouts that almost drowned out the transmission.

"UNITE! UNITE FOR THE CURE! DEATH TO THE COMPANY! Remember: Love Free or Die!"

Music pumped on as the strobes lit back up. The crowd seethed with a fever pitch of excitement. I stood still amid the dancers, pushing people back as they knocked into Leon and me. Something was off. I could feel it.

Raine...I found him across the room, cornering another man.

"Stay put." I released Leon to Cannon's care, well aware Leon would've flayed my flesh with his glare if he could have.

The man Raine talked to had rings through every visible part of his body—nipples, nose, lips, ears…His lips thinned as he shook his head at whatever Raine demanded. Gone was Raine, the *comme ci comme ça* Freelander. He looked harsh now, his shoulders drawn up tight.

"Problem here?" I asked when I reached them.

Raine glanced in my direction. He visibly relaxed. "Not at all, my friend."

The other man looked scared shitless.

"This is Colt, Darke." Raine's smile unsettled my gut. "You can talk with him later. Right now I think he needs a drink—don't you?"

Colt slipped away in the direction of the bar.

"He looks a little nervous."

"He's got the shakes." Raine lit a cigarette, taking a deep drag. "Opiates are his thing. Hard to come by when the Company trawls our waters and black-markets our wares to line their own pockets."

"I need to find out if he has this plant you talked about for the cure."

He put an arm around my shoulders. "No doubt. You will. Just let him get a few drinks down his gullet first to loosen him up. Hey, I could use one, too. You?"

I allowed Raine to steer me to a different bar and accepted a cold bottle. My first sip relaxed my throat. The second spluttered all over the floor. Leon was pushing my patience to the breaking point, dancing directly in my line of sight…with that mother-fucking Colt. His red lips were curved in a teasing smirk. Colt's hand slid up Leon's chest. My vision turned red. Forget questioning the snitch. I was gonna kill him. I banged my beer to the bar and barged right between the two.

Leon whirled on me. "I jus' wanna forget. *Mais* yeah, I already did dat, didn't I?" His laughter harsh, he slapped a palm against my chest to push me away. I didn't move. "Forget the war. Forget the virus. Forget for tonight. I ain't dead yet."

"Then dance with me."

"What?"

"Dance with me." My hands found his hips.

"I don' think—"

"You never think. That's what I lo—" I inhaled briskly, stopping myself. "That's what I like about you. You feel without considering the consequences."

His head cocked back. "Dat ain't a compliment."

"Yes, it is." I palmed the back of his head, my fingers sifting through his hair. "Dance with me, Leon. Feel me now."

I groaned when his hands slowly linked behind my neck. Our chests pressed together. "Yes, baby."

His skin was the smoothest I'd ever felt. As I dragged my palms down his back inside his vest, Leon's muscles were firm, flexing beneath my touch. My thumbs circled the dimples above his ass, easing him closer. Our cocks rolled against each other through our clothing, and my breath stopped momentarily just to speed even faster.

"I want you so much, Leon."

He scattered kisses up my throat to my chin. "You break me into pieces."

"You put me back together." The almighty ache for him reached much farther than the exquisitely painful rush of blood pounding through my body. "I'll put you together again."

We danced together until I was practically making love to Leon on the floor, one of his legs wrapped around my thigh. His shallow gasps made me groan, his hands floating all over my body, under my shirt, making my skin burn with arousal. I pumped against him again, watching his eyes roll back.

"Tonight. I'm going to have you tonight." My voice was gritty.

Leon slid his leg down from my thigh. He peeled away from me. My mouth had left a red-purple mark on his throat, and I leaned forward to give him one on the other side. But he placed a hand against my chest, holding me back.

"I just wanna get a drink. You asked for time. I need space. Five minutes." He patted his hip "'Sides, I got my gun."

I allowed him the space he wanted and called all the others from my D-P. The ping back was immediate—no threats, nothing learned, and Colt vamoosed. *Waste of time.* A few minutes passed, and I grew anxious for Leon's return. My anxiety took a turn for the worse when a sudden spike of fear jetted through me. *Leon.*

"All points on Leon, now!" I shouted into my D-P. I waited a heart-stopping moment for the others to get back to me. I scanned the overcrowded room, searching for a shock of black hair. *I swear to God if he's getting himself groped by another loser with happy hands, I'm gonna—*

"I've got no visual," Liz called in.

"We have nothing. He's not near the entrance or the stage." Cannon sounded like he was pounding pavement in his haste to locate Leon.

Darwin checked in. "The bars are clear!"

I was at the back of the palace, Leon nowhere to be found. Worry reached so deep inside me, it made my hands unsteady, and I almost dropped the gun I'd raised on instinct. Scattering people before me, I ran through one of the twisty passageways—closest to the dance floor where we'd been. More of Leon's fear arrowed at me, sharper and clearer the closer I got to an opening in the long, cool stone corridor ahead.

It led directly into an enclosed courtyard, empty except for two men. Colt had a gun aimed at Leon.

"G'on. Do it so I don't have to when the time comes." Leon's stubborn chin thrust up.

I barreled forward and brought the side of my hand down on Colt's arm so fast and so hard that I broke his wrist with a snap. His gun clattered to the ground. His scream died quickly in his mouth as Raine came out of the shadows and unloaded a bullet into Colt's head.

"I got him," I reported over the D-P, scooping Leon into my arms. "We're gonna exit on the east side of the palace. Make tracks. Meet us there."

Raine tucked his weapon into the back of his pants. Standing over Colt's prone body, he lit a cigarette. A thin blue cloud of smoke trailed from the red glowing tip. "I guess he figured it out."

"Figured out what exactly?" I asked.

"Leon's infected."

I stared at the man. He'd already discovered the one thing I didn't want anyone else to know. I didn't think he was half as laid-back as he wanted us to believe, and perhaps that made him a more powerful ally. At any rate, I owed him.

Stepping forward, I put out my hand. "You helped save Leon's life. I am in your debt."

He shook my hand.

Leon wriggled, trying to set his feet on the ground, but I kept him cranked against me.

"You can let me go."

"Not likely." I dipped my mouth to his ear. "And you oughtta know, we're gonna have words later about you and your death wish."

"You're an arrogant sonuvabi—"

I cut him off with my lips, molding them to his. Leon was safe, but the tension wasn't dispelled. If anything, I needed to get him alone even more.

"Get us out of here," I said to Raine.

We moved swiftly down the courtyard, keeping behind a line of crumbling colonnades. Minutes later, we finally exited the palace through a thick metal door to a deserted alley outside.

Shortly after our exit, Linc, Liz, and Darwin busted through the door, keeping low and scanning for any threats.

"We're clear." My forearm flexed around Leon's middle when he tried to move away from me.

Nathaniel and Cannon cleared the exit next.

I nodded to them. "Leon's cover's been blown. We need to get out of here. We don't know who else knows."

Raine led our escape as we slipped away from the palace and its bright lights and noise. "We need fast transport." Raine stubbed out his smoke and quickly lit another.

Cannon scratched his beard. "Fuck the donkeys—"

"Camels," Linc corrected.

"We need a vehicle." Liz drummed her fingertips against the butts of her guns.

A loud engine roared up behind us. Our raised weapons were met with flashing headlights. Then Darwin's face appeared from an open driver's side window. She pounded her fist on the roof of the hot-wired, desert-ready Cruiser.

I hadn't even realized she'd done a disappearing act.

"She's slick." Liz grinned.

"Get in," Darwin called.

CHAPTER TEN

Raine rattled off coordinates to Darwin, who lead-footed it through Omega under his direction. She took hairpin turns with the same precision she handled the Predator, cool under pressure.

"We can't go back to Karesh." I stuck my face between the two of them in the front seat. "It's not any safer for Leon there than it was at the Amphitheater if someone's already been picking off the infected."

"I've got a place in mind." Raine peered out his window, his weapon cocked and ready.

I sat back, rearranging Leon on my lap. Scoping out the back window, I noted a Cruiser tailing us, gaining on us. The crack of a rifle sounded before stone dust blew across the windshield, a bullet having narrowly missed our car.

Darwin cursed and swerved to the left, trying to shake the unwanted armed escort. Linc and I rolled down our windows and swiveled behind to take aim from either side of the vehicle. His Heck made sweet music with one of my Smith & Wesson 500s.

With the accuracy of soldiers trained to dole out death, we took out the tires first. The best part was the fireworks when the engine block went up in flames and the vehicle crashed into the wall.

Darwin sped away from the explosion, and we calmly holstered our weapons.

Between me and Linc, seated on Cannon's thighs, Nathaniel wryly commented, "I'm beginnin' to get the feelin' people don't much like us around here."

Leon made the first noise he had since we got in the car, a small chuckle.

"Maybe it's a sign you should keep all your southern charm for me," Cannon said, tightening his arms around his husband.

"I don't think that's ever been a problem, big man."

Liz coughed, "Ass kisser."

Nathaniel grinned, dimples digging into his cheeks. "Yep. In every single sense of the phrase, Lizbeth."

I smoothed Leon's hair back, hiding my smile at Liz's crimson face with a kiss to his temple. The eight of us squished inside the stolen vehicle made for cozy quarters. I didn't mind Leon sitting on my lap where he couldn't get away, but I for one wasn't ready to snuggle up to Cannon's backside.

We didn't encounter any more threats in the form of Corps troopers or assassins or whoever else had it in for us. Leon's shaking body slowly stilled, his breaths evening out before sleep overtook him. In a couple hours, we passed through Omega and out the other side, across yet more barren desert, where nothing and no one resided. Darwin gunned it over high dunes that shined silver in the moonlight. On the other side of the sandy hills was a fantastical sight. The wide tires of the vehicle slipped and spun, but Darwin eased it down to an endless beach. She rolled to a stop just out of the crashing tide's reach.

In his sleep, Leon's arms had slid around me, his head resting under my chin. I woke him gently. "We're here."

His nose twitched and he rubbed a hand across his mouth before his eyelids fluttered open. His gaze was so sweet and dazed; I tried to forget the worry that hounded us, that time was running out.

"Where, here?" he asked.

"Haven't got a goddamn clue. Take a look." I nodded out the window.

His slumberous eyes widened as he took in the scene. We were all stunned to silence as we piled out of the vehicle, assaulted by the warm, salty air. I pulled Leon along with me, sniggering when he stumbled in the untouched white sand, his mouth agape. Not too far out in the surf, an island castle rose from a surrounding sandbar—stone blocks, turrets, and all. A slim causeway from shore to door was the only route to and fro.

"This is…" Nathaniel rubbed both hands across the shaved sides of his long hair.

"Wild," Leon breathed.

"Fucking weird." Cannon's brow furrowed as he canvassed the area for imminent tangos or more sand dunes.

Liz started walking toward the nature-made jetty. "I think it's romantic."

Cannon did an about-face. "Did you hit your head or something?"

A smile tugged at my lips as I led Leon forward. An air of reluctance hung over him, but I wasn't gonna let him get away with hanging back. It was clear his earlier anxiety had been replaced by a sense of wonder at this otherworldly place.

Waves lapped the sides of the rocky pier as we filed across. The castle was even more imposing up close, reaching high like the Beta Territory skyscrapers—except instead of glass and steel, this structure was built of rough-hewn stone and was utterly out of place in the blistering landscape.

"It's not a mirage, I promise you," Raine said, pushing open the massive timber doors. The rusty hinges let out a loud creak.

The ceilings were high, the rooms cavernous. A combination of dust and sand tickled my nose as we made a pass-through from the bottom level to the top three stories. During the recon, nothing could be heard but quiet calls of "clear" echoing through the vast vault-like castle. We reconvened in the main room on the bottom floor.

"How the hell did this place come to be?" I asked Raine as he sat cross-legged on one of the cushions tossed across the floor.

"An environmental anomaly caused by the Purge. It seems this castle drifted across the oceans to settle here. Amazing that it survived the trials of earth-wide destruction, just like our ancestors." He rolled a cigarette and lit it, his auburn hair glowing in the light. "Good thing for us, too. We're always safe at sea."

Leon lingered on the far side of the room, refusing to look at me.

"We should get some shut-eye," I said.

Linc stood at attention, no doubt thinking what I was thinking. I couldn't wait to get my hands on Leon, possibly to throttle him. Linc probably wanted some alone time with his new wife, too.

"Just as long as we're as far away from the Fuck Bunnies as possible," Linc said.

Liz's eyes danced. Cannon flushed to his hairline. Nathaniel took his brother in a tackle that landed them in a mass of limbs on the floor. He rolled off Linc, puffing his hair from his eyes.

"Someone has to stand guard while the others rest," I said before anyone could retreat.

Nathaniel pointed at Cannon. "We got it covered."

Cannon helped Nathaniel to his feet, grumbling about being volunteered as he none too gently brushed off his backside.

"C'mon, big man. We can have that second honeymoon later."

Everyone else claimed rooms while Leon tried to skedaddle past me on the first landing. I hooked him around the waist. "Not so fast. You're with me."

He started cursing up a storm.

"Swear all you want, and don't think I don't know what you're saying. You're not leaving my side." I barely concealed my fury about his asinine antics from earlier.

I marched him upstairs. I'd done my surveillance well, scoping out a room that not only had a lock but also an adjoining bathroom and—one odd miracle after another—warm running water. I assumed it was collected rainwater, heated by the sun somewhere in this whimsy of a castle. Inside the bedroom, I turned the lock behind me. Leon wrapped his arms around his body, looking down at the floor as he shuffled his feet.

"What's wrong?"

Dropping his arms, he thrust his chin forward in challenge. "You're pissed at me."

More than pissed, I was troubled. He'd asked to be killed, for fuck's sake. I forced myself to relax. The hot button I wanted to push tonight wasn't his temper. I stripped off my shirt and tossed it on the bed. Just because I wanted to goad a reaction other than fear or despair out of him, I lifted my arms for an allover stretch, my back to him. Every muscle in my body flexed. I listened to Leon's guttural response.

I closed the distance to him and brushed my hands down his arms to join my fingers with his. His gaze roved over my face—awed, worried, maybe wondering if I was gonna beat his ass for his brash *Go ahead and kill me* move. But I had better things to do with that incredible ass of his, and I couldn't wait to show him. Once I rid him of that hideous fucking hair dye.

Then I was going to teach him a lesson about when to beg and why: only for me, to make him come.

The bathroom was little more than a small flagstone rectangle holding a commode, a sink, and a shower stall. I tugged Leon in after me, our chests brushing in the enclosed space. I divested him of his clothes. I loosened my trousers and let them drop to the floor, standing in full erect glory before him. The darkness of my body against the tan of his never ceased to make my heart pound, longing and lust uncoiling within me.

That damn tat on his groin, beside the sweet staff of his stiff cock, taunted me. My fingertips trailed over it. His skin dimpled and he braced a hand on my shoulder. I turned on the water and walked into the cubicle, beneath the spray. When I looked back, Leon's gaze wandered over my body, stopping at my ass. I flexed the globes and groaned when he clasped me in a firm grip.

I dislodged his hands. "Come on. Let's get you cleaned up."

We warriors always traveled with a light pack—ammo, socks, dried food. Tonight I made use of the sliver of soap I'd brought. Later I had plans for the lube. I stood Leon under the spray, washing his hair of the ugly black dye. I cleaned his entire body, stopping only to soap mine. When our chests met, they were slick with hot, sudsy water.

The more I revealed of him, the more I was overwhelmed by fear for his survival. My hands slowed, reaching down to his ass so I could pull him against me.

"I am mad at you." I skimmed my hands up his back and cupped his face between my rough palms.

"It's bad enough to die, but 'cause of what I've done, because Cutler's out to get us, other people are gon' get infected." His large eyes blinked up at me. "I don' want anyone else to die because of me."

I returned my hands to his rear. I grasped him harder and he gasped loudly. "And what about me?"

He tried to back away. "You don't want me!"

Pushing him against the slick wall, I punched beside his head with both fists. "Does this look like I don't want you?" Our cocks strained together, mine butting against his. I wrapped my arms around him, whispering against his ear, "Does this feel like I don't need you? More than I've ever needed anyone?"

He shook his head, a moan on his lips that I swooped down and swallowed on my tongue.

"Don't you ever fucking ask for a bullet again." I shuddered against Leon

I lifted my head, not caring if the water failed to hide my tears. Our kiss was a languid mesh of salty tongues, our touches so terribly tender it felt like my heart was beating in my hands, his for the taking.

"*Cher.*" His tongue traced the cords of my neck to my ear. He had no idea what that forgotten endearment meant to me. Another slip of tears welled in my eyes. "I don't know what I mean to you no more."

"Then let me show you."

There were no towels when we stepped out of the shower. I licked the droplets from his body with the flat of my tongue, holding him still when he quivered and groaned. In the bedroom, I shook out the blankets to get rid of the dust and quickly remade the bed. I laid Leon in the middle of it.

I lit a candle and placed a tube of lube and a condom from my ever-ready pack beside him, making sure he knew my intentions. He spread his legs to invite me on top of him. The sunny warmth of his body was the antidote to all the darkness in me, all the despair that had sucked me into a black hole for so long I'd forgotten about loving and touching and living.

With death and disaster so close, I needed to show Leon I was worth living for. That he was worth all my care, all my attention, and he could have what he wanted, if he still wanted me.

Leon looked like a tiger as I moved over him. His hands

cruised into my short hair, scraping my skull. I lowered myself on top of him, crying out when his hard cock aligned with mine. We were both slick and ready, hard and wanting, but I wanted more. I wanted all of him. I wanted inside of him.

I kissed him for a long time, fucking my tongue into his mouth where he licked it like he had my cock the other night. Our wet lips audibly parted. "I'm gonna love you so good, Leon."

He moaned, tossing his damp hair about.

This time I didn't go for his beautiful shaft. I was after his glorious ass. I flipped him over and laid him spread-eagle. Leon immediately lifted up, presenting himself.

I spread his cheeks wide and slapped the perfect rounds of flesh. "No one's ever gonna have this sweet ass again but me. Got it, baby?" I shoved aside the constant worry he might've been raped at Taft's hands. I'd stop everything if Leon showed the slightest discomfort about what I was doing.

"Yes!" Leon's voice was muffled in the mattress.

Goddamn if his ass wasn't the hottest thing I'd ever seen. My tongue skipped down the length of his spine while I dangled one finger over his little hole. I kissed the top of his cleft. I tongued the tight crease, roaming to nip and slap and massage his peach-like ass on every pass closer to his pucker. His cheeks were so muscular I needed both hands to spread them fully apart so I could get my face right in there where I wanted it.

His ring expanded when I breathed on it. His groan reverberated when I moved back up to tease the dimples above his ass. I took a side trip to his balls, sucking the pink orbs into my mouth and running figure eights around them. When he humped back against my face, I lashed my tongue from his perineum to the pretty pistil-like opening and speared deep inside.

"Ohhh!" Bracing even wider on his knees, Leon wiggled his butt in front of me.

"Nice. So beautiful." I spanked both sides with soft slaps, leaving a pink mark on his flesh.

Diving into his taut divide, I ate his ass, loudly slurping. I loved his taste, his wanton reactions, his wild writhing. I licked, bit, lightly chewed his crinkled tissue until it swelled and expanded. I bet his cock was leaking precome like mine, but I wasn't going to touch either of us, not yet. My finger ringed his moist entrance, and Leon begged for more.

"Relax, baby," I shushed, my soft words at odds with the loud spank I unleashed against his flank.

"Uh, uh!"

"I'm gonna be here a long time."

He reached a hand back to drag my face closer. "Oh yeah! Get in dere, *beb.*"

I ate the holy hell out of his ass, stopping only to catch my breath, wipe my mouth, and start again. His loud vocals spurred me on from gentle teasing to full-fledged feasting on his divine cherry. "You've got no idea how long I've waited to be in here."

My jaw pressed against his scrotum. I tongued inside, curling and flicking. My fingers opened him, too, until I was kissing, biting, eating. "So fucking tight. How long's it been?"

Leon's long, guttural groan finally formed breathless words. "A long time. Since before I had a hankerin' for Cannon, far as I can remember."

A pure shot of jealousy possessed me. I growled and nailed his prostate with a finger. "You still hot for him?"

"*Non!* Oh fuck, Darke…fuck me…"

"Not yet." I maneuvered beneath him and went for his cock. Levering his length toward my mouth, I said, "And I said I don't fuck. I make love." I took him straight down my throat, caressing him with my tongue.

Leon's shouts echoed off the stone walls. His firm thickness filled my mouth as his thighs quivered on either side of my head. I grunted around him, tempted to stroke myself, but one touch and my dick would shoot off. Pressing on his clenched abs, I pushed him from my mouth. He gasped and trembled. His back arched in the most beautiful form I'd ever seen. He glowed with a light sheen of perspiration and was flushed with lust.

I craved him like nothing else.

I rolled Leon to his back. His sumptuous lips were too much to resist. I kissed his mouth, his neck, his jaw, where a light sprinkling of stubble rasped my lips. As I reared up between his legs, the tendons on my thighs were tight and my cock was a darker shade than the rest of my skin, the flesh stretched taut and shiny. It reached beyond my belly, its girth wider than ever before.

"Holy hell. That's goin' in me?" His voice cracked. With his hands cupping my shoulders, he bent up to capture one of my nipples between his moist, pink lips. His movement brought the head of my cock into contact with his pucker.

My eyes slammed shut, and I held his head against me. "I can come all over you instead."

He pulled back and grabbed the lube. "Like hell you will."

Leon held himself up and open, his cock pulsing against his stomach, a pool of clear release sticking to his skin. His bud mesmerized me. He poured lube over my fingers and into my palm, his eyes never leaving the big black staff throbbing from between my thighs. I slowly glided my fingers up and down my shaft, tempting him. His fingers came forward to teasingly polish the broad cap of my cock, gathering the slick from my fingertips to use on his own. I breathed fast and shallow, on the verge of coming from that light touch alone. I let him work on my dick while I joined three wet fingers to slowly plunge them inside of him.

With a moan, he looked down his body. My first knuckles breached him. His pelvis tilted farther up, aiding my ingress.

"Look at that, boy." My balls churned, and I needed to take my place inside him.

When I said *boy*, Leon's gaze flipped to mine. He liked it at times like this because he knew he was mine and I'd take care of him in all ways. His arousal saturated my mind, pulled my features tight, and made my muscles strain.

All three of my fingers deep inside him, I wiggled and pumped slowly. His hips swiveled, always chasing my retreating fingers. The cover was in disarray because of his writhing. When I started banging harder and faster, spreading out my fingers, Leon went wild. He shouted and scratched and bit at my neck and arms.

"You ready for my cock?" I asked, rolling the condom down my throbbing shaft.

"*Oui*. Yes, yes!"

"Leon, love."

His dazed, hungry eyes found mine.

"I need to know you want this." The head of my cock was primed at his tender opening. My arms shook. My abdomen tightened. "I need to know you want me."

"Feels like I've always wanted you, *cher*." His hands smoothed my cheeks, then joined at the back of my neck.

It was excruciating to go so slowly with him, but I wouldn't force him. I wouldn't rush him. Little by little, I entered Leon. He stretched around the crown of my cock until he accepted me inside that first ring of muscle. I gripped the base of my shaft, so close to exploding I had to lock down on all my muscles and shut my eyes from the sight of him taking me in.

I curled forward around him, breathing in his heady scent. His palms smoothed down my back, and I felt him moving his hips, loosening slightly, wanting me.

Inhaling deeply, I looped my arms around him. "Just a little more, angel."

"Why do you call me dat?"

I turned my head for a kiss. "Because you are mine, my saving grace."

Leon sucked in a breath and moaned. His passage relented, his legs locked around my waist, hands clasping my shoulders.

I rose up on my arms and grunted, "You're also a dirty, hot fuck." I thrust all the way inside him.

The tight intensity was almost too much to bear. Being inside Leon, finally, for the first time, I couldn't move for fear of coming. I watched him frown, his mouth fallen open. Kissing and licking and nipping all along his throat, I stroked my hands down his sides to his hips, around to his pert round ass.

He relaxed with a gasp.

I drew out a bit, massaging more oil along my cock.

"Oh…oh…*m'dieu*…" he stuttered when I slowly pressed deep again.

The heat coming off his skin was no match for the inferno of his channel that wrapped around me so closely, stars burst into my vision. I stilled inside, desperate to hang on to my control. Leon started to groan and beg. I looked down to see my thick black cock stretching his pale pink hole to the max and Leon loving every minute of it.

"Do it. Fuck me. Have me. Make me yours." His harsh words ran like fingertips up my spine and down to my balls.

I withdrew at a treacherously slow pace and slid back inside with another languid thrust.

He grasped my neck, biting my shoulder hard. "*Merde!* Fuck me! I need you!"

That was it. I took a giant breath and drew out only to slam inside, knocking the next words from Leon's gasping lips. "Like that?"

He clung to me, his eyes hazy and gold-ringed with wide circles of dilated black. "Yes. Yes! Lose it. I need you to lose it in me."

I roared, shedding my tightly strung control. I hadn't let anyone inside emotionally or physically since Wilde and Tam. Now I nailed Leon so deeply he clawed my back, his cock jerking between our slapping bellies. The savage consummation of six months of flirtation and play, of loss and powerlessness made me snap. I took what Leon had offered in the early-winter months over and over again. I took him hard and fast despite my need to make love to him. I couldn't contain myself. I wouldn't lose him.

I pulled out, gasping for air. My chest heaved. Leon's cheeks were red, his neck covered in love bites. His shaft leaped up. I slapped a broad hand down on his upturned ass and slapped my dick across it. He was so tight, so taut, my cock bounced off him.

"Put me inside," I bit out.

Sure hands and long fingers guided me to his passage. Once he had me snug against him, he lifted his ass, taking me in.

My breath fell from my lips with a gasp. "That's right, sexy boy. Fuck my cock."

He whimpered. His hands pulled me forward until I tunneled deep inside. Then I wrapped one hand around both his wrists. Raising them above his head, I started slamming. "You still wanna forget?"

"No." He mewled at the sensation of my cock pounding inside of him.

"That's right. No more running. No more forgetting. No more flirting with anyone else."

I wrapped a hand around his shaft, using quick squeezes just under the ridge of his head. He came quickly, screaming my name, spurting across both our chests and spurring me on.

I sucked my come-covered fingers into my mouth and then slanted my lips over his. "And no goddamn dying on me."

The constrictions of his throbbing passage shredded the last of my control. I came with rapid bursts, overflowing the condom until it leaked out in a sexy, sordid mess. My world went white-hot, my hearing filled with the sounds of his deep-voiced moans and my yells.

I fell to my back, bringing Leon across me in a tangle of arms and legs and labored breaths. I filled my hands with his hair, dropping a kiss to his forehead. "You okay?"

"You din't break me, if dat's what you're askin'."

I kissed the willful smirk off his lips, content when he curled against me. "No one should ever break you, angel."

His hands drifted up and down my back and sides and I stretched into his caress. My shaft rose again, prodding his thigh. He grasped it in a fist that couldn't completely close around the girth.

"*Merde*. So big. I can't believe you put dis all the way inside me."

His words and his touches turned me on until my legs tensed and released fitfully. I lowered my mouth to kiss along the tops of his shoulders from one side to the other.

My voice dropped to a deep tone. "That cock you're stroking wants to be inside you again."

He abruptly stopped, pulling his hand back as if my shaft burned him. "I think my ass needs to recover first."

I chuckled into his hair, teasing out the soft lobe of his ear with my tongue.

Leon leaned on to an elbow. "How well did I know you before?"

Laughing with a deep rumble, I skimmed my palms over his rear. "Not this well."

"We never made love?"

"Leon, you'd remember if we had, if nothing else."

He grinned. "I can believe dat." Then his smile disappeared. "What about your past?"

"There was nothing before you." I lay back and shut my eyes.

"Dat ain't true. I know dat ain't true, Darke."

"Sometimes I wish there was nothing before you." If I opened myself up to him, I risked more than just loving and losing him. I would feel him, his emotions, even more intensely the tighter we were bound.

"Your *maman*, your dad…please, *beb*. Let me in." He knocked a fist against my chest. I opened my eyes to see his, shadowed and serious.

"What do you want to know?"

"Just about every'ting."

"That's sure asking a lot, sweet baby." I dragged him across me, watching a blush spread across his face. "My mother was a blues singer, famous in her time. It turned out to be her downfall. It got her noticed by the Company, and nothing good ever comes of that."

Leon snorted. "Don't I know it."

"Music and arts were immediately outlawed when the Company came into power. They could've imprisoned her or worse, so at first, when they made her perform in their clubs, she counted herself lucky." I rode my thumb across his pouty bottom lip. "Skin color caused race wars in Old History. Now the new government came along and claimed their way was better, more egalitarian, if you can frigging believe that." I gave a dry huff of laughter. "They might not have discriminated based on race, but they sure as fuck tyrannize in every other sense, don't they? All they did was trade one oppression for a host of others."

"What was her name?"

"Soleil."

Leon popped up. "But dat's French!" He frowned. "For sun, and she named you Darke?"

"It was about the nature of things." Lacing my fingers through his, I watched the play of our skin. "Light and dark. Like you and me."

"And what was your papa called?"

"Reginald."

He spluttered a laugh. "Well, I'm glad you aren't Reggie Junior. Darke suits you." He kissed my knuckles.

It did, except when I was with Leon, like this.

"What happened in the Company clubs? When did she meet your papa?"

"You weren't kidding when you said you were curious." I pressed our joined hands to my chest. "Her freedom was stolen from her. She was their caged bird with her brilliant voice, their pet, made to perform. Song kept her alive, and occasionally she was accompanied by my father. He was one of her fellow musicians. A saxophonist, very talented. His emotions were vibrant and colorful, lighting up her gray world the few times they performed together. She felt emotions from others, you see. It was part of what made her music soulful."

"She what now?"

"She was an empath." I'd never told Leon about this unusual trait I'd inherited from her. I decided to give him honesty, in one form or another tonight. My voice lowered when I said, "Like me."

He sprung up like a jack-in-the-box toy. "You what?"

"I can sense the emotions of people I'm closely connected to."

He sat across from me on the bed. "Okay. Dat's not creepy at all."

My cheeks grew hot as he sat there, staring at me. "Go on. Ask it."

He clapped his hands, more lively than I'd seen him in a long time. And I was just so happy to be there for his entertainment. "Can you feel what I'm feelin' now?"

"Amused." I raised an eyebrow.

Closing his eyes, he was quiet for a moment. Then he stared at me with a serious look. "And now?"

I rolled my eyes, indulging him a second time. "Trying to be solemn. Still amused."

His lips quirked in delight before he frowned hard. "Now?"

Laughing, I pulled him back into my embrace. "You know you can't change your moods just because you want to, baby. You're still *highly* amused."

"I get the feelin' I won't be laughin' in a few minutes."

I shook my head. "No. They fell in love, the chanteuse and the saxophonist. With all musical practices illegal outside the government's sanctions, they had to stay as performing monkeys to remain alive."

"Did they get married?"

"They couldn't. It wasn't allowed. They weren't even supposed to have sex. This time it wasn't about race but about simple control of Company commodities. They didn't want their assets distracted by anything other than providing entertainment to the patrons."

Leon stiffened in my arms. "They survived through all dat hell and the Company couldn't let them be together?"

"They didn't survive enough, though. Not enough." I tried not to let the story burn me, but it wasn't just a story. It was my past, how I came to be. "When it was discovered she was pregnant, they tried to escape. My mom knew they'd take the baby from her; they couldn't let an infant interfere with her performances. With the help of some underground Freelanders, she made it out. My father was shot in the back because at the last minute he wouldn't run. He had to make sure she had the best chance. That meant serving himself up."

I cried as I hadn't before because I'd trained myself to grieve in silence. Being with Leon made my emotions claw at the surface, dragged them from the darkness.

Leon's fingers tenderly took away the tears. "But your mom's not at the commune."

"No. She never fully recovered from my father's death. She died when I was eleven." I pressed my mouth to his in a gentle kiss. "They say she died of a broken heart."

I captured him in a deeper kiss, giving him my desire and need. Like my mom, I thought I'd die when Tam and Wilde did, only to discover my heart beat more proudly than ever with Leon in my arms. But their ghosts still stood between us.

When he drew back, his lips were slick, his eyes hooded. "Eden and Hills raised you?"

"No one raised me, angel." Before falling in love with Tam and Wilde, I'd become unreachable, pushed into isolation from the boundless feelings pressing in on me from all around. "I'm untamed." Especially with Leon, when I felt the uncontrollable urge to have him again and again.

He felt the press of my erection rising from my groin. His eyes twinkled. "Somethin's not tamed, dat's for sure."

We kissed and caressed slowly, kindling the fires that would ignite again if I didn't let him fall asleep. His heavy eyelids finally started to drift down when he broke our lingering kiss.

"Did I know all this before?"

"No, angel." I pulled him deeper into the blankets.

"Why do you keep callin' me dat?" he asked for a second time that night.

"Because you give my heart flight."

* * *

When I woke, it was to the arousing feeling of Leon's lithe body molded against mine. His hot erection was a brand against my hip. I slipped my hand beneath the blanket and ran my fingertips up and down the pulsing shaft, knowing I'd make good use of his ass again if I didn't get out of bed soon.

I left him sleeping and quickly washed and dressed. Arrested by the sight of him burrowed under the covers, one arm beneath his head, I walked out the door before temptation made me lose all my gentlemanly restraint.

I wondered if Cannon had slept at all when I found him in the large room downstairs, fully alert. He seemed to thrive off tense situations.

We pooled our meager rations, and I set some aside for Leon.

"How's Leon?" he asked.

"Better." I kept my face clean of all emotion.

"Fucked it out of him, did you?"

I stared right through Cannon.

"Hey, you don't need to talk. I heard it all. Don't know why we get dubbed the Fuck Bunnies what with the noises you got out of Leon last night."

"I don't kiss and tell, no matter what you think you heard."

"No. You just screw in front of the whole commune." He looked instantly regretful. "I'm sorry, man. I didn't mean to bring up—"

I waved his apology away. "That won't be happening with Leon."

Both his eyebrows lifted. I was saved from any more interrogation when Nathaniel entered the room.

He settled beside Cannon, rubbing sleep from his eyes. "Where's Raine?"

"He left real early to retrieve our shit and get Farrow and Sebastian." Cannon fed a bite of dried fruit and grain to his partner. "And he for damn sure better stock up on some provisions, because any more of this trail-mix bullshit and my stomach's gonna gnaw a hole clean through to my spine."

A sudden sound interrupted us from outside the mammoth door. A possible intruder. We three took careful aim, arranging ourselves around the room to hit the target from all sides.

Raine strolled into the keep. Alone. He kicked the door shut behind him, seemingly unperturbed by having several weapons pointed at him. "Well, folks, I've got some good news and some bad news." He shook a small leather bag in his otherwise empty hands.

CHAPTER ELEVEN

Cannon, Nathaniel, and I lowered our weapons.

"Please tell me that Sebastian and Farrow are on their way in." I started right in with questioning Raine.

"'Fraid not." He stuck the mysterious leather pouch in his pocket and quickly rolled a cigarette.

Cannon glowered. "So that would be the bad news, then."

"'Fraid so." He exhaled two perfectly concentric smoke rings.

Linc and Liz entered the room. Liz immediately began digging through the food supplies while Linc asked Raine, "'Fraid so what?"

If this kept up we'd never get to the bottom of Raine's intel. "Why don't we put a lid on it until the others come down?"

"Aye-aye, Cap'n." Darwin slunk in with a salute in my direction. All eyes locked on her. "What? We're on the water, aren't we?"

Raine stubbed out the butt of his smoke with his boot. "Can I just say—?"

"No!" I barked.

Leon loped around the corner. "Don't think you should be cranky after last night, *beb*." He sent a shy smile my way.

His hair was tousled, his expressive eyes dancing. I wanted nothing more than to throw him over my shoulder and take him back to bed for the entire day.

Those plans were shot to shit when Raine started talking. "Karesh was raided. They mostly managed to decamp before the troopers swarmed."

"Define *mostly*," Cannon said.

"There weren't any casualties, just a couple prisoners." As Raine divulged his info bit by bit, he made himself comfortable on the floor.

"And the prisoners were?" My heart started pounding.

"Your people."

A round of expletives sounded off.

"Anyone else?" I asked.

"No."

"Chief Shehu, his family, they're all safe?" I'd felt an affinity with the warrior.

"Just yours." Raine reclined on his elbows. "They were hauled to a war camp on the outskirts of Omega. The chief had them tailed. He's keeping an eye on them."

"An eye isn't good enough. They'll be dead meat or beaten up for Revolution secrets if they're detained much longer." Linc strode around the room. He'd been raised as CEO Cutler's one rising star, known to be a ruthless and cunning strategist. He knew the CO's ops inside and out.

"Maybe you'd like the good news now?" Raine pulled the satchel from his pocket.

"Get on with it." My nerves were tighter than a slip wire at this point.

Juggling the bag from hand to hand, he said, "I managed to find what I think is the final ingredient for the cure."

The tension released from me so fast I felt dizzy. My palm sweated against Leon's, or maybe that was his getting damp as he gasped beside me. "What is it?"

"A rare genus of plant found only in the most rugged desert terrain. It won't be identical to the Company's synthetic antidote, but it should do the trick." Raine tucked the bag away again, fully aware that the item was more valuable than all the scrip in all the Territories. "I told you Mother Nature always provides."

I smiled against Leon's lips when I kissed him soundly. He gripped my back, laughing between soft nips of my teeth. When I pulled away, I asked, "How long?"

"Eh, I don't know. Measurements, test runs, this and that..." Raine lounged idly, as if he were talking about the fucking weather and not the cure to a disease that was set to kill my man. "The other good news is I retrieved your gear and weapons as well as my mobile lab."

"Then you should get right on it." I struck for the door, ready to carry anything he needed into the castle so he could set up and start work.

Linc stood in my way.

"Move it."

"We need to consider our options," he said, always the tactician.

"Here are your options: Move your fucking feet out of my way or we're gonna go a round or two."

Practically climbing up my arm, Leon tried to drag me away. Linc's chest heaved in and out, but he wasn't as full of rage as I was. He was being cool in the face of a twofold crisis, whereas I had only one goal.

"If we fight, it's gonna get real ugly in here, real quick. We're all on the same side." Linc left his hands down at his sides, as unthreatening as could be except he still blocked the door. "We have a choice and it could affect the entire war, if not our collective consciences. Stay and work on the antidote or save our friends. People we consider to be our family."

My teeth clamped down hard. "Leon is my family. I want to save him. We're staying." It was a no-brainer.

The others immediately objected, Leon most loudly. One of these days I was going to have to teach him to choose self-preservation over playing the goddamn martyr for the cause, preferably before he ripped my heart out and shredded it apart.

I took a step back from Linc. My shoulders were stiff as I turned to face the room. "Leave Raine here so he can work."

Nathaniel attempted his peacekeeping thing. "We aren't splittin' up again. Not after what just happened. Two of our people were caught, man."

Their protests did nothing to budge me from my decision, not until Leon drew me away. "*Cher.*"

God, he was pulling out all the stops this time. The second he called me that, he had to know he tied me in knots, wrapped me around his finger. I let him back me out to the hall, where he leaned up to glide his lips across mine. The way his tongue teased into my mouth to tangle slowly with mine caused a splintering ache that started in my chest and leaped to my groin.

I grunted when he drew back, chasing after his seductive lips.

"There's a week and a half. Plenty of time for Raine to make his medicine." Nuzzling my neck, he whispered in my ear, "You won't be proud of yourself if you insist on him stayin' when we need him to save the others. And dat's one thing I love about you, my big, righteous warrior."

His soft touch and low words were more persuasive than any gun at my head could've been. He knew it, too. Several more drugging kisses had me agreeing to anything. Hell, I'd go out on my own to extract Sebastian and Farrow.

I nodded my assent.

Leon pulled me back to the room. "We're solid."

The others quickly rearranged themselves in casual stances as if they hadn't been watching the whole show with avid interest. *Dickheads.*

For the next fifteen minutes, I lugged our shit from the stolen vehicle to the castle along with the others. Amid our gear was Raine's lab equipment.

Leon lifted a wide-bottomed glass vessel from the box he set down inside. "Dis looks like a bong."

"Beaker, bong, same thing. We can have a toke after our mission." Raine wiped an arm across his perspiring brow.

Pothead, tour guide, shaman, same diff. Jesus.

"No one's smoking anything and we're not going anywhere until Leon eats something." I delivered Leon's and my packs to the bottom of the stairs.

Liz took a break from checking her cases of ammo to heckle. "Whoa ho! Looks like there's a new big papa in town."

"I'm not his daddy, Liz." I glared down at her while a blush crept up the back of my neck.

She hummed softly, reloading her Eagles. "That's not what he was screaming last night."

"Suits me fine." Cannon interrupted. "Gives me time to shave this fucking fuzz off my face." He scratched his jaw.

Nathaniel's eyes lit up. "Well, I volunteer for that duty."

"Hop to, then, Blondie." Cannon gave him a lascivious wink. "I guess the honeymoon really isn't over." They raced up the stairs.

"Horny-moon, more like." Leon snickered.

I swatted his ass. "You'll get yours, too, later tonight."

He gingerly rubbed his backside. "Dat still hurts, ya know?"

"I'll make it feel better later."

Leon moved into my welcoming embrace and suckled on my bottom lip until my knees were one suck away from buckling. This playfulness between the two of us was brand-new, lighthearted even amid the fear and stress. "Dat's what you said last time."

"And I was right. You certainly weren't complaining."

* * *

Regrouping in the room downstairs before heading out, we all wore similar kaffiyeh—the women in hijabs—disguising our hair and faces. Our lightweight robes hid our weapons well.

The mood was tense on the trip back to Omega, and the ride seemed quicker than our escape had been. Probably because we were racing toward danger instead of fleeing from it. We couldn't make a solid plan until we saw exactly what kind of shitstorm we were facing.

We stopped a quarter klick away from the coordinates Raine had gotten from Shehu's man. After hiding our transport behind a dune, we crabbed up the small sandy hill and passed three pairs of binocs around. That's when we figured out the shitstorm looked more like a full-blown she-devil in the making.

"Fuck's sake." Cannon swiped an arm across his brow. "It's a goddamn war camp over there."

He wasn't lying. The area we watched was a well-maintained prison camp made of tall barbed-wire fences on the perimeter that multiplied into little square boxes inside, dividing up a number of holding pens. There was no overhead cover from the sun's overwhelming heat. In the few minutes we lay at our lookout point, the searing rays baked through cloth to my skin. I could only imagine the hellish conditions inside. To make matters worse, large solar reflectors in each corner of the huge structure shined the torturously bright sunlight toward the POWs from all angles.

"That's inhumane." His nostrils flaring, Nathaniel handed the binoculars over to Linc.

"What if they're infecting more people in there?" Liz spoke in a broken voice.

This was a doomsday scenario, especially as we timed the short intervals between the guards walking the boundary. The place was totally open to the elements. There could be no covert approach or any way to sneak inside without being made.

"It's crawling with hostiles." I gave my binoculars to Darwin. "Shit's gonna get hairy."

"Hairier than Satan's asshole, that's for sure," Darwin muttered.

The guard on our side turned in our direction. Perhaps he'd caught the reflection of our binocs.

We hunched down until our faces were half buried in the sand and Linc whispered, "Fall back."

Completely hidden by the sand dune, we took stock of the situation. The entire area—inside and out—was built to be visible from every angle. The troopers were heavily armed and not snoozing on duty, not to mention the fact almost all of us were recognizable enemies of the CO. The math was simple: We were fucked. But not a single one of us had ever backed down when the odds were against us, and with two of our people inside, we weren't about to start now.

"Plans?" Linc asked.

Nathaniel chewed his lip. "We need to be wily."

"Bullets won't help. There's too many of them and not enough of us. We need to outsmart them somehow." Liz drew a quick diagram of the prisoner camp in the sand.

"How many civilians do you think are inside?" I wondered.

She totaled up the numbers. "If every pen holds five people…by my reckoning that's at least two hundred."

Linc watched his wife lift her over-robe to pull her high-powered sniper rifle from her back. "How many guards can you take out quickly?"

"Not enough." She placed the expensive rifle in his hands. "Our position would be compromised before I was through, and they'd retaliate on the prisoners. Then they'd get to us."

Cannon had keenly observed Liz hand over her beloved sniper rifle. "Just what the fuck are you thinking now, Liz?"

She sent a look to Darwin, who nodded in that woman-to-woman way that made absolutely no sense whatsoever to the male species. "What Nate said. Being wily."

"Using our wiles." Darwin sat up straight, her interest sparked.

"Yeah, I didn't mean put your life on the line, Lizbeth." Nathaniel was the target of two sets of glares coming from Linc and Cannon.

"Hey. Caspar always did call me foolhardy." She popped her knuckles, her wide grin nestled in her black headscarf.

"Dat's a bad move." Leon, who had been quiet, piped up. "I'll go in. Got nothin' to lose, right?"

Linc turned his attention to Leon.

I instinctually grabbed for my lover. "Yeah, you do have something to lose. It's called your life."

"*Mais*, it's worthless now. Might as well put my last days to good use."

How he could be so fucking insouciant about his existence when it meant everything to me made veins pop up in my neck. "You are staying put." Before he could volunteer for another hair-raising, heart-attack-inducing sortie, I looked at Liz. "What's the plan?"

"I thought we'd just stroll up to the place and see if we could flirt our way in."

"Flirt? You?" Cannon almost choked.

With a harsh frown, Linc tried to shove her rifle back at her. "That's a no-go."

"In other words, those men look hot, pissed off, and dusty. We're gonna offer up sexual favors in return for entry. Does that make it any clearer?" Darwin's explanation did not settle Linc's objections.

The two women wouldn't be waylaid. Both were highly skilled soldiers well versed in the art of undercover ops. It went without saying that none of us approved of their scheme, but we were out of options.

Darwin and Liz wriggled out of their long robes to reveal much less confining clothing underneath.

"Tell me you two weren't planning this back at the castle," Linc said.

Liz put her hands on her hips. "We weren't planning this at the castle."

Jumping to his feet, Linc swooped her into a sudden kiss that left her panting. "Remind me you're on my shit list later, when you get back safe and sound."

Resituating her clothes, she saluted. "Roger that."

"Woman," he growled.

"What? I was responding to a direct order from my commanding officer."

Liz and Darwin clambered over the dune, arms raised in the air.

"Use your assets!" Linc instructed.

"Don't worry, baby, we'll be using those and plenty more." She wiggled her ass and tapped her thigh. "I've got my party favor. And a little flash bang goes a long way."

"Righteous babes," Raine said.

He was caught in the crosshairs of every scowl. He only shrugged in response, taking out his cig papers to roll one up.

"You want to send up smoke signals or something?" I snarled, knocking the rolley out of his hands.

Linc was to cover our two interlopers. He was almost as much of a crack sniper as Liz. He followed the women in his sights as we scrambled up the hillside beside him.

Liz and Darwin made it safely to the fence, approaching a trooper. I focused the binoculars for a closer look. The women talked. He lowered his aim to the ground. A healthy length of feminine leg was flashed. The soldier licked his lips, nodding.

"Those are some serious assets." Raine must've had a death wish, making a comment like that.

Without so much as looking, Linc reached over and knocked him on the back of his head. "Shut the fuck up about my woman."

"Would it help if I said I was talking about Darwin?"

"No," we all replied.

We continued to watch in near silence, holding our breath. Seeing former First Lieutenant Liz Grant playing coy was certainly an eye-opener.

Beside me Linc muttered a long string of curses until he couldn't hold it in any longer. "I swear to fuck, if that grunt so much as touches Liz, I'm gonna put a bullet in his head."

Cannon looked away from the binocs and glanced at Linc. "You could just kill him now."

"I'd blow their cover."

"Better than her blowing him," Cannon joked.

"You are seriously not helping," Linc gritted out.

Leon watched beside me, barely breathing, his lips moving silently, perhaps in prayer. I briefly took his hand in mine.

"They're in!" Linc reported.

"And the guards?"

"Following like slaverin' dogs on a dick leash." Nathaniel got into a crouching position.

"All of them?" Cannon got into position beside his man, ready to hoof it.

"Affirmative. Move out." Linc motioned us forward, keeping the rifle at his shoulder while he started down the dunes.

Keeping low to the terrain, we sprinted across the open plain with our weapons raised. I tore off the headdress; it interfered with my sight. The others followed suit. Subtlety was off the table as we rushed the prison camp.

We took our positions along the edges of the fenced structure, each of us with a C-4 pack set to blow. Every corner and interim location turned hot when the red light went green. I only hoped the POWs had been corralled in the middle.

After a twenty-second countdown, the outer barriers blasted wide open. My ears rang and my sight pinwheeled, but as the shattered glass from the solar mirrors projectiled around us, I had only one person to keep track of: Leon. I covered him with my body, wrapping my arms around his head. The din of explosives echoed in my hard-beating heart when I felt his long draws against my chest.

I pulled him to his feet, giving him a quick once-over to ensure he was in one piece. He already had his pistol in hand. It took more than a bomb to fuck up my baby, as I well knew.

The retaliation came fast—the inner fences fell like dominoes to the sand. As we were swarmed by a mass of prisoners and guards, we herded the friendlies outside and went hand-to-hand with the enemies. Back-to-back we moved as one. Leon was more than capable of taking on the Corps troopers.

A sudden onslaught shoved us apart. I knocked out two of my assailants with my fists, swinging around to throw the third motherfucking limpet off my back. That's when I heard Leon's raised voice. He was being driven into a corner where spikes of glass jutted from the sand like swords. One stumble and he'd be impaled.

With an almighty roar, I yanked the soldier off my back and snapped his neck. As I raced forward, I realized that I couldn't kill the trooper on the attack and save Leon at the same time. There was no backup. Adrenaline jetted through me. I crashed into Leon sideways, covering him as we flew through the air and clear of the biggest threat, the mirrored shards. I braced for the impact of bullets in my back, sure they'd hit me before the ground did.

I landed on my side with Leon in front of me and scrambled

quickly around, almost certain I was dead. Gun raised, I started to pull the trigger when Sebastian appeared from the smoke and dust. The soldier who would've killed me bled a red puddle into the sand, care of Bas.

He leaned over us. "We're clear."

My head thumped back and I laughed weakly. "Shit, man. We were supposed to be saving you."

Sebastian stuck the Corps-issued weapon in his waistband. "I told you I wouldn't let you down."

Wiping my eyes of grit, I took a second to thank the motherfucking Lord for Sebastian's quick reflexes. Leon helped me to my feet, but something in his stormy gaze haunted me.

There was no time to unravel what his look meant as Linc came up to tell us the others were preparing to make tracks. We rendezvoused at the main entrance to the camp, which was now little more than twisted wire and metal.

Cannon stood beside Liz, surveying the damage. "That was a goddamn close call."

"Those glass shards missed us by a cunt's hair," Liz replied with her usual expressive language.

I tried not to think about how close Leon and I had been to death, because it was bound to give me the shakes.

"Ah fear mah skin got a little toasty." The soft southern lilt came from Farrow.

Sebastian pulled his sister into his embrace. "I didn't think we'd get out of there."

They held on to each other for a moment before Farrow drew back. "Are you gettin' prissy on me?"

"Hey, you're the one standing here complainin' about your sunburn."

And we were all back to normal again. Normal dysfunction, anyway.

"Enough small talk. Time to put some distance between us and this bust-up." Linc marshaled everyone toward our hidden vehicle.

"What about dem people?" Leon pointed to the multitude of prisoners filtering through the fallen battlements. Some of them were not in the best of shape.

He posed a solid question no one had an answer to…until Darwin drove up in a large military transport followed by another with Raine at the helm. The pair located a couple of copacetic-looking POWs, gave them the keys, and directed them to the new Karesh coordinates. Hopefully Shehu and his people could handle the influx.

After commandeering an extra vehicle to accommodate the rest of our group, we tore the desert to hell scrambling back to the castle. Concern for Leon was foremost in my mind. Like the solar panels, I felt him shattering apart inside. He couldn't be remembering the last time we'd been caught with our pants down in an explosion. That had been the night in Beta when Taft had blown up his bio-bot factory. The night I'd saved Sebastian, Liz, and Leon. When my back had been burned and scarred, the moko with Tammerick and Wilde's names forever marred.

* * *

There were ten of us now at the island castle, but I didn't have time to play hotel concierge or chatty host. As soon as we were inside, I grabbed an armful of food, some fresh water, and Leon's hand. I banged up the stairs, towing him behind me. His seething glare was a living brand on my back.

I quickly shut the door behind him and dumped my armload on a table before turning to face him. I ran my hands through his hair and jerked his head up. The need to kiss his pouty lips crashed through me. I hesitated before our mouths met, waiting for him to tell me *no*.

With a hungry moan, Leon gripped my shoulders and slid our lips together. The silken mesh of our tongues, the hot glide of our lips tore a rumbling groan from me. I drew back with a growl. Every part of me hummed and throbbed. My balls ached for a quick release, but I wouldn't find relief that way. I sensed Leon's arousal…anger…fear.

"What are you scared of?"

"Why don' you tell me? Ain't dat part of your talent?" His words were scathing.

"You do not want to play this game with me tonight, Leon." I dragged him against me.

He lashed out. "I'm scared of losing you!"

"Unless you pull another stunt like asking to be shot in the head by the next hippie with a handgun, that *ain't* gonna happen." His anger sparked mine. "So why don't you tell me what this is really about."

He locked his jaw and looked away.

"You gonna make me fuck it out of you?"

"You don' fuck, remember?"

"I do now, if that's what you're asking for."

"Yeah, *beb*, maybe I am."

I all but tore the clothes off him. Pushing him face-first against the wall, I kissed and licked and sucked my way down his long, lean body. By the time I reached the top of his ass, he panted. He grinded back against me. He cried out when I ran a lone finger down his sleek trench and another teasing fingertip up the underside of his hot, heavy shaft.

Pulling back, I stood up. I ripped off my clothes and flung them aside. He peered over his shoulder at me, licking his lips until they were full and shiny.

I sat on a high-backed chair and beckoned him to me. "If that's the way you want it, get over here. And bring the lube and condoms with you."

Leon gasped, eyes widening, then fanning low. He swaggered my way, supplies in hand. Moonlight through the open windows highlighted his bronzed skin, loose hair, long muscles, tall cock.

When he stopped in front on me, I treated him to a good look at my thick shaft as it stood straight up. He moved to touch me, but I didn't let him. Instead I stroked my jutting rod with long, hard pulls, sighing with pleasure. His groan was a sound of pure frustration.

"I don't know about you, but I thought about doing this all day long. Thought about you doing it for me."

"*Merde.* Please, Darke. I want to."

"What if I want to suck your cock?"

He had no smart-ass reply. His mouth opened and closed with a snap as he nodded.

"Put it on my tongue." I leaned forward, opened my mouth, and waited for him to probe inside.

Leon was so erect he had to force his shaft down and between my lips. His firm length snuck into my mouth. I hollowed my cheeks, tonguing the tight cliff around the head, pressing it to the roof of my mouth. Taking him completely inside, I swung my head from side to side before pulling back. I still worked my cock; my knees spread wide so Leon could stand between them. Lowering his pelvis, he bucked inside from a different angle, one that made him shout. I sucked him off long and hard, easing up every time he thickened and swelled as he got close to climax.

Leon watched it all with gleaming black-gold eyes. This time it was the fury of arousal blazing out at me, not the fail-safe of anger.

He released his dick from my mouth a final time, and I turned him around. I gripped the high crescents of his ass, my thumbs tickling his hanging ball sack. Then I spanked him, on the left side, the right, with an open palm, and then with the back of my hand.

"*Aahh!*" His back arched. He stepped into the slaps, bracing his feet farther apart.

Another swing, another smack. I even went at his swaying balls with the lightest flips of my hand. "Is this what I need to do to get you to talk?"

He didn't answer. I bit and sucked the sensitive skin at the top of his cleft, reaching between his spread legs to pump his wet cock. Releasing both my teeth and my hand, I pulled the tight orbs of his ass apart and licked from his perineum to his spinal column. Then I leaned away from him.

"Is this what you need?" I growled.

"I need you!"

"That's better." Kissing to the middle of his back, I caressed up and down his inner thighs. "I need you, too."

The final furious tension dissipated from him as soon as I said those words. Parting his ass, I got him as wet as I could with my tongue and then even slicker with the lube as I powered my fingers into him.

When he was ready and I was dripping long, clear strands of precome, I turned him to face me. "You're my sweet sexy baby, aren't you?"

His hair hung in his face. I smoothed it back. "*Oui*. Yes."

I guided Leon over my lap. I lowered him slowly until the muscles in his thighs trembled and his abs twisted. His breath gusted across my neck and he watched my cock get closer to his pucker.

"Stay like that," I ordered.

He hovered just above me, not making contact, straining at the thighs to keep the position. I ran my hands all over his soft skin. I tweaked his nipples and licked them. I caressed his arms and shoulders and back. I circled the infinity ring of his tattoo with one fingertip over and over while his hips dipped and danced, trying to make a connection with my rigid cock.

I pulled his mouth to mine and lashed him with my tongue. He returned the kiss with feverish desire. When I had him grunting with each breath, I sheathed my shaft in a condom and slathered it with lube. Finally I touched the broad tip to his hot hole.

"Now, remember, I don't play around, boy. Fuck me."

It was only the second time we made love. Like the first time, we eased into it, now completely at Leon's pace. I held his ass cheeks open. He used my shoulders for leverage. Our lips coasted together as the teasing slow glide of his tight channel opened for me. Halfway down, I used another drizzle of slick liquid along my cock. I pooled more into my palm and took his erection within my fist. My length was slippery, Leon was primed, and the rest of the way down was a fast glide that punched the breath from my chest and a yell from his throat.

He squeezed me so tight I saw stars.

"That's it. Ride me, angel," I husked in his ear.

He gave a high gasp, arching his back, driving me even deeper.

I ran my hands down that slender, sculpted body and around to his backside, grasping his gorgeous ass. "Fuck, Leon."

I rolled up so our chests heaved against each other. Licking and biting and sucking Leon's neck, I skimmed my hands down his perfect chest to his nice hard cock.

When I took him in hand, Leon breathed against me. "Don' lemme go. Don' lemme go."

I took over his rhythm, mating our bodies together. My heart stuttered and my voice broke. "Jesus Christ, baby. You get inside me like no one else. Never letting you go, never."

His eyes opened wide. They shined with unshed tears. He whimpered and tensed. "Darke!"

I tightened my arms around him. Rocking my cock up and

down, in and out, I threw my head back. His tears hit my cheek the same time his come jetted over my stomach. As his channel squeezed around my cock, I brought him down on me one last time. An orgasm so strong zipped down my back and then straight out my shaft. It shredded my senses, toppling me off a cliff I no longer wanted to hold on to.

This wasn't just undeniably hot sex. It was life-affirming love-making. The comedown was slow, filled with murmurs and kisses. On unsteady legs, I lifted Leon in my arms. I swept the blankets aside to lay him down. I crawled in beside him and gathered him to me.

I kept touching him, talking gently, sharing a litany of lovers' whispers. "You are so good, angel."

I was so drugged on the feel of him, I didn't notice at first when he removed his hands from my chest to pull them to his sides. With my eyes closed, I didn't see the stiffness of his jaw or the hot temper in his gaze.

A harsh huff of breath dragged me from the warm haze enveloping me. I opened my eyes to find him watching me with resurgent anger.

"Angel?"

"Don' call me dat anymore, goddammit! I know what you did to me, how you tried to get rid of me." Jumping from the bed, he shot a finger in my direction. "I remember every'ting."

CHAPTER TWELVE

Leon stood in front of me, naked and enraged.

I pulled some pants on quickly and approached him cautiously. "What did you say?"

He spit some virulent-sounding Cajun curse at me before stomping over to yank on a pair of loose trousers. His back was ramrod straight, his gaze furious and fiery bright. His hands gripped the chair behind him until his biceps strained.

"I said I remember." He spoke low and forceful.

"What? How is that possible?"

"Yeah, how is dat possible? Considerin' you've been trying to keep me in the dark." He snorted. "Darke, how fittin' is dat?"

I sat on the edge of the bed, gripping my knees so he wouldn't see my hands shaking.

"It was the explosion. Musta knocked some sense back into me." He glanced away from me, his shoulders drooping.

"So…you remember…?"

His voice emerged in a stark whisper. "The night of Cannon

and Nate's handfasting. When you laughed at somethin' I told you and you let me kiss you on the cheek before you said good night."

His face turned pink. Mine heated as well, remembering that first, innocent flirtation and how good it felt. "I'm glad, baby. It's one of my favorite memories."

Flashing eyes flicked to mine. "Too bad the memories didn't stop there, huh? Is dat what you wished for? Dat I wouldn't know about every'ting that happened afterward?"

I shot up and strode over to him. "No. I wish you'd never been abducted. I wish I'd been there to kill Taft or make him take me instead, infect me instead!" I forced him to look at me. "How can you even ask me that?"

Both his hands swinging up to my chest, Leon pushed me away. "Because you've been hidin' shit from me! You've been manipulating me. An empath? How the hell do you think dat makes me feel, Darke? You *feel* every'ting from me, but you never told me a goddamn thing!"

"We had a bad few months, Leon. I thought maybe we could begin again instead of going back there." The excuse sounded pathetic even to me.

"A bad few months? Dat's what you call it?" He wiped angry tears away and glared at his wet fingertips, betrayed by emotions he couldn't control.

The sight of him crying made my voice crack. "We were getting to something good together here."

"You don' just get to pick and choose! We don' get a fresh start." He slumped on the bed. "We probably don' get no start at all."

I hunkered in front of him. "That's not true. We have one now."

"Just so I can die?" He reached for my face but stopped before making contact. "Every'ting from dat first night at the celebration, all the times we kissed."

I brushed the back of his hand with my lips.

He pulled free, moving farther away. "All the times you made me believe somethin' was happenin'. *Mon Dieu*, then you'd go off an' ignore me for days, unless someone else took an interest in me. What the hell am I to you?"

"You're more than I was looking for, more than I ever wanted."

Staring at me with hurt and disbelief, Leon held up a hand to hold me off.

"That's not what I meant. Dammit. My words always get tangled up around you."

I clasped his face. "You're more than I ever hoped for."

"*Mais*, not enough to make it permanent." He rested his fingertips on my upper back.

I always welcomed Leon's touch but not there, not in this context. I jumped away from him.

As I searched for a shirt, I listened to his low, sad chuckle. "'S'what I thought."

"It's not what you think at all." After taking a ragged breath, I started to pull the shirt over my head to cover my back and tats, to conceal my guilt and blame.

Leon stopped me. He'd approached silently. Now he caressed me there with his lips. The sensation on the puckered scars made me shiver.

His husky voice slid into my overwhelmed senses. "You tried to get rid of me."

"I came to Beta to get you."

"After you made me give you these moko. I wanted so much for you to honor me the way you did them." His fingers skated away from my skin.

I turned to find him chewing his bottom lip, a frown creasing his forehead. I dropped my shirt on the floor, and his gaze followed the soft swish of fabric, the only sound besides our jagged breathing.

"I couldn't. Not then."

He flashed a bittersweet smile. "I remember. I remember all dat stuff you said to me, Darke. You couldn't have me, *mais* you weren't willin' to let me go. Maybe you should've. It would make dis easier."

"Leon, stop—"

"No, you stop. You din't want me. You made me fuckin' tattoo you with the names of your lovers!"

"I shouldn't have asked you to do that."

He tossed his head back. "Yeah, well, too late for that, ain't it? Just like every'ting else. Dat don't answer the question about what you're doin' with me now. Pity fuck? Last fling? Gettin' it while it's still hot?"

"I didn't want you to remember because I thought it would be better if you forgot it all! You'd find someone better for *you*." The idea made me choke. I'd kill any man who dared to touch him the way I had. "I thought it was for your own good."

"So what happened? Din't wanna give up your trophy boy?"

"Trophy boy? Trust me, honey, you are not a trophy boy. If you were, you'd stop giving me so much grief all the time."

His mouth gaped open, then snapped shut in one firm line. "Well, I do apologize for makin' your life difficult, O Great Warrior Darke."

"I'm trying to save you, angel."

"Save me? Save me for what, *beb*? So I can pine over you for another year with no hope of you feelin' anything for me?"

He pivoted to storm out of the room. I blocked the door before he reached it.

"You make me crazy." He watched me, his arms folded across his chest.

"I never say the right shit around you. I always wanted you to be mine, more than anyone else. I thought I could let you go." I beat my skull against the door. "I was wrong. The thought of you with another man makes me want to snap his arms off and feed them to wild animals."

A slight smirk appeared on his lips. "Dat'd be the crazy talkin', then."

"Leon," I entreated. "I'm scared, too."

"You never act like it."

"I'm petrified. I can't stop thinking about you. It's not just want, nothing so simple as that. It's pure need. It's…" I thumped my hand against my heart, whispering, "It's here. You are here."

His lips quivered. He moved next to me, where he slid down the floor. "You should say shit like dat more often."

My laugh was short.

"Dat ain't all I remember."

I wasn't sure I wanted to know what else was hiding inside his mind, waiting to bite me in the ass. Nevertheless, I sank down across from him. I risked reaching over to encircle his ankle with my hand. His palm rested over my hand, replacing the warmth that had been sucked from the room during our fight.

"I know what happened to me when Cutler had me grabbed."

I scrabbled next to him and brought his chin up beneath my fingers. "What did they do to you?"

"I…Taft snatched me before I knew what the hell was happenin'. It was all planned out. Later, in the tank, Taft told me he knew who I was as soon as I appeared on the Posse scene. He had every intention of takin' me dat day in Beta."

"That's why you are not putting yourself in harm's way again."

"Has anybody ever told you you're *un petit peu* overbearing?"

"No one's ever told me I'm *putty poo* anything."

He rolled his eyes. "It means *a little bit.*"

"Exactly. I'm not a little bit anything." I kissed him briefly on the mouth, then urged, "Tell me what happened."

Leon took a breath. "Taft was unhinged. I spent more time alone with him—when I was conscious—than anyone else."

The very thought of Leon alone with the cracked-up fanatic who outright said he had plans to fuck Leon brought my overbearing side to the forefront, but I prodded it down for the moment.

"He talked nonstop, mostly about Sebastian. He wanted to know if I'd been with him, if he put out for everyone but him. He'd get downright vicious and then tell me he was sorry. After that, he'd threaten to sodomize my ass if I so much as spoke to Sebastian again."

My hands tightened on Leon.

"I think he was in love. Weird, sick, twisted love." Sliding closer to me, Leon dropped his voice. "I don't know where I was taken. I was pumped full of somethin' in the tank. Woke up in a white room on some sort of surgical bed. Tubes down my throat and hanging off my arms, and dat's when I started to scream. Tried to anyway. I met Doc Val when she came in to sedate me."

Leon's terror squeezed around us both like a snake tightening its coils around our bodies.

"She…I don't think she did any of it willingly, Darke. Somethin' wasn't quite right. It wasn't like she was a robot, but her motions were automatic. As if she wasn't really there. Dat scared me at first. I thought they were gonna turn me into the same thing, whatever she was, whatever they'd done to her. I guess I shoulda been so lucky, huh?"

"What did she do to you?"

"Oh, *beaucoup de* shit." He laughed low. "Blood tests, body scans, around-the-clock-monitoring, sleep studies. Then, for an extra kicker, they pumped my heart full of a drug dat made it feel like it'd jump right out of my chest and run around the room until it spluttered to a stop and died on the spot. I guess they needed to know if my body was capable of handlin' the virus." He shrugged. "I was told I was the first test subject. If I survived the early implant and incubation, all other infectees would be modeled after me. The entire motherfuckin' downfall of the Revolution would be on my head."

I pulled him onto my lap, wrapping my arms around him. "That's a goddamn lie. The entire motherfucking end of the war and their defeat will be because of you, your bravery, your courage…." My forehead dipped to his. "Your heart."

"She infected me over and over again with a rapid formula of the Plague. She monitored how quickly it took effect. She kept me conscious through each trial. Val—" His voice faltered. "She took me to the edge of death over an' over again only to give me an antidote, magically fuckin' revive me, and start again several hours later. Felt like my entire body was liquefied from the inside out. At the end, I couldn't feel anything but pain. I couldn't hear, but I'm pretty sure I was screamin'."

I'd become a boulder of rage. I could barely speak when I asked, "How many times?"

"What?" Leon resurfaced from the trauma-filled trap of his mind.

"How many times did Val infect you?" My voice scraped in my throat, sharp as saw blades.

"Five. Five times until she found the perfect formula dat infected me but didn't take root immediately…the one that's dormant, dat's in me now." He shivered. "So, you see, I know how it's all gonna go down. I know what my death looks like, feels like. And I don' want you there at the end. What if you die, too?"

I crushed him against me, running my hands all over his body. He was so pure, so alive. I couldn't believe death was on his doorstep. I wouldn't believe it. "The only end is gonna be the Company's. I promise you that."

He shook his head but stayed within my embrace. His words

rushed out. "Taft told me too much. He *told* me he was tellin' me too much, but it didn't matter 'cause Dr. Val was gonna erase it all from my mind." When Leon glanced at me, his eyes were wet and shiny. "Dat scared me the most. I din't wanna forget you, *cher*."

"Oh, angel. Angel." His words destroyed me. I curled my arms around him until he pressed deeply into my body. Desperate sobs heaved between us.

"When they told me about their plans to destroy Beta with the minibots, I lost it. I tore apart my room until nothin' was left but broken glass and shredded bedding." He gasped. "I worried about you dying because I knew you'd come to rescue me. I *knew* you would. I couldn't warn you. They told me I wouldn't remember you even if I saw you. I'd never touch you or hold you or kiss you again, and I went crazy."

He huddled against me until the tears ended and our rocking stopped. Leon rubbed his cheek against mine.

A few minutes later, I drew slowly away from him. "Did Taft ever make good on his threat?"

Leon flew to his feet, his emotions firing all over the place. "Is dat all you care 'bout? Someone mighta got to my ass first? Wouldn't have as much to brag about then, would ya?"

"What the fuck are you on about? I'm terrified Taft might've abused you. And for the motherfucking record, I don't talk to anyone about what goes on between you and me when we're alone. I never have." I jumped up after him.

He regarded me with a withering sneer. "Dat's right, 'cause you don't talk to no one. Least of all me."

"What's gotten into you?"

"You, for starters. You got in here"—he knocked his head—"and here." Leon thumped his chest as I had earlier. "Stupid *fils de putain*." Muttering to himself, he finally looked at me with somber eyes. "You got inside me deeper than any virus ever could, *cher*."

"That's where I want to be." I reached for him.

He shrugged me away. "You were married to two people, Darke."

"Tammerick and Wilde. Yes."

His lips pulled thin. "You loved a man and a woman at the same time."

With a sigh of frustration, I said, "I did love them, Leon. That's got nothing to do with us."

"Don' it?" He raked both hands through his hair. "What's it you call it? Polyamory? How can one person be enough after dat? I don't got no pussy, no tits. No soft lips."

I almost laughed. Leon had the plumpest, softest lips I'd ever tasted, man or woman. "That's your problem?"

"Ain't a problem. It's a fact. And stop gettin' empath-y on me."

"You feel inadequate?"

"*Ta gueule*! You had a three-way relationship, asshole. How the hell am I gonna live up to dat?"

I opened my mouth to reply. He slammed a hand against my lips. "Fuck you." He took a swing at me. It hit my jaw with a crunch. He hit me again and again. Each time I did nothing to block him, which only magnified his wrath.

I silently took it all as my due.

When he slumped against me, I trailed my hands down his back.

"If you get it all now, like you think, you'd know I cleared out all of Tam and Wilde's belongings from my caravan before we left Chitamauga. I gave everything to Eden to distribute. I gave their things away so I could bring you there, with me, Leon, without them between us even though you couldn't remember." I smoothed the wild tumble of hair off his brow. "I just wanted you."

"You din't. You don't.'"

"You are so goddamn stubborn."

His chin shot up. "And you're too stuck in your ways."

I released him and paced a ring around him. "Am I?"

"Yeah. I'll never be enough for you. I understand why you tried to let me go."

"You don't have the first fucking clue." Worse than his anger was his fucked-up sense of self-worth. It ripped my heart in two. "You think I can't love you? I'm a fucking coward. I didn't want to love you because—"

"'Cause I'm gon' die." Those big, sad eyes, so knowing, struck my soul with a piercing blow.

Someone pounded on the door.

"Not now!" I glared between the door and my man.

The knocking became insistent. If it were Liz with nibbles or Raine with another outfit change, I would not be held responsible for my actions.

I flung the door open to see Raine. Not the man of the hour. "Goddammit! I said not now!"

"I think you might wanna hear this."

I was about to grab him by the shirt and shake him when he drawled, "I think I've got a working antidote."

CHAPTER THIRTEEN

I regarded Raine with a healthy dose of suspicion. "That was quick."

His hair stood in red corkscrews around his head as if he'd twisted his fingers through it repeatedly. "Like I told you, Mother Nature—"

"Provides. Yeah, I got that." Just like she seemingly provided him an endless supply of spliffs, judging by his red-rimmed eyes and pinpoint pupils. No way was I about to let him inject Leon in the middle of the night with some half-baked cocktail of a cure he'd dreamed up while he was half-baked himself. I was ready to slam the door in his face when Leon budged between the door and me.

"Let 'im in." Leon's hand glided up my arm until his fingers tangled with mine and he tugged me back.

As I moved out of the way, he shuffled in front of me, one foot over the threshold.

"Where do you think you're going?" I grabbed his wrist. "We're not done here."

"It's all about the cure, right?" he said with false brightness.

"And finding Cutler," Raine added.

I wasn't into violence just for the fuck of it, but right then I wanted to knock Raine flat on his back.

"I can at least be a guinea pig for this since you keep sidelinin' me when it comes to the important stuff." Leon stood half in and half out of the doorway.

"I am not letting you be another test subject for another test-tube yahoo, babe."

"Don't see how you can stop me."

Raine considered our exchange with one eye on us and the other aimed at the cig he rolled with one hand.

"I'm pretty sure I could find something to make you stay put," I said.

Recognizing my sexual intent, Leon arched an eyebrow. "Maybe later."

This was not the time to get all horned up over the man who teased out all my most intense reactions from anger to arousal. "Wait," I ordered.

Amusement curled his lips. "Aye-aye, sir."

I brought my face to his, my mouth landing in the hollow beneath his ear. "You call me *sir*, you better mean it."

His response was a ragged moan. Better than his moaning about how I was overbearing and bossy. I stalked through our room to throw on a shirt so we could get this shit over with. Raine trilled a low-pitched whistle behind me. I glanced back to see him staring at the relief map of scar tissue on my upper back and shoulders.

My spine stiffened.

"That looks painful." Raine lounged against the doorway.

"It's healed." Brushing past Raine, I grabbed Leon's hand. "This thing between you and me tonight? It's not done yet. Think of this as a reprieve."

He mumbled something under his breath, but he didn't yank his hand free.

We followed Raine down three flights of stairs, taking a turn at the bottom landing, where we came upon Liz, who had the midnight watch.

"Just out for an evenin' stroll." Raine nodded at her.

"Not a threesome?" She winked at me.

Leon pulled up short in front of her. "There's no orgy. We're not gettin' our rocks off. And Darke said he could make do with me alone."

Dipping her head, Liz made herself nice and comfy in her tidy corner. "Well, okay, then."

"*Oui. C'est ça.*"

I grinned at Leon for schooling Liz. He prodded me along, venting more steam along the way. We maneuvered another staircase, this one leading down into the musty innards of the castle keep. As soon as Raine led us through a timber door, we were surrounded by muggy, smoky air. With no windows for ventilation, a thick blue haze of pot smoke surrounded us. His mad-scientist lab resembled a hookah den more than a doctor's workplace.

"Quite the little chem lab you've got down here," I said.

"*Hmm?* Oh yeah. Freeing the mind through chemical aid lets the ideas flow through me." He gestured toward a bong bubbling away over a Bunsen burner and burping out sweet-smelling fumes. "I call it liquid meditation for the brain."

Free his mind? More like freebasing. I was not going to let Leon take anything this double-talking doped-up douche bag prescribed. My senses went on high alert, but as hard as I tried to get an emotional read on Raine, I got nothing. All that came back was an opaque veil. He either knew how to block me, or he was simply empty of that which defined humanity.

I pushed Leon in front of me so we could we get out of the room. "This is a waste of time."

Leon wouldn't budge. "If I can do one thing for the people, Darke. Please."

I relented. "Let me see this cure."

Raine loped to a table cluttered with test tubes and measuring apparatuses. He lifted a rich purple piece of fabric from over a vial, which he handed to me. I swirled the contents. Glinting diamond-like shards shot through the thick liquid. Far too pretty a thing to have been cooked up in this dank and murky basement. I lifted the tube to my nose and sniffed. Despite the beauty of the colorful pearlescent liquid, I expected to catch a whiff of a vile-smelling brew.

I closed my eyes as the perfume swept over me. It was neither antiseptic nor noxious but lightly floral. The scent spun the most pleasant memories to me. My mother singing to me in the safety of the commune, playing with the animals with the other children, watching Leon approach me with definite intentions at Cannon and Nathaniel's handfasting. It was…magical.

Still, a shaman that did not make him.

"Give me the gear." I plugged a cork stopper in the vial top.

"I should be on hand to monitor him," Raine said.

"You should go upstairs and raid the food," I said. "You'll be getting a case of the munchies soon."

I handed the tube to Leon. He carefully pocketed it.

Raine loaded me up with hypodermics, rubber tourniquets, swabs. His primitive system was so not happening, not tonight. We still had a little time before the virus detonated in Leon and all the others Cutler had infected.

Supplies in hand, we retreated upstairs. On the first level, we came across Sebastian. Sleep slowed his smile.

"Late night?" he asked.

"Early morning," Leon answered.

Sebastian lounged against the wall. "I wanted to thank y'all."

"There's no need. You saved our asses," I said.

Sebastian tucked a lock of platinum-blond hair behind his hair. "Yeah, there is. You know, we don't get a lot of second chances. Those Corps goons separated me from Farrow. She's all the family I have left." His vivid violet irises flipped up as he ran both hands down his face. "She talks so hard, but she's so soft and no one gets that." His throat bobbed. "I couldn't bear it if she were tortured."

Beside me, Leon shuddered.

"I know everyone thinks of me as the newbie, but I'm not. I'd stand in front of a bullet for my sis."

"I hope it never comes to that, Sebastian." I clasped his shoulder.

After exchanging quiet good nights with Bas, we headed to our bedroom. Once inside, I placed all the injection paraphernalia on a table and turned to Leon.

"What are you thinking?" I asked, leaning against the table. "You pulled away from me when Bas talked about not wanting Farrow to die a bad death at that camp."

"Tammerick and Wilde." He hung his head. "They were your only family in the commune."

My eyes stung. "Oh, angel."

He hugged himself, becoming smaller than I'd ever seen him. "I'm sorry I said all dat shit about you, about them. I got no right bein' jealous of ghosts, huh?"

"You've got no need to be jealous at all." I pulled him into my embrace.

"*Mais*, you din't answer me. How'm I gon' be enough for you?"

With a smile, I placed a fingertip against his lips to quiet him. "You're more than enough. You're a handful, babe. Hasn't anyone ever told you that?"

"*Ma mere*… She don't make it sound like a good thing, though."

"And now me." I led him to the bed and began easing him out of his pants. "Trust me, it's a good thing."

Leon gave a start, pushing off the bed. "What are you doin'?"

"Getting ready to sleep." I stepped out of my clothes.

He made a beeline for the table. I blocked his way.

"I wanna do it tonight."

"That's too bad, because I'm not going to let you. You haven't had anything to eat or slept a wink."

He treated me to a glare that could've seared the skin off my body. "I'm gettin' tired of you orderin' me around."

"Maybe you'd like it better if I tied you down." And put a gag in his mouth for good measure.

Leon showed a flash of interest at that idea before he renewed his piercing stare. At least I shut him up long enough to get him to open up and eat some food. Afterward, we crawled into bed. It was nothing less than fucking awkward because he continued to fume. I could leave him the bed and sleep on the floor, but screw that. I wasn't ever gonna waste another night with him. Even if he lay rigid beside me.

Turning on my side, I stroked his chest. "I'm being selfish. I'm scared. I'm worried Raine's fix won't work, baby. Did you see what he's using down there? The conditions he's working in? The place is a shambles, he talks in brain teasers, and he's high half the goddamn time, too. I don't want you to pony up for this because you feel responsible. Not tonight."

"He ain't the first shaman to dip into the hallucinogens, Darke, lemme tell you." Lying on his back, Leon crossed his arms behind his head. "Now, I once met a voodoo priestess—she would've been Shehu's counterpart, if not Raine's. She used the iboga root to talk to the higher realms. Dat's how they reach their magic."

"I don't think he's reaching magic down there." I cantered on top of him, sliding my body over his. "I just want one final night of hope."

"Why din't you say that to begin with?" Leon whispered.

"I don't like admitting I'm afraid."

He lifted his head and kissed me, punctuating each soft sweep across my lips with a flick of his tongue. One leg thrown over mine, he settled in the nook of my neck. "Dat makes me feel better."

I chuckled. "What? That I'm pissing my pants over here?"

His arms tightened around me, and his knee nudged my erection. "Not wearin' any pants," he teased, his words sluggish as he let out a yawn.

I was repeatedly reminded of the fact that we were lying together naked until I finally drifted to sleep after him.

* * *

I woke late in the morning to the sound of the shower running and Leon whistling. I smiled and stretched. Then I remembered I had promised to give Leon the supposed cure today.

I kicked out of bed and joined him in the shower. Wet, slippery Leon—he reminded me of the night I'd seen him skinny-dipping in Chitamauga Lake, the night I'd convinced myself I could let him go. What a fool I'd been. The muscular lines that ran from his back down to his ass knocked the breath from me and dragged a groan from my throat.

I stepped in after him, pushing my body tight against his.

"Mornin' to you, too." He peered at me with a grin from behind long, wet locks. His hands roamed low to my thighs, which he gripped and stroked between soapy fingers.

I washed his hair, rubbing against him the entire time. I stroked his rigid cock in a sudsy fist, watching his hips grind into my loose, teasing hold. Soapy flesh, wet hair, bodies covered in teardrops of water, our breaths grew shallow and ragged.

I spread his ass open, sliding a knuckle to his entrance. Kissing his shoulder, I wet my fingers with more soap and snuck inside. Leon gasped and wriggled. He writhed on my fingers while I teased his nipples with the flat of my palm. I sent my hand down his wet belly, playing with the soft hair before grasping his shaft. It was hot, completely stiff, filling my stroking fingers.

"You're cock is incredible. Might have to let you in me one day," I growled against the nape of his neck.

Leon shuddered hard. "Oh God."

A warm gush of precome ran down my hand. I grinned. "You like that idea."

He nodded and mewled. "*Oui*. Jesus, *cher*."

"Not today, though. Today you are mine." I ran my cock up and down his ass, testing his tender pucker. "You're mine, right?"

"Yeah. Yes." Head thrown back, Leon moaned.

"Too tight, babe. Let me grab some lube." I left him with his taut ass swaying in invitation.

I raced back to him, quickly sheathing my cock in a condom and slicking my length until it was dripping. In my hurry to take him, I squirted the liquid straight into his chute and he jumped when he felt it wetting his insides. I spread him with my fingers and then took my place.

"You want this?" The flared head of my dick brushed his dainty hole.

Leon braced against the wall, legs spread, ass displayed, suds running into his tight cleft. Looking over his shoulder, he smirked. "What's it look like?"

"Smart mouth."

"I can suck you off with it if you want."

What I wanted was his lips on mine. I dove down to capture them, easing my tongue into his mouth. I entered him at the same time. The first thrust trapped me in exquisite torment, his ring tightening around the head of my cock.

Leon tried to push back.

I placed my hands on his hips, dragging my lips to his ear. "Easy, easy baby. Take it slow."

I watched, spellbound and just this side of exploding inside him when he eased his gorgeous ass back a bit at a time. My fingers clenched on his skin, my short nails leaving marks as I fought against thrusting inside him.

Leon rolled his hips in a slow rhythm until he'd slid me inside to the root.

"Jesus Christ." The words burst from me. "Fuck me."

I stood as still as I could. Leon swiveled back and forth, taking me in and out, gathering speed, moaning every time I bottomed out inside him.

I couldn't take it any longer. Reaching around him, I got a good grip on his hips and used that leverage to plunge into him. Leon howled. The hot spray of the shower splashed off his face like warm rain. Each thrust was all the way in and all the way out while he wailed and writhed and wrapped his hands around my ass to force me to go faster.

I dropped my mouth to his shoulder and licked up to his neck. "You feel so good, so good."

His hands clawed at the wall in front of him. "*Ah!* You too. *Oh, oh…*"

"Don't you ever think I don't want you. Does this feel like I don't want you?" I sheathed my cock inside of him again.

He shook his head.

Wrapping my arms around Leon, I pulled him against me. The new languid pace of our fuck made my voice break around all the words I wanted to say. Words that came easier like this when nothing stood between us.

"Say it."

"You…you want me."

I nipped his ear. "I need you."

"You need me." He cried out as he came. I captured his seed in my palm, bringing it to my mouth, where I soaked it up with my tongue.

His clenching ass coaxed my orgasm with unbelievable force. I lunged inside of him a few last times as come spiraled out of me. The blinding climax almost dropped me to my knees.

When we'd toweled off and had something to eat, Leon sat propped on the bed, shirtless. He had that devil-may-care look on his face, yet thick tension rolled between us. I gathered the syringe and the vial, swabs doused in alcohol and the tourniquet. I set them beside him and then sat down.

I kissed the soft skin of his inner elbow, running my tongue down to his wrist, along his palm, and to his fingertip. Cradling his face in my hands, I kissed his lips. "I want you more than I ever wanted anyone, angel. And that scares the shit out of me."

He took a deep breath. When he met my gaze, all the anger from the previous night was gone. *"D'ac."*

"Duck?" I frowned.

"D'accord. I get it." His voice gentled, and his mouth moved to my neck. "I understand."

"Good."

As I prepared to administer the dose, I willed my hands to be steady. I couldn't allow myself to think about what would happen if it all went wrong. I had to believe there truly was magic in Raine's little vial—the magic I'd felt last night. It was our best hope, our only hope right now.

After cleaning the thin skin at the bend of Leon's elbow, I filled the syringe. I held his arm steady, my gaze darting between his eyes and the narrow blue vein I'd puncture. I licked my lips nervously as I set the needle against his skin. The point almost pierced him when loud banging sounded on our door for the second goddamn time in twelve hours.

The syringe skipped harmlessly across his skin. I held the needle aloft and shouted, "What the fuck now?"

Liz busted the door open and strode inside. Her eyes widened when she saw what I was about to do. "You can't!"

I placed the hypodermic carefully aside, wondering if it was contaminated.

She located my weapons, shoving them at me while I sat, completely confused. "Cutler. He's here. He's been sighted."

"What?" I began to arm up.

"He was seen at the POW camp we nailed to the ground before he headed to the Corps compound, some kind of goodwill bullshit visit. We gotta jet."

I halted and started stowing my guns away. "I can't."

Liz dragged me aside. I didn't know why she bothered. She talked loud enough that fucking everyone had come to the open doorway, where they eyed her, me, and Leon playing patient on the bed.

"You can. You will."

"Fuck off and no."

"Go, Darke," Leon called over. "Go. Get Cutler. Waste him. I'll wait."

I rushed to Leon and dropped to my knees in front of him. "I'll stay."

"Dat don' make sense. You can't stop the Revolution to look after me."

"I'm not stopping to look after you. I'm staying because I—"

Pressing a kiss against my lips, Leon stole my words, stole my breath. He drew back. "I want you to fight. You're a warrior, not a nursemaid."

"I would rather be with you," I snarled.

"Den use that anger to cut Cutler's nuts off." Leon wasn't as confident as he wanted to appear. His speech was unsteady.

"I swear to God, if you don't wait—"

He interrupted me. "Leave Raine behind. He can keep watch."

Yeah, because I had so much faith in the shyster shaman.

Liz tapped me on the shoulder and I barked, "Gimme a damn minute, woman."

The room emptied. I guided Leon to his feet. Grabbing him

with shaking hands, I choked, "I haven't said everything I need to yet."

His smile didn't reach his eyes. "There's still time."

"You promise me." As I tried to keep my emotions in check, I felt as if my face would cave in under the strain. I was so close to losing it.

"I promise."

Leon's back bowed beneath the force of my kiss. I touched his face, his neck, his chest, landing on his hips, steering him to me. I tasted his lips, his tongue, his earlobes. I drove into his mouth again, making sure he'd remember me, his promise, our passion.

"So much I want to tell you."

"You will." He clung to my shoulders. "You will."

I dragged my hands away from him, finding my ammo, my boots, my shirt. All the while I regarded Leon, fighting the fear this might be the last time I saw him.

CHAPTER FOURTEEN

As we crammed into the desert Cruiser once again, I demoted Darwin to passenger and took the driver's seat. I needed something to stomp my foot on, even if it was just the gas pedal. My throat felt like someone had tightened a screw on it. My breaths coming short and fast, I concentrated on the cold, hard facts. Cutler was in Omega. Cutler needed to take a long dirt nap for all the evils he'd perpetrated on Leon.

Cannon slid in beside me. Turning the ignition, I looked back at the castle.

My wingman inspected my no-doubt-distraught visage with a long, slow, "Duuuude. Maybe you should stay."

"Fuck off."

Leaving Leon behind—with Raine—already twisted my heart up and wrung it dry as this desert earth. I did not need Cannon getting inside my head. As I'd been reminded every hop, skip, and jump of the way, our quest was twofold, and I was an emotional, sappy, sad-case fuckwit when it came to Leon. In the high beams of Cannon's scrutiny, I clamped up tight for the remainder of the drive.

An hour or so later, I braked gently on a sandy hillside just outside the Corps compound we'd landed at. Nathaniel rolled up beside us in the second vehicle, nodding through the window to Cannon. If they started getting kissy-face on the glass to each other, I was going to go ballistic. The nervous rumble in my belly winched tighter and tighter, a clear sign we had to proceed with caution.

"Nice rides," Darwin said, nodding out the rear window at the foursome of dune buggies racing in our direction.

Cannon hooked his head around for a look. "Sure beats a camel."

Scanning the low-riding, high-powered transports, I felt a loosening in my taut nerves. "Our backup is here. Look lively, people."

Each of us armed to our eyeballs, we disembarked from our vehicles, hidden behind the hillock. Shehu and his band of warriors cruised to a stop, barely disrupting the swirling sand. Greetings were exchanged between our two groups before Shehu and I convened.

"You are unsettled." His glossy black eyes pinned me.

"You're less than relaxed yourself."

"I must apologize for allowing your people to be taken." He bowed, the long Mohawk-style braid dripping over his shoulder.

The chieftain of the Karesh Freelanders didn't need to show me such deference. "We know the risks."

"I am responsible for all in my care, as are you. Where is the young Leon today?"

"He…" I made sure my back was turned to the others. "I cannot endanger his life like this."

Stroking the long blade of his deadly machete, Shehu gave off the impression of a predator on the hunt. "The risks will get higher today."

"That is the fate of our venture."

He raised his voice. "To war?"

"To war!" Around the two of us, soldiers and warriors, our combined Freelanders and Territorians, raised their firearms in a gesture of solidarity.

As a unit, we moved across the hot, prickling sand to the topside of the mound shielding our vehicles from view.

Weapons were drawn. Binoculars were pressed to eyes. Then hisses sounded all around.

Cannon broke the ugly spell to curse, "*Fuuuckin'* A."

Really, there were no other words to describe the scene we came upon. It was impossible to believe any sight could be as repulsive as the one we'd witnessed at the POW camp or as viscerally horrifying as the Beta Corps's brutal ambush of my own militia not quite a year ago. I rubbed my eyes, hoping grit and sand had blurred my vision to the point of delirium.

Sure enough, my eyes maintained the same gruesome visual. Zoomed in, the open-sided makeshift combat hospital was heavily guarded. What made us all squirm in the sand were the patients housed inside on plastic-wrapped cots. Except these sick people didn't look like war-wounded soldiers but innocent civilians. They didn't wear Corps insignia but the rigor of cadavers on their strained features.

The worst part was, they seemed aware of the disintegration of their flesh from the inside out. They hadn't been drugged up, doped up, or given any reprieve. Even the ones walking around in jerky, zombified movements had a sick pallid alertness about them.

Dark horses of death galloped at their gravesides.

"Cutler did this." My voice came out gravelly.

"Total annihilation." Nathaniel grimaced. "Leave it to Father."

Liz didn't handle binocs but used her CheyTac rifle to dial closer. "Mass extermination. Cutler's infected more, hasn't he?"

"If that motherfucker's even here…" Cannon spat.

"Who put us into play here?" I asked.

"Raine reported it. This." With a snarl, Linc narrowed his eyes at the tent.

Before we had a chance to regroup, we noticed a group of brick-faced soldiers herding the civilians who were still mobile toward a big transport.

Shehu slid forward with the ease of one accustomed to this landscape and the ways in which to blend in. He dodged behind scrubby brush barely big enough to conceal his mass, but his painted face and slithering tactics made him invisible to the enemy. Two of his warriors followed him.

Darwin hauled in a hasty breath the same time I saw the scar-faced, scruffy commander stroll between his troopers, shouting orders. The same man who'd put Darwin through her paces when we'd touched down in this Territory. His eye patch today was embroidered with the InterNations standard.

"Stand down, soldier," I whispered to the Alpha Elite woman while maintaining a read on Shehu and his men creeping closer to the backside of the Corps hospital.

With my attention split, Darwin decided to go balls-out blazing. Barreling across the terrain, she laid tracks toward the trucks.

My entire crew, and Shehu's warriors, too, pounced to their feet with me. Talk about putting up a red flare to our whereabouts. I hunched low, hoping their instincts would kick in and they'd follow suit. Lo and behold, the hotheads hit the sand beside me.

"You, you, you, *and* you don't need to be ID'd." I met the flinty glares of Cannon, Nathaniel, Linc, and Liz, aka personae non gratae to the millionth degree. "Stay put and cover us."

I turned to Shehu's remaining warriors. "Back up your chieftain."

I didn't wait for replies. I was off and running after Darwin. Fuck me, that woman had more balls than brains. I dodged behind her footsteps. My longer legs almost overtook her fast footfalls, and then we were there. With no plan, little artillery support—nothing but her mouth gunning off.

The Omega Commander's craggy face turned in our direction with a look of pure bewilderment. "Flight Captain Darwin, you've been cited as MIA."

"What the fuck are you doing?" Apparently Darwin didn't give two shits about *all* the weapons cocked, aimed, and one trigger away from party time with our brain matter. She went bared-teeth and bald-faced bitch in her former commander's face.

Confusion scuttling across his face, the commander jerked up his creased tan pants. Sweat dripped from his temple.

"What is this?" He pointed at me as if I were three-day-old trash no one had taken to the dung heap.

"*This* is Darke. A Freelander. My bodyguard." Faced with extreme danger, Darwin braved a grin.

"You are one step away from being court-martialed, hanged, or worse."

"And you're about two-dozen meters from being stretched out naked on the hot tarmac of the landing zone and having your nuts poached." As Darwin talked, the commander blanched, and eight severely pissed off troopers took aim at us.

It was like we were in the middle of a pressure cooker placed on top of an open fire. Darwin kept stoking the flames with her feisty attitude.

The kill-or-be-killed instinct rushed over me, but before I had the chance to push the bad end of my S&W 500s into the leader's empty eye socket, we were surrounded on all sides by glinting, gleaming, sharpened steel.

Shehu had marshaled his forces as silently as a reaper.

The troopers took precision aim at the Freelander newcomers.

With a clipped voice, Shehu advised, "You can stand down or get run through. Your choice."

"Ease off, soldiers," Eye Patch ordered. Once his command was followed, Shehu's people gave a little leeway from their encroaching circle. Eye Patch turned to Darwin. "What the hell is the meaning of this?"

"I'm asking you the same thing."

"This?" He glanced disinterestedly at the dying civilians.

Some of them had stopped their march to the transport, and the close-up view was even worse than I'd imagined. The skin of their faces was not just hollow and sunken, but shrunken and sticking to their skulls. Their droopy eyes dripped a thick yellow substance. Mouths gaped open, and I knew the stench of their breath would be that of fetid disease.

"It's Cutler's new plan to root out insurgents or kill 'em before the real virus even goes live." Eye Patch smiled.

"These are innocents." I craned forward.

"Not anymore. The minute the bleeding manifests, after they're released in the streets of Omega's bazaars, they're home-grown killers. Kind of perfect, beautiful human bombs."

"What do you mean, when the bleeding manifests?" Darwin asked.

"That's how this new one spreads. Airborne toxicity from some kind of—" He stopped and scratched a finger under the bars-and-stripes eye patch. "Whatever. They're gonna start leaking blood. That blood contains the contaminant. From there…it's unstoppable."

"A death sentence to all in Omega." Shehu twirled his machete so its shiny blade reflected the sun in diamond patterns.

"Oh, probably all the Territories after Cutler sees this thing go live. We were chosen to undertake the test subjects, to see if it was a success." Pride seeped from his skin like tainted oil. "I'm thinking it will be."

"Hey, Commander? I'm pretty sure it won't." The razor edge

to Darwin's soft voice should've been his warning. "Ever heard of the Reformed Corps? You're looking at them."

There was no saluting or sweet-talking from her this time. She drew her gun and bored a hole into his brain before he even had a chance to say a prayer.

His deadweight slumped to the sand, and Darwin used his lifeless body as a stepping-stone to his shocked and shitting-in-their-britches soldiers. I guessed I wasn't much needed as her supposed bodyguard, but I did a clean sweep with my weapons around the quivering idiots to make sure no one got high-and-mighty ideas about becoming a hero. Shehu and his men moved with us.

Darwin launched herself at the lieutenant with her gun at his temple. "Here are your options, sir." She spat the word with venom that shook her body. Her hand remained steady. "Join up or die on the spot."

The douche bag shook in his boots for a full ten seconds before capitulating. He gestured his men—his troopers to command now—to follow his deed and decree to the Reformed Corps by removing his Corps insignia and tossing it to the ground.

The arrival of Liz and Linc, Cannon and Nate, Sebastian and Farrow heralded the end of our tête-à-tête. Taking charge with Bas and Farrow beside her, Darwin ordered the defecting troopers toward the barracks, where they'd get the rest of the battalion on board double-time or go another round of dead-dead-dead.

Shehu and his men hung close to them, tightening the feeling of Freelanders and Revolutionaries with one specific goal: to unite in the fight for freedom.

Left beside the idling truck, I huddled with the people I'd made this journey with. They ignored me to take a closer gander at the infected civilians who were aimlessly wandering. To say my comrades were visibly unsettled was an understatement.

"What now?" Linc asked.

"We can't let them spread the disease." Liz popped her knuckles one by one.

"We have to kill them." As soon as the words left my mouth, I felt my knees buckle, but I managed to remain on my feet.

"That's drastic." Nathaniel slipped a hand through his hair.

"So's your fucking father," I replied. "Do you think I take this decision lightly? Do you think I will sleep in peace ever again if we do this? There's no other choice."

"Kill the few to save the thousands?" For the first time, Cannon looked unsure.

"They have to die," Linc whispered.

Whipping toward her husband, Liz hissed, "That's a bit fucking cavalier!"

"Why are you surprised? You know what I am, what I've done." Linc grabbed Liz's shoulders. "You said yourself we can't let the infection get out."

"I didn't mean we had to murder them."

"If it were Leon?" Nathaniel looked at me, his voice cutting through the maelstrom of emotion. "Would you decide the same?"

If it were Leon...My heart stopped. I swayed because I'd

closed my eyes and lost that one compass point to all this endless
misery. If he had to die, I would be right behind him. Very few
got second chances at life. No one, least of all me, deserved a
third. I would honor our…love…and go at peace to be with him
forever.

"If he dies, I die."

"What about the cure?" Liz spun toward me. "Raine has it
ready."

"It's too late, Liz. It's too fucking late for that." Linc hooked
her chin so she focused on the infected. "These people are gone."

"There's not enough time, even if it works," I said. "We have to
replicate it, and they're already in the advanced stages." The sense
of my argument didn't make the reality of what we had to do any
easier.

I watched a tear slip down Liz's cheek. I felt as helpless as the
people whose fate we were about to decide.

One of the infected approached us.

"Do it. Kill me." The black-haired woman appeared wraith-
like before me. Her skin was nothing more than thin parchment
over bleached bone. "I don't want to be responsible for"—her
bone-rattling cough full of phlegm bent her in two before she
straightened—"the deaths of others."

"Jesus motherfucking goddamn Christ." Cannon rattled off all
the curses on the tip of my tongue.

I took her skinny arm in my hand and gently drew her into the
shade of the truck that had been set on a collision course with
Omega. "Is there anyone with you?"

"My husband was among the first subjects. He died." She

coughed, collapsing against the truck at her back. "No children."

"You understand what you've asked for?"

"Please. Now. I won't be part of the Company's agenda. I'd rather die."

I placed my hand on her cheek. "You are a brave woman. A warrior before all."

I returned to the others. "We do this now before it can't be contained."

Despite their previous objections, it was clear there was no choice. The sag in all our shoulders said everything.

Nathaniel dialed up Darwin on his D-P. "We need insta-euth hypodermics delivered fast. There will be a supply in the medic building. Bring them all." He ended the call. "We can't do it…" He linked his fingers with Cannon's. "We can't let them bleed out; can't let them bleed at all."

"No guns." I nodded.

The safeties locked into place with resounding clicks.

Darwin raced across the bald terrain, a big olive-green satchel slapping her back. She delivered it to my open hands.

"How goes it inside?" I asked.

"Better than out here."

No doubt.

As Darwin sprinted back to the barracks, we passed out the doses and swirled the deadly liquid contents of the syringes. Puncture the vein, end suffering. So easy, so…enervating.

We broke ranks and began the cull. I heard every emotion in my head, in my heart. Terror of the unknown, hopes for a serene afterlife, silent good-byes sent to husbands, wives, children. And that was just the people we were…killing. On our side, I battled through an emotional miasma of disgust, shame, self-hate, and maybe a small glimmer of hope we were ending suffering.

The first plunger I sent home was to the woman I'd comforted. "This won't hurt."

"I know." She watched me lower the needle to a vein in her elbow. "Do not worry. You are giving others life."

As I depressed the plunger, I thought of doing the same to Leon, except with the cure. That was the only thought I allowed myself, the only way I'd get through this.

The drug hit her quickly. As her head rolled back, I cupped her skull and laid her out on the ground. My fingertips were no more than whispers upon her skin when I closed her eyelids.

I looked over to the tent and saw Cannon and Nathaniel inside. Neither was moving and Cannon's face was corpse-white.

"What is it?" Nathaniel's concerned voice pricked my resolve.

"She…That girl…" He pointed to a brunette laid out on a cot. Her face was so still it looked like a mask. Her open eyes stared unblinking. A locket hung around her neck. She was pale, possibly already dead. "She looks like Erica did, my sister, the night she…" Cannon swallowed. "Like my mom and dad when the Plague killed them all."

Jesus Christ. How many more reasons did we need to stop CEO Cutler? Families ruined, lives destroyed, populations wiped out.

No more.

Rubbing Cannon's shoulder, Nathaniel leaned in to whisper to him.

"I'm solid." Cannon came back online just as another of our toughened crew got a bad case of the shakes.

Perched on the bed of a civilian, Liz's entire body shook from earthquake-sized chills. As she struggled to hold her injection steady, Linc placed a hand on her arm.

"I won't let you do this." His voice was low and soft.

Liz stared blankly ahead. "I'm a soldier. This is what I do." Tears ran down her face while she raised the needle for a second attempt. Shame and sadness wafted off of her like misty clouds before an incoming storm.

"Not this time, sweetheart." With the gentlest movements, Linc plucked the syringe from her hand.

"What about you?"

"I'm capable of coming out of this in one piece." Linc sneered at himself. "Think of all I've done before."

"Don't say that." She stood abruptly to put her arms around his stiff form, but he backed away.

He jerked his head in the direction Darwin had taken. "You go help the others. We've got this."

I couldn't watch anymore. I became nothing but a robot carrying out a task. There was no honor in this. None at all as we made sure to euthanize everyone inside and out of the combat hospital.

On the drive back through Omega city, black twists of smoke spiraled into the air behind us. We'd burned the field hospital to the ground to contain the germs. The civilians gathering in the open bazaars of Omega knew the location from which the smoke billowed. It was a visible symbol of the Corps's defeat. The crowds amassed in celebration, but even as we heard the sweet rush of their cheers, our vehicle was filled with an ominous air.

The mass graves we'd grimly dug and gently filled provided no solace, only cold comfort for what we'd done. I felt unclean. Dirtier than I'd ever been. Never had I killed innocents. Judging from the bitter metal tang of distress threatening to drown me, neither had the others.

My foot stammered on the gas, then stuck on the brake.

Sebastian reached for my shoulder. "We had no other choice."

Even though my head believed him, my heart practically turned upside down in my chest. *Sure. How to tell this to Leon? By the way, we just happened to slaughter a bunch of people infected just like you. But it's okay, babe, because—you know—they had that rapid strain. And, oh yeah, I was the one who gave the kill order.*

The only prescription to make this whole shit situation better would've been to find Cutler sitting pretty and ready to receive his own fair share of payback at the Corps camp. But of course there'd been absolutely no joy there either—he was not on site and probably never had been.

We figured out why quickly when the massive citywide D-Ps flashed to life and the giant mocking face of the CEO himself appeared in real living color, probably on a different fucking continent.

His smile was supercilious and his eyes, piercing. His fingers were steepled just below his chin as he relaxed in a big cushy chair in front of a giant glossy desk with an arrangement of InterNations flags hanging on the wall behind him.

"I have a special message for my people today."

Gag.

"The infection is spreading, the virus multiplying. You have only the Revolutionaries to blame for this new infection. If they would simply give themselves up for the greater good, my friends, everything would return to normal."

Normal as in having no personal rights, no freedom to choose, no electoral power, no prospect of a better future.

"And now I speak directly about the insurgents responsible for today's batch of deaths in Omega. You see, my people, the cause for your celebration is not a victory against the Corps or the Company. Today, at the Omega Corps combat hospital, a group of rebels killed civilian patients in cold blood."

Jesus Christ. Apparently he had eyes in the skies and just about everywhere else, too.

"You cannot win this war. Any further rebellion or anti-military action will only end in the loss of civilian life…and more often than not it will be caused by Revolutionary fighters."

"Well, this is a clusterfuck of the highest order." Cannon stared mutinously at his father-in-law in front of us.

I couldn't agree more.

Cutler's diatribe was cut short when the D-Ps fizzled and frazzled with static interference that always introduced a sound bite from the so-called Voice. What a relief. At least listening to a broadcast from him-her-whoever wouldn't make me want to yank my ears off my head and throw them out the window.

I started to slowly ease down on the gas, maneuvering the vehicle through the crowded streets, when Cannon laid a hand on my arm. "We should probably hear—"

My foot slammed on the brake, hurtling everyone in the Cruiser forward.

The faceless Voice didn't start in, no. Leon, *my Leon*, was up on the screen, bigger than life.

Foreboding didn't so much as creep up on me as crash into me like a ten-ton weight. It was magnified by the fact that Raine had been the one to feed us false info about Cutler being on the scene. Leon was with Raine. And right now, Leon was getting a shitload of face time on the InterNations D-P.

"What the fuck?" Cannon shouted.

"Raine must've rigged something up..." Sebastian said.

"I'm going to rig something up. His neck with a rope..." I stared at the screen above, hoping like hell my instincts were way the fuck off-kilter, because at that moment every single sense inside me screamed with mortal fear for Leon's life.

"Yeah, I don' know 'bout y'all, but I got sick of listenin' to dat asshole Cutler." With a slight smirk, Leon started right in. His first words made me bark out a laugh. I wondered how many channels this was going out on. If, like the Voice, his reach was InterNations wide, wouldn't that just yank Cutler's nuts up to this throat?

"*I* got some really important news to tell you. I'm a rebel, a Revolutionary. I'm a freedom fighter, 'cause I believe everyone gets the right to love who they love and live how they wanna live." His eyes shined with the beautiful truth. Pushing the sun-streaked locks off his face, he frowned. "Somethin' else I gotta say. I am one of the people CEO Cutler personally infected with the new Plague. He thinks he can use us to kill our own people!" His gaze wavered off to the side and then returned to the screen. "I received an antidote today. I tried it."

"He said he would wait, goddammit!" I yelled in disbelief.

"It din't work." Leon's voice rang clear.

All the air was sucked from my lungs. I shook my head, shook it again, but I could barely make out the rest of Leon's words through the buzzing in my ears.

When Cannon gripped my hand until I thought he'd crush my fingers to dust, I focused on what Leon was saying.

"I won't let Cutler use me like this. I will not let dat bastard make my body his weapon." His jaw set at a hard angle, he all but repeated what the female patient had said.

Cannon whispered, "The little shit's gonna fucking sacrifice himself." He sagged in his seat with tears pinging on his eyelashes.

Leon leaned forward. "I'm gonna do what I need to for the greater good. I'm encouraging anyone who was infected, like me, to do the same. We can make a difference dis way!" His fist came up to pound on his chest. "I will kill myself before dis goes any further."

My chest started pumping like a bellows. That was the only way I knew I was still breathing. Other than that, I was dead. I knew tears were pouring out of my eyes because I had to swipe them away to make sure I could see Leon. Because I had to see him.

To think this might be the last time I see him alive…

A sob broke out of my throat before I wrenched open the door and evacuated the contents in my stomach onto the ground.

I was dimly aware of Cannon pulling me back inside the vehicle and saying, "Maybe Raine's putting him up to this?"

My head was shaking again, and tears were flying everywhere. I had no voice. But I knew this was Leon's choice. Thinking back to our fight when he'd thought he could never be enough for me, my heart squeezed until I thought it would simply shrivel right up in my chest and expire.

He'd flat-out told me he didn't want me around to watch him die, didn't want me near him at the end. This was deliberate.

He wasn't going to wait.

With an almighty roar, I slammed my fist on the dash. The whole vehicle shuddered. He was still alive. He was still on the D-P. I cranked forward in my seat, my face almost up to the windshield.

What I witnessed wiped any last spark of hope from my heart. Leon started to talk, but he choked up. Tears slid in twin paths from his eyes, and he hastily brushed them away. He couldn't smile. He was thinking about me. I knew he was. He was trying to say something to me, but I didn't want to hear it. If he said it, I'd know this was all true and I was too far away to stop him.

His voice cracked. "*Tiens-moi serré*, Darke." *Hold me tight*. It was what he'd wanted Liz to tell me the day Taft abducted him.

The screen went blank.

"NOOO!" My shout silenced all the others. I exploded inside the vehicle, arms flying, feet kicking out.

A hard punch to my cheek knocked the hysterics out of me. Cannon's face appeared in front of mine. His bleak eyes and low voice carried through my heaving breaths. "Pull it together, man. We've gotta drive fast, right goddamn now if you have any chance of reaching him."

CHAPTER FIFTEEN

I didn't trust anyone else to drive. My hands melded to the wheel and my eyes peeled on the horizon, I waited for the break between sand and sky that meant water was near.

The ocean. The castle. Leon.

My fear that I wouldn't get to Leon in time was off the charts as I jammed my foot on the gas and shifted through gears. I didn't give a shit if I pulverized them to dust. Everyone else wisely remained quiet except Cannon, who was trying to get in contact with someone at the fortress to no avail. No one answered his repeated messages on the D-P. Not Leon. Not Raine.

That kind of silence added oil to the fire racing through my veins.

"Try again," I punched out between my teeth.

"There's no ping back."

I snarled at Cannon, "Keep. Fucking. Trying."

Driving gave me purpose. If I'd been in the passenger seat—Cannon's seat—I'd have destroyed the goddamn D-P. I might've torn up the entire motherfucking vehicle.

I didn't keep tabs on the Cruiser that was supposed to tail us, which held Linc, Liz, and Nathaniel. If they were behind us, good. If not? I didn't care.

Leon, Leon, Leon. I almost puked again but managed to swallow the bitter bile before it hit the back of my throat. It felt like hours when finally the castle reared up—the mirage before us.

"LEON!" I thundered the second I jumped from the Cruiser. I didn't stop yelling his name the entire time I sped across the causeway that never seemed to end.

Bursting through the door, I took bearing of the empty rooms with the fastest visual ever. I bolted up the stairs. Boots pounded behind me. At the top of the castle, I turned the doorknob. It was locked.

"GODDAMN YOU!" I pounded on it once, twice. Then I simply kicked the hundreds-years-old thing in.

I barged into the room on legs that all but fell out from under me when I saw Leon.

"NO!"

The chair I'd sat in the other night was knocked on its side on the floor. A rope looped over the open beams knotted around Leon's neck. His face was hidden behind the tumbling locks of hair, hands wide open, head hanging limply.

I moved in a flash. "Not you. Not now. Not ever. Not like this." I grappled with his legs and swung them over my shoulder to take the weight off his neck. "Get the rope. CUT THE FUCKING ROPE NOW!"

Cannon was there. His KA-BAR sliced the thick twine like it was melted butter. Leon's body slumped into my arms.

I laid him out on the floor, inspecting him with my eyes and my hands while I throttled back the roar rumbling through my body.

His eyelids were closed. His features were relaxed as if in repose. His arms and legs were limber.

I reared back and smacked his face with enough force to wake the dead.

He didn't so much as twitch.

My palm burned.

"Oh God. OhGodOhGodOh…"

The others rushed forward, boot-shod feet standing all around us. Too close. Too much. Too many.

I jerked up. "Get the fuck back! Don't touch him. Nobody touch him. I got this. I got him." Boots shuffled back. Bending over Leon's still form, I pulled him into my lap. "I've got you. I've got you, I've got you." Blabbering, sobbing, reeling from dread.

I felt for the pulse in his neck, willing it to send up a strong throb beneath the pad of my thumb.

Nothing.

I bent for his mouth and his chest immediately. Hands pumping up and down, breaths filling his lungs at intervals. I gave him my breath as I'd lay down my life for him, but not yet, not now. I wasn't ready for him to be gone. I'd never be ready.

My arms creaked two minutes later. My heart cracked open. Instead of puffing breath between Leon's lips, I kissed him. I kissed him and cried over him. I kept a hand on his neck and one on his chest and I willed him to live. I filled him with the all the love I'd never shown him. I clung to him like a wave breaking over a rock.

"Darke?" Liz's voice sounded clotted, thick.

I shook my head and started another round of compressions.

"Darke." That was Linc.

I ignored him, too.

Cannon started in. "Maybe it's time to—"

Leon gasped. He inhaled and cried out. His eyelids shot open and he stared at me.

"Keep those eyes open, baby. That's right. Do what you're doing. There you go. Perfect, just perfect." I gently coached him through his first seconds back in the land of the living with tears coursing down my face.

I choked. "He's okay. He's okay. He's alive!"

His breath warmed the hollow of my neck when I drew him to me. I watched Liz fall into Linc and Cannon accept the ready-and-waiting embrace from Nathaniel.

"You're alive. You're okay." I cradled Leon in my arms and kissed all over his face. "I'll make sure you're okay."

Minutes later, I lifted him from the floor and made him comfortable on the bed. I turned to the others.

My voice dropped low. "I'll take care of Leon. You find Raine. I think I need to have words, or maybe a reckoning, with our shaman."

With one last relieved look at Leon, everyone filed from the room.

After propping Leon on the pillows, I retrieved some water. I made him drink from the cup I held to his lips, and then I wiped his lips with soft touches of my fingers.

Ligature marks that had been red from the rough rope were shading into deep purple bruises circling the column of his neck. The more the marks surfaced on his skin, the more my fear, and ultimately my anger at his rash actions, consumed me until I slammed the water down.

"How could you do this? What the fuck were you thinking?" He blanched, but that didn't stop me. Maybe I was supposed to treat him with kid gloves, but I couldn't. "You promised you'd wait."

"I'm a hustler; you know dat," Leon whispered back in a voice raw from the rope's wounds. "It's easy enough to lie."

I had to distance myself before *I* did something rash. I leaped off the bed, pacing back and forth. "That's it? That's all you've got?"

The door swung open, Liz behind it. "Maybe you two shouldn't be alone right now."

Her concern had the effect of cold water splashed on my face and I sat down. I tried to breathe evenly like a normal human being, not a wild savage animal. "It's okay. I'm good. We're fine."

I sounded so, so solid with my two-word answers.

Liz glanced at Leon, who gave her a small nod, letting her know it was okay to leave.

The pain, the fear, the all-encompassing panic rushed over me. I moaned. "How could you do this? Why, Leon? Why?" I looked up to see his eyes filled, and he kneeled before me. "Why do you want to leave me so much?"

His remorse was like a blanket smothering him. "Because I don' wanna leave you at all." He bowed his head until his cheek lay on my thigh.

I reached under his arms, lifting him to my lap. There I rocked him. "Why?" I asked against the soft hair beneath my lips.

His face hidden in the lee of my neck, he said, "I had to know if it worked. *Possédé*—dat's what *Maman* always said I was."

"What?"

"Possessed by the devil, always gone my own way quick as I could."

Arms gliding around my neck, he slid his cheek against mine where his soft whiskers rubbed my rough stubble. "I injected myself as soon as you left."

I'd felt it in my bones while we drove away from the castle. I opened my mouth to rip into him again, but before I could speak, he pulled back.

"I got in touch with Hatch. He put me on the line with Doc at Chitamauga. I wasn't bein' completely stupid, Darke."

Hatch. Another name to add to my shit list. My hand moved to Leon's neck and stayed on the heated, bruised flesh.

"Doc talked me through it. And there's somethin' you don't know."

"What?"

"Hatch gave me a module for my D-P before we left. It sends a blood sample to the Doc so he can test it immediately."

Slipping off my lap to sit beside me, Leon wrapped his arms around me. Instead of relaxing into his hold, I remained upright as if I had a stick jammed up my ass.

He huffed, a long gust that sent his hair off his brow. "So I did it. Sent the results to Doc. He tested my blood. Still positive for the Plague."

A shiver raced over his body. His emotions that had run bright since he'd come around dimmed like candle flames dying out.

I leaned back and pulled him with me. I couldn't believe I'd found him dead such a short time ago. Now he was here and living, alive and breathing.

Tracing the lean lines of his back, kissing him until his trembling stopped, I warmed him, soothed him, held him. "We'll have other chances. There will be another antidote, one that works."

Tension loosened from his limbs all at once.

"What was the deal with the broadcast?"

"I din't wanna die without making a difference. I din't wanna die without sayin' good-bye to you."

My heart slammed up into my throat. "You do not say good-bye to me, ever." I drew his head back to lance him with my stare. "How did you manage to set it all up?"

"Hatch connected me just like Nate did when Liz's stuff went live from Beta."

Hatch again. Double Hatch Death. I might even use my hatchet on the man when we got back to the commune. Call it poetic justice.

I paused before asking the hardest question. "Why not wait for me?"

Leon stepped onto the floor and moved away.

I shot up. "What?"

"I din't think you'd care."

"That right there better be one of your perfect fucking lies." Another current of rage blasted through me.

He backpedaled. "I...I can never be sure with you."

My voice quiet, I asked, "Is that so?"

He swallowed and nodded.

In two steps I was right in front of him, grasping his face in my hands. "I love you! I love you, you shortsighted son of a bitch. Jesus Christ, I didn't want to, but..." Dragging him into my arms, I lowered my voice to whisper against his ear. "I think I fell in love with you that first night, angel."

His fingers reached for my shoulders and dug in. His tense body clung to mine. He said nothing. I don't think he even breathed.

I drew back and cocked my head. "I say I love you and you've got nothing?"

Leon chewed his bottom lip to hide the sweet smile forming. He shook his head a little and sighed. His nose nuzzled my throat and a long breath moaned out of him. "Say it again."

"Don't I deserve something in return?"

He pushed up to pop a kiss on my lips, beaming with self-satisfied delight that settled my heart solidly in my chest for the first time in months.

I didn't let him duck his head, instead going for his lips with my own for a deeper, longer, lustier taste. I kissed his cheeks and temples, his quivering eyelids when the dark fans of his lashes swept low.

I murmured against his brow, "I love you so much, Leon Cheramie."

He gave a rumble before launching himself into my arms. His legs wound around my waist, and his searing kiss nearly knocked me off my feet. I groaned when he pulled back, trying to recapture his suckling mouth.

He nibbled my bottom lip. He slid his tongue along my jaw with a hum. Leon lapped my parted mouth and retreated when I gasped.

"*Je t'aime*, Darke."

I cranked my arms around him and let out a resounding *whoop*! If Liz busted in now, I was going to bust a cap in her ass. Joy spread through me like warm sun rays after a long, dreary winter. I sealed our love on Leon's lips with a kiss that seared my soul.

Spinning toward the bed, I eased him down and crawled on top. His mouth was plumped up, glistening. Irises coin-sized and dilated. Body waiting, ready, especially when he stretched and rolled his hips, drawing attention to the hard ridge in his pants.

I wanted to get him naked, consummate this moment. I wanted to take him and stamp my essence within his body and all the hell over him until he knew without a doubt no one would ever reach as far inside him as I did.

First I needed to make sure he saw sense because—*fuck*—he'd very nearly succeeded in killing himself in the name of the Revolution. For a second time. Tumbling aside with a groan, I willed my erection to stand down.

Leon propped onto an elbow beside me. He idly played his palm beneath my shirt, tugging his hand over muscles, tickling my nipples. "What?"

I clamped down on his wrist to stop his toying motions. "You know what."

He shook his head.

I leaned over and stretched his arms out. "Yes. I need to make sure you're okay in your head, not just your heart."

He tried to snatch free. Good thing I was stronger, bigger, and had been through a few more battles than him. He was going nowhere.

"Whatever."

I ignored his response. "I'm not saying I have the first clue about what you're going through, but I am saying I will be here every step of the way." I captured Leon's tears when they fell, then his lips when he sighed. "I *want* to be with you. I'm choosing you. I need you to choose life."

"I choose you, too."

I relented with a kiss, retreated with a question. "And life?"

The battle within him was not black-and-white. It came across in bright bursts of feeling where hope warred with fate, a destiny he'd already accepted.

I cupped his face. "I'm going to be completely selfish here, baby. I love you. And my heart is tethered to yours now." I figured out right away I wasn't above using his emotions for me, or guilt about our circumstances, to make him stay put, in this life, on this earth. "I already decided that if you die, I die, because I am not doing this again. I've never loved anyone as much as I love you. I never will."

Gone was my guilt over Tam and Wilde. They would be happy for me. I knew that. As long as the little prick with my heart in his hands stopped trying to put an end to his life.

Leon's head knocked up. "That ain't fair."

I didn't care one damn bit. "Guess you better decide to live, then."

His nod was slow. *"D'ac."*

His pronouncement was so quiet, but my God, it was a victory. One that meant everything to me.

"You do not do anything like that again, angel." I shook him. Then, afraid of hurting him, I gentled. "Don't, please."

"And if it's just another week?"

I forced a hard swallow before I could answer. "It won't be. It'll be forever for you and me."

Leon broke from my hold. He rolled me onto my back and straddled me, suddenly flirty and sexy. *"Lâche pas la patate*—we'll hang in there. You're a romantic fool, Darke."

"For you. Only for you."

* * *

After Leon fell asleep, I disentangled from his arms. I stepped into the hall, shut the door, and collapsed to the floor. I needed a minute to regroup, sit down, and possibly pass out without him waking up to witness my total mental breakdown.

The stark terror of seeing him suspended from the ceiling with a rope around his neck crushed me. Leon hanging. Long bare feet swinging. Hair falling to cover his face. I'd now witnessed the deaths of three lovers.

I groaned, hugging my arms tighter around my body. Pain made me immobile as I saw the scene over and over again. It was a good thing I'd puked everything up earlier, because I broke out in a cold, nauseating sweat.

I rubbed my face and rose to my feet. I did my rounds of the castle, making sure everything was locked down, before I finally headed back to the bedroom.

Inside, Leon hogged the bed from one side to the other. I smiled, shucked my clothes, and slipped in next to him. He shuffled in his sleep as I filled all the empty spaces around him, as he did me.

* * *

It was still dark when I woke, and Leon wasn't next to me. I kicked off the bedding, intent on tracking him down, when I heard the shower running.

I used the basin to clean up the dust and dirt and tears from yesterday. It was barely dawn. Leon appeared from the bathroom just as I'd finished washing my face. He smelled of soap and the heat of silky skin.

As I patted myself dry with a towel, I glanced over at him. He didn't have a stitch of clothing on. His cock was hard, and a jewel of precome welled from the slit. I watched as that clear drop formed a perfect diamond before slithering down his shaft in a meandering path.

My jaw went tight. I licked my lips. I struggled to breathe when he ambled around the room, displaying every sexy part of his taut, toned body.

"Jesus Christ, Leon. Don't you think you should get some more sleep?"

"Sleep is for the—" Stopping abruptly, he shook his head. He bent over the foot of the bed, angled from his hips, pushing up his ass.

Looking at me, he ran both hands up the backs of his thighs to his buttocks. When he spread those firm cheeks to reveal the smooth crack between, I gasped.

"I don' wanna sleep. I wanna feel alive with you. I want you inside of me."

Cherry-red and slick, his tiny hole winked at me from between the swells of his ass. I dropped my hands from where they clenched under my pits only to clamp them on my thighs. He dipped a finger inside himself with a soft, wet squelch.

My cock lurched forward, dragging me behind it.

"Holy hell." I stared at his backside as he speared an extra finger inside.

Moaning and fucking up and down on two fingers, Leon threw his head back.

"You prepared for me?" I gripped the sides of his cheeks, mesmerized by the slick visual and slurping sounds.

"Din't wanna wait." With a dip of his knees, he sent a third finger home. The back of his hand brushed my cock, which had clear ideas of doing all that filthy-hot work for him.

My palms on his inner thighs spread his legs wider. He withdrew his fingers to brace both hands on the bed in front of him. I roughly fondled his hanging balls, then inspected his sleek open asshole. I teased the broad black-purple cap of my cock against his pucker, clasping that pert ass wide.

Leon's whole body shook from shoulders to toes. He turned his head, trying to gauge my intent. While he watched, I greased my palm with spit. I curled my fist around my meaty erection and made it glisten. Backing away enough to fit my entire cock against the deep, hot valley of his ass, I decided to go for a little ride since he was being so acquiescent.

I grabbed his hair in one hand, wrenching him up, his hip with the other, and pulled him to me. The first long slide made me shift closer and rumble deep within my chest. The second made Leon wiggle his ass around me. The third caused a globule of ejaculate to stretch from the tip of my cock down his cleft.

I stilled. My dick thudded against him, the black rod wedged between his paler cheeks.

"Mon Dieu."

Reaching around, I gripped his cock and squeezed. The head was engorged above my fist, filled with blood and need. I bit his shoulder and licked it before jerking his shaft in quick tight strokes that strangled his voice and made him rise to his tiptoes. Then I released him and stepped away.

"Get back here." Groaning with frustration, he fell forward to his hands on the bed.

"I'm not fucking you raw. Lube and a condom." Sweat beaded along my torso and dripped down my stomach.

Leon scrambled to find it, but I stopped him. "Oh, no. You wait right here. Stay just like that." I swooped down for one long lick of his trench, stopping to twirl my tongue at his furled opening.

My cock covered and coated in lubricant, I returned to my man. His back arched for me. His ass lifted. The vision of his ruby entrance when I slid my thick shaft toward it made me swell even more.

There was no more teasing, just a slow pop through his ring and a long howl as I slowly seated myself completely inside him. I withdrew immediately and lunged back in.

"Yeah. Just like dat, *cher*."

My breath coming in rasps, I fucked him right down onto the bed. I shifted him forward, keeping him attached to my needy cock, and crawled up after him. My arm around his throat—protecting it—his hand grasping my flank, I dug my toes in and rocked in and out. His round buttocks lifted up and sank down with each thrust and retreat. Muscles bunching and bulging, bodies banging together, we drove across the mattress and almost fell to the floor.

With a grunt, I slowed my pace. The underbelly of my cock caused a pause and the most heated friction every time I sucked out of him. It made Leon yelp in a throaty voice before I plunged deep again.

I stopped. Kissing across his shoulders, licking the nape of his neck, I said, "I'm not going to fuck you from behind, baby." I dismounted, moving back.

Disappointment cracked his voice. "You're not?"

Flipping him over, I settled above so his cock was a hot spike between our stomachs. He lifted his legs to my hips, bracketing me with his body. We touched in all places, in all ways.

My lips against his, I whispered hoarsely, "I want to make love to you, just like this."

I entered him with a groan. The slick slide inside was perfection—hot, tight nirvana. We held our lips open and close, our mouths sometimes missing the mark and landing on chins or cheeks or sensitive earlobes.

Leon voiced the sexiest little moans amid a litany of nonstop mumbles: *ooh yeah, ahhh, please, please, oh fuck, more…*

"I like being inside you." I lifted up to push deeper.

"I know." His grin ended in a groan when I pumped long and slow.

I leaned down to kiss his chest, above his heart. "I like being inside you…*here.*"

His sooty eyelashes fluttered down. His lips parted for my kiss. His arms tightened around my neck, bringing me toward him.

I rolled into his body with lingering thrusts, awed by his beauty, his strength. Sinking inside with such care and love, I felt our communion light up inside my body. I swiveled my hips to grind my stone-hard balls against his upturned ass, breaching him deeper than before.

His breath hitched. His eyes flared wide. "Oh! I'm gonna come!"

A sudden flash of sizzling heat squeezed my cock. Unexpected. Too much for me to withstand as Leon's back arched, driving me deeper. It was impossible to stop the fast snap of my hips and the all-encompassing desire to fill him with my come. It lashed out of me for so long and in such magnitude, I hollered in my release and left fingerprint trails on his skin.

But I wasn't sated. Not by a long shot.

Leon whistled through his teeth when I grasped both ankles, drawing his legs wide. "Darke?"

"Now I'm gonna fuck you." *Mark you, own you, make you mine.*

I managed wet kisses on his lips between our full-bodied writhing.

I volleyed into him, my blunt-headed length a torpedo engulfed by his grasping hole. It was easier to pound into him, his narrow chute used to me, nice and wet and sloppy. Lush sounds comingled with his uncontainable moans. And I was overtaken by my driving need to inhabit his body any way I could, to take away the fear and pain and fury and replace it with love and peace and forever.

Pulling out my thick cock, I pushed it against Leon's. He was just as hard as me. Wet with come and lube, I smoothed my hand up and down both shafts. His stomach clenched. His body strained upward. When his throat arched, I cupped the back of his neck and sent my lips sliding all over the purple-colored flesh he'd hurt.

"You want to give this up?" I lunged back inside of him.

Leon shook his head.

I hauled him on top of my thighs. I fucked into him again. "Remember this feeling. Me inside you. You inside my soul." I lifted his hand to the hard-beating pump of my heart.

He nodded frantically, his fingers digging into my flesh.

"Because I love you. I love you so goddamn much." Unbidden, tears rose in my eyes. I captured his lips, his gasp, his vow of requited love.

I withdrew completely from his ripe round cheeks and slid back inside. Once, twice…I bent over his body after watching my dark, glistening cock dive deep and retreat into the hot pink hold of his ass.

Leon looped his legs around my waist as I lowered us both down.

"Good. So good, baby." Then I wrapped my arms around him. I brushed my lips over his and cried out. My seed sped into him as his spread between our bellies.

Minutes later, I loosened my arms to slide off of him. I flopped to my back.

The sole of Leon's foot rubbed my calf. He squeezed and massaged the muscles of my pecs down to my abs. When I lifted sleepy eyes, he was squinting at me.

"What?"

"It's so different with you."

"Why?" Lifting up to an elbow, I captured his hand against me. "Because I'm black?"

Leon sniggered. "No. *Mmm.*" He bit his bottom lip. "That just makes it hotter. No, 'cause I never…"

"You never had a lover?"

His face, already flushed from exertion, turned rosy-colored. "Nah. I just screwed a lot of people."

"Why?" A tight fist of jealousy cramped my stomach.

"Too busy workin'. Then I felt dirty. You know me, the Company whore." His head lolled toward me. "Had to make money. Had to survive. Wanted to make sure my *maman* was safe, 'cause if you think I'm trouble—*merde*—she'd shoot her mouth off at anyone, anywhere because she never believed the must-do rules. We could barely make the government rent on our poverty-row house with her work at the factory. 'Sides, I'm cute and I got a great ass, *non?*"

"Leon." I groaned. I wasn't sure I could handle this, but trust and love and complete honesty had to be on the table between us.

"Sold my soul to the devil. Pay was good. And since I was in demand, the Company left *Maman* alone." His eyes drifted shut. "They made me go with men and women."

"You don't like women." Renewed anger aimed at the CO ripped through me. He'd been through so much, a war of his own.

He smiled, only one side of his lips curving. "I like 'em well enough to be friends with 'em. Wasn't too thrilled to fuck 'em. Not at first. But ya know what? It was easier with the women than the men. The executives wanted to own me, and I din't want them…inside of me…in my body or my head like that. The women? They were nice, usually fed me afterward. I could get it up either way, but I had control when I fucked a lady. The men took all dat control away from me."

"That's not something to feel blessed about," I said.

"Sometimes you gotta take what you get an' make the best of it."

"Not with me."

"Not with you. Never like that." Rolling onto his side, he ducked his head. "But I know what it's like to have pussy, Darke."

"If this is about Tam again, I will tell you every single day I don't want a woman. I'm not looking for anyone else—male or female. What happened with them, my love for them had everything to do with circumstances. I loved them. I miss them."

He shuffled away.

I scooted right behind him until my chest met his back and my arms rounded his body. My lips skittered across his cheek to the corner of his mouth. "What happened with you? It was unexpected. I tried to turn you away because I convinced myself I couldn't have you, didn't deserve you, didn't want you." I tipped his face so he couldn't hide from me. "You know what? That was all bullshit. You alone made me whole. *You*, just you. You are the one I want."

He dropped his head. "I still feel dirty." His words were muffled by a pillow, but I heard them.

"You can be as dirty as you want with me. Trust me. I like it. You turn me on so fucking much it's a wonder I didn't bang your ass wide open the night of Nathaniel and Cannon's handfasting. Christ, it damn near killed me to keep my hands off you these past months. My palm is thick with callouses from beating off to thoughts of you…"

"Really?" He breathed in wonder. He pushed onto his side, once more tangling long limbs with mine.

"You've got no idea what you do to me. And I love it." I ran my fingertips along the hollow of Leon's cheek. He glowed with my praise. "There's not a single dirty speck on your spirit, angel."

He hummed, lowering his face to my neck.

I drew my hand down his back to grasp his ass in a firm hold. There was one more thing we had to cover before heading off to la-la land. "You're not to fuck anyone but me ever again."

That might not have been the smartest move. Leon reeled up and snapped, "As long as we're throwin' out edicts, same goes for you."

"Won't be a problem."

"For me, either."

"Good."

"*Bien.*" He resettled himself with me as the cushion for his body.

"And you let me take care of your every need from now on," I tacked on just as Leon relaxed.

"And if I say I'm fully capable of takin' care of myself?"

I snagged his chin and kissed his lips. "You'll let me do it anyway because you love me and you're a generous person."

"*Hmph.*" In a shy whisper, he said, "I wanna take care of you, too."

"Oh, you will."

"*D'ac.*"

Duck meant *okay. Good.*

"Tell me you love me again," I whispered against his ear, thrilling when little chills rose on his skin.

"*Je t'aime. Je t'aime.*" Each time he said the words that joined us together, he kissed me with soft pecks. "I love you, *cher.*"

With the covers drawn over us, I hugged him tightly.

"Am I allowed to sleep now, *monsieur?*" he asked with a large yawn and a twinkle in his eyes.

I suddenly felt bad about haranguing him. Not enough to stop from adding, "Only with me. Every night. In my arms."

CHAPTER SIXTEEN

When I woke up, Leon was right where he was supposed to be, safely nestled against me. I must've slept for a long time, because bright sunbeams slanted into the room. I watched him for a while, measuring his breaths, his little snuffles. Pushing the hair from his face, I kissed him every so often, trying not to wake him. Everything was so new and fragile; I took the time to appreciate him in my arms.

Finally easing out of bed, I had a thorough cleanup. After checking on Leon one last time, I headed downstairs. The smell of food cooking hastened my steps.

Nathaniel manned a frying pan over the fireplace. I took a seat at the long wooden table next to Cannon, who watched his man with the usual unwavering attention.

Liz pushed a cup of coffee at me. "Good afternoon, sunshine."

I blew across the piping-hot black liquid and tried to dial back my smile. Cannon inched away from me on the bench so he could get a good look at me, then nodded with a grin of his own.

Nathaniel and Linc did the cooking, serving up plates of fish and some kind of creamy, grainy mush. During the next ten minutes, the only sounds heard were grunts of approval, forks scraping plates, and coffee being gulped and refilled.

It was only when Cannon got up to clear the table and Nathaniel joined him across the room that I felt all eyes turn to me.

"He's good. Leon's fine. He's sleeping."

Liz folded her hands on the table. "How good? And I'm not talking about the sex this time."

"We need to know if he's solid in his head, Darke. Or should we put him on…?" Linc left his thought unfinished.

"We talked. I may have bribed him with my own life-and-death scenario if he ever succeeded in hurting himself." I leaned back and folded my arms across my chest. "He doesn't need to be on a suicide watch."

"You're sure?" Nathaniel asked.

"Yes. But that doesn't mean he's not all fucked up in his head about this shit, you know?"

"I think we're all a little fucked up in the head about what might happen to him, man." When Cannon's gaze pierced mine, the dark brown of his irises glistened before he closed his eyes. "Seeing that, seeing him like that last night…" He clasped his hand over his mouth.

"I know." My voice was rough.

Cannon looked up, weaving his fingers through Nathaniel's.

"My lover, Alejandro, was caught and killed by the Company five years ago. He…" Cannon chewed on his upper lip, letting his head fall back. "They hanged him in front of a huge crowd in Epsilon. Made a whole event out of it. I was there."

"Jesus Christ." Liz reached out to grab his free hand. She pressed it to her face. "I never knew. All those trips to Epsilon?"

"I went to see him. No one knew. I only ever told Blondie." He searched his husband's face before putting an arm around him. "I've been there, Darke, so if you need to talk, come find me."

I walked to him and clasped his hand. "I appreciate that. And I'm sorry for your loss."

Cannon peeked over at Nathaniel before lifting his palm to kiss the heart of it. "Jesus. Yeah. I'm sorry I brought that up."

"Don't be. I only wish you hadn't gone through that." Nathaniel kissed him on his mouth, earning a red blush Liz cackled over.

"Okay, uh, so…" Cannon stuttered.

"I told Leon I love him." I filled in the gap before I even realized my mouth was moving.

"No shit?" He wheeled back toward me.

A grin stole across my face. "No shit." Then I laughed, and damn, that felt good for a change.

Their voices swelled as everyone began talking over one another. I couldn't make out the specifics, but the message was clear: the usual ribbing mixed with a healthy dose of pure happiness.

When everyone settled down, Linc asked, "So, Darke. You want the good news or the bad news?"

"The bad."

Elbowing my ribs, Liz said, "Always did peg you for a morbid SOB, when you're not being all lovey-dovey and shit."

"Nice. Your man lets you kiss him with that mouth?"

She waggled her eyebrows in Linc's direction. "That's not all he lets me do with it."

Linc flushed pink from his neck to his hairline and cleared his throat. "The bad news is Raine's not so mysteriously missing."

"Surprise, surprise," Cannon muttered.

"Who's on it?"

"Darwin went out with Bas and Farrow," Nathaniel reported. With the sun shining in behind him in this stone cavern kitchen, his blond hair glowed and the earring at the peak of his ear picked up the light.

"Is it safe for them?"

"Let's face it. It's not exactly safe for any of us." Cannon scratched irritably at the stubble shading his jawline.

"So we wait. What's the good news?"

Nathaniel rummaged in his pack, retrieving a bigger D-P than the handheld devices we carried. He set it up in the middle of the table, the one-dimensional tablet going 3-D and upright at the scan of his thumb.

"We watched this earlier. The Voice put together a little promo of his own following yesterday's events."

"Does anyone else think the Voice is a lame name?" Liz leaned one elbow on the table while Nathaniel fiddled with his fancy gear.

"Here, here." Cannon winked.

"Really. He *or* she—we don't know for sure—could at least have put a little spin on it when *the Voice* started to get popular. I mean—"

"Lizbeth?" Blondie smoothly cut in.

"What?"

"I'm tryin' to work here." He scrolled back through the incoming data and the day's notification history.

"You know, that's the same thing I tell your brother when I'm—"

Linc hauled her onto his lap and clamped a hand over her mouth.

"It's on."

Everyone became serious as the Voice began his broadcast.

"The CEO tried to drive the Revolutionary leaders out into the open today by forcing them to do something that went against their honor. He grows impatient. The fact is CEO Cutler is the one killing us, not the rebel angels of mercy."

"I think this Voice has a hard-on for us," Cannon said in a wry tone.

"The fact *is* his ploy backfired. Here are the scenes from all around the world. The aftermath of Cutler's threats."

The triple-sided screen burst into vibrant life with events I watched in openmouthed wonder.

Shehu and his warriors along with a hundreds-strong battalion of Omega Corps infiltrated the Omega Quad. Executives, soldiers, medical officers stood down. We saw similar action take place in Territories across the world, the names of Kappa in Central Europa, Sigma in the Southern Americas, and Zeta in the Siberian frozen land running across the bottom of the D-P monitor as they fell to the rebel army.

I blinked at the screen, unsure if what I was seeing was real.

The best part came next and—holy hell—I jumped off my seat and plastered my face to the D-P to get a closer look because retaliation of this magnitude was sweet.

"The Company's getting shut down, shut out, locked up. You, the citizens and Reformed Corps combined with the Revolutionaries and Freelanders, are standing up! Pushing back! Changing our world!"

Triumph on this massive scale was so much more effective than the invasive Plague Cutler was ready to unleash. Citizens all over the world, on every continent, throughout all the lands, were shown celebrating. Not running scared, not hiding in their gray government houses, not hunched over and shuffling along to their next workhorse assignment. Then the scene zoomed out to show six squares, each from a different Territory. In every one, all at once, red ribbons lifted to the sky. They flew on the wind like the raised voices we listened to: *Live in Freedom! Love at Will!*

"I'll be goddamned." I plunked into my chair and shook my head, overcome by emotion. "How many Territories are left?"

"Eight," Liz answered.

"And Cutler?" I asked as Nathaniel turned off the D-P.

"On the run, in a hole—who knows?" Cannon tapped his fingers restlessly on the table.

"I don't think Father was ever here. It's not his scene." Linc pushed back from the table. "Not enough amenities."

"Or a big enough population to brainwash," his twin added with a twist of his lips.

"So Denver sent us on a wild-goose chase with Raine as well as Cutler."

Placing both palms on the arms of his chair, Linc met my stare. "And he'll get his comeuppance, too."

"Darke?" Leon's throaty voice called from up above.

I hit my feet before my coffee cup clattered to the table. Smirks were plastered on every single puss in the room.

I pointed my finger at them. "We stay put today." That was another one of my edicts.

"Aye-aye, Captain." Cannon saluted. Wiseass.

"Good to have you back in the saddle." Nathaniel sucked in his cheeks to stifle his grin.

"That's what Leon said." Liz just couldn't help herself.

"One last thing." I turned at the threshold. "What'd you do with the rope?"

"How do you think I started the fire?" Nathaniel gestured behind him to the big open hearth.

Although I'd made plans to use that hanging rope to hog-tie Raine, burning it was good enough.

"Go check on your man," Linc commanded, placing a covered plate in my hand.

* * *

Leon was fresh from a shower, alert, clear-eyed. After I set the tray down beside the bed, I couldn't resist sampling his pouty lips. "How are you feeling?"

He winced as he sat down on the bed. "A little sore."

"Aw, shit. I'm sorry. I was too rough." I kneeled in front of him.

"Nah. I like it. I like knowin' you were in me, all the way."

My cock plumped up. I swallowed thickly. My eyes strayed from the slow lick of his lips to the discolored purple skin encircling his throat. "How's your neck?"

"S'okay. Remind me to use a gun next time. Less hang time." He gently fingered the bruises.

"Jesus, Leon. That is not funny."

"I know. I'm sorry. I didn't mean to hurt you like dat." He urged me up to the bed next to him.

"Don't. Don't say sorry again. I've got to tell you what happened yesterday." Getting up to retrieve the food platter, I tried to distract myself from his growing apprehension.

"It's bad."

"It's not good, that's for sure." Guilt spread its ugly disease through me. "Here." I handed him the plate and a fork. "Maybe you should eat something first."

He tucked in with a hearty appetite that pleased me. Nathaniel's breakfast disappeared in a matter of minutes, leaving me with nothing but the truth to tell and no way left to stall. A frown burrowed into my forehead as I faced him.

"G'on. I can take it."

I settled beside him. "The coordinates Raine gave us led to a field hospital on the Corps base. We had to kill a lot of people."

"The enemy."

"I don't think there are any enemies anymore. Just Cutler and…Raine." My lips curled in disgust.

"He's still missing?"

"Yeah, but not for long. When we find him, I'm gonna—" I stopped myself. The need for revenge and retribution cranked up my rage.

"He din't do anything wrong."

"The hell you say."

"Nothin' worse than what I did." He dropped his head.

I tilted his chin right back up, high in the air, where it belonged. "Bullshit. He used you, and I need to know why. What he did was practically murder, knowingly giving you a fake antidote. What you did? That was misguided and goddamn stupid and…At least you were trying to save others, not kill them." I grasped his chin harder. "Not that I condone that shit. You are not to try anything like that ever again."

"I know," he whispered.

I released him to burrow my face in his hair. "The people yesterday, they were…like you. Not military, not the enemy. Civilians infected with a new, even more rapid strain of the Plague."

When Leon pushed me away, I wasn't surprised. As I replayed what we'd seen and what we'd done—my voice subsiding into a gruff, hoarse tone—his eyes grew as big as the dinner plate I'd brought to him, then as empty as it was after he cleared it.

He folded his arms around his chest and sat away from me. "Why did you revive me?"

"I don't know how you can even ask that question."

His chin notched higher. "If you can kill them, why not let me do it to myself?"

"It's not the same thing. It was ugly, Leon. What Cutler did to those people and what we had to do. But there was no choice. They were about to be sent into Omega. They were going to die in a matter of hours, only after they spread the infection." He remained silent and I forged on. "You…you cannot kill yourself. I won't let you."

He gave a derisive snort.

I grabbed his face. "You have to live."

His laugh was harsh. "Just 'cause you say so?"

"That's right."

"I'm not sure you're strong enough." Suddenly his stony face shifted into such utter sadness, it overwhelmed me. I let his face go to bring him to me. He didn't resist.

"I assure you, I am." I cupped the back of his head. "You are, too. You know you are. Only a powerful man could pull that shit you did yesterday. The broadcast? Standing up against what Cutler did to you? You are a hero, Leon. And I need you to be heroic for me."

He pressed his face against my shirt. *"Couillon."*

"Cursing me again?"

"Crazy fool."

"Crazy in love." We reclined together. "What happened yesterday was not done lightly."

"If it comes down to me?"

Even though I assured him it wouldn't, I had a sick feeling that was CEO Cutler's plan from the start.

"Will we ever be okay?" He blinked big honey-brown eyes at me.

"Yes." I cuddled him closer. His hands skimmed over my shoulders, landing on the sensitive scar tissue on my upper back. I shivered with his warm caresses and something more potent. With time running out, there was one way to convince Leon of my love. "Do it…the moko."

"What?"

I ripped my shirt off. "I want what you want. You, on my skin."

His gaze roamed over my chest. Pink tinted his cheeks.

"You sure this is a good idea? If you gotta fight, you'll be in pain—won't be at your best." His hesitation didn't mask the over-whelming joy radiating from him.

This felt so right.

"I'm not going to cry, if that's what you're worried about." Emotion made my voice brusque.

"*Oui.*"

Leon practically danced from the bed to his rucksack. I barked a loud laugh at his eagerness. *Joie de vivre.* That's what this was all about. I remembered that long-lost term, something my mom had said to me once about how it felt when she was singing—no matter who her audience was. *The joy of life.*

The will to live. I could give that back to Leon as he'd done me.

"Where?" When he returned, his hands trailed along my back.

I lay down on the bed and placed my hand on my upper chest. "Right here."

"What do you want?"

"Angel wings. And your name."

Nodding, Leon said, "*D'ac*. Okay. Dat's good."

I spread his palms across my pecs. "You sure you want your name here?"

"*Mon Dieu*. Yes." He leaned in to my mouth, flitting his tongue along my lips and deep inside. "'S'all I want."

"My little devil with angel's wings."

"Not so little." He grabbed his crotch, highlighting the hard-on clearly visible beneath faded denim.

"Not so little," I agreed.

With his tools laid out, Leon shaved my mostly smooth chest. To sanitize me, he used the same alcohol swabs Raine had given him for the injection. Each touch was tantalizing torture. Keeping still made me ache while my cock hardened to full capacity, getting slick and thick inside my pants. Leon knew it, too. His hands grazed my groin, multiplying the exquisitely sensual intimacy of this moment.

The first puncture was the worst. He started at my sternum, moving slowly outward over my left side. As the bone chisel and small mallet gouged into my flesh. Leon's gorgeous face was lined with intense concentration. Blue-black dye dripped into my skin while his eyes screwed up over every painstaking detail. He swiped away the blood and the sweat on my face and his.

He was an artist at work, the masterpiece of our love on my skin. My chest puffed up, and he slapped my side. "Don' move."

"Yes, sir," I blurted.

He arched one of his eyebrows in amusement.

An hour elapsed. Two and then three. He designed my torso freehand. Every so often, he pressed a kiss to my lips. Those light brushes were powerful enough to be some sort of numbing agent or aphrodisiac. I didn't know. I didn't care. His kisses soothed me into a mindless substate of relaxation beneath the continuation of pain.

Leon got up and stretched so high that his shorts rode dangerously low. Just the sort of hot visual I needed to keep this statue-like stillness up for the rest of the moko. When he hunkered over me again, his fingers were less sure, like he'd lost the moment.

"If your hand shakes, you're gonna fuck it up."

He gave me a *tsk* and steadied himself.

I grinned.

He'd tied back his hair, so I had an unimpeded view of his artistry. The design spread across my breastbone, over my pectorals, down my diaphragm. The lines on the outside were thick. On the inside he etched smaller, tighter patterns. At one point his forehead rested against my neck so he could get close enough to put in the fine detail. That was when the enormity of this deed delivered a pure shot of emotion to my heart.

I shuddered beneath his touch.

Leon raised his head. "You said you weren't gonna cry."

"I'm not crying because it hurts." I brushed the backs of my knuckles across his cheek, careful not to disrupt his work but desperate to touch him. "You are so damn beautiful. I am honored to wear your mark and your name on my body. I love you."

He beamed with warm pleasure and pride. "I don' think I'll ever get tired of hearing you say dat."

"You won't have to. Gonna say it every day."

"I thought you din't want me to fuck this up."

"You won't. We won't."

It took grueling hours. It was painful. It would need finishing touches. But watching Leon throughout the entire process, I was enamored. Daylight was long gone by the time he finished, but I didn't regret a single minute of being spread out and at his mercy.

After his careful cleanup, he led me to the mirror in the bathroom. He lit the pillar candles and stepped back.

The black-indigo ink stood out on my skin. Wings opened in flight from one side of my chest to the other. In clear script, his name wound through the feathers that looked like they ruffled in a breeze.

I touched my tender skin, grazing his name. It was such a heavy moment, yet it made me feel so light. "It's perfect. Like you."

"Like us." His fingers rested at the shallow dip at the bottom of my spine.

Stiff after being still for so long, I gave my back a stretch. I bunched my arms forward, clenching and releasing muscles.

Leon hissed behind me.

I glanced at him. The same immediate famished need reflected back at me.

Quickly losing my pants, I stretched out on the bed. My body was stinging with pain, but the hurt was so damn good, and the love resonating between us was worth every moment of it. I couldn't wait until my skin healed over and his name was right there for all to see, front and center on my chest, intertwined with the wings that represented everything he was to me.

But right now I needed to claim him. Give myself to him.

"Get over here."

"Maybe you shouldn't do anything too strenuous." His eyes were glittering and deviously dark.

"If you don't get over here and fuck my cock right now, I'm gonna show just how strenuous I can get." Arching my back, I stroked my aching rod.

"Well, I guess. Since you aren't givin' me any choice."

He took his damn sweet time undressing. Swiveling his hips, running his hands down his well-muscled body, covering his cock, cupping his ass.

The final straw was when he sucked a finger into his mouth and let out a small moan.

The second Leon stepped next to the bed, I hefted him on top of me. With lubed fingers I quickly stretched his wanton ass to accommodate me while he sheathed me in a condom and stroked slickness over me.

I gripped his hips as he straddled me. "Ride me."

There was no tease or buildup. The entire day had been fore-play. He squatted above me, grasped my cock, and sent it home with a guttural cry. Each time he rose up and sank back down, I pried him open. His head fell back. His velvet tunnel enveloped my shaft.

In heat. I was in heat. I sat up until we were face-to-face, close enough to kiss. He linked his ankles at the base of my spine, using the leverage to force me deeper, faster.

"Leon!"

He dug his fingers into my hair and yanked my neck back. Teeth nipped at my throat and across my collarbone. The heated wet passage of his ass contracted. He thrust upon me, his dick slapping my stomach. Balls banging my groin. The thatch of his pubes rasped mine. I grinded into him and reveled in his bite—the one from his teeth and the one that sizzled grooves of heat from my cock all the way up my back.

Our hands clasped around each other's biceps. We longed to get closer, but the fresh tat prevented it. Our skin was slick, and my chest burned. With my hands skimming on to both sides of his ass, I opened him further and sunk so deep inside there was no turning back.

His eyes opened wide. He arched in my arms. "Yes!"

Leon's moans and whimpers came faster and louder and longer, my cock dragging the incredible sounds out of him.

"No one's gonna be inside you like this, angel," I grunted.

The high-pitched moan that met me was music to my ears. "Only you, Darke. Always."

"Damn right."

I smoothed my hands over his back, doubling them across him, holding him, covering him, loving him. Forever.

I lost it. As I pounded up into him, I fisted his shaft at the same punishing pace. Crashing my mouth to his and moaning within the wet heat, I gave everything. My skin for his name, my soul for his heart, my love for his life.

"Angel, angel." As I pulsed into him, seed propelled from my shaft in an outpouring of one soul to the other.

Leon shuddered on top of me. The sweet scent of his come sprayed between our bellies.

My thrusts slowed. I flopped back. "Holy shit, baby."

"Yeah."

"Okay?"

"Ungh."

"I'm not moving tomorrow." I was all loosey-goosey. I managed to just about bring him to my side, where the wet tip of his cock hit my hip. He was still firm and hard for me. I stroked another few drops from him, bringing the lush male taste to my mouth.

"Today." Leon gathered more of his release and fed it to me one finger at a time.

I lapped and sucked and asked, "What?"

"It's way past midnight."

"God. What did you do to me?"

And please do it again and again.

* * *

Of course, life waited for no man, and neither did former First Lieutenant Liz Grant of the Alpha Elite Tactical Forces.

Too few hours later there was a rap of knuckles on the door, quickly followed by, "Knock, knock." Surprise.

"Fuck off," I returned by rote.

"Darke." Leon hopped to his feet, completely naked.

"What?" I rolled into his warm spot. "Can't I just have a few minutes alone with you?"

"You had the whole day and last night, too."

Of course Liz chose that moment to stick to our old routine, opening the door and barging right in with everyone behind her and Leon naked as a jaybird. I wrangled him to the bed and covered us up.

I was relieved to see the group that had gone after Raine were present and in one piece, lingering on the side. But when everyone gaped at me instead of Leon, I had to make sure I wasn't busting a new tent-by-erection beneath the blankets.

Leon laughed against my ear. "They be lookin' at the moko, *cher*."

"Finally got my angel wings," I said to all with a sweet affirming kiss on Leon's lips.

I felt like a goddamn leader of my people. Truly capable for the first time with Leon my consort, my lover. We sat side by side in the bed. Pride puffed my chest as I held Leon's hand above the blankets for all to see.

"Report," I ordered.

"Fuck. Are we supposed to bow now?" Cannon said to Nathaniel, who gave a little smirk.

"I don't do curtsies." Darwin shot one eyebrow up.

Liz heckled, "Oh, that's okay, because Farrow does."

Sure enough, Farrow performed a small dip of her knees with the elegance and grace of her fine breeding, all the while shooting a simmering glare at Liz.

"Is there news on Raine or not?" Because if not, I had other plans that had to do with Leon's hand, which was wandering up my inner thigh.

"Shehu spotted him in Omega," Cannon said.

"So we move out together." Linc tapped his holstered weapons.

"No one's moving out but me." I wriggled from the bed, intent on finding clothes, weapons, bullets designed to make Raine's brain splatter.

Everyone was quick to voice their support, but Leon's low voice drew me in. "I don' want you to do dis."

I turned toward him as I dragged on my pants. "This is about avenging you, and that's mine alone to do. There's no telling when or if we'll be attacked here. Everyone stays."

"Just take a backup, man. I volunteer." Cannon thumped his fist to his chest.

All the rest stepped forward.

"No. This is something I've got to do." I strapped a knife to my waist. "Give us a moment?"

Leon's anguish swirled around us as the room emptied. He unrolled gauze and tape. Then he carefully sheltered my new wings under clean bandages. Afterward I drew on a shirt and finished arming up.

"I'll be back soon. Nothing and no one can keep me from you." The kisses I stole from him pulled a deep groan from my throat. I moved back, but he followed, landing in my lap on the bed. I twisted strands of glossy hair between my fingers, helpless beneath the onslaught of his mouth. "I can't get enough of you."

The delicious curve of his bottom lip nudged against mine.

His tongue swooped inside, seeking me out. Our faces angled for a better fit. Each twirl of his tongue, every murmur from his lips was seared in my mind when we broke apart.

"You are too damn sexy," I said.

"You are too dangerous." He yanked me against him by my shirt when I tried to stand up on unsteady legs. "Remember last time? The explosion in Beta? I said *no more*. I don' need my honor defended or whatever. I need you alive, so you best be careful out there."

CHAPTER SEVENTEEN

I roared off in the Cruiser on my way to Omega. I wasn't thinking. I was working on blind fury, the kind that ate up every other emotion and spit it back out, leaving a red-black rage in its wake.

A pinging on my D-P made me ease back on the gas. It was a message from Darwin. Seemed our little mole Raine had had the forethought to sneak back and cut the brake lines on both vehicles.

Oh joy.

I tested the brakes, and sure enough I got no traction in return. I added that to the latest *Oh shit* crisis. Looked like I had no option but to keep up my headlong, breakneck speed. *Shame.*

Coming up on the now wide-open gates of Omega, I spied a nice little parking spot off to the left—aka a hilly sand dune. I took my foot off the pedal and braced myself in my seat. This was going to hurt.

The car slowed in the troughs of deep sand, enough to lessen the impact to a mere body-rattling, teeth-clattering crash when I collided with the dune hood-first.

Leaving the vehicle behind in a heap, I plugged Shehu's coordinates into my D-P and raced off.

* * *

The city hadn't slept since the Quad had been repurposed and the old rule kicked out. I slithered through high-lit streets, which were teeming with revelers who would be put to better use organizing their militia.

I located Shehu and my prey on the rooftop of a vacated building in S-4, where the quietness was pronounced after the heaving atmosphere of the inner city.

Raine was quiet, too, an improvement on his usual chatterbox.

He didn't look scared enough to satisfy my kill-him-dead urges, though. In fact, he leaned casually against an upended crate, puffing on a cig.

He blew a smoke ring up to the pitch-black sky. "I expected you sooner. The fierce warrior and all."

Before I could retaliate, Shehu smacked him on the side of the head with a hand as big as a brick. The blow made Raine cough, and his cig dropped to the floor. I stomped it out on my way to getting in his grill. Standing over him, I wasn't just a fierce warrior. I was a harbinger of death.

"That was for your insolence," Shehu coldly commented.

"And this is for your ignorance." I slammed my fist into his gut, causing another round of coughing and hacking. "You know, smoking will kill you. But not before I do."

Spluttering and shaking in his sandals, Raine looked to Shehu for support that wasn't coming. He started in with the begging, but Shehu remained stoic and unmoved.

"I'm one of your tribe!" Raine wailed.

Shehu spat at his feet in a gesture of disgust and disownment. "I do not know you. You are no more than a rat in the streets."

Not two seconds passed before the slippery shit made a run for it.

"Fuck!" I pounded after him, Shehu at my heels.

Raine leaped across a gap between the tight buildings, falling to his knees as he landed. He punched right back to his feet and took off in a zigzag.

I briefly appraised the four-story drop between one roof and the next and then went airborne behind him. My landing was a little clumsier, but I was in much better shape than my pot-toking, cig-smoking quarry. I just hadn't taken his familiarity with the city into account.

One rooftop led to the next. Clotheslines, potted plants—even people in pretty little terraced gardens got in my way. As far as the Territories went, Omega was nice. I felt bad that I didn't have time to sightsee or say sorry, especially when I knocked over a table laden with food.

By the time Raine drew me into a mazelike menagerie of live exotic animals, my patience wore thin. The animal part would be okay if it were simply parrots or monkeys or other nonlethal vertebrates, but no. I almost fired off my Smiths when a lion reared up in its cage, rattling the bars and roaring at me from two paces away.

"Oh, you gotta be kiddin' me."

I bolted away from the only other predator that was bigger than me. I was gaining on Raine. Finally, I cornered the traitor in the heart of Omega. There was no escape. No other roof to jump to, no ladder down. Raine was huffing and puffing in near exhaustion, and his hair stuck in thick, sweaty clumps to his face.

Shehu came up behind me, and then he sidled past. He was pissed, judging from the sharp copper emotion he gave off and the sharp metal machete he brandished in his hands. His long braid swung down to his hips. He was bare-chested apart from two crisscrossed leather straps on his torso and a boatload of scars that marked him as a man of action.

Not a dude to mess with.

The flat rooftop overlooked the city and the desert. It was secluded, and the only sounds carrying to us were Raine's whistling breaths and the susurrations of the breeze.

"I will contain him," Shehu said, his teeth glinting like the metal of his weapon.

"How?"

The blow from the butt end of his heavy machete to the side of Raine's head was enough to rock Raine on his feet, but not enough to knock him out. Torqueing Raine's elbows behind him, Shehu forced him to his knees with arms high above, pulling painfully at his shoulder sockets.

"That is how."

Grasping Raine's hair in my fist, I hauled his head back. I

couldn't wait to fuck him up so badly that even the devil in hell would take one look at him and turn him away—but first I wanted answers to my questions.

"Let's start, shall we? What was the real deal with Colt?"

Raine was keeping his mouth shut for once, so I helped loosen his lips with a swift knee to the jaw.

He spat blood to the rooftop with a whimper. "Colt was gonna talk. He'd helped with the cure because he thought it was for a good cause. He'd followed all of you Revolutionary assholes since Cannon's first speech to the masses."

"That doesn't tell me why he had a gun to Leon's head."

"I drugged him, messed with his mind, and made him think Leon was out to get him."

"You evil little cunt." My lips curled in disgust. "What else?"

"When he found out I had no intentions of giving you the real cure, Colt threatened to tell you. No amount of opium could keep him quiet."

"Back the fuck up for second. You mean you staged the whole Amphitheater night?"

Raine's face shot up in defiance. "Yeah. Colt needed to be silenced. Leon needed to die. I'd planned on killing two birds with one stone that night, without even lifting a finger. Once you found your pretty boy dead at Colt's feet, you'd retaliate."

"Too bad your plan backfired. So that's why you killed Colt."

"I had to plug the leak before he came to his senses and told you the truth."

"With a bullet."

He shrugged.

"You threw us off the scent and solidified your position as a good guy by murdering an innocent."

He smiled. "One of my finer moments."

"This is one of mine." I grabbed him by the neck, cutting off his air. "This is what Leon felt when he hanged himself."

I watched his mouth gape and his eyes bulge.

"Darke, we're not finished with him yet," Shehu cautioned when the traitor's face turned purple.

I relented and stepped back. Raine's breath exploded from him.

"Give me the real antidote."

"I can't. I sold it to the highest bidder."

"Who?" My fingers clenched, aching to be wrapped around his windpipe again.

I received no answer.

Shehu swiftly splayed Raine's right hand on the rooftop. His machete swung down with a whistle. It sliced through three fingers, unleashing spurting blood and bloodcurdling screams.

"You won't be needing those. A shaman would never sell out his brothers. You have brought shame to your calling."

He kicked the dismembered digits aside.

"Cutler," Raine said through wheezing breaths. "I sold it to him in return for sanctuary. I'm the only one who discovered an antidote to rival the one he had cooked up in the chem labs."

Cutler had struck once again. And didn't this sound exactly like Taft's excuses for turning tail, selling out Sebastian...and giving up Leon. The only difference was, in the end Taft had died with some semblance of honor. The same would not be said of Raine.

I pressed my boot heel down on Raine's mangled hand, deaf to the sound of his caterwauling. "Why the setup with Leon? Why did you send us to the field hospital?"

Sweat dripped down Raine's face when he glowered up at me. Between panting, pain-filled breaths, he gasped, "It was part of the bargain, another one of Cutler's mind games. He wants to invade your psyches, and since he's not close enough to do it with his usual pharmaceutical methods, he's getting creative." He cradled his stumpy hand to his chest when I let up. "He wants you all broken down before he puts the bullet in your brains, or before you're infected. So you know with your last dying breath he has won. And I had to get you out of the way. You were plastered to Leon's back night and day."

"What about Leon?"

"The CEO wanted to watch him crumble, see his will break, then watch you fall to pieces. Worked, didn't it?"

He had just enough stupid pride to pull off a defiant glare.

Defiance I happily knocked off his face with my fist.

"On the contrary, you worthless piece of shit. Leon's alive, he's well, and he's going to live to tell the truth. Whereas you will not."

Shock overtook his smugness. I paced slowly back and forth, making sure to mash his missing fingers beneath my boots to his long, low whimpers.

"Quite the little acolyte, aren't you?" I teased.

"I prefer entrepreneur."

"How about you interpret this?" I jabbed his unprotected belly, then pulled his wounded hand from his chest. I punched the meaty, bloody mass over and over again while Raine writhed on his back.

"Wait. Wait!" His voice weakening in the wake of my violent outburst, Raine started to cry. He looked to his chieftain.

That time Shehu didn't step in. His lips lifted off his teeth in a feral snarl.

"There's more."

"This better be good. Where the fuck is Cutler, and where is the cure?" I leaned over Raine.

"The unholy trinity, the triumvirate of evil—"

I gripped his neck and snarled in his face. "Fuck off with the word games."

"Dr. Val, Denver, and Cutler are all in Delta."

Fuck. Delta was on a totally different continent, a small island in the northern seas. Formerly known as a big city by the name of London, pre-Purge Delta had been home to places called Piccadilly Circus and Canary Wharf. Now I nearly smiled, listening to Raine sing like the yellow-bellied canary he was.

"When you get to Delta, say hi to my old lover for me."

"Who?"

"Cutler's henchman. Denver."

Denver. The man who told us to locate Raine. The one who knew all about Leon's abduction. Then there was the lovely Doc Val, who had not only brainwashed Liz's father years ago but had masterminded this entire germ warfare against Leon and all the others infected. Raine would be the first to pay for the pain he'd put Leon through, but he wouldn't be the last.

My hands closed around his throat once more. Now it was *his* neck in a noose; one I tightened as rage coursed through me.

He grabbed clumsily at my wrists. He flailed at my feet.

Shehu watched dispassionately for half a minute before lowering into my line of vision. "He has more to say."

I dragged in deep breaths before I broke my hold. "This better be worth it."

I was glad the marks of my strangling fingers bruised Raine's neck. He deserved to die in so many horrific ways I'd lost count.

He could hardly whisper after my assault. "Leon's going to have an InterNations-wide target painted on his back, thanks to his broadcast, once word gets out he's still alive. And it will, now that I've leaked the location of your stronghold."

"What did you just fucking say?" I yanked his head back by his hair.

"You heard me. Cutler wanted you flushed out. I already made sure that's gonna happen. I leaked your location to some anti-rebel groups." Beaten up and on death's door, Raine watched me with the last ounce of glee he'd ever feel. "Turns out you're on a lot of hit lists, Darke."

"Bullshit. Cutler wanted us out in the open. Instead we're going to land on *his* doorstep."

"He will win, you know."

"Too goddamn bad you won't be around to see just how motherfucking wrong you are." I lifted Raine to his feet, delivering him to Shehu's arms. I had all the intel I needed from him. There was only one thing more I wanted. I withdrew my knife from its sheath at my hip.

Finally sensing the end, Raine started sobbing.

"You tried to take my lover from me. For that I will take your heart." I looked to Shehu for permission.

"Yes. It is just."

"Please don't," Raine cried. "I'm sorry! I—"

Raine's wheedling was cut short when the knife pierced his chest. Shehu caught him, silencing his gurgling with a merciful hand suffocating the last breaths. He kissed Raine's temple and laid him down. "I will take care of the remains." The devastation of this night finally showed on my mentor's face in deep lines.

"Will you bury him?" Everyone deserved finality in this war.

"He will receive last rites." Shehu rested his hand on my shoulder. "Godspeed, brave warrior."

CHAPTER EIGHTEEN

Goddamn Raine. If I hadn't already killed him, I'd have ripped his head off and chucked it into the streets of Omega. Leaking the location of the castle to the mob-hungry masses who could find out Leon was still alive. They wouldn't be too keen on letting a human time bomb walk among them.

Sprinting back to my pitiful Cruiser, I continued to grumble to myself. This was bad, very bad. Worse was the state of my vehicle. Thank God it started on the first try. The radiator hissed only a little, and the front fender only fell half off. Shame about the brakes still not working. I could just drive it into the ocean to get it to stop once I returned to the keep, except we'd need the piece of shit along with the other Cruiser to get clear of whatever was headed our way.

I just hoped I got there first.

With one hand, I pinged everyone at the castle from my D-P while I made my way there at breakneck speed. After giving my crew the heads-up, I pounded the gas. If I never saw another particle of sand, I'd give thanks to every god ever known to man.

If we got out of Omega and off of Aafricans without getting caught in the incoming onslaught, I'd make a goddamn shrine.

Stopping was even more fun this time. The seat belt grabbed at my torso. My hands braced against the dashboard. My knees locked in place as I jolted forward and then back. Such a bitch. I didn't bother cutting the engine. The others were already racing across the causeway.

Leon threw our rucksacks in the rear and leaped in beside me. He leaned across the console to kiss me hard and fast on the lips.

His whisper was throaty. "I love you."

I gulped and nodded, then exhaled all the pent-up breath in my lungs. Those three words made everything worth it. I clenched his hand and held it against my heart.

"Raine's dead."

He chewed on his lip for a moment as his eyelids lowered. "Okay."

"I'm not sorry about this one."

"If he'd done the same thing to you, I'd have fucked him up, too."

I reached over to clasp the back of his head, bringing our foreheads together.

Cannon and Nathaniel hopped into the back. Darwin was last in with a curt, "Break it up, boyfriends. Airfield, pronto."

She didn't have to tell me twice.

"Are you sure you're not Liz's long-lost sister?" Cannon asked her.

As the rest slid into the other vehicle—Sebastian, Farrow, Linc, and Liz—I backed up and revved the engine. I could already see bright headlights beaming at us from across the beach.

"This isn't gonna be pretty," I warned.

And it wasn't. The chase back to the Corps Outpost and landing strip found us hurtling forward, swerving side to side. I kept a grip on Leon's leg and one on the steering wheel. The vast flat land was crisscrossed with bouncing lights from other vehicles, Linc's closest behind us. What I wouldn't give for a motherfucking reinforced tank stocked full of RPGs.

At the base, tarmac smoldered as our tires squealed across it. Ten more vehicles skidded behind us. Luckily, we didn't have to bribe, steal, or whore our way onto a plane. One lone Predator—sleek, black, monstrous—was prepped for liftoff, its rotors already turning because now we had allies.

I didn't give a shit if the Cruiser kept driving into the pitch-black night, but I slowed it enough through zigzag maneuvers so we could jump out without getting brained on the pavement.

Pulling Leon by the hand, I grabbed both our duffels and ran toward the underbelly of the beast. I looked behind long enough to watch the others drop and roll from their vehicle and haul ass in our direction.

Darwin shot back, "Watch your heads!"

Because decapitation by rotor would cap my night off just right.

I ducked Leon under my hand and shepherded him inside. The nine of us barely made it to the jump seats and controls before I felt the burst of the thrusters. Gunfire crackled outside.

Taking off from the airfield in a transport made ready for our use was a heady feeling, but it wasn't enough to quell the topsy-turvy of my stomach rolling upside down.

"This is your flight sergeant. We want to welcome you to the unfriendly skies—"

Darwin squawked over the electronics. "Sebastian, I swear to fuck…"

"Feel sick?" Leon asked.

"Not from the flight."

The crack of gunfire continued outside.

"In three, two, one…"

"Delta, here we come!"

I'm going to puke.

A minute later, airborne, Leon pulled a gnarly-looking root thing from his pocket and started peeling it with his knife. When he had a shaving between his fingers, he pushed it at my mouth.

"Here, chew on dis."

"No."

"C'mon. It'll settle your stomach. Just suck it for a second."

I shook my head, trying not to smirk. "That's what you said last time."

"And you liked it."

I squirmed in my seat from immediate arousal overtaking the woozies in my belly. I listened to him hum and peered at him. He grinned, whittling another section away.

"Maybe I'll have to take you over my knee again."

He blinked at me, his wide gold-toned irises shading into wicked darkness. "Maybe you will."

I hummed. "And *you* liked it."

"You'll like dis. It's ginger root." He waved the sliver in front of me again.

"I'm not biting." I glared at the fibrous white flesh.

Leon sat back with a huff. "You're really a stubborn bastard sometimes."

"Yep. But you love me, so that's okay." I opened my mouth, biting the skin of his fingertips when I took the slice of ginger inside.

Maybe it was the look of total satisfaction on his face as I savored the sharp flavor, or maybe it was the ginger working its magic, but I felt almost instantly better. Making Leon feel good swelled me with a new kind of pride, unlike any I'd ever felt before.

Later I heard a muffled one-sided conversation coming from Linc on his D-P. He plugged some coordinates into the mobile device and tucked it into his pocket.

"So you have another airfield lined up in Delta?" I commed Darwin in the cockpit.

"Not exactly."

* * *

Not exactly was right. What a little prankster Darwin was. Our landing strip was an enclosed green space. We narrowly missed trees as we landed, and this time touchdown was so rocky my bones rattled in their joints.

Sebastian's voice came over the comms. "We hope you had a pleasant flight with Rebel Airways United. Please enjoy your stay in Delta T, where you can be sure to get your head fired at and maybe your ass stabbed, too. But not in a good way."

The only things that stopped me from punching Sebastian's grinning face when he took off his helmet were (a) my legs were still too wobbly to move and (b) Darwin walloped him on the back of his head so his smug smile slipped right off his face.

"Where are we headed?" With night fully descended, we quickly changed into full blackout garb.

"It just so happens, Denver gave me Dr. Val's location." Linc tapped his D-P.

"Fucking great. Did you miss the part when I said he was Raine's ex-lover? Raine, the backstabbing murderer who set us up? Raine, who Denver sent us to in the first place?" I wasn't moving out until I had damn good reason to. "How do we know this isn't a setup?"

"It's the only lead we've got."

Where had I heard that before? Oh yeah, when we were led directly to an ambush in Omega.

"Not good enough."

"Fine, Darke. You take point. We check out the location. If you think it's a bullshit mission, we pull out. We all know you can read people, right? Use it on Dr. Val to see if we're getting fucked over." Liz settled the tension between her husband and me.

"Fucking dandy." I motioned everyone to disembark from the Predator.

Out of the park, we moved in silent single file through the Territory streets. The InterNations slogo was everywhere—shining pristine and clean. *Regeneration, Veneration, Salvation.* Flags hung from all the streetlamps. The city was constructed of high buildings in old cold stone and narrow roads. After the colorful, almost festival atmosphere of Omega, Delta felt regimented, locked down.

Once upon a time, this land was a cultured city of theaters and shopping, palaces, and gardens. Home to royalty. Cutler was the new self-imposed InterNations aristocracy. Hopefully he was here, too.

As we approached Sector One, the home to every Territory's government seat, evidence of Delta's Corps influence picked up. We hastened toward Denver's coordinates, the roads more and more heavily occupied by a strong military presence. The tight buildings and low sky, the soldiers on patrol and the halogens lighting up every thoroughfare felt oppressive, almost suffocating. Apart from the park we'd landed in, there were no green spaces or trees, no night sounds from insects, birds, or animals. Just the stomp of boots on pavement and the damp mist of fog.

We climbed up a metal fire escape to avoid the heat in the streets. I led the way, and we came to an out-of-place tree-lined neighborhood of big, sprawling mansions. On the ground, we slipped from tree to tree, finally stopping at a corner across from a once-impressive private residence.

The dilapidated structure had a sloping tiled roof, turrets where stones were missing, and several boarded windows. A high iron fence seemed to be the only barrier until several guards converged at the gated entrance, exchanged words, and went about their patrol around the unkempt grounds.

It was too risky to let Liz shoot out the blazing halos shining down on the place. One whiff of interlopers and our fate would be sealed. I lifted a finger to my lips, raised my fist, and gestured forward as soon as the last guard cleared our sights. They were all swiftly taken out by three teams of two with knives and garrotes. We piled the bodies behind thick shrubbery before performing a final sweep of the perimeter.

Assured it was all clear, we climbed over the fencing and slunk toward the entry as one low-moving mass.

"Are we blowing this thing or what?" Cannon whispered as we gathered in the shadows of the colossal double front doors.

"Save the C-4. I got this." Liz dipped a hand into her pack to find her lock-picking tools.

Leon tried the doorknob fashioned in the shape of a large lion's head. "It's open."

I grabbed his arm, halting him before he stepped across the threshold.

"Think she's expecting us?" Darwin asked as she aimed her weapon inside.

"Didn't someone mention a setup earlier?"

That was me. I pushed the door open. "Step lively and stay close."

Inside the foyer, guns drawn, we tracked across the marble interior. A double staircase of dark wood covered in a bare-threaded runner climbed up three floors. Doors opened in rows to either side of us.

I waved my gun toward the first chamber, from which orange firelight glowed. We moved silently, filling the doorway to find Dr. Val perched on a dainty sofa.

"I've been waiting for you." Her refined accent complemented the antique atmosphere of the manse.

A fire roared from an open hearth set within pink marble surrounds. The rug looked ancient, something made in a distant and long-lost FarAsian country. Paintings covered every square inch of richly papered walls. Only their tattered, curling edges showed the wear and tear of intervening decades.

Likewise, Val looked a little dog-eared, her upper-crust appearance wearing thin. Her elegant up-do allowed a clean shot to her carotid. Her fancy pastel blouse bared enough leeway for a knife through her breastbone. I gripped my gun in a tight hold while Leon, Liz, and all the others prickled beside me.

She laid a bound book down with all the care one would give a newborn child and straightened as if to rise.

"Don't. Fucking. Move," I hashed out.

She stilled into a statue. "By all means." She held her hands in front of her.

Stalking forward, I quickly searched and bound Val. She kept up the regal posture, but there was a cloudy haze surrounding her—some intangible sorrow I couldn't grasp.

"You must be Darke."

"That's exactly who I am." *Or death knocking on your door, if we want to be precise.*

"There's really no need for restraints."

"There's really no need for you to speak unless you're asked a direct question, *unless* you want to talk to the barrel of my gun." Black rage deafened me to all but the roar of blood through my veins. Every atrocity she'd committed against Leon flashed through my mind.

I felt a similar seething anger coming from Liz. A stabbing darkness. This was the woman who had helped create the first Plague, the one who was behind this new malignant manifestation. Dr. Val had scrubbed Liz's father's mind into a blank slate.

The bitch who'd infected Leon again, and again, and again. If I had to kill a woman tonight, so be it. If I could take her to the brink of death, do it over and over again, even better.

With at least twelve guns trained on her, she remained polished and poised, everything I hated about the CO's minions, but behind her wealthy elegance there was sadness. It blanketed her gray eyes. She wore a melancholy smile so small her bright white teeth were barely visible. Underneath all the sheen, she looked far too young to be complicit in such horrific deeds, capable of creating a monster of mass destruction.

I shook my head of sympathetic thoughts. They had no place here. I wanted the cure and Cutler, in that order.

Because Liz was equally incapable of doing anything but paralyzing her twitchy trigger finger, Linc walked forward. He hunkered down.

"You've hurt a lot of people. You understand you will die for that?"

"Yes." She bravely met his gaze.

"We need information from you first."

"I understand."

"Wait!" Farrow sheathed her KA-BAR. "Wait, Lincoln." She touched his shoulder. "We should start with *why* first."

"Shoot first, ask questions later." Cannon banged the door closed, shutting us inside.

"And I'm jes' sure Nathaniel appreciates your single-mindedness, you big bull. However, everyone has a reason." Farrow was not doing herself any favors, getting close to the enemy.

Val looked around the room we filled. We bristled with hostility and more weaponry than could be counted. She glanced at Farrow, who nodded encouragingly.

"This is my family's home from centuries ago." For the first time, Val's voice trembled. "I was far too keen, far too smart, and far too ambitious for my own good. When the CEO first approached me, I was in awe of his brilliant campaign. We'd been minor nobility and lost it all during the uprising—"

"Uprising? The Purge was earth-wide destruction!" I boomed.

"It was…unfortunate. And we fell on misfortune. I was promised my parents' and my sister's safety, and if I didn't comply, he told me they would all die."

"Cutler." I choked on his name.

"Many years ago, yes. I traveled to Beta, where I worked under Dr. Robie Grant."

Liz jerked her gun. Linc gently pushed it to her side and took her in his arms.

"Robie had such vision. Everything he talked about was to better peoples' lives. He was torn in two, just as I was." Her eyes glazed over. "I'm sorry, Lizbeth. I'm so sorry. Robie was a man of honor."

Liz looked coldly in Val's direction.

"What's your first name?" Farrow joined Val on the sofa.

"Elizabeth—Elizabeth Valary. And you are Farrow Monroe?"

I cut in. "You know us all. You have our dossiers?"

"I do. I did. Now all I have are these walls, this home, memories, and heirlooms, and a past filled with arrogant mistakes."

I paced a ring around the rug in front of the fire.

"I'm not afraid to die. I deserve it."

"Fuck!" I punched the wall in front of me, hoping some part of me would bleed. "You created this shit. The new strain that's about to go on the rampage. You infected people!"

"I've repented."

"That's not enough. You better have a fucking good reason why I shouldn't just shoot you now."

"Copy that." Liz slipped away from Linc to stand by my side.

Elizabeth Valary tried to rise to her feet, but Farrow soothed her down. Then she rounded on us. "Maybe you should give her a chance to explain."

"Are you kidding me right now, Farrow? What the hell? She coerced my dad. She infected Leon!" Liz shrieked, at breaking point.

"You know I love you, Lizbeth. But you better back off." The hard glint in Farrow's green eyes reached all the way to her thinned lips.

I forced a shoulder between the two. "Opposite corners. Now." I pointed my weapon at Val. "Talk. And do it quickly unless you want me to set Liz free to go off mission."

She spoke softly but strongly, an all-pervasive air of hopelessness shrouding her. "I can get you to Cutler. Or I could, except

I'm on house arrest. He confiscated all of my laboratory equipment, and of course, there are the guards outside."

"We took care of them." Cold corpses were all they'd be come morning light.

"And there's Leon. How are you feeling?" She struggled to stand with her hands tied behind her back. The first step she took toward him found her face-to-face with the muzzle of my gun.

Throughout all of Dr. Val's interrogation, Leon was stationed behind the thick wall of Nathaniel and Cannon—well guarded—but his face peeked out and his features were sheet-white as he watched his torturer.

"Don't do that," I gritted between my teeth. "You nearly killed him five fucking times! You do not get to do the concerned-doctor act here."

"I was brainwashed, too, with my own formula. I tried to extricate myself long before Cutler made me use the same mind-altering components on Robie." Her head swung to Liz. "You must believe me. I never wanted any of this to happen. None of it. When Leon was brought to me, I was controlled by drugs. I'm just as much an unwilling participant in this as all of you."

"What about my dad?" Liz's voice was a rough whisper.

"I thought it would be better for him. For you and your mother, too. Lizbeth, he was used and used up. Robie was so bright, a truly affectionate man, a remarkable scientist. When he started falling apart...I wanted to give him a clean slate before what we'd done together destroyed his humanity. I wanted to give him his old life back. I was capable of carrying all the blame."

"I don't know what's worse—my father coming clean for the

cause or you not being completely successful in keeping his memories at bay." Liz turned a tearstained face into Linc's shoulder.

"I'm sorry, Liz. All we can do now is focus on the new strain."

"Once again, the one you created." The Smith on my hip was burning a hole in its holster. I wanted to raise it so badly and pull the trigger. Leon's sudden presence at my side calmed my blind fury enough that I had the presence of mind to ask, "What is the plan?"

"Leon is Patient Zero. His body holds all the answers."

He flinched beside me, and I moved in front of him, blocking him from her sight. "No. No more testing on Leon. Try again. If there's not another viable option, you're dead tonight. I promise you that."

She sat forward. "He's the *key* to all this."

"And I'm going to lock your mouth shut with a bullet." My patience wore thin. Leon huddled behind me, shaking. "You've got about two minutes to come up with an answer I like."

"The first Plague strain was reborn from a virus introduced in 1918. We used that superbug as the prototype. Perhaps if I go back and research the first wave…"

"Ticktock. Not enough time." My teeth clicked together.

"Then it's getting to Cutler, all or nothing," she said, squaring off her shoulders. "He has the stashes of the antidote."

"Are you saying you can get us inside? Close enough to kill him, to vaccinate everyone?" Cannon marched toward her, his Glock inches away from her face.

"Yes. If you trust me."

"You'll have to earn that," I snarled.

"I can start right now. I think there's someone else here you should meet."

None too gently, Cannon yanked her up and prodded her forward. We formed a cage around the doctor as she led us down long hallways. Her heels clicked on the marble, her skirt swayed from her hips, but she moved awkwardly with her hands tied behind her back. Pre-Purge artifacts lined the passageways: disintegrating statues, frayed framed Old History artworks nothing like the ones fed through the D-Ps and deemed suitable by the Company. Cobwebs hung from doorways that might not have been opened for decades.

At the end of the very last hall in the vast mansion, she nodded. "In there."

With our sidearms aimed and at the ready, we waited while Linc pushed the door open.

Inside the soundproofed room sat one solitary male figure at a long steel desk topped by D-Ps and snaked by wires.

"Fucking hell," Liz breathed.

"It's you!" Linc burst across the threshold.

CHAPTER NINETEEN

Denver?" Liz strained forward.

He continued to sit with his back facing us, long black hair barely swinging over the chair when he turned his face briefly, unconcernedly. He swiveled away again, raising one hand to silence us, as if we didn't have an armory of weapons trained on the back of his head.

"It seems it's time for me to sign off. I have unexpected visitors tonight. Remember, citizens of the world, victory is within our reach. Love Free or Die!" His tone—heard unmodulated for the first time—was rough and slightly lilting with a foreign accent.

"That's Denver?" Fury mangled my words. I was surprised blood vessels didn't pop in my eyes.

"Holy shit! You're the Voice?" Liz hooted.

"The voice of wisdom and reason." The man stood with a flat stare and gave a slight bow.

"The bastard who had it in for Leon." I growled.

"I know I never had *Monsieur* Cheramie. I'm fairly certain I'd remember that." He appraised Leon with one eyebrow hooked in interest.

I bucked as Cannon's hands suddenly gripped my arms.

"Here we go again," Cannon muttered.

"You set us up at the water tower in Beta. You probably set up his goddamn kidnapping, you know, the one that got him infected by your fucking pal over here."

Denver casually leaned against the desk behind him and crossed one foot over the other. "You don't really get a lot of choice in your evil deeds when you're Cutler's aide-de-camp."

I vaulted past Linc, jerked Denver up, and drove my fist into his face. His body flopped in my arms, and I dropped him like a deadweight.

Cannon came up beside me. "Knocked him out, huh?"

"Yeah." My chest chugged in and out.

"He has a little pent-up anger," Farrow said to Val.

"That's becoming apparent," the doctor replied.

"Feel better?" Leon ran his arm around my waist and looked down at the man I'd just laid out.

I flexed my knuckles. "A bit."

After a couple minutes, Denver came around. Linc helped him to his feet while he brushed out his hair and checked to make sure he still had his weapons on his body, which he didn't.

Meanwhile, I stayed busy emptying all the cartridges from his fancy, custom-made pair of handguns, pocketing the ammo.

Denver hungrily eyed his weaponry, then relaxed his shoulders. "*Daijobu.*"

He was a big guy, at least as tall and as broad as Linc, Cannon, and me. His slanting eyes and unusual skin tone marked him as FarAsian. A bright synthetic tattoo of a dragon slithered up one side of his neck, and his face bore a fine crosshatching of pale scars. Something about him reminded me of the kind of quiet calm before a snake strike.

I didn't trust him for an instant.

Sebastian, on the other hand, eagerly bounded up to him. "Shit. Your setup is righteous." Denver watched as Bas inspected his monitors and couplings. "You know, I might have some ideas about how we can network the Voice faster. You're coaxials are way outdated."

"Who is this kid, and why is he touching my stuff?" Denver hit several buttons that flipped his expanded DPs shut.

"Sorry, man. I get a little crazy when newbies get nosy with my shit, too. No offense." Undaunted, Sebastian grinned at Denver, whose lips curled into a little smirk.

Linc stepped between the two and slapped Denver on the shoulder. "So, the Voice, huh?"

"Ah, *irasshai*, good to see you alive and whole."

Beckoning Dr. Val over, I asked, "I'm assuming there's food and beds."

"Water, too," Denver added with a grin.

"Of course. I'll make sure everyone is well tended." Val headed for the door.

"Farrow, I want her kept detained. She's to have no contact with anyone else inside or outside of this house. And you." I pointed at Sebastian.

"Hmm?" He blinked from his latest detailed inspection. This time it was Denver, not the computers he focused on.

"Fuck off out of here so we can question Denver. Stay with Leon. Keep your hands to yourself."

"Seriously?" Pretty boy punched his hands to his slim hips.

"I wouldn't mind keeping his hands to myself." Denver's gaze traveled up and down Sebastian's body, appraising the lean blond man.

"Out, Bas. Now," Linc ordered.

"Uh…okay." Bas stumbled over his words, pushing his white-blond hair from his deep purple eyes. "C'mon, Leon. Let's get you sorted."

Before leaving, Leon slinked to me. With a half smile, he looped his hands around my neck. "You could try bein' a little less—"

"Possessive?" I ran one palm over his firm ass. "Not a chance."

He left, thoroughly pleased.

Left in the room were Cannon, Linc, Nate, Denver, and me. I swung into a chair and raised one of my guns on the Voice. "Start talking. Or start running. Your choice."

All air of familiarity and friendship fled when Cannon and Linc barred the door.

"You don't want a drink first?" Not a single muscle moved on Denver's scarred face.

"We don't need your type of hospitality, not when it usually comes with one of our own being taken."

"He's a hostile one," Denver said as he sat down across from me.

There wasn't a goddamn twitch or tell on the man. His emotional reading flatlined.

Linc stalked toward him. "Darke's not the only one. You captured Liz!"

"Then I saved her for you."

"That's goddamn debatable."

"Semantics, my man, and you know we speak a different language."

"Yes, and yours is all about Cutler politics." Nathaniel's voice cut like a sharp blade through all the others.

"Nice to meet you, too, Nathaniel Rice. You should hear your father speak about you."

Without another word, Nathaniel lashed the butt of his Glock across Denver's cheek.

Denver spat a dark red stain on the floor. "*Y'all* better hope I'm not infected."

"You better goddamn hope you can get us to the cure." I moved behind him and grabbed a chunk of his hair. "You sent us to Omega. You set us onto Raine. Just whose fucking side are you on?" I shouted in his face.

"What are you talking about? What about Raine?" A flicker of emotion crossed his indecipherable eyes. "He was working on the antidote, and he was closer to solving it than anyone else. He had the resources to keep you safe."

"Until he sold us out."

"To who?"

"Who the fuck do you think?" I rasped.

Denver stared at the twins. "Daddy Dearest."

"That's right. So you expect us to believe you've switched sides, too? The bad bodyguard going clean for the good of all mankind?" I laughed bitterly. "I don't think so."

"Raine was my lover many years ago. I never made him for a rat." There was finally a chink in his stoic armor, revealing the depths to which he felt Raine's betrayal.

"Raine said to tell you good-bye when I stabbed him through the heart." Cruelty bred cruelty. In this instance, I wasn't sorry.

I dropped back as Denver's head fell from my grasp.

"That is not an honorable death."

"No, it wasn't. He was fortunate to get an honorable burial."

"That is something to be thankful for."

Linc squatted in front of Denver. "You've double-crossed us so many times I don't even know where the line is with you anymore."

"I have been burdened under the fealty of ownership just as you've been buried beneath the bond of blood. Our deeds and actions are not always just."

"You're English is getting better, old *tomodachi*," Linc said.

"Your Japanese still sucks," Denver returned.

"Yeah, and just because you're the Voice doesn't mean I trust you." I interrupted their buddy-buddy moment with the barrel of my Smith & Wesson.

"I am not surprised," Denver said.

"I take it you still have access to our father." Linc began pacing while Cannon glowered in our general direction.

"I am his most trusted guard."

"You have access to the Quad?" Linc asked.

"Yes. In fact, I'm expected back later, along with my weapons."

"No," I said. "How do we know he's not going to turn us in?"

Rising from his seat, Denver padded softly around, ignoring the pistols tracking his every move. "You don't."

"You're not helping your situation here, Den," Linc cautioned him.

"I am with Cutler every day. Every moment I'm free, I'm here, with Val. There's a reason we're together in this. All of us, at the end. To bring the CEO down. I'm risking my life to start a new one. A life where I'm not forced to bow down and make innocent people bleed. There can be only one end to this."

"Cutler's," I said.

Denver nodded. "Besides, do you honestly think I like being called *the Voice*?"

"It is a pretty crap name," Nathaniel allowed. "And you are a damn good hacker."

"I used your schematics."

Nate barked a loud laugh.

"My weapons, if I may, Darke."

I reluctantly handed them over, watching while he reloaded.

"You will get us inside, pronto," Linc said. "And we need to know every move from here to FarAsian Nu that he's planning." Clasping Denver on the shoulder, Linc ushered him to the door.

"I'll be in touch tomorrow."

The bastard had just earned his life back.

Sebastian was waiting outside the doors when we emerged.

"Where's Leon?" I growled at him. Screw manners. It'd taken every last reserve of civility to not go for Denver's throat.

"Upstairs. Liz's watching him." He yawned.

I patted him on the shoulder. "Thanks, Bas."

He smiled, but his attention was on someone else. I glanced around to see Denver returning his look.

Oh, Jesus.

Cannon dragged me to the opposite side of the hallway with him and Nathaniel to lay down a few plans for the next day. All the while I overheard Denver speaking to a very interested Sebastian. Denver towered over the paler man, who turned his face up as if he were catching the last rays of the sun. When Sebastian's fingers ghosted over the discolored bruise on Denver's cheek, Denver's eyelids slid closed.

I wondered if that's how I'd looked the night of Cannon and Nathaniel's handfasting, the first time Leon had touched me. Perhaps Denver deserved some leeway. Or perhaps I'd knock his teeth loose tomorrow.

Sebastian led him away, ostensibly to care for his swollen cheek and possibly other swollen things by the looks of it. I wanted to intervene, but it wasn't my place. Linc trusted the man. And after the shit Tate put Sebastian through, he wasn't as naive as he used to be.

"They looked cozy," Nathaniel said.

"You know sexy gearhead talk gets me off, too, Blondie."

One good thing came of it: With Linc heading away, Cannon and Nathaniel saying their good nights, and Sebastian otherwise occupied, I could be sure there wouldn't be any interruptions between Leon and me. I'd hardly had a chance to talk to him, let alone hold him since Raine had done a runner in Omega.

Unfortunately, I spent what felt like an hour lost in the maze-like house of high walls, tall windows, and Old History furniture. The place was fascinating, a time capsule filled with relics dating as far back as the mid-1800s, near as I could tell.

Eventually, I turned the corner in one of the sloping upstairs hallways to come across Liz leaning opposite a closed doorway. "Sebastian said I'd find you here."

She stretched her arms above her head, pursing her lips around a yawn. We were all running on empty, but still running. "We're on rotation. Me, then Darwin, then Cannon. In case anyone comes after Leon."

So they could each have some downtime with their lover while they protected us.

I swallowed roughly. "What about the house?"

"Sorted."

"Val and Denver?"

"Oh, I think the Monroe kids got it under control."

"You caught that already?" No need to ask which particular asset Sebastian was guarding while his sister probably tucked Elizabeth Valary into bed.

"I have a nose for these things."

"Just not when it comes to yourself." I tweaked her nose until she slapped my hand away.

"I take offense to that. It didn't take me that long to figure my head out when it came to Linc."

"And your heart."

Her smile skipped away. She reached for my hand and brought it up to her chest, where she held it. "We were lucky, me and Linc.

Funny to think that now, when I was pretty sure one or both of us would…die in Beta." She let me go to turn her head aside, but I knew what she was hiding, the brightness of tears filling her eyes.

"I'm sorry," she said.

"Maybe I should—"

"Go. Be with Leon." She knocked her shoulder against mine. "We'll keep you safe. And whatever Leon tells you, just remember how much he loves you, Darke."

"Are you okay?"

"Oh sure. You know me. I live for the doom and gloom."

I took Liz in my arms. She always appeared so in control and unaffected. It was only while holding her that I realized how much she took on, and into herself, without letting it show.

"Darwin is relieving you soon?"

"One hour."

"And Linc's waiting for you?" I watched her check the ammo in her gun belt.

"Sure as the cock crows."

"You're a good woman, Liz Grant."

"And you're a damn good man, Darke. Now, go be with yours before I get weepy and shit because Cannon would love hearing all about that in the morning."

* * *

In the bedroom, Leon lay curled on his side facing the opposite wall. One candle glowed, illuminating a small space simply furnished with a high bed, a washstand, and a rolltop desk with a chair.

I shed my weapons and clothes, placing one of my Smiths near where I'd sleep. I dipped my hands into the warm water of the washbasin and cupped them over my face, rinsing off the day's travel-weary grit.

Sliding behind Leon, I let out a low moan. He was naked, his skin silky. My hand moved down to find the tat on his groin by memory. He stirred and sighed my name.

Nuzzling the nape of his neck, I placed a kiss on his shoulder. "Hey, angel."

He turned in to me and pushed one of his thighs between mine. His slow, sensual kiss made me scoop him closer. Tilting his face, I lashed my tongue into the wet heat of his mouth. He bit my bottom lip and tugged. That pull shimmied all the way to my stiff cock. With his fingers clasping my neck, he licked my top lip and the seam between before I took control of the passionate tryst of our tongues.

I rubbed my thumb over his mouth after he slipped his lips from mine. "Did you eat?"

"Yeah. Did you?"

"Yes," I lied.

"Bullshit. Just 'cause you're the man with emo abilities doesn't mean I can't tell when you're lyin.'"

I went back to trailing kisses over his neck and jawline. I'd eat tomorrow or the next day. Food wasn't a high priority at the moment.

He pressed me away. "At least lemme take a look at the moko."

I lay on my back while he retrieved the salve. He kneeled beside me, his thighs open. The deep pink column of his delicious cock rose hard and upright. He tended my moko with gentle sweeps of a warm damp cloth while I brushed the backs of my fingers across his soft sac. He shivered and squirmed. My fingertips danced behind, finding and flirting with his opening. His mouth parted on a gasp.

I took his length in a tight fist and slowly began to stroke it. Leon grasped my shoulders. "That ain't helpin'."

"Ain't it?"

"I gotta tell you somethin'." He wrung the washcloth in his hands, peering at me from beneath his eyelashes. "Will you hold me?"

Without a word, I took the cloth from him and tossed it on the floor with a wet slap. I gathered him to my side as I lay down and cupped his face to my chest, sifting my fingers through his hair.

Sadness flowed from him, enshrouding us both.

"It's going to happen in seventy-two hours, *cher*."

"No, it's not."

"You can't will it so. 'Sides, we already had dis conversation." His fist hit my ribs.

"I'm not willing it. I'm going to make sure you're free of this fucking infection." My voice rose above his.

"Darke. I love you. I want to stay with you. I've tried." He propped himself up, his face ravaged by emotion. "It's August sixteenth in three days."

I kissed my way to his mouth. "I'm well aware of the date."

He wrenched free. "I don' want you near me when it happens. The chance of you being infected..."

A groan tore from me. "I am not going anywhere, *god-fucking-dammit*!"

"Promise me, *cher*."

"I can't do that. You can't leave me. No one's gonna make me walk away. Not even you."

His hands caressed my face. "Liz will take the kill shot on me if the virus goes live. She agreed," he whispered.

That was why Liz had told me I needed to hear him out, why she was drowning in misery. My heart dove down to my stomach. I pulled Leon beneath me where he couldn't get free. I kissed him until he couldn't talk anymore.

His lips moved to my ear. "She'll make it clean. Dis is the only way."

"Don't you ask me to give you up." My voice broke.

"Don't keep my ghost around when I'm gone, *cher*."

I was undone by huge, terrifying sobs. My body racked against Leon's. He comforted me, the stronger man in this. Soon all that was left was a dry tightness in my throat and his body surrounding me, awakening mine.

"I want you to make love to me," I husked.

"What?"

I curved my arms around him to lick a path to the shell of his ear. "I want you all the way inside of me."

He moaned. "But the virus? What if I'm not safe?"

I cut him off with a chuckle. "Baby, you were never safe for me." I suckled his earlobe between my lips.

He shoved me back with his hands on my chest. "I'm serious."

"So am I." I gripped his arms. "You haven't had any symptoms.

And I don't care anymore. I don't care about anything but you. I already told you if you die, I do, too."

Leon suddenly melted against me with a cry of need. I felt the hot stab of his rigid length against my thigh, an echoing spear of need making my cock stretch upward.

He bit and lapped at my neck, growling and wild. "We do dis my way." He thrust against me.

I heard a low whimper, after a moment realizing the unlikely sound of deep-rooted desperation came from me. I nodded.

"So I can suck you until you come. Den fuck you until you come again."

"Please, angel, yes."

Leon pulled the sheet down my legs, and his mouth followed. He sucked my inner thighs and lapped the sensitive backs of my knees. His hands drifted to my abs, feeling each divide of flesh with fingers that stoked my desire in their wake. Come dripped from the slit of my cock—clear trails ribboning down my engorged shaft.

"Stand up." He urged me to the floor, taking a place on his knees before me.

I pulled on his hair before he could draw my cock into his mouth. "I don't want you down there."

"Too bad. My way tonight." He knelt up to lick me with the tip of his tongue. His determination to have me the way he wanted trumped everything that sought to tear us apart.

His hardness pressed against my leg when he sucked me to the back of his throat. The wide oval of his mouth stretched into a smile when I grunted his name. Pulling my cock down with the tight hold of his lips, he sat on his heels. In that position, his throat opened. My entire thick length tunneled into a wet constriction that made me shake from head to toe.

I yanked back. Thrust back in. I listened to him moan and suck. Before I lost all control and became a savage, insane beast of pure fucking, I pulled out.

"You said I could eat your come." His hoarse voice and swollen lips tipped me over the edge.

Without responding, I tossed him onto the bed. I couldn't articulate anything but grunts at that point. I backed my cock up to his face as he lay beneath me, then grasped his thighs and split them wide. My mouth was swallowing him before he had a chance to yelp.

When Leon did yelp, it was after I was so deep inside his mouth, the noise traveled up to my tightening balls. Circling my hand beneath his balls, I cupped everything, all of him in one fist. As I feasted my face on Leon's dick, he responded in kind with a frenzy of licking all over my cock.

He massaged my balls while slurping me down. Saliva and pre-ejaculate dampened my groin. I started pumping my hips. He spread my ass with both hands. My dick deep in his throat, I came in shuddering, yelling, yowling pulses the moment he circled my ring with a slick fingertip.

Leon pushed me off of him. His hard cock waved in my face before he flipped me over to my belly. I balled the sheets in my hands and rose up to my knees, giving him absolutely full fucking access to my ass. Feeling the hot wash of his breath against my backside, I laughed and dropped down.

His fingers raked along my hips. "Get back up here."

"You wanna shove your face in my ass, angel?"

"Now," he demanded.

Swinging my head back, I saw Leon focused on my cock, balls, and ass. I drew up and bent over, pulling my cheeks apart. Positioned for his pleasure, I was already on the brink of coming a second time.

His hands skimmed down my back. His lips, too. I arched and groaned. I spread my legs wide, lifting my ass the second his tongue touched the top of my divide. He kissed and sucked and gripped me open. He bit me. I watched as long as I could, stretched back, as his long fingers and pink mouth moved against my flexed muscles and ebony skin. When he licked my hole, I pulled a pillow to my face, hunkering down, humping my lower half up for more.

Oh Christ, did he give more. I bucked my ass against his face and then pumped my hips into thin air. His wiggling tongue lunged so hard, I shouted. Then he added fingers—three or four—coated in lubricant. He laughed like I'd never heard him before, splicing those fingers open and pushing on my inner glans.

"You dirty little bitch." I gnashed when he palpated my nut. My cock stretched and strained to be touched. A funnel of clear fluid fell from the tip to the mattress.

"Who's my little bitch now?" He leaned low and grabbed my balls with his teeth, almost chewing on them.

His words, his fingers, his mouth were so fucking crazy wild hot, I almost shot my load.

"Where are the condoms?"

"Huh?" I could barely function. I just wanted him in me.

"Rubbers."

I heard him moving off the bed, rummaging in my pack. "Don't need 'em."

"Like hell we don't." He returned with a fistful. "They're more important now than ever."

I watched him wrap from tip to base. As I waited for him to take me, all the love I felt for him pulsed through me.

I shuddered when Leon moved between my legs. His hands swept down my back, to my thighs, which he prodded farther apart.

Leaning over me, the tip of his cock brushing my hole, he said, "*Mais*, I don' wanna hurt you."

Reaching around, I slid him up and down over my bud. I'd never felt so open. "You won't."

He took his time, inching in, sliding out, adding more lube.

His balls finally slapped my taint and I shoved back.

Leon held on to my shoulders, his long thrusts making me dizzy. No one had been inside me for so long. No one had ever been better.

"Is dis good?" He conquered me with another thrust.

When I managed to lift my head, Leon shined with triumph, taking me, having me. He grinned with exultation, with ecstasy, with sheer eroticism that thundered right down to my balls.

We'd fought so hard for each other.

"Baby. Angel…"

He thrust again. *"Bien?"*

"Fuck yes. So fucking *bien*. I can't…"

My breath caught and held. That was all Leon needed to hear. Rough, hard, no-holds-barred sex tore yells from my throat and come from my cock within writhing, loud, hungry minutes.

His thickness hugged by my clasping channel, I fell to the bed. "Flip over."

I rolled to my back and took him inside again. He lifted on top of me, pinning me down with my hands in his. His swiveling, plunging cock never let up. He was the most amazing lover I'd ever had. My incredible love.

I kissed his lips and his neck. I bowed up to scrape my teeth across his nipples. I roused again, my dick so hard between our slamming pelvises, I shivered.

I was sure I could save him. He was certain this was the end. Our gazes searched into the other, and we never lost contact through his long, powerful thrusts. The intensity was almost too much to bear, but nothing in my life had ever felt so good. It was close to painful. Ecstasy soared through me as he stretched me, took me, owned me from the inside out.

My feet rode along the backs of his legs when I lifted my thighs around him. Sweat and come slipped between us with every deep pump of his hot cock. He took my hands in his, twining our fingers together.

Leon kissed me through heated, panting breaths and little moans of, "I love you. *Je t'aime toujours.*"

When he climaxed, I etched the thousand expressions crossing his face into my mind. I held his hair back and kissed the column of his neck.

"My God. You are so beautiful, Leon. So beautiful."

After, he lay across me, motionless but for the rise and fall of his chest as he took in deep drafts of breath.

"You are so beautiful," I said again. I'd say it forever.

Shimmying so his legs parted over mine, he moaned.

His eyes met mine, dazzling in a moment of serenity before they shaded with the hurt we both carried. There were no more words to say and only one way to connect where we couldn't be ripped asunder. We lay side-by-side and face-to-face, holding each other. I moved so tenderly inside Leon. I knew the day that would never end would ultimately bring morning too fast.

And too few days left after that.

Another orgasm broke over me while my heart tore apart.

CHAPTER TWENTY

Time moved at an alarming rate from that point forward.

On the afternoon of August 14, 2071, we all gathered around the large front room of Val's mansion. We checked our weapons once, twice, three times. We scoured over maps on our D-Ps, studying Delta's Quadrangle, looking for ways in while waiting for Denver's latest incoming.

We discussed how to get the cure from Cutler, who would take him out. Tomorrow night was go-time. That afternoon, everyone grew increasingly antsy but tried to hold it together.

On the periphery of my vision, sudden movement caught my attention. Leon had been standing by the grand fireplace, talking to Sebastian. As I watched, he swayed in slow motion, left then right, before his legs buckled, crumpling beneath him to the floor. Bas caught him before he landed. I rushed to Leon, taking his weight in my arms.

Laying him on the sofa quickly vacated, I inspected him. He was out cold. His eyes closed, skin pale and clammy, respiration a little haywire. It reminded me of the way he'd looked after we cut him down from the rope.

"What the fuck's going on?" I barked at Doc Val.

She crouched beside him, scanning him with her D-P.

"It could just be exhaustion." Farrow swept the hair off his brow.

I wished I could believe that, but one glance at Val and her tense face put an end to that notion.

"His pulse is reedy but stable," Val said. "Good O2 levels. No outward presentation of the infection."

"Yet. You mean yet." I grabbed her wrist in a punishing hold.

She didn't try to pull away from me, which was a good thing. I was liable to snap her bones in half. "All the data I researched on the virus and the special strain injected in Leon supports what CEO Cutler has told you. His infection will not become live until tomorrow, midnight. I specifically engineered it that way."

"Can it be triggered any other way?"

She looked away from me.

"Answer me, goddammit!"

"No. There was no one else working on this. Cutler may be a political genius—"

"Tyrant," Cannon spit out.

"But his is not a scientific mind. He could never have advanced the infection that far without my aid."

"Well, thank our lucky fucking stars for that." I released her to clasp both of Leon's hands. "So now what?"

"We monitor him. This is probably a side effect of the virus filtering into his body."

I bowed over him, breathing slowly to hold my sobs deep inside my chest. "Please—" I broke off. I kissed each of his fingers, both of his palms. He didn't respond. "Please tell me he's going to wake up again."

"Oh my God," Liz whispered.

"I can't say for certain, Darke. I'm—"

I reared up. "Don't you fucking say you're sorry! Don't you dare. If you value your life at all, you will shut the hell up and get away from me right…fucking…now."

Farrow and Cannon pulled Val away. I hunched over Leon, covering him.

"If I can say one thing?" Dr. Val asked.

I nodded my assent.

"I'd like to monitor his vitals on the hour."

I must've growled or something because she stood straighter, holding her D-P with all the medical modules out to me.

"Or you can do it. I'll show you how. I also think it might be a good idea to quarantine Leon. You won't want to risk anyone else's lives."

Lots of grumbles resounded, but I tucked Leon against my chest and stood. "Fine. And I'll be quarantined with him in our room."

"And I'll be taking watch in the hall," Liz said.

"So will I," Linc joined in.

"And Blondie and me," Cannon volunteered.

Sebastian rose last to stand beside the others.

They all followed me out the door with my precious cargo. I grabbed Val's D-P on the way. I thought my knees would buckle like Leon's had, not because of his slender form in my arms but from the family surrounding me. The friends who didn't give a shit about any infection. The people who would always fight for my man.

* * *

The intervening hours were interminable but not wasted. I cherished every moment with Leon throughout the night and into the next day, even though he never so much as moved. His stillness terrified me. In the absence of anything else, I tried willing him awake, willing him as I said I wouldn't. I begged him to open his eyes. He never did.

Talking to him in a low voice, I took those hours to tell him all the unimportant little things about me that I could think of—stupid shit I'd have died of embarrassment over had he been awake and listening. That my favorite color was gold because it reminded me of the glinting specks in his eyes. How I wished he'd wear those godforsaken threadbare cutoffs for me alone. That I wished I could sing like my mother had or play saxophone like my father, simply so I could put to music the way he made me feel so alive. That he was so sexy, he made me speechless; that he was so loving to those who'd earned his loyalty, I was humbled.

I lay next to him, placing his head in the crook of my shoulder, while I whispered the most important things to him. How I'd spent almost every night since I first met him dreaming about him. How he enthralled me with his courage and his heart and his soul. That his desire to look out for me hit me as hard as his desire to be with me as my lover.

I held his hands, caressed his face, cooled his skin. I even managed to catch some shut-eye when sheer exhaustion snuck up on me and pulled me under.

A soft knock on the door woke me to instant alertness. I checked on Leon. Still unconscious. Pulling on a pair of pants, I edged the door open to find Cannon pacing outside.

I left the door ajar and joined him.

"Cutler knows we're here."

"Here in Delta or here with Val?"

"Delta." He stopped marching and hauled back to punch the wall. Eyeing the cracked door, he halted his fist just before he made contact.

I bit out a harsh curse. "Do you think Denver—?"

"No."

"Val?"

"No. I don't. You know I don't trust most people as far as I can fucking throw them, but I got a feeling about them, Darke. Besides, there are eyes and ears everywhere." He backed up against the opposite wall. "There's more. Lots of shit's going down in Delta."

"Care to elaborate?" Like I really wanted to know. He rubbed a hand over his jaw. "Other names have been released. There are about twenty more right here in Delta getting ready to unleash the virus tonight at midnight. Surprise."

"He's backed us into a corner." I didn't show Cannon's restraint, slamming my fist into the wall.

"It's bad, man. Everywhere. Riots in the last CO-held Territories. Names and faces of all the infected on the promos. Cutler says he'll inoculate every citizen who turns in a rebel. And vaxes for the whole extended family of the person who captures the biggest rebel crew."

"That would be us." The hope for a cure had just turned into a tool to defeat the Revolution—and us. Despair roiled all the way down to my stomach. I thought I'd retch all over the carpet. I must've looked like it, too, because Cannon took a step toward me. I held it in one more time, warding him off with my hands raised. "You shouldn't come any closer, just in case."

"As if I give a fuck about that bullshit. You're gonna make it. So is Leon."

I tried to believe his confident words, the same ones I'd been repeating to Leon. "It's at critical mass now."

"Yep."

"What time is it?" I asked.

"Sixteen hundred hours."

"Eight more to go. Any word from Denver?"

Cannon crossed his arms over his chest. "Nope."

"I need to know as soon as he makes contact." I finally straightened, having conquered the churning nausea in my gut.

"How's he doing?" He nodded toward the bedroom.

"Same."

"Darke—"

"Don't…" I met his gaze. "Man to man, don't feed me any lines right now. Just tell me when we get word from Denver so I can be ready to move out."

He pushed out his fist and then opened his fingers at the last moment. Our hands met with a loud clap.

"Beb?" A guttural voice escaped from the bedroom. Leon's voice.

A wide grin bloomed across Cannon's face as he grabbed my shoulder and pushed me inside.

Leon sat in the middle of the bed. I crawled up in front of him, taking his lips in a ferocious kiss that seared me to my soul. He leaned back with a gasp.

"What? You act like you haven't seen me in days." Confusion and disorientation wafted from him in thick clouds.

I didn't answer. Instead, I placed my hands on the sides of his face and kissed him more slowly, letting my tongue linger against his inside the wet heat of his mouth. Leon awakened completely. He grasped the back of my head, returning my kisses. On his knees, he rubbed against me, all that sleek tawny skin against my steel-hard muscles. Blinking, he pulled his lips from mine with a soft suck. He was seemingly unaffected by whatever had laid him unconscious for more than twenty-four hours, as if he'd just woken from a long, restful sleep.

I remembered then stories of people who were at death's door experiencing a few last golden hours of vitality. I swallowed through the stone in my throat, whispering nonsense in between kisses I placed on his shoulders up to his cheeks.

"What happened?"

"You passed out downstairs. Almost twenty-four hours ago. Val thought it best to quarantine you. I stayed."

"You're just determined to get yourself killed." His fingers trailed to the seat of my pants and he squeezed my ass. "Bad timing, eh? *Mais* yeah, now I got you to myself." He peeked at me through the tumble of hair, licking his bottom lip.

"We're headed to Company Headquarters as soon as the sun sets."

"A couple more hours. I'll take 'em." Sliding his hands inside my pants, he sent his fingers down my cleft.

"Leon…" I groaned.

"*Shh*. I already know every'ting you wanna tell me."

"Not everything." I disengaged his hands and eased off the bed.

His head tilted to the side. "You gave me a bath while I was out of it."

"Yeah." I smiled. Heat surfaced on the skin of my chest and face.

"*Hmm*. What else? Oh, you love me."

"Yes, I love you, Leon." My heart began to pound, and I returned to him after shedding my pants. "I love you," I murmured against his mouth.

Those final hours with him awake were treasures. Talking, savoring soft touches, making the gentlest love…before it became more and more difficult to ignore the enormity of what might transpire.

In the end, we twined around each other and held on through the pain of knowing we'd be parted soon. Possibly forever.

We were both aware of the clock counting down. The moment daylight turned to dusk, Liz peered inside.

"Denver's ready. We've got an in."

"Give me ten."

I dressed in black from head to toe. Leon handed me my guns.

"You take one." I laid the butt of a Smith & Wesson into his hand. "It's better than your Colt. We'll get you a proper firearm when this is over."

"I can't. I'm not…" He holstered the weapon at my side. "I'm not a killer. Even if they're makin' me one."

I draped my arms around him, hating the armor and artillery between us. "No, you're not. You are a survivor. Val is staying with you. She's the most capable of—"

"Taking care of me?"

"Give me two hours, angel, and I'll be back."

He nodded without saying a word.

I pushed him against the wall. "Just need you to be sure." I covered his mouth with mine. "This beats for you." I pulled his hand to my heart. "This will die without you. I love you."

"*Je t'aime.*" His eyelashes lowered over his eyes.

Twisting my fingers in his hair, I guided his head up. "And I need you to know, this is not good-bye. It's not the end. We are not finished." Every word I said cracked my voice.

"*Bien sur.*" Reaching up, he fervently kissed me. "It's not good-bye. Just *à tout à l'heure.*"

Leaving him was the hardest thing I'd ever done. As my boots hit the top of the stairs, I turned back. He watched from the hall, trying to hide the haunted look in his eyes.

No more words were said. Nothing else was possible. We had covered every contingency. All that was left was winning his life back.

* * *

We performed our good-luck rituals before heading out of the mansion. Liz double- and triple-checked her Eagles. Linc patted a small pocket where he had something secret tucked away. Cannon rubbed his wedding band around his finger three times while Nathaniel slipped his fingers along the suede cuff of his wrist. It was all meant to ward off bad omens that could fuck with our mission. We'd need all the luck we could get.

I closed my eyes. All I thought about was Leon, briefly kissing my fingertips and bringing them to my heart. Then I centered myself as the focal point for the feelings of my comrades, getting a read on each and every one of them. This group was tight. Everyone was solid, as determined as me.

On the way into city center and the Quadrangle, we skirted every possible tracking device. The night was as black as soot, a dusting of Delta's permanent cloud cover keeping the moon under wraps. If our faces were captured on one of the many cameras lining the streets, our mission would be dead in the water.

Unrest was alive and well in the streets of S-2 and S-1. Unlike several days ago, the civilian presence was as strong as that of the Corps soldiers. We remained in the cover of blackness, winding around the high walls to a section that faced the unpopulated side of Delta. Denver assured us he'd make sure this particular piece of the Quad wall was unmanned, that the razor wire on top would be cut to provide an opening, that the wire itself would be shorted out from its electrical current.

Such assurances meant little to me.

We scaled the four-meter-high defensive barricade on ropes hung from grappling hooks easily enough, but time was already whittling away too fast. I was the last one through the small aperture in the circular death trap of barbed wire. I skimmed down the opposite side, landing soundlessly on my feet.

With silent motions, Linc herded us along the interior wall toward CO HQ. We listened to the growing disturbance coming from outside the Quad, waiting for entry into Company Headquarters. The service entrance steel doors we huddled against wouldn't budge unless seriously blown up, or if Denver followed through with his promises to deliver us straight to Cutler in his eagle's nest.

During the minutes that elapsed, we tested out comms links to one another and quadruple-checked our rounds. Even though I wanted to focus solely on getting the cure for Leon and getting the hell out—regardless of anyone else's fate—I couldn't forget my comrades. The mule-headed idiots who had pledged their lives and love and honor to save Leon.

The Revolution had brought us to this point. I scanned the faces of Liz and Linc, Nathaniel and Cannon, Darwin, then lastly Sebastian and Farrow. They were cool and calm, willing to risk their lives to save Leon's, ready to die in the fight for freedom.

"For Leon, my man." Cannon held out his fist. I hit it with my own.

Similar strong words echoed all around. Their conviction instilled new confidence in me.

The door opened without a sound. Denver, his hair in a long braid, stood inside the black marble corridor. He waved us in. Shivers of excitement raced up my spine, replacing the chills of dread. Once we were inside, we all locked our guns on Denver.

He huffed a dry laugh, swinging the door shut behind us. "You all have trust issues."

"Hardly surprising given your track record." Liz lowered her weapon only when he raised his hands to show they were empty, not that he couldn't go for the wicked-looking blade glinting along his thigh.

Denver scanned his thumbprint on a wall module and moved us into an empty room.

"We wait here," he said. "Cutler's surrounded by advisers and para at the moment. Too many threats."

"Then he better be quick about it," I hissed. "I'm not a very patient man tonight."

"I could tell you a story to pass the time." Denver lounged against a long table.

"Not interested."

"Not a man of curiosity, warrior Darke? But I find you very curious."

"I'm a killer." I flickered back to what Leon had said. I *was* a killer. Tonight I would be again, asking very few questions, if any.

"I'm interested." Sebastian sidled up to him.

"Why don't you just blow him while you're at it, baby boy?" Liz wryly intoned.

Sebastian had changed during the course of our mission. Where before he would've blushed and stammered, now he merely rolled his eyes.

Denver's dark eyes widened at the suggestion. He ran the backs of his fingers down Sebastian's arm. "*Hmm*, sweet one. For you I will tell the tale of how I came to be here."

"How the fuck long is this gonna take?" My nerves started jangling all around.

"Until we get to the end, yours being the end of the CEO."

"You could just KO him again," Cannon suggested.

Ignoring Cannon, Denver continued. "I used to be just like your Leon, Darke." His black gaze drilled into me. "A rent boy in Nu Territory, many years ago. There was one problem: In addition to selling my ass to the highest bidder, my pimp whored me out for cutting games. He assured all my johns I enjoyed getting sliced, even got off on it. So this happened." He shifted his face toward the light of a halo, and his ghostly scars shimmered.

"I didn't have a warrior or friends to take me away from the street corners, where men practically stripped me bare in public so they could ram their cocks up my ass after they added their notch on my face. That was the real game to them. These scars are how many times I was used against my will simply so I could eat one meal a day and perhaps sleep on a mattress instead of a piece of pavement a few nights a week."

His story made me feel sick. Cold waves of horror from everyone else drowned me.

"One day, Cutler rescued me. He was on a political junket in Nu. Of course, he meant only to make a public spectacle of the man reaming my ass out in the open, yet he took me under his wing. He didn't use me, not that way. Not ever, not to this day.

He merely made sure I cleaned up after him, kept the deviant homosexuals at bay, and used my rage for his betterment—well out of the public eye."

"Christ Almighty, Denver. I never knew." Linc stared at the man.

"Why would you? I am simply your father's bodyguard." Denver smiled. "I do appreciate the times you have spoken to me in the language of my people, though."

"What about the tats?" Sebastian asked in a soft voice, his fingertip trailing along Denver's neck.

"The dragon tattoo was so I could rise up one day and tear apart those who used me. It's taken ten years of planning to get to this point. Trust me"—his hard gaze never wavered—"I killed the rest of them. Over the years, as silent as a reaper. I made sure they all knew why before I slit their throats wide open. Cutler exploited me in a different way. Though he was my savior, he was also my captor. You are not the only people who seek revenge. I will make sure this is seen out."

"What did he do to you?" I asked.

"It's not what he did, but what he made *me* do." Denver focused on Sebastian, carefully caressing his cheek and forehead as if marveling at the unmarred beauty of him. His lips quirked when he said, "Ah, and Cutler did change my name. He got tired of pronouncing my given name, Deyama."

"Deyama?" I held out my hand. "A pleasure to meet a fellow rebel."

Silence followed our handshake until Sebastian pulled that darkly handsome, scarred face into a kiss. Denver lifted Sebastian to him, winding his hand down his back, following every passionate move of his mouth.

They were interrupted by the sound of a D-P.

Breaking free of the blazing kiss, Denver spoke into his mouthpiece. "What?" He held up a hand so we would be silent. "He's what?" His mouth tensed. "Got it."

He signed off and turned to address us. "Civilians are inside the Quad. Cutler let them in. They know rebels are here. They know it's you. Cutler's making a break for it."

That was our go.

When we burst from HQ's main doors, the formerly quiet Quad was a wall-to-wall, foaming-at-the-mouth insurrection. Black ops or not, there was no fucking way we'd keep our cover in the fomenting crowd. Troops and civvies meshed together. One group shoving, kicking, screaming their way forward, the other shouting, shooting, sending them back toward the gaping gates.

Denver came over the earpiece. "Need to locate Cutler in this melee."

Ditto that, except things got real hairy, real fast. If we didn't want to be compromised, we needed a way through.

A fist flew at my face and I knocked it aside. Guns rattled off from every direction. The black night was lit by bright pops of live ammo. We ducked and ran.

"Diversionary tactics." The order came down from Linc. Rules of engagement were in place. We couldn't—we wouldn't—engage the civilians. Cutler had outfoxed us again.

But we sure as fuck engaged the Corps para, who roamed like black bugs throughout the rebellious crowd. This was not a time for mediation or trying to talk people into seeing our side of shit.

Nathaniel wielded his machete. Liz let her sniper rifle guide her. Linc and Sebastian pulled up the rear, and we all forged forward.

Drones dropped out of the sky, popping out enemy fire that razed through fighters on both sides with no consideration whatsoever for civilian life.

We made it to the ramparts of Corps Command. Another endless round of drone machine guns chewed up the pavement just in front of our feet. Above the whistles of bullets, Darwin let loose an almighty squeal that almost burst my eardrums.

"Tone it down, soldier," I commanded. "Undercover, remember?"

"They're not after us," she replied.

"What?"

She shoved her D-P in my face. "The fine, upstanding citizens of Delta T are chasing Cutler. They're following *him*, not us. Look! They're uplinking his location to the D-P network. Denver, you old dog, you opened the airwaves to all?"

There was a bright spark of white from his teeth as he smiled in the dark.

"I'll be goddammed." Cannon watched Cutler's infrared sat image like a predator on the scent.

My mouth hung open in shock. For once, an InterNations-wide manhunt was not targeting us.

Darwin snickered, gently pressing her fingertips to my jaw.

"MOVE OUT!" I shouted.

"Aye, Captain. Where to?" Liz asked.

"What's his position, Darwin?"

"En route to the medical building."

"I've got to cut loose here." Denver broke free of our group. "I'll see you inside. Just follow the trail."

He disappeared like a wraith into the masses. But as we prepared to follow, the masses parted for us. They created a tunnel of human bodies, pushing us forward, shouting us on. Guns clicked all around, but they weren't aimed at us. As another formation of drones banked over the Quad, gunfire crackled into the air.

Plane parts rained down in showers of hot metal. Sparks spit at our feet. We blasted open the door of the med building with all weapons firing. Crouched as one, tracing the pristine white surrounds, we tracked blood and sweat and death inside the hushed emptied enclosure.

An open door at the end of the hallway beckoned us. Cold white light shined from within. I took point with everyone else at my flank, spreading out.

We entered the room.

The sight of Cutler, sweat-free and smug, reached down into my gut and jerked me upright. Our almost victory over him had backfired. He'd led us exactly where he wanted us.

Behind him, Doc Val was strapped to a chair, at gunpoint.

Beside her, bound and gagged, was Leon.

CHAPTER TWENTY-ONE

W e were immediately surrounded on all sides by troopers who had been waiting just inside the room. Outmanned, outnumbered, out-fucking-maneuvered again.

With my head down, I glared at Cutler through slit eyes that were surely sharp enough to cut through him.

CEO Cutler looked a lot more gaunt and aged in person than on the daily promos. Must've been some nifty tricks with lighting or tech enhancements. Across the room, he had the haggard look of an old buzzard, not the white-crested eagle talking down to us from the worldwide D-Ps. But that didn't matter one damn bit, because once again the cunt held all the cards.

I swung my gaze toward Leon. His arms and legs were strapped to the chair, and the rag was stuffed too deep into his mouth. He coughed, his eyes widening like an animal led to the slaughter. His face turned red, then purple.

Inside I was dying. My heart lurched in my chest. All-consuming, all-firing rage burned from the top of my head to the balls of my feet.

Leon blinked rapidly, a tear leaking down his cheek. I clenched my hands to keep from rushing to him, my own eyes filling. I watched him draw in a breath, then another until his skin color returned somewhat to normal.

It was only then I took note of the large dark figure looming over Val. It was none other than Denver—our last hope—holding the gun to Val's head.

Seeing him standing there so unperturbed thrust me over the edge I'd been hanging on to by my fingertips. I barreled toward him, bullets loaded, guns drawn. I gave a mighty war yell and jumped across the space separating us—only to be taken down and relieved of my weapon by a tangle of troopers.

"Disarm the rest of them," Cutler instructed.

He casually walked around our group as we were pushed into the center of the room. Hands behind his back, he inspected each of us with a superior slice of his eyes, a taunting tilt of his lips. He paused far longer in front of his twin sons, who matched his stare with withering glares, undaunted by the man who had beaten their mother and tried to usurp their lives.

I strained to peer past the blockade of soldiers to Leon, ready to go feral to get to him. Before I could find an opening, Cutler called out, "Restrain them."

It was Denver who did the honors. He moved swiftly, with certainty. This obviously wasn't his first hostage situation. I surged toward him with a snarl when he came near me, but he merely raised an amused eyebrow, so like his mentally unstable mentor.

The eight of us were bound together by the wrists in a circle, with our backs facing inward. A fantastic defensive position if we had our weapons, the worst possible scenario in a situation where we had no access to firearms.

If Denver were truly on our side, he'd have shown one small mercy and left the knots loosened. I tested the bonds as inconspicuously as I could. Every movement from one of us tightened the wire already biting into our wrists. We weren't going anywhere, and it looked like Denver was the one making sure we went down.

Circling his quarry, Cutler once again appraised each of us.

"An interesting, if mongrelized, group you have here. You know how I hate the mixing of races and the abominable acts within the sexes." His voice was tinged with revulsion. He pinched the bridge of his nose, as if our Freelander-Territorian smell offended him. "I can understand some of your motives. Darke here, for instance. You simply have no choice but to act on impulses like an untamed animal. As for the rest of you…noncompliance with Company laws is strictly forbidden and goes against the grain of normal human behavior. Which brings to me to our dear Farrow Monroe."

He stopped before her, worrying one finger over his thinned lips. "I must say, I'm concerned for your well-being. If they pressured you into this abhorrent position because of family ties—"

Farrow interrupted. "Actually, Lysander, Ah'm a lesbian." She spoke in her soft, lilting drawl, with the blunt force of a weapon. "And the only thing abhorrent about this situation is you and your ignorant, blinded bullshit beliefs."

"What?" His mouth fell open in shock.

"I make love to women. I love women, their sweet bodies and even sweeter taste." Her angelic features never wavered, but he looked at her as if she were possessed by the devil.

Disgusted, he turned to Sebastian. "Surely you can talk some sense into your sister."

"'Fraid not. See, I'm gay."

"Insolent boy!" He whipped out and backhanded Sebastian. "This is what must be stopped."

Our shouts rose. Our shoulders strained, only tying us tighter together. At least that kept Bas upright when the unforeseen blow would've knocked him off his feet.

Cutler smoothed both hands down the sleeves of his suit jacket, calming himself. "It's seems I misjudged the malleability of my citizens, all of you as well as those traitors outside." He shrugged. "I'm not certain what I should do here. We can watch Leon die in a few hours. Then you will all be infected. Of course, my people are inoculated. How I wish you—Lincoln and Nathaniel—were still my people, my sons, but your deeds and actions speak too loudly to be ignored."

"You fucking asshole!" Cannon savagely stamped forward, dragging us all with him.

He was stopped short by the metallic click of guns prepared to fire on us.

"Commander Cannon, I've waited almost a year to see you again. I'm sorry to have missed your splendid captivity at the Outpost. I hear waterboarding didn't set well with you."

"Shut up, Father," Nathaniel said with deadly malice.

"And I heard you were too much of a pussy to do your own dirty work," Cannon returned, blazing right ahead. "You fucking coward. Can't even get your own gun out, and you probably can't get it up anymore, either. I don't give a good fuck what you do to me; this fight will go on."

"Ditto that, Commander." Liz stood directly behind me, clasping my fingers.

We all agreed loudly, strongly, with our shoulders drawn back. *Fight to the end. Die for love. Die so Leon could live.* I shoved my chin up, my jaw made of stone. *Die for Leon.*

"Ah, Lizbeth. It's so nice to see you again. You seem as outraged as ever. It appears even my son can't domesticate your baser instincts."

She bared her claws at him. "As it so happens, Linc doesn't think I need to be tamed. And you are not allowed to call him your son anymore, you cocksucking, motherfucking pig."

"You know you're going to burn in hell for this, Father." Like Nathaniel, Linc astounded me with his cool, unflappable presence, but inwardly, I felt the tension brewing within the two brothers.

"I'm so disappointed in you boys. So disappointed. I can see now there's no convalescence to cure you. You were made in your mother's mold. It's why I had to adopt a son of my own making. A killing machine of sorts. My Denver. He who has never questioned me, back-talked me, or broken his promise to serve me and serve me well. I saved him once, and he keeps me safe in return. I prefer his methods to yours. He does not bow to the useless futility of emotions."

Stationed once again at Val's side, Denver allowed a fleeting smile to cross his features.

Cutler moved away, leaving us at gunpoint. He jerked Leon's chin up. "Alas, I think I will have to wipe everyone off the face of the planet again and start virtually from scratch. I really didn't want it to go this far." His milky blue stare arrowed on me. "And it will start with Leon."

I held myself caged within the tight bonds of emotional restraint, a perfect mirror to the physical ones tethering me to everyone else. I gave no response other than to dive deep into Leon's eyes so he could see the truth of my intentions.

His expression smoothed over in acceptance of his fate. Seeing his hopelessness made my heart race in my chest. *He will not die today.*

"You asked if I carried my own gun. If I know how to wield it, former Commander Cannon, dismissed from duty in contempt of court." He drew out a Glock. "I assure you, I do."

Sound exploded in the chamber—the gun going off with a bang, curses flying from our mouths. The bullet whizzed through the air and hit Farrow in the thigh. She pulled us back with the impact.

Beside her, Darwin shoved a shoulder beneath the wounded spy. We pulled outward against the bonds only to snap back to one another.

Cutler holstered his weapon. He smiled a snake's smile.

"This is wrong, Father," Nathaniel shouted, pushing forward.

"You are wrong. I am right."

He was insane, completely fucking insane.

I listened to Farrow bite off whimpers of pain, to Leon pounding the chair legs against the floor.

Cutler spoke into his D-P. "Bring in the trolley."

The doors rumbled open to reveal a lab table on wheels, covered with a cloth. It trundled between our circle and Leon, Val, Denver, and Cutler. Cutler flipped off the cloth to reveal hundreds of vials separated by a thick red line on barren white fabric.

"This is the antidote serum." He lifted a small glass ampoule. There was probably one milliliter of liquid inside. That was all I needed. *It's so close.*

He held up another vial from the opposite side of the table, clinking the tiny capsules together. "And this is the virus. It's our special new rapid strain—isn't it, Dr. Valary? Even faster than the one used in Omega. It takes mere minutes to overload the body's system.

"I cannot abide by you *people* any longer." Cutler's eyes turned glassy and his breathing shallow. Spittle dripped from the corners of his mouth like a dog gone rabid. He wiped it away as an afterthought.

Leon eyed the table as hungrily as me. The martyr in him probably wanted to inject everyone else in the room with the serum before himself.

"I don't even have any demands tonight. You can all go to your graves." He stoppered the bottle of antidote, gently guiding it back between the glistening glass columns.

"Cure Leon and infect me instead. Make me Patient Zero," I said.

Cutler turned a curious look on me. "Why should I do this?"

"I'm the bigger prize." I heard Leon make a choking sound, but I didn't look at him.

"That is true in the grander scheme of things, but you're all going to die anyway." He peered between Leon and me for a moment before he shook his head. "No. I'm not convinced. You really have nothing to bargain with, Darke. Whatever will you do?"

"You have a very special hate for Leon"—*a sickness*—"why not keep him around? With the rest of us out of the way, he'll be yours to use as you wish. I know you get off on it." I spoke through gritted teeth.

"He would certainly be a tortured little soul after you all died on him." Cutler grinned as if he knew how much those hated words cost me. "But that means Leon will be forever safe from the outbreak. That wasn't my plan, and you're wasting what little time you have left."

"Why wait for Leon's Plague to go live? Infect me now with the new one and you get a front-row seat to everyone's death." I upped the ante.

I watched Cutler consider for a moment. "That was almost a decent trade, Darke. But I'm afraid I have to decline."

I growled in frustration.

"Eden. She'll come back to you. She will. She'll do it for Leon's life." Linc's offer made my head snap toward him.

"What the fuck, Linc?" Nathaniel hissed.

I wanted to oppose Linc's suggestion, but I couldn't. He knew his father better than anyone, and Cutler showed his first true spark of interest.

"That's the best idea I've heard all night. Perhaps you have some of me in you after all." He gave a fond slap to the side of Linc's face. "You all die and I get to keep Leon as my pet and Eden as my wife? How do I know she'll agree to it?"

"Call up the commune."

"You call." Cutler produced Linc's DP and put a call in to the commune. He held the device near Linc's mouth.

I couldn't listen to the conversations as Hatch located Eden. I couldn't think about the implications as she agreed to sacrifice herself to the monster who had made her life a living hell. When the comms ended, no one spoke. Morbid tension held us still and silent except for Leon. Pronounced veins stood out in his arms as he struggled in the chair. His muffled shouts echoed throughout the cold, white room.

"It appears our little whore has something to say." He pulled the gag from Leon's mouth and dropped it to the floor.

I stamped my feet, trying to get closer to him.

"Darke, what're you doin'?" Leon barely forced the words through dry lips.

"Saving you." I felt silent sobs shaking those all around me. I didn't care. All was lost, but at least Leon would live. *Oh God, I want to touch him one more time.* "I love you."

Someone would come up with something—a plan to get them out of this. They'd all been through impossible situations before. Releasing Leon from the virus was the only way I could ensure he would survive. He'd get out. He was wily.

"Self-sacrifice in the name of love. It almost warms my heart." Cutler shook two vials at me. "I think it's a fair trade, especially

69666666 66 66 66

with my wife coming back to me. You are more valuable to the Revolution, Darke. Leon's just a slut."

I'd made my peace. I nodded.

Leon's chair screeched across the floor. "NO!"

"Or I could just infect Darke, too. I don't really see the point of one or the other."

"Don't you fucking dare, Cutler," I threatened. "You give him the antidote first, then infect me. Otherwise you can fuck my gun sideways."

"Strong words from a strong soldier. I would expect nothing less. We have an agreement." He gestured between Denver and Val. "Let her go so she can get to work."

Dr. Val looked sick. "I don't think I can infect another person…"

"Do it now!" I yelled.

Leon was cut loose, but Denver maintained a tight grip on his left arm. Val prepared a needle, poked it into an ampoule of the serum, and approached Leon.

"I don' wanna do this." Leon's low whisper carried to me.

"I don't care. Give him the drug," I demanded.

Once his vein plumped up, Val punctured his skin, plunged the shaft. Tears fell fast down Leon's face. "It won't take long. It's fast-acting, less than two minutes."

"Where's Leon's D-P?" I asked.

Cutler held his hand out to one of soldiers. The slim black tablet appeared.

"Take a blood sample and send it to Hatch." I didn't trust them for an instant. They could've just double-dosed Leon.

"Very thorough." Cutler nodded at me.

"You bet your fucking ass I am."

Impatience nagged at the corners of my brain until Cutler answered an incoming bleep on Leon's D-P. "Hatch says he's clean."

"Show me."

He held the D-P in front of my face. *Clean, clear, and free of disease.*

Relief soared through me. "Oh God, yes." My head fell back and I smiled.

But Leon's reaction knocked the relief right out of me. His pain burned bright inside of him until it turned so dark in the center it was nearly a black hole.

"Darke, please, no. What good is my life without you?"

His emotions, his words, his stark expression crippled me.

Denver, placid as ever, cut me alone out of the captive circle, ratcheting the others even more closely together. He placed me on a gurney that had been wheeled into the room. Not a blip colored his emotional radar. I detested the man even more.

"This should provide a few moments of entertainment at least." Cutler looked positively giddy.

Liz swore over and over again at me, her face distorted in pain. Linc's fierce stare never shifted from his father. Cannon's muscles rippled with the immensity of power he put behind trying to get free of the wire. Their emotional output overwhelmed me. I blanked them out. Watching Leon's bright spirit getting dimmer was already more than I could take.

Dr. Valary hovered beside me. "This will hurt." She swabbed my skin before preparing the hypodermic.

"You bastard!" Leon shouted at me.

The virus couldn't hurt any more than the obliteration of my heart.

"I love you," I said as I focused on my angel.

"*Cher*, no!"

CHAPTER TWENTY-TWO

S top, Elizabeth," Denver ordered.

The needle puncture I expected never came. The point hollowed my skin for an instant before it skipped away.

Leon looked at Denver, surprise lighting his features.

"What? What is it?"

Denver glanced at me. "We're not going anywhere, and you're not going to die."

Leon bounded over and covered me with his body, gripping me fiercely.

Cutler whipped his head to Denver. "They are going to die. All of them!"

"Not this time, Boss." He discharged his weapon once. It hit at a precise nerve point in Cutler's shoulder, making him drop his Glock as his fingers twitched lifelessly.

"Denver?" Confusion scuttled across the CEO's face. He pulled a red palm away from his wet wound.

"The name's Deyama."

A vengeful Denver appeared from the cold depths of calm encasing him. This one was furious and fiery. He strode to Cutler and grabbed his hair. His fist primed, he slammed it into the befuddled face. "It's time for a new fate, Cutler-*sama*."

During the chaos that ensued, troopers shouted orders at one another:

Stand down.

Let's move out!

Stay. We fight to the end.

Denver yelled for Leon, who looked up in time to catch a blade flying end over end at him.

Deftly holding the handle, he cut me free of the gurney before springing across the room. Sliding under the circle of our friends, he came to his feet amid the wiry web holding them together. He sliced them free faster than I could blink.

The sound of glass shattering pushed me into action. I hoped like crazy it wasn't the serum…or the virus…

I swung to my feet and sped to the table of goods, the one getting knocked around by the jostle of bodies. I protected the vials while Nathaniel and Cannon barred Cutler's escape. Denver was immobilizing him with the same systematic motions he'd used on us. The rest of my people kept wary eyes and raised weapons on the soldiers huddling like cattle before a butcher.

Cutler wasn't getting out of this. At least not alive.

"I want that fucking antidote in Darke now!" Denver bellowed.

"I'm good. The needle didn't break skin."

"Close enough. We're taking no chances. You get the antidote first." He tossed his head toward Dr. Valary. "Elizabeth?"

She started toward me. At the same time, the troops opened up with a wild spray of fire. Hit somewhere in the middle, she landed on the hard floor. A bloody stain bloomed from her stomach, spreading across the torn blouse she wore.

Leon hurried to me. He lifted a needle to prep it, but I closed a hand over his wrist. "I'll do it. See to the doctor."

Leon handed me my gun and the syringe before dropping down to tend to Val. I quickly administered the serum with one eye on the action across the room, the other on Leon.

The others surrounded the trigger-happy troopers.

Denver held his weapon in Cutler's face as the CEO kneeled on the floor.

Farrow's dark pants stained with blood leaking from her thigh down.

Leon lifted Val to the gurney and bandaged her wound with strips from his shirt. He glanced at me, and my heart stumbled a few beats before returning to its normal rhythm.

Liz wiped her eyes when she looked back at us before she faced forward to say, "Fuck the Reformed Corps. They're not invited."

With her decision, bullets rang out. Soldiers in midnight blue dropped like floppy puppets to the floor but not before another of ours was hit in the crossfire. Denver spun off his feet and then went down flat on his back. Sebastian ran to him, searching his body, slapping his face and calling him every curse word in the book.

A husky voice broke through tight lips on the cadaver-still body. "Vest."

"What?" Sebastian moved his ear to Denver's mouth.

"I'm wearing a vest." Denver groaned.

"Holy fuck." Linc pulled a trembling hand over his face. "He pulled a Liz move."

"Not as dramatic as me, though." Liz marched over, prodding the man with her boot.

"Did you leave it close enough to the wire, *tomodachi*?" Inspecting Denver's bared and wound-free chest, Linc rocked back on his heels.

"No other choice. Cutler can smell a rat from ten klicks. I had to make sure the serum was on the premises and get it into Leon in time." Lifting his head from the floor, Denver peered at me. "Nice work, by the way, offering yourself up. I wasn't sure how this was going to play out."

"Reassuring, as always," I muttered. "There's still one rat on the loose."

We watched Cutler crawling across the floor. Cannon kicked him over to his back, stomped his boot on the CEO's sternum, and then pulled the gasping man to his feet.

InterNations CEO Lysander Cutler pitted his glare at us. "I still own this regime."

"But you set me up as your second. I am fully capable of installing a new, more humane government, Father," Linc delivered in an even voice.

"And I'll be right beside him. Wasn't that the Cutler vision?" Nathaniel placed himself shoulder to shoulder with his brother.

"You're really going to murder your own father?" Actual real terror was trapped in his voice for the first time as he watched his Freelander son.

"No. I am," Linc said.

"No way." Liz marched forward. "No one should kill their own father, no matter how heinous his crimes."

"Roger that. I won't let you do this, live with this, Nathaniel. It's bad enough you'll see it." Cannon joined Liz.

Nathaniel whispered into Cannon's short hair, his arms looping around his body.

I heard Cannon whisper back, "I will do everything to keep you whole, my love."

As Nathaniel and Linc retreated, I strode into place beside the commander and the lieutenant. Liz, Cannon, and I filled in the space the brothers vacated.

"We'll do it," Cannon announced.

Denver approached the CEO—the political genius, the genesis of this entire Revolution, the Plague, the virus, and all the hate against free love. Ripping through the wires at his wrists, Denver allowed him some semblance of an honorable death I didn't think he deserved. A shot in the back was too good for this cold-hearted cunt.

"I'll be happy to." My voice sounded hoarse, and I was shaky with relief, but I was certain I could hold my Smith steady enough to shoot this bastard dead once and for all.

We took aim.

The only last words were ours.

"Head." I called out my target.

"Heart." Cannon tilted his barrel down.

"Spleen." Liz spat the word out.

Fear flitted across Cutler's eyes one final time. I took enjoyment from his last moment on earth. We fired as one, plugging him with three neat holes. He dropped instantly, a lifeless bag of bones who would never fucking hurt us again.

CHAPTER TWENTY-THREE

I clasped Leon to my side, crushing him against me.

Linc walked to his father and kneeled down. "You will never take anything from me again."

He removed the fat silver ring with the Rice family crest from Cutler's finger. When he stood, Liz was there. Kissing the palm of his hand, she finally rested the Freelander signet home on her husband's finger where it belonged.

"He wanted to be embalmed to lie in state." Denver shifted his long black braid over his shoulder as he joined Sebastian, piling the dead.

"No one needs to mourn him or make pilgrimages to him." Nathaniel closed his father's eyelids. "You reap what you sow."

A fresh wave of troops burst into the room. Far smarter than their predecessors, they took one look and dropped their weapons with metallic clatters to the floor. They held their hands high while their unblinking eyes took in the scene: Thirteen

Revolutionaries standing over crumpled bodies of soldiers and one man laid out alone—the way he'd lived his life was how he'd go into the afterlife.

Linc marched up to the group. "Tell your comrades the CEO is dead. The antivirus serum is viable. It will be distributed immediately. There's a New Order. It's called democracy."

"Commander Linc Cutler?" One brave soul strutted through the throng of dark blue Corps uniforms. She saluted with crisp movements.

"Lieutenant…" He inspected her badge. "Alexia." Returning her salute, he regarded her curiously.

When she removed her cap, she revealed a bright stripe of white hair that would possibly be styled into a Mohawk. "My sister, Moxie, has spoken highly of you. It's an honor to meet you, sir."

Linc nodded. "Moxie is one in a million. Welcome to the Reformed Corps, people."

Turning, he addressed us. "All right. Let's get the word out! We need to distribute the serum, round up the last of Father's cronies, and start to work on our new InterNations government."

Cannon gave a grumble. "Thought we'd have a little downtime first."

"I'm a little hungry, myself." Liz winked at her former commander and then beamed a grin at her husband, who squinted in response.

"Not to mention tired." Nathaniel yawned wide.

"And bleedin' out over here," Farrow shouted through

clenched teeth. She was being attended to by Darwin. Val had been stabilized. Both women were lucky. All major organs and arteries missed by the smallest fractions.

Denver stepped forward. "How do you stand such insubordination?"

"It's not insubordination when we're all brothers and sisters in arms and at heart, my friend."

Sebastian linked his fingers through Denver's with a wide smile.

"This will take some getting used to." Denver touched Sebastian's cheek.

Beside me, Leon hummed as he always did when he was happy.

"*Je t'aime*, Leon Cheramie." I drew him into my arms, turning my back on the room. Wrapped around him, my body shook as relief gusted through me.

After the all-too-brief interlude, it was down to business. Each of our crew was inoculated first. With Farrow and Val's wounds dressed, the doctor gave directions to Darwin, Sebastian, and Linc to the stores of serum within the med building. She asked them to break into her office to retrieve the formula. It would be handed to Denver so he could broadcast the solution over the D-P as the Voice.

Denver wasted no time sending out a victory call.

"The war is over. CEO Cutler is dead. Triumph is ours! Democracy is taking root as I speak, and the antidote to the virus is in hand. We will be distributing it to the early infectees first. Instructions for replicating the serum will follow shortly and all citizens will be inoculated, the strain destroyed. Know this, citizens of the InterNations: The Revolution is won! We will love freely! We will not die!"

I'd never seen the man so impassioned. His lively speech raised cheers from our squad and a thrill to my heart.

As we hobbled from the medical building, the dazzling scene outside was like nothing I'd ever witnessed. Our shoulders straightened and our strides lengthened as the thousands-strong throng parted for us.

They chanted as one voice:

"Live in Freedom! Love at Will!"

InterNations flags were being replaced by Freelander colors already. Soon there would be one standard for all of mankind.

And that was just within the walls of the Delta Quadrangle.

I shook from the tidal wave of triumph hitting me from all quarters. This time I let the vibrant emotion wash over me, cleanse me, carry me along.

Out on the streets, the celebration amplified. News had spread at the speed of light during the dawn hours.

I wiped tears from my eyes, locking my arm around Leon's waist. The building-wide D-Ps glowed with updated images from the last Territories to topple the CO government. *VICTORY! LIFE! CURE! EQUALITY! FREEDOM!* The words unfurled across the screens and resounded from the massive crowd lining the streets of S-1, S-2, and all the Territories and all the communes from continent to continent.

Music began beneath the swell of the chants. It started with a single, shockingly clear female voice. The song of victory gathered volume, leaping from person to person. Instruments joined the mix—trumpets and tambourines, flutes and finger cymbals.

The scene on the D-P cut into six equal squares where the same musical outpouring flooded back at us from InterNations Territories far and wide. The sounds we heard weren't those of Old History heralding a change of arms but a boisterous chorus of people using any noisemaker on hand to signal the dawn of a new era.

My steps faltered from the sheer majesty of it.

"Let's go home." Leon tugged my hand.

"There's just one thing I've got to do first." I cupped his face. "I love you, you foolish, sweet, beautiful man."

"I know." His chin rose. His eyes sparkled. Defiant. Stubborn. Sexy. All mine.

I dipped my head to meet his lips, pulling him to my deep kiss. His arms wound around my shoulders. He moaned as cheers exploded from the rooftops to the roadside. And I knew the image of us kissing was being broadcast all over the world.

Two men in love, at the end of a war.

With no fear of reprisal.

For the first time in our New History.

CHAPTER TWENTY-FOUR

The early-September evening when we approached the forest surrounding Chitamauga was crisp, the sky a breathtaking array of incandescent violets and golds. The sunset wasn't nearly as gorgeous as the man walking beside me, though. Leon hadn't been this relaxed since the very first days I'd known him. His loose gait made his ass sway inside the tight jeans, but every time I tried to linger behind a pace or two to admire him, he pulled me forward with a wicked grin. He gabbed a mile a minute in a husky mixture of what Liz called *Cajunese*.

I fell in love with him all over again.

We'd remained in Delta for two weeks, just long enough to bury CEO Cutler's remains in a small cemetery with an even more negligible headstone. No one else was in attendance. His sons had wished him dead, both for years of deception and for the devastating acts he'd perpetrated—not just on his own family, but their friends and lovers, as well as an entire nation. But each murmured a few words aloud before his coffin was covered in dirt.

We stayed a bit longer to begin the long slog of turning another authoritarian stronghold into a viable democratic assembly, including key people from all communities on the continent.

Two weeks during which Leon and I had done little more than hold hands and softly kiss. We'd abstained from lovemaking in equal agreement because the next time we were together, we wanted to be as close as we could, skin to skin, soul to soul. We needed to make sure we were both completely clean after the botched virus attempts, and we didn't trust anyone more than Doc back at the commune.

Just because we'd agreed to these measures didn't make it any easier. I was bone-hard almost every waking moment. I went to sleep with an erection that had Leon's name on it and woke up in the same state.

At least I knew Leon was as hard up as me. Literally.

Leon's eyes went wide and his free hand pumped into the air in time to his shouts. I looked ahead, where his gaze was aimed. Chitamauga. It was the first time the big wooden gates protecting our village were open and unmanned. The people of Chitamauga hadn't waited in the town square. They streamed out of the commune en masse. Their whoops and hollers roared, deafening my ears as my eyes filled.

Altogether, eleven of us returned, and our three new additions—Val, Denver, and Darwin—were enfolded with the rest of us in arms that hugged, hands that shook, smiles that broadened ever wider. People passed us from one embrace to another.

It was a beautiful sight that nearly rivaled Leon.

I kept my hand resolutely on his waist lest he get tugged away by the tide of friends and family and Freelanders who never thought they'd see him alive again. Children swarmed his legs. He laughed boisterously, beaming at all who surrounded him, blushing from time to time, awed and humbled by the love he inspired in people.

He had no idea the effect he had, on me most of all.

Evangeline appeared like a whirlwind before us. Her summer-green eyes were wet and hazy as she grasped Leon to her. Just as quickly, she shoved him away with a whack on his arm.

"*Grand beede!* You make your *maman* scared like dat when you say you're gonna kill yourself? Next time I kill you myself."

Tears overtook her, and Leon wrapped her up close. "Sorry, *Maman.* I didn't mean to cause *la misère.*"

"*Mais,* yeah! You always make *cette misère.* Dat is why I love you. *Si embêtant.*"

I heard Miss Eden giving similar treatment to her two sons and their spouses before she broke down, too. When she recovered, she took every other person in our crew—new or not—to task as well, her hand raised, finger pointing, strawberry-blond hair falling into her eyes during her tirade. As was Eden's way, she then forgave each of them with a kiss and a warm hug that made even Denver stumble over his polite words.

Sebastian snickered at his discomfort.

"Miss Eden?" I called to her as I approached.

Her hands lifted to my face. "What is it, son?"

"I owe you thanks. Cutler never would've agreed to the deal without you."

"I would've done anything, just like you. You don't owe me anything except a hug."

My arms wrapped around her. I held her tight for a brief moment, a lump of emotion in my throat making any further thanks impossible.

When I released Eden, Leon's mother rounded on me. "Big handsome, dat be what my son call you. C'mere."

I didn't have a choice. Evangeline hustled me right into her arms, giving me a moment of soft maternal comfort I'd been lacking for too many years. My face heated with her canny regard as she clasped both my cheeks.

"*Mm-hmm.* Tall, dark drink of water. Now I be wonderin' about your intentions with Leon de Bellisle Cheramie."

I stuttered over words that tangled my tongue. "I'm sorry, ma'am. I tried my best to keep him safe. I…I love him."

"*Maman.*" Leon interrupted, getting himself *tutt*ed by several stern village matriarchs.

"*Alors.* He say what I wanted to hear. You hush up, Leon." Reaching up on her tiptoes she didn't even brush my chin, but Evangeline's expression was fiercely emotional. "*Merci. Merci.*" She rubbed a suddenly damp cheek against my shirt, where her whisper was both felt and heard. "He survived 'cause of you, Darke."

I leaned down to her. "I live because of Leon," I said quietly. "Thank you for being his *maman*."

As soon as she released me, Leon launched into my arms. "You survived the inquisition."

I laughed, dragging him against me. "Is that what that was?"

Old Man Hills made his way toward us through a tunnel of familiar Freelanders. Micah, Kamber, Hatch, Smitty, Lyra, Gruff Tommy, and Gal the mutt were there.

Hills had his dandelion-fluff hair tucked behind his ears. I'd always thought of him as the sun. Tonight he was the moon preparing to let a new sun rise in his wake. I recognized his time was waning. He accepted it with satisfaction for the years he'd been given. I hoped one day, in the far-off future, to know the same sense of contentment with a life well lived and well loved.

It all started with Leon, whose palm I lifted to my heart.

Tommy, on the other hand, crackled with crisp energy. He'd probably outlive us all.

Regal as any monarch in these down-home surrounds, Hills raised his palms to the heavens. "We have learned through the ages there are no spoils of war. There can be no winners when blood is spilled and life is taken. But tonight I count you all as victors! It was not just one battle. It was a war for the heart of humanity.

"When we got the word from Darke, from Delta, I..." He bowed his head. "I gave many thanks for your lives, warriors. We also felt the sorrow of those who passed by your hands as need be, by the soldiers who undertook a fight they did not understand, and by the man we will also mourn because celebrating death is not just.

"Warrior Darke." Hills pulled me tight against him, where I felt his frail bones. "Welcome home.

"Leon Cheramie. Savior." He motioned my lover forward. "Thank you."

And so he gave his benediction to each and every one of us while I committed to memory his many blessings on former Corps soldiers and commanders and even those who had worked for Cutler in order to bring him down in the end.

"Welcome home…and welcome to your new home."

The cheers were cut short.

"There's someone else I cannot neglect," Hills continued. He lowered his head. "Jonquil died in childbirth. We thought it wise to wait until you returned from your mission to tell you."

"The baby?" Cannon croaked.

The cry of an infant pierced the air. Eden came forth, and she passed the squalling red-faced parcel to Caspar and Nathaniel. Their hands seemed too big to comfort the tiny crying package. Cannon rocked unsteadily on his feet. Nathaniel passed a hand over his mouth, stepping back from his husband.

Cannon swore. "Fuck. Don't leave me alone with it. I'll drop it!"

A few titters passed around the engrossed onlookers as Nate crept back to his side.

"Not it—she. She's a girl." Eden hovered close enough to wrap the little girl tighter in her swaddling before pressing her fully against Cannon's chest.

He looked aghast for a moment, then immediately in love. His huge fingers rested lightly, oh so gently, on the creamy skin of her teeny puckered face.

"Where's the father?" Nathaniel asked, appearing both reluctant and enraptured.

"He turned out to be a no-good layabout," Evangeline said. "He wasn't ready to handle the responsibilities of bein' a papa. Took off a couple of days before Jonquil went into labor."

A ferocious frown cranked down Cannon's brows, and Nathaniel similarly scowled.

"That ain't right. What kind of a man does that?" Nathaniel peeked with so much longing at the baby in his husband's arm. "Who's lookin' after her?"

Lyra came forward to kiss the baby girl and then both men. "This was Jonquil's last wish. That her daughter would become yours."

"Wait. She's ours?" Cannon looked up from his mesmerized study of her small fingers wrapped around his thumb.

"You are her fathers." Eden nodded, wiping the tears from her eyes.

"She's ours." Cannon turned toward Nathaniel just before his face crumpled.

Hoarse sounds came from the massive man. Nathaniel cradled the baby in one arm, his other one looped around the stoic military commander so overcome with emotion it spilled onto everyone in sniffles, soft words, sighs.

The wee thing screeched again, much louder than a person that size should have any right to do.

Cannon jerked his head up to peer at the baby buffeted between their bodies. "She's got a temper."

"Should be right at home!" some smart-ass or other called.

They cuddled and cooed at their newborn daughter as we

made our way into Chitamauga proper. Torches shined as bright as the night stars constellating the sky above. Trestle tables had been filled with a feast for the stomach and drink enough to sate any kind of thirst.

Cannon considered the vast spread of roasted meat and vegetables, the tankards of mead waiting to be drunk. He swayed in a slow side-to-side motion, watching as the infant brought his finger to her mouth to suckle on it. "How the fuck are we gonna feed her?"

Eden smacked him on the ear. "Language."

Guffaws came from all quarters of the town square.

"She has a wet nurse, Caspar," Eden explained. "No one's expecting you to start a'lactatin', but we do expect you to make sure Liberty doesn't grow up with your bad mouth."

"Little Liberty, is it?" He smiled down at the child. "On my honor, I'll be on my best behavior around Liberty."

At the dawn of a new freedom, the child's name seemed only fitting.

Cannon and Nathaniel found a bench to park it on, where they ignored the rest of the carousers. When Nathaniel began to sing in his rich, melting voice to the daughter in his arms, everyone turned to stare.

Cannon carefully kept his finger within Liberty's tight fist, but now his gaze wandered over his lover's face. As the song ended, he leaned in to Nathaniel, kissing him with slow fire before whispering something in his ear that caused the blond man to blush.

Sometime later, Leon strolled up to me, the baby in his arms.

I'd kept my eyes on him the entire night, but my hands off of him. I wasn't at all sure I'd be able to stop once I started touching him. He was talking to the baby while she kicked and gurgled in his arms. He looked so comfortable with her, so adoring. I took another knock to my chest.

He pressed a kiss to my lips, letting out a soft moan. I slipped my fingers through his thick, wavy hair, trailing a hand down his back.

"I'm just gonna help them get Libby settled. Dey ain't got a clue what they're doin'." He jerked his thumb back at the pair of parents, who were looking sheepish.

"And you do?"

Leon sent a seductive fingertip down the center of my chest, leaving me gripped by a rush of arousal. "I can sweet-talk just about anyone. You know dis."

I did.

It was the first time I'd let him out of my sight since we'd moved out on CO HQ in Delta, but I didn't think my heart could withstand seeing him with adoration in his eyes for anyone but me, even if it was a child. I wanted Leon to myself first. I was a selfish bastard where he was concerned.

He returned a half hour later, coming to stand in front of me. The swells of his ass jolted my cock to life. My lips skimmed along the back of his neck, raising goose bumps I licked with my tongue.

"Time for bed." I dipped my mouth to his ear, letting my deep voice rumble across his sensitive skin.

He turned in my arms. "Where?"

I snorted in disbelief. "With me, of course. Tonight." I kissed his cheek. "Tomorrow night." I grasped his bottom. "Every night." I took his lips in a possessive kiss, barely keeping myself in check.

Boisterous catcalls interrupted our caresses, which were growing more daring by the second.

"Get a room!"

"Get a caravan."

"The lake works for me."

"Oh, Christ," Tommy grumbled. "Don't tell me I'm gonna be shacking up next to another Love Hovel."

* * *

We headed to our caravan, and I guided Leon inside.

"Home," I said.

Evangeline and Eden had been through, tidying the rooms and airing them out in my absence. I'd also asked Evangeline to deliver Leon's belongings. His spare boots rested beside the door, and the moko tools he hadn't brought overseas were displayed on a shelf next to my books.

"Our home," I pronounced in a gruff voice.

Leon shook his head slowly, turning to inspect the two rooms. His fingers ran across my belongings and his. My heart was filled with pure love and peace. I turned away to hide my emotion, lifting our packs to a low table. I removed the guns and other weapons we'd tucked away earlier in the day, knowing we wouldn't need them here. With Leon watching me, I opened a wooden gun case I'd carved years ago. I'd never shared it with anyone before. Inside I placed our weapons side by side before stowing it on a high shelf.

Leon leaned against the wall, his smile growing.

I shed my clothes with deliberate slowness while he watched, his eyebrows rising higher and higher the more flesh I revealed. When I went to wash briskly from the water in the ceramic basin, I heard him mutter an oath. Then I reclined on the bed, naked and inviting.

"Come to bed, angel."

He skimmed out of his gear faster than I had, joining me with a bounce of the mattress. I laughed and pulled him tight against me before draping the blankets over us.

"You arranged all dis?" His thigh crossed over mine, and his warm words sent damp kisses across my chest.

"Yes. Is that okay?" My hands roved across his bare, silken skin and flawlessly muscled back.

"*D'ac.* I should thank you."

"Leon," I muttered in warning. We still needed to see Doc tomorrow, and my cock couldn't stand any more foreplay without payout.

"Just a kiss." He spun on top of me; then he lowered himself over me until every part of our bodies touched.

My head flicked back. My hips snapped up. Breath whooshed from me in a groan. "That's not a kiss."

"Dis is."

He cajoled my tongue into his mouth after thoroughly nibbling my lips. Once inside, he sucked on me the same way he sucked my cock. Unsurprisingly, my cock pulsed with every pull of his lips.

I fell back when he released me, all my muscles coiled with restraint.

He snuggled against me. "I love you."

I slit one eye open, taking in his flushed face and bright eyes and mussed-up hair. "I love you, too. Now go to sleep."

"Still bossy."

I cupped his ass, the two globes muscular enough to withstand my teasing squeeze. "Extremely fucking horny. The sooner we sleep, the sooner tomorrow gets here and we can get the all clear."

It took a while for my body to calm down, but he was out almost immediately. I didn't mind the ease with which he shut off; it gave me time to hold him, knowing he wasn't going anywhere.

* * *

We showed up at the low-lying wooden medical building washed, fed, and watered well before lunchtime. I went in first and underwent an examination more thorough than I'd ever had before or ever wanted again. That was after Doc took a maddeningly long time looking over my moko, those that had scarred on my back as well as the fresh angel wings on my chest.

"Our Leon did this in Omega?" Doc wore a pair of spectacles that kept sliding down his nose, and his curly gray hair formed a close cap on his head.

"Yes." I turned toward a mirror over the sink and once again took in the sight of the unfurled wings, swelling with pride.

He gave a low whistle of appreciation. "Damn fine work. Talented young man."

"He is." I nodded my head.

I waited with Leon, bouncing my legs, for the time it took Doc to process my tests.

Eventually he stuck his head out the door and grinned. "Clear." Pushing up the glasses that wouldn't grip his nose, he peered at Leon. "Your turn, son."

I went outside and paced around the building for the duration. My fists clenched and unclenched. I should've brought my weapons and done some target practice, starting with the same stand of trees I kept passing. The wait was infuriating.

What felt like hours later, I rounded the building for the umpteenth time to see Leon walking toward me.

"Well?" The kick of adrenaline galloped through my veins.

He smiled. "We're good."

I let out the loudest yell before wrapping him in my arms. Then I growled, "Caravan, now."

We almost ran down the roads that were bustling with midday activity. Heads peeped out of buildings—the kitchens, the forge, the barns, town hall. I heard murmurs, knowing our good news would be all around the commune in less than an hour, especially if Tommy the town crier had anything to do with it. He spat a glob of tobacco juice when we sprinted past, dipping his head, which did nothing to hide his toothless smile.

"Go get 'im, boy."

The door of the caravan banged against the wall, and I booted it shut. It bounced back in protest. Leon laughed until I latched it closed and came at him with the full force of all the want I'd ever had for him.

"*Mon Dieu.*"

He stood his ground, a moan rippling from his throat when I ripped his shirt down the center and flung it aside. Called to action by my greedy haste, he kicked off his boots. One almost went through the window. His laugh that time was breathless. He yanked at my pants while I dragged my top up and off. The zipper stuck, but that didn't stop my lion from palming me through the rough cloth barring his way. Then he crouched down to nip the thick, hard roll of my cock, and I lost it completely.

Shouting in a hoarse voice, I knocked his hands away. I backed him to the table and tore at his jeans. His engorged shaft was in my mouth in an instant. The taste of his precome made me moan. He swore as his hands steadily guided me.

I looked up over the lean, hard lines of his body. The sun worshipped him, making him tawny and smooth except for the sprinkle of hair that thrived in soft curls around his throbbing cock. I lifted my mouth from him, giving one long, languorous lick around the leaking head. Another bead of moisture appeared from the tiny slit. I sucked that up, too.

He cursed again, throwing his head back, eyes shut tight.

"Got a problem, baby?" I asked, nuzzling low to his pink balls. They smelled so earthy, so masculine.

"Get your goddamn pants off."

I stood to my full height, pushed his thighs open, and stepped between them. "You do it."

His hair shimmered on his shoulders. His lips looked so

plump, like he'd already blown my cock. I pushed my thumb into his mouth, my eyes rolling back when he sucked fast and hard.

His fingers didn't fail this time. Belt off, button undone, zipper down, he bunched the fabric to my thighs and then took me tight in hand.

"Fuck!"

He smirked around my finger.

"All fours." We weren't making it to the bed. The floor would have to do. The first time, at least.

Leon complied, head thrown back, back arched, ass raised, and his cock lying flat and rigid against his belly. I crawled beneath him, my head between his thighs and my dick rising up to his lips. His hungry moan made me buck.

"What're you doin'?"

"Taking the edge off. Suck me," I demanded.

All that was left were grunts and groans and swallowed moans. There wasn't another word, just the noise of hard, hot, wet male flesh thrusting in and out of sleek tight mouths. I curled my shoulders up and dragged his thighs wider. I took him to the base and back over and over. Leon devoured my cock just as relentlessly, his hair draping over my legs, his back bowed, his body writhing above me.

His scent and his cock and his taste and his sounds drove me to the brink just as fast as his powerful lips and the fast flicks of his tongue before he engulfed me each time. I slapped his ass twice with both palms, warning him I was going to come—and come fucking fast.

Those loud spanks were enough to set him off. He lifted his

head up to howl the same time he sank his cock all the way into my throat and blasted ropes and ropes of seed. My hips grinded up into the air, pleasure shooting up my spine. My saliva-wet cock danced before the first jet raced up my length to shoot out the head. Leon took the first hit on his neck. He guided my wild cock into his mouth, moaning with each load to hit his tongue while I swallowed everything he gave me.

I slid from beneath him, my thighs quaking. With him in my arms, I tasted his lips. The leftovers of warm, wet come rolled between our tongues, and he made me hard again, just like that.

Leon leaned from my arms to drag the covers down on the bed. I pushed the pillows to the floor and laid him down. He lifted his legs, immediately pulling his knees to his chest.

"Encule-moi."

"What?"

"Fuck me." He licked a single digit before pressing it inside himself.

My eyes slammed shut at the insanely hot sight. When I could speak again, my voice had dropped an octave lower. "Not this time."

I licked around the pink aperture where his finger disappeared. I made my way up to his round balls, sucking on each, slowly lipping across the delicate stretched skin. "You're gonna be inside me this time. No protection and no precautions."

A predatory grin slid across his puffy, well-kissed lips. He pulled his finger free with a gasp and a wiggle of his hips. Then he pounced on me, throwing me to my back. I chuckled, but the laughter shifted to a groan when he skirted his tongue—so soft and wet—around my nipples.

He shimmied lower, slinking down my body, led by his tongue and puckering lips. Down the flexed muscles of my abdomen and along the deep cuts of my pelvis. He kissed his way along the tight black curls that thinned to my groin. I held his hair back to watch him. His face full of pleasure, he seemed to be sipping from my heated skin.

Each touch lifted more fire to the surface. It flamed even brighter when he raised my cock to the side, bypassing the thick length to feast around the base of my shaft, wetting my pubes and nosing the root where I was heaviest. Moving fast, he jerked my legs open wide in rough palms, biting at my rump until I rolled my legs up to provide him open access to my twitching hole.

The bites became softer the closer he roamed to my opening.

Looking up with heavy, heated eyes, he curled his lips in a half smile and then licked his lips. The next thing he licked was my entrance. My head dropped back. All the air left my lungs. I raised my ass higher, seeking his mouth when he pulled away.

His hands gripped both sides, holding them apart. "So fuckin' tight. So fuckin' delicious."

Leon pinned my thighs to my chest with one strong forearm and swooped down to slake his need on my hole. My channel opened more and more to each long lunge of his tongue. I shouted, thrusting up, when he dragged his softly whiskered chin down my taint, using the same friction to torment my aching ring.

By the time he got to lube and fingers, splicing me open, I was delirious. Gulping for air, I alternated between squeezing my eyes shut and watching his every move. He talked through everything, tantalizing words about how good he was gonna love me and how long he was gonna fuck me. He slowly stroked my cock in a loose circle, finger-fucking me and nibbling on the dam of muscle leading from my scrotum to my ass.

"Please fuck me now. Jesus Christ, Leon, please!"

He stopped his torment with a double-handed swat to my ass. I almost shot right then. He kneeled beside me, his cock bigger than ever.

"Get me wet."

I opened my mouth, ready to take him deep inside, but he pushed my forehead back with a low chuckle.

"Touch me with that mouth and this is all over, *beb*. Use the lube, an' get me nice and slick."

I briefly wondered how long he'd waited to order me around. But I didn't care. Leon in charge was the fucking hottest thing I'd ever seen. Once I'd coated his cock until it shined with oil in the afternoon's sun, he moved me where he wanted me—on my back, legs spread, my feet in his hands.

"You know, I went easy on you the first time."

Holy Christ. My stomach tightened. My cock rose up from my abs. Leon trickled a line of lube over the broad cap, avidly watching it streak to my nuts.

"Does that mean you're going to take it out on me right now?"

He brushed his wet tip against my contracting hole until I moaned. Then he visibly relaxed, held his gorgeous cock with one hand and my neck with the other, and slipped into the ring of muscle.

"*Non*. It means I'm gonna love you like it's not the last time." He eased inside, eyes glittery. "It means I'm gonna love you so good, love you forever, *cher*."

"*Oh!*" The tantalizing strength of his cock, bare and hot, opened me up.

My thighs rose to his hips as his heavy balls slapped my ass. I could barely breathe as this gorgeous man throbbed inside of me, spellbinding me.

"Touch me," Leon breathed.

"You feel so good." I pulled him to me, my hands sliding up and down his back. I loved him this way, something masterful in his movements he'd never unleashed on me before.

"*Mmm*. I could get used to this." He bit his lip, swiveling to the left, to the right. Leon pulled back and thrust in with brute force that belied his smaller body.

My toes curled and my hamstrings strained.

He pushed me back to the bed with his palms flat on my chest. He grunted with every long, hard lunge but lingered inside, gyrating, grinding my cock between our bellies. Folding over on top of me, he kissed me between sharp gasps and sheared-off words.

I gathered his hair in my fist, his pumping ass in my hand. "I can't wait for you to come in me."

He didn't go faster, but his thrusts deepened, punching my glans, making me swell and shout. His face took on the sharpest look of desire when I screamed in my climax. It catapulted up my cock and took me by surprise. Took my breath away. Gripping Leon within my seizing body, I released all over both of us.

As he got closer, Leon let out a series of harsh grunts interspersed with soft mewls. Overtaken by pleasure, he opened his eyes wide, the pupils swallowing all the color of his irises.

"Ah, ah, oh, oui. OUI! Darke."

He came a moment later with shivers and jerks and thrusts that powered his come inside of me, where I wanted to capture it. Leon's arms trembled. His throat corded. His mouth fell open. He was so stunning my heart stopped.

When he dropped on top of me, I wrapped all the way around him as I had while we'd made love. Every sated moan pulled him more fully into my heart.

"Sticky," he murmured.

"Do you care?" I kissed the top of his head and then wiggled down so we could be face-to-face.

"No. Feels good."

Our hearts knocked against each other, our pulses still racing. I kissed his fingers, then his palm, then his lips. I caressed his spent cock gently, waiting for the whimper he breathed out.

"Lie down, my love."

With his eyes closed, his arms and legs spread from one end of the bed to the other, he seemed to be asleep when I returned with a warm, wet cloth to clean him up. He mumbled sleepily with a smile. He laughed outright when I jumped onto the bed, sending the washcloth sailing somewhere across the room.

I kissed his chest, rubbing my lips over his heart, which boomed in response. "I want you to be mine."

"*Mmm*. I am."

I nipped his chin. "I want you to marry me, be my forever-more."

Still sleepy, he caught his lip between his teeth without opening his eyes. "Bein' impulsive? You?"

I took his face in my hands. "I'm not being impulsive."

Hearing the serious tone of my voice, he slid his eyelids open. He wound one leg around mine to bring me back against him. "I am yours, forever. You know dat. Don' need a ceremony."

"I want one," I rumbled.

His breath hitched. "I don' want it to be too soon for you, *cher*."

Dammit. When had my *impulsive* man become so fucking annoyingly wise?

"It's not because of our circumstances, if that's what you're wondering, Leon."

"*Je sais.*"

"Then?"

"I think you need more time." His tranquil smile absorbed all my frustration.

Gone was the impetuous kid who'd caught my attention and held it fast for nearly a year. The man beside me wasn't rash. He wasn't totally reckless.

He was smart, sure, confident…and sexy as hell. He'd been reborn, the same as me.

We weren't going anywhere, and I had all the time in the world to woo him.

CHAPTER TWENTY-FIVE

Leon was strangely old-fashioned in his ideas about courtship. I liked it. Though we lived together, slept together, and made the most mind-blowing love, he wouldn't agree to marry me, not yet. Finally, my man had realized his worth. Not as a pawn in play, not as a rent boy paid for, not as my relief from a troubled past.

It'd taken him so long to become this self-assured man, there was no fucking way I'd overstep the boundaries he set.

I took him to the lake, where we sat on the shore at sunset with old ceramic mugs of hot cocoa in our hands. We spent afternoons beneath the autumn sun in the meadow, colorful wildflowers the only witnesses to our picnics and kisses. Our hikes outside the commune were filled with the wonder of being able to enjoy the bounty of Mother Nature instead of looking over our shoulders every time a twig snapped. In those moments, during all those days, Leon became the most precious gift in my life. We didn't need anything grand. Holding hands, listening to him whistle and hum, sneaking off for a kiss that would lead to much more in bed later…all those small details of life in love grounded me to this existence, bound me to this man.

Leon packed his guns away for good—we hoped—along with his past as a hustler. He began working in the school with Kamber. The kids followed him around the village, seeking his easygoing attention, and when he turned that attention on anyone—on me—he invested every bit of feeling fizzing through him.

He was, without doubt, singularly captivating.

The more I thought about it, the more I understood. He wasn't ready yet. He needed to be his own man first before he could fully be mine. And Leon needed to be certain he was the one person I wanted above all others. I redoubled my mission to make sure he knew how much I cherished him, honored him, and respected him.

Fall went from cool nights and mornings to days of crunchy, ground-covering hoarfrost. The apple harvest was reaped. The war we'd fought so recently seemed so very far away but remained present in our thoughts.

Just like our relationship, the restoration of the liberated Territories took its first baby steps during the months of September and October. The InterNations League was born, a worldwide representative group that mirrored the smaller geographical coalitions. Created from elected officials who came from the Territories, the communes, and the Reformed Corps in equal measures, they hammered out a functioning democracy. Our world was to be integrated on all levels.

The artifacts recovered from staunch government strongholds and top-tier CO mansions—the music, art, and literature that had been banned decades ago—found new homes in buildings being made into museums and libraries open to all and on the airwaves that were no longer controlled by the government. Instead of becoming obsolete, the D-Ps sang with life, news, and novel information.

Jobs were not appointed but applied for. Education took a more personal turn, where children weren't forced into a calling early on. History and future, fact and feeling all mingled into one burgeoning InterNations movement.

That didn't mean our new world was a utopia. Far from it. Every day a new batch of problems cropped up like weeds in the field. But the field was fertile. The new leaders of one united government tangled with the infrastructure issues of military and police, judicial and legal, agriculture, health care, and education.

Above all, there was hope for a better future, for us, for our children, for the generations all over the world to come. The overwhelming spirit of a valiant people, the survivors of near total annihilation, guided us.

Of course, some of our core group would soon be pulled away to take on new responsibilities.

* * *

I carried a handful of late-autumn blossoms to the Chitamauga cemetery, making my quiet rounds to my mother's and to Tammerick's and Wilde's markers. I touched each headstone with reverence. Since I realized how much I loved Leon, my mind was unclouded and clear as the bright blue day.

I was thinking about my father, the man I'd never met, when another father walked into the graveyard. He headed to a far corner with one flower tucked in the hand curled around a little baby enclosed in his arms.

Cannon and Liberty.

I didn't want to startle him; nor did I want to interrupt him. I moved cautiously toward them.

"This is your momma, Jonquil. We bring her flowers every Sunday because she liked bright things, as bright as you, Libby." He ducked his head to the pale yellow knit cap that covered a sweet ring of black curls. He kissed her rosy cheek and she reached up, patting his face. When he frowned, it was less fearsome than before.

"'Course, you could try to take it a little easy on me and your other daddy and let us go to bed at the same time."

I stifled a laugh and the patch of ground beneath my boots crackled. Cannon pivoted around, covering Liberty's head with his arms. Seeing me, he settled back on the cold ground.

"Sorry, man," I said.

"The old reflexes are hard to forget."

"I hear that." I grabbed my own seat of frosty grass beside him. "We had some bad times out there."

Cannon tucked Libby beneath his chin, covering her ears with the yellow hat. "We don't talk about the war in front of Libby."

"You do understand Auntie Liz will have her holstered up by the time she's ten."

"Not in this new era."

"So you're an idealist as well as a romantic."

He snorted in disagreement and then nodded. Libby was hugging his thumb with her round pink fist. "Yeah. Maybe."

"Liz and Linc have to head out soon?"

"They think so." His mouth hardened. "I think everyone should just stay put."

I pointed my finger at him. "Idealist."

"Idiot. Fu—I mean, eff you."

I'd taken on a new role as active war turned to rebuilding—I was a military adviser and aide. Likewise, Cannon had opted to keep with his Corps training. Nathaniel worked most of his days with Hatch as they sought new ways to smooth over old fears with technological advancements. Both Cannon and Nathaniel were staying in Chitamauga, although they'd travel as needed for training to help any way they could.

Denver, who knew most of CEO Cutler's secrets, had been called to testify against the biggest war criminal who ever was at Cutler's posthumous trial. With our signed affidavits for his character, he hadn't been charged, but he was required to fill in a hell of a lot of blanks.

Once that obligation was fulfilled, he was taking Sebastian on a trip to FarAsia.

Farrow and Val both would spread their time between Beta Territory and Delta. Val, important in the medical field, would continue to work on pharmaceuticals and vaccinations for the good of the people. Farrow had already been appointed a coalition adviser.

Darwin would return to Alpha. Although she daily lamented her lack of boyfriend material, it was common knowledge she'd won over one of our commune men's hearts with her sharp wit and perhaps a talent for more than just the mechanics of engines…

It was Liz and Linc who weighed most heavily on my mind. There would never be another single InterNations ruler, but Linc needed to put his face out there, show people how to lead, take up a politician's life. They were readying to depart to Beta. Both would be profoundly involved in all aspects of ongoing reform.

I'd miss them more than most.

"I asked Leon to be my husband as soon as we got back here."

"And you call me the romantic." Cannon showed no surprise at all. "It's not a mistake, you know. I loved before, too. Just the one. I'm not greedy like you."

"Says the man with the baby in his arms."

"She's even more beautiful than Blondie, isn't she?" His voice softened with wistfulness before he laid a glare on me. "Are you wooing him?"

"Yes, I'm wooing him." I fell back to the grass where the morning's frost bit into my jacket.

He covered Liberty's ears with cupped hands. "I mean with more than your cock."

"If there was any more *wooing* of that kind going on, I'd be limping. I'm dating him. I'm courting him. I'm being careful but not *careful* with him." I dragged an arm over my face, muffling the next words. "What if I can't be what he needs?"

"Darke, he only needs you."

"I want to have the ceremony before the others leave the commune."

"Well, maybe a little bird told me he's coming around."

"You've been talking to him?" I careened up.

"Nope."

"Who? Liz?"

"Yup. And Farrow. And Bas…"

"Fuckers. All of you."

"Dude, language. Little pitchers have small…*ah shit*…I can't remember. Let's just try not to swear around Libby."

"I believe the sayin' is *little pitchers have big ears*, big man," Nathaniel said, striding over. He leaned over to kiss Cannon and then his daughter, whom he retrieved from Cannon's arms. "Hey there, gorgeous."

Her bell-like laugh was half gurgle, half bubbles.

"You sweet, sweet thing. Now we gotta talk about this stayin' up all hours of the night. Papa Cas needs some sleep. And don't be goin' all precious on me, sweetheart. You try usin' those dimples against Uncle Linc. Now, he's the one you gotta charm."

Listening to Nathaniel talk to his baby girl leveled my heart.

"Would you like to hold her?" Nathaniel asked. Libby's aqua-blue eyes locked on mine, luminous with amusement.

"No."

Nathaniel pressed her into my arms.

"I said no."

"We're not on a mission, so I don't have to listen to ya. Besides, she's met Uncle Leon and she needs to meet Uncle Darke."

"Fuck."

"I won't tell her grandmama you said that," Nathaniel drawled with a wink.

Curling my arms around Liberty's small body gave new meaning to fragility. Nevertheless, she kicked her bootie-covered feet free of the blankets and squirmed with vitality.

"She's lively."

"I know." Cannon's forehead crinkled. "Wait till you try changing a diaper on a moving target."

"You're a little hoyden, aren't you?" Keeping her in my hands was like handling a live grenade.

"A hoyden?" Cannon asked.

"A firebrand. Sassy," I explained.

"That about covers it." Cannon chuckled.

Nathaniel lifted the little princess from my arms and snuggled her against his shoulder. "How's she been this mornin'?" he asked.

Cannon's gaze skipped between his husband and their daughter. "Um, five by five. And possibly soiled."

Nathaniel smiled. "How are you, big man? You were up half the night with her." The loving look passed between the two of them clashed into something hotter.

Their need snapped the air into a tight band.

"I could take Liberty for the afternoon," I offered.

As soon as the words left my mouth, they began grilling me as if I were taking on the entire Corps Elite on my own.

"Do you know how to swaddle?" Cannon peered at my large hands.

"Nope."

"Warm a bottle?" Nathaniel bounced Libby in his arms.

"Probably."

"Please tell me you can sing a frickin' lullaby, because I really want to fuck Blondie right now." Cannon stamped to his feet.

"Can do," I assured them.

* * *

Having no idea what to do with the baby, I took her sight-seeing through the commune on our way to Leon's and my caravan. Her sparkling eyes took in everything from cardinals in flight to falling red leaves. This little girl was going to be so much trouble.

Her pack of bottles, binkies, blankies, and nappies was almost heavier than my rucksack of socks, boots, ammo, and guns. I dropped it on the table inside the caravan and took her to the chair.

It didn't rock, but I did, in slow motion. Liberty broke free of her blankets, and the odor that hit me made my nose curl. *Possibly soiled.* If I could, I'd put Cannon back on manure duty for this. Libby was all over the place once I freed her of the swaddling. I had to hook her delicate ankles in the fingers of one hand and sing to her to make her stay put until I changed her diaper. After she was cleaned up, I decided to tell her a bedtime story, about what the world would be like when she grew up.

"There'll be an environmental rebirth, Territory green spaces."

Her face pinched tight as if she'd sucked on a lemon. I eased back in the chair, holding her on my legs, where she could squirm at will, free from all blankets.

"Now, that's going to screw your face up, Liberty. It's all good, okay? You just gotta listen to your daddies. They know what they're doing."

I popped a bottle between her rosebud lips for good measure, and she sucked the milk down with a hearty appetite I approved of. "You don't know yet how lucky you are to be born in world completely different from the one I grew up in. But you will.

"Life will have changed for all of us. It already has. Access to new technologies and medical advancements. In return, we'll exchange our knowledge of the land and husbandry. You'll get to choose how you want to live and who you want to live with."

Liberty's features relaxed as she toyed with my hand. I talked softly and slowly so as not to startle any more cries from this wild and weird creature.

"You shouldn't be scared, Libby. Change is good. Even if curious city dwellers come to our haven. The new roads will bring them. Those highways will tempt our people away, too, though I reckon not so many." She spat out the nipple of the bottle once it was emptied of milk and I placed it aside. "You know this is a special place, Chitamauga, where we work hard and love even harder."

I lifted her to my shoulder to coax a burp from her as I'd seen Leon do. When her soft cheek rested against my shoulder, I whispered the final truth of her wonderful future to her. "You, Liberty, are a symbol of hope and the new tidings of a new world."

She didn't seem sleepy at all when I finished, so I tried another tactic, blowing a raspberry on her tummy. Her giggles were as bright as the light shining from her, so vibrant I did it again and again before I finally sobered.

"Your daddies wanted you to nap."

She squinched her nose.

Calling upon my mom's songs—stored deep within me and stirring to the surface—I sang to Libby. The words and tunes came effortlessly, as if they'd always been waiting for this moment.

Leon strolled in after I'd sung Libby to sleep. I hummed the final refrains while he took in the sight of me with the baby in my arms.

"She's not that impossible," I whispered.

"Did you use your emo magic on her?"

"No. She's happy. I can feel it. She loves her daddies."

"You look good holdin' her," Leon said, quietly pulling off his boots.

"I do?"

"*Oui.*" Trodding to me on bare feet, he drew my head back for a kiss that shivered from the dipping tip of his tongue straight to my groin.

"I'm not ready for a baby yet." I ran my thumb to his chin, hooking him to my gaze.

"I know."

"I will be."

"I know." Leon turned his back and started to undress for bed.

"After you're mine."

"Already am." He sent me a smile over his shoulder.

"Not enough for me." I wanted to get up and grab him, but I couldn't wake Libby. "Say yes."

"*D'ac.*"

"No, no, no, none of that *d'ac* shit. You say, *Yes, Darke. I will become your husband.*"

Leon carried the sleeping baby to the makeshift cradle—our drawer of shirts I'd laid out on the floor—and set her down, smiling and crooning. He returned, guiding me to my feet. My heart hammered.

"*Oui*, Darke. I will be your husband and you mine." The impish gleam in his eyes became something smokier as he led me to the bed.

I needed Cannon and Nathaniel to collect Liberty now. "We'll wake her."

"You'll just have to be quiet."

Several minutes later, I bit my lip to stave off a deep guttural groan when Leon swooped beneath the blankets and between my thighs to take me in his mouth.

* * *

I was waiting at the altar in the meadow on the afternoon of November 1, 2071. Dressed in a deep red shirt, with a black tie that flapped in the wind and a pair of charcoal-gray trousers, I rubbed my hands together. Darwin had somehow summoned my wedding clothes up from Alpha Territory in the week between the betrothal announcement and our handfasting.

Hills and Eden stood off to the side of me, their presence

calming. Evangeline had kissed me on both cheeks when I'd taken my place. The Chitamauga people—grandparents, aunts, uncles, families in all shapes and forms—spread across the field as far as the eye could see. My own crew—Leon's, too—were among the closest circle.

Though Chief Shehu had been counseling me via D-P how to control the flow of emotions from others, I couldn't escape the onslaught of joy that matched mine and magnified it hundreds of times over when Leon appeared on the crest of the small knoll. Nor did I want to. The rich outpouring of love made the luxuriant autumn colors of the decorated meadow stand out as bright as the sun.

Leon paused at the head of the aisle that was no more than our friends and families parting a path for him down the center. Today everyone held a candle guarded against the flirty breeze by a small glass cylinder. But none of those flames could hold a candle to my angel. He wore sleek leather pants and a tight white shirt, his jacket zipped low. His hair was down around his shoulders, and the honey-brown waves danced in the wind.

He walked alone and I stood by myself. For this we needed no backup or help. He nodded when he was touched or spoken to, but once he locked his gaze on me, it never left.

When he stepped onto the wooden platform, I reached out and cupped his face. I kissed him with years of yearning, desire, and love swelling inside me. Swallowing his moan, I finally parted from his lips to delve into his clear gaze. His irises bloomed with a bright sheen.

Liberty squalled in Nathaniel's arms, all red-faced and pumping fists. He and Cannon didn't look one bit bothered as they attempted to quiet her cries with soft touches and murmured cajoling, and neither was I.

"Feed the kid already!"

"Check her diaper."

Cannon took the small scrappy bundle against his chest with gentle care. "Shut the hell up. Libby's just overwhelmed. Now, pipe down so I can hear Leon's and Darke's vows. I didn't fight a goddamn Revolution for nothing."

"What'd I tell you about the use of bad language, son?" Eden pointed her gnarled ceremonial wand at Cannon.

"Sorry, ma'am." He ducked his head to Libby's pink cheeks.

"That's Mom to you."

"Yes, ma'am."

Hoots and hollers followed, and Liz sidled over in a slinky dress—Desert Eagles strapped to her hips. "Give her to Auntie Liz."

Taking hold of the baby, Liz did that maternal thing, hushing and patting and swaying. Big Man Cannon linked his arm around his Blondie's waist, jerking his chin toward Liz as if to say, *Told you so.* Linc watched his wife—the sniper, the soldier, the confidant—with fresh fascination. Even I did a double take.

Leon's warm lips pressed to the side of my neck, bringing my full attention back to him. We turned as one, facing Hills and Eden, both in their flamboyant ceremonial garb revealed only on the most special occasions.

Hills intoned, "We gather before the wind, the ocean, the earth, and the sky to join these two men in a union that shall never be torn asunder. Not by laws, not by religion, not by the hardships of a life such as ours."

I squeezed Leon's hand. I tore my eyes from Hills, placing a small kiss along Leon's clean-shaven jaw.

"*Bien*?" I asked, my throat clicking with tight emotion.

His fingers slid along my cheek, and one tear escaped the long black lashes. "*Oui*. So *bien*." He winked.

I exhaled noisily, and he laughed.

Hills bowed. "If there any here who would wish to object—"

"Fuck no!"

"Get on with it!"

Our elder smiled, clearing his throat. "We recognize a love that was fought for. It didn't come lightly to either man. Their desire to pledge their lives to each other demands our ceremony, our care, and our celebration."

Hills touched both of us on our foreheads and then stepped back. Eden came forward, draped in her moon-silver gown. She rolled a red satin ribbon between her fingers, then wound it up and down our right arms.

"I bind thee now from North to South and East to West, where your love will carry on all winds. I bind thee from hand to hand and heart to heart." Eden's palms rested against our chests. "The Goddess has blessed you, as you two have been blessed in finding each other."

The red ribbon of unity tethered us together as a physical symbol of our everlasting promise to each other—one never-ending ribbon of love. Being superstitious—something that came part and parcel with my abilities—I recognized this was fate. All the obstacles in my course and all the people who'd been part of my life had brought me here. To this place where my existence intertwined with Leon's into a long future governed not by fear...but by freedom.

"You may now speak your vows."

I was up first. My palms sweating, I felt peaceful and...nervy all at once. Reciting the intimate verse I'd written myself, I had to stop and start again more than once because Leon sang to me with his love and passion and pride and possession.

"I want you to know, I will give you all that I have. My angel, Leon." I kissed his palm, his wrist, and the bend of his neck. My left arm ran up his back, pulling him against me. I spoke to him as softly as possible, as if every word were sacrosanct. "I will lay down my life for you. I give all my love to you."

A sob caught in his throat. I lifted my free hand to his face, sweeping the moisture from his cheek. "Please don't cry."

"It's because I'm happy."

My heart leaped as a smile burst over my lips, lips I quickly pressed to his.

"If you're ready, Leon," Hills prompted.

As unsteady as his reaction to my vows was, Leon's voice surged strong and clear. "I remember every'ting."

Shock rattled through me, since the last time I'd heard those words, he'd spoken them in anger. But now Leon's fingers curled around mine.

"I regret nothin' 'cause it brought us to dis moment, dis place, these people, and most important, to each other. I, Leon de Bellisle Cheramie, promise to love you with all my heart."

I held him closer by the wrists, feeling our skin heat where our palms rested against each of our thundering hearts.

"I vow to live beside you, to take care of you in all the ways I'm capable of, to protect and to cherish you." He murmured the final vows against my lips, completing the infinity circle of our bodies, our pasts, our love. *"Tiens-moi serré."*

"I will hold you forever," I whispered.

Full circle. The war begun and the Revolution won. Love lost, love gained. I lifted Leon off his feet. He tilted his head, moving in for the slowest, hottest, wettest kiss he'd ever given me.

"That ain't fair! We had to wait until after the rings," Cannon complained, a smile in his voice.

Eden stood in front of us, gently unwinding the ribbon from our arms. She folded it before passing it to me. "Do you wish to exchange wedding bands?"

"Fuck yeah." Leon dug into his pocket. "Me first dis time."

He presented a wide band of hammered copper, gold, and silver. It bore the unmistakable marks of Smitty's naturalistic work. "This is a symbol of how much I'm gonna own your ass."

I exploded with laughter, as did everyone else.

Twirling the circle between his fingertips, he became serious. "I read dis a long time ago in a contraband book. I've always wanted to say it, never thought I'd get the chance." Shy eyes shined at me when he pushed the ring down my finger. "With dis ring, I thee wed." The metal warmed against my skin as he slid it home to rest. "With my heart, I thee pledge."

"May I?" My hands shook when Cannon placed the ring in my palm.

"Yes, *cher*."

"This was my father's."

Leon pressed a knuckle to his mouth, and I dragged it back down.

"Now, don't do that, baby. I need your ring finger." I spun the ring slowly down his finger and kissed the very tip. "My heart, *mon coeur*, my angel. Be mine."

He nodded his head, accepting my ring. "Always."

"Forever," I said with conviction.

I sniffed so as not to cry, but my small effort was futile. With Leon's hand clasped in mine, we turned to the congregation. Everyone began pumping their fists to the air.

Hills beamed like the last blazing night star from the middle of the altar. "Today we rejoice!"

"To Leon! To Darke!"

Leon leaped into my arms, laughing, crying, kissing. I set him down to do the final duties, to give honor to my elders, Eden first with a kiss to her cheek. Hills last. We both knew this would be his final handfasting.

I clasped his palm. "Thank you."

"You will take care of our people, Warrior Darke?"

"I will." With those two words, I accepted my future place as commune elder.

Hills's head snapped up when the red ribbons unfurled from each person's hand in so many dancing arcs across the sky. Their shouts raised in unison: *Live in Freedom. Love at Will!*

Leon and I walked the long rows, hugging everyone who had stood witness to our marriage on our way to the town hall. Festivities were our specialty when we weren't knee-deep in Revolutionary shit. Tonight the party was in full swing within minutes. Freelander banners hung from the rafters. Lanterns were lit, illuminating the room with a soft glow. Food and drink were abundant.

Leon was dragged from my arms as soon as we'd entered. No amount of grumbling had swayed our friends from pulling him to the middle of the dance floor.

I drank from a mug of ale, unable to wipe the grin off my face. I kept catching sight of Leon's lissome body moving amid the throng as he danced from one person to the next. As long as he didn't rub against that Jack-anapes or Dixon Dickhead, I could deal. Besides, he was my husband now.

"Congrats, my man." Cannon leaned against the trestle table next to me. He held out his hand.

"Just following your lead." I shook his hand before pulling him in for a hard hug.

There were very few people who could understand what this chance at second love meant. Cannon was one of them.

"You two looked good up there at the altar," he said, taking a swig from his cup.

"Felt good. It felt…"

"Right." Squinting at me, he clanked his mug to mine.

I dropped my voice. "I don't feel guilty anymore."

"And you shouldn't. It took me even longer than you to figure it out, but the wait was worth it—don't you think?"

I agreed with another taste of my drink. "Where's Libby?"

Rolling his eyes, Cannon pointed across the room, where

Micah's twin daughters, Calliope and Dauphine, had Liberty set up between them, taking turns whispering in the baby's ears.

"Built-in babysitters. Nice."

"Where's your husband?" he asked.

The moment Cannon said that, my throat squeezed. My hands shook so much I had to set my mug down.

He gripped my shoulder. "Yeah. It's pretty fucking amazing hearing that for the first time, isn't it?"

My voice was uneven. "You could say that." My laugh was tremulous, too. "Leon's dancing, of course. Where's Nathaniel?"

"Singing, of course."

"Do you ever think we got really goddamn lucky?"

His gaze hooked on Nathaniel, who sang alongside Miss Eden. "Every day."

Smitty and his banjo had been booed offstage less than a minute after he took it, but the resident blacksmith had taken no offense. He'd joined Old Tommy and Hatch, who was concocting some new green, bubbling alcoholic drink in a tall beaker just inside the town hall's wide-open doors.

"You're in trouble now," Cannon mumbled, hiding his grin behind his cup.

Leon was making his sinuous way over to me.

"I sure hope so," I replied. "Sweet Jesus, this man's driving me insane."

I snapped to attention. Leon's hair was in a damp disarray, and he'd lost his jacket somewhere along the way. With the short white shirtsleeves bunched up on his biceps, his tawny skin glowed.

I took one last swallow of ale before I forgot how to swallow altogether. I'd already lost the ability to speak, my tongue tied in knots over his graceful approach.

"I think I better cut out of here." Cannon clasped Leon's arm and quietly said something to him, which only made Leon's eyes glitter even more.

I felt overdressed, but his hungry eyes let me know he appreciated the sight of me in a suit and tie.

Leon gave a slight bow. "Dance with me, *cher*."

I gulped. "Aren't you thirsty?"

"*Non*. Nate's gonna play that gee-tar, and I wanna dance, *mon mari*."

"My name's not Marie."

"Dat means husband."

Oh. Yes.

As was part of a tradition lost half a century ago, the dance floor emptied when Leon walked me to the center. Our friends and family stood along the walls. Liz pressed up to kiss Linc. Cannon looked longingly at his lover, who was preparing to sing the next song for us. Farrow flirted with Val. Denver raised Sebastian's hand to his lips in a courtly gesture.

With everyone in position, Nathaniel began to strum his guitar.

The lyrics didn't matter, nor the tune. What held my attention was the man in my arms and the hush around the hall. Our bodies fit perfectly together, and even though I had never felt comfortable dancing, Leon made it easy.

More than easy, it was intimate…and beautiful.

His hands remained on my shoulders throughout the first song, and mine rested lightly on his hips. Our gazes never parted, but we didn't speak. I breathed him in, the feel of him, the look of him, loving him.

Nathaniel left the stage and let Eden continue with the romantic songs. Before long, we were surrounded by a mash of bodies. The tune picked up, and with it, my hands wandered over Leon's ass.

"Remember the last time we danced?" he asked.

The space between us melted away. Where we touched, I sizzled with yearning. The last time was at Madam's Amphitheater in Omega. Jealousy had fueled my need to brand Leon as mine. That dance had almost made me come in my pants. It wouldn't take much longer to get to that point again. Care of Leon's quaint ways, we hadn't fucked for a few days or spent last night together.

I groaned. "Don't remind me…"

"You wouldn't let yourself have me then." He brought our joined hands up between our chests. Our rings chimed. Our hearts pounded. "Now you have all a' me."

His fingers slid around my neck.

I tilted my face, touching his lips with the softest brush. "I love the way you move with me."

"I love the way you move inside of me."

"Fuck. You can't say shit like that and expect me to just dance with you all night, angel." I growled with desire.

"I expec' you to make love to me all night long."

My muscles stiffened to make a move out of this place, but he gentled me with the caress of his fingertips along my arms. "Or we could just keep dancin'. You don' wanna party all night?"

"I'm not as young as you," I groused.

His laughter was sultry as a summer breeze. "*Mais* yeah, I could teach you a thing or two."

I yanked back with my face heated. "Oh really?"

"*Mm-hmm.*" He licked his lips with the pink tip of his tongue. "That's it. We're done."

With his hand grasped in mine, I plowed through everyone in my way. Leon sent our apologies to anyone I trampled in my hasty exit. He pulled me up short when we reached Liz and Linc. I glared, impatience winning out over any semblance of manners.

"*Merci.*" Leon shook Linc's hand and accepted a hug from Liz. He looked at me, lifting his eyebrows.

"Look, I know you're taking off in a couple of days for Beta, but we gotta go." How long could this night go on? I gave back-breaking hugs to both of them and hoped that was good enough.

Cannon watched it all, a smirk on his lips, Libby asleep in his arms. *Asshole.*

Liz wouldn't let me pass. "Oh, don't think you're getting out of sending us off, Darke, just because you think you're gonna be spending the next three days inside Leon's ass."

"I don't plan on coming up for air." I gave my short reply.

"Not even for me, your old pal?" She batted her eyelashes, to no effect but a rumble of amusement from Cannon.

"No," I bit out.

"*Bien sur.* We'll be there," Leon promised right before I whisked him out the doors.

* * *

At first I couldn't locate our caravan. The village dickheads had pulled the same stunt on us as they had on Caspar and Nathaniel. I was desperate enough to use the solid trunk of a pine tree as a bedstead, but not on our first night as husbands.

We'd been relocated to the meadow. When I glimpsed the lights shining across the frozen field, I took off at a run, Leon racing beside me. At least Tommy wouldn't have to worry about being kept awake, especially since our caravan was the subject of one more commune tradition. Tiny silver tinkling bells looped in strands all around our home.

I stopped at the steps, where candles lit each side of the stairs. Wood smoke pumped from the chimney, its gray trails wispy. "Grab on to me."

"What?"

I lifted Leon to my hips. His thighs curled around my waist. His lips meandered up my neck.

I took the steps carefully because of my precious cargo, and when we ducked inside, I faltered. "Did you do this?"

"Some of it." He craned his neck to see the bed in splendid new linens. To take in the many lit candles. To smile at our red satin ribbon displayed in a carved case on the table.

"How'd you get the ribbon?" I patted my pocket, where it'd been folded flat.

"You were a little distracted when we were dancin'. I passed it off to Tommy." He winked.

I slid him down my body and he led me to the other room. A

giant claw-foot tub filled with steaming water took up most of the space.

"It's beautiful," I murmured.

"Has anyone taken care of you?"

"I..."

"I din't think so." Leon swirled a hand around the hot water, beckoning me closer. "Look at you, all suited up and perfect."

I shoved out of my boots and hooked my thumbs into the waist of his pants. "Why don't you undress me, boy?"

"You ain't called me that in a while." His shirt dropped off first, then his pants, underneath which he was completely naked.

I wondered if I could go blind from the sight of his sheer perfection. "You didn't like it."

"Depends." He quickly loosened my tie and let it flip behind him in a black arrow. "If you say, *Boy, get over here and suck my cock*"—moist lips peppered around my throat—"*Ça va*, I don't got a problem with dat."

My clothes hit the floor as he undressed me. I stood as still as I could, a statue when he dragged my pants down. Leon bit his lip the moment my cock lunged upward in front of his face, but he didn't touch me.

He motioned me to the warm water, waiting until I settled in. With my knees against either side, there was enough room for two, yet he knelt on the braided rug, lathering his hands, soaping me all over until my breath rasped and my knuckles turned as white as the porcelain beneath my grip.

Every time he rose up, I sucked on his skin, dewy and damp.

His stomach, his thighs. His balls dangled over the edge and I
slurped them, too.

Foam dripped off my chest and down my back. I shivered.

"Dis is how I love you. Dis is how I care for you." He kissed my
chin, his hand dipping lower beneath the water to tangle in the
hair at my groin.

The water waved as my body moved to his every teasing touch.

"Let me love you, too." I pulled him into the tub, settling him
on my thighs. "Let me."

"You gave so much for me."

"No more than you." I wrapped Leon in my arms as our wet
skin found a new rhythm.

We kissed, taking our time to feel the smoothness of each
other's mouths and the sleekness of bare body to bare body, buffeted by the bath's hot water.

He sat back, his cock aligned with mine. "The wings healed
perfectly."

His lips were firm and wide and sensuous—and oh so talented—as he traced the shape of my angel's wings in flight, the
moko on my chest. I shuddered as a volley of need lit its way
down my torso. I let him play with his lips and tongue and
hands and fingers until I was tense as a wire unraveling with
desire.

We slowly toweled each other dry, rediscovering the valleys,
the hills, the dips of bare skin. Mine ebony, as dark as night
against his golden sunniness.

"Maybe we should start callin' you *light*." Leon smiled from
the bed he climbed onto.

"Hmph." My face heated with a blush barely visible beneath my skin.

"What? I'm serious. Look at you. Grinnin', whistlin' all night."

"Leon." Grumbling, I fought a smile.

"See? Leon and Light."

"Leon." I stalked him, and he leaped off the bed.

I chased him to a corner of the caravan. He may have sprinted faster than me, but I had longer limbs. "Gotcha!" I threw him over my shoulder and swatted his pert ass.

I tossed him onto the bed and jumped on after him.

Leon rolled me over and pinned me down. "Uh-uh. I got you."

"Yes, you do." I captured him against me.

There was very little preamble to our lovemaking. The need to consummate our union with our bodies made me slip wet fingers into him after kissing up the insides of his tensed thighs. Leon's gaze drew low as he watched along the length of his body. He arched and twisted, gasping, pumping against my coned fingers.

"Love me!" He shuddered.

When we joined together as one, I lay slowly on top of him. Our bodies met from lips to chest to groin. His thighs rose to my circling hips and my arms hooked around his shoulders.

I gasped against his mouth. "I love you so much, Leon."

I languidly withdrew, his strong legs curling me back to him as he bowed into my hold. Our bodies, always in sync during times of battle, were completely in tune with our lovemaking, too.

"We made it." Leon's eyes took on dizzying depths. His channel pulled me deeper.

"We made it together." I thrust inside of him. His body

wrapped around me like the red ribbon had, with nothing that could come between us.

Hands and hearts. Mouths and mumbled sighs and moans, the music of lovers.

I cried out when I came, lowering my lips to his. Leon climaxed in the next instant, clutching at me. His heat and warmth and wetness spread over my palm and onto my stomach.

I'd always loved the clean, salty scent of him after we made love—I didn't want to wash him from my body, and he looked too sated to move. Dragging a blanket over us, I thought about banking the fire in the woodstove. Instead, I fell back to the bed with my beautiful husband lying across me. We'd keep each other warm through the night.

And in the morning, when only coals remained from the crackling fire, I'd tiptoe from bed and start up the kindling. I'd bring him breakfast. I'd have the bath refilled. I'd soap him and caress him and love him all day long, and for all the days and nights to come.

About the Author

A Yankee transplant via the UK and other wild journeys, Rie happily landed in Charleston, South Carolina, with her English artisan husband and their two small daughters—one an aspiring diva, the other a future punk rocker. They've put down roots in the beautiful area, raising children who meld the southern "y'all" with a British accent, claiming it's a comical combination.

After earning her degree in fine arts, Rie promptly gave up paintbrushes and canvas for paper and pen (because she decided being a writer was equally as good an idea as being an artist; of course it was). That was fifteen years ago that her writing career started. With a manuscript of super-epic proportions! Safely stored under a lace doily in a filing cabinet. Possibly in England…

Since then she's done this and that, here and there, usually in the nonprofit arena, until she returned to her dream of being a writer. Even though Rie basks in the glorious southern sunshine as often as she can, she's mostly a nocturnal creature, adjourning to her writer's atelier (spare bedroom) in search of her next devious plot twist or delicious passionate tryst.

No matter what genre or gender pairing she's writing, she combines a sexy southern edge with humor and heart—and a taste of darkness. Enjoy!

www.riewarren.com

Twitter: @RieWrites

Facebook: https://www.facebook.com/RieWarrenRomance

CPSIA information can be obtained at www.ICGtesting.com
Printed in the USA
BVOW02s0132160215

387759BV00001B/4/P

9 781455 575190